I0636302

The Manchester Bradshaws:

A Family Through Time

The Manchester Bradshaws:

A Family Through Time

SARAH LYSAGHT

Elusive Spirit Publishing

Copyright © 2018 Sarah Lysaght

All rights reserved. No part of this publication may be reproduced or transmitted in any form or by any means, electronic or mechanical including photocopying, recording or any information storage or retrieval system, without prior permission in writing from the publishers.

The right of Sarah Lysaght to be identified as the author of this work has been asserted by her in accordance with the Copyright, Designs and Patents Act 1988

First published in the United Kingdom in 2018 by
Elusive Spirit Publishing

Produced by The Choir Press

ISBN 978-0-9571850-2-9

In memory of Janet,
a woman of high standards.

Contents

Background   ix

Introduction   xv

Part I   1761–1797   Platt and Bradshaw Union   1

Part II   1771–1817   Samuel Bradshaw   45

Part III   1817–1874   William Platt Bradshaw   79

Part IV   1867–1913   Frank Bradshaw   151

Part V   1912–1960   Harry Greaves Bradshaw   235

Acknowledgements   313

Background

Centuries ago British landowners used their land for the rearing of sheep. The wool provided by these animals was used to clothe the people both at home and abroad. During the sixteenth and seventeenth centuries Manchester became a cloth town, a centre for linen and woollens.

When the manufacture of a mixture of linen and cotton called fustian cloth was introduced, its popularity and production soon spread throughout south-east Lancashire. The raw materials needed to manufacture fustian were imported into Liverpool from the slave plantations in America. These materials were transferred to Manchester to be manufactured into thread and the cloth then traded on London markets, increasing the wealth of its Manchester merchants. As Manchester expanded and produced more fustian, its woollen trade fell into decline.

Manchester can be found south-west of the Pennine hills. Its centre is on the east bank of the River Irwell. Manchester also occupies the land between two smaller streams called the Irk and the Medlock. Before the Industrial Revolution, Manchester was surrounded by open countryside and fast-flowing rivers. Its population lived in a handful of streets and most had views of the Pennine hills.

The road we know today as Deansgate, which runs through the city, was at one time a quiet country lane also known as Alport Street. Around 1750 near the Knott Mill end of Deansgate was Alport Town. Alport Street was named after this area and ran from the Knott Mill end up to where Quay Street and Peter Street now cross Deansgate.

By the beginning of the eighteenth century Manchester had become a town of national significance. Its cotton industry prospered, dominated by the merchants and manufacturers who controlled how the cloth was produced. A large number of independent weavers worked from their own homes or small workshops and managed to earn a fairly decent wage.

Around this time many inventions and discoveries were made in Great Britain which were to change all this. Described now as the Industrial Revolution, it was a time of great progress in engineering.

Major changes were taking place all around the town, one of these being the building of the Bridgewater Canal. Francis Egerton, the third Duke of Bridgewater, had toured Europe as a young man and returned to England impressed by the workings of the canals on the continent. The Bridgewater Canal opened in 1761 after an act of Parliament was obtained by the Duke allowing him to construct a canal from Worsley to Manchester. This enabled the Duke to carry coal obtained from his pits to the increasing population of Manchester who demanded it. He spent the remainder of his life extending, improving and repairing this waterway, and it wasn't long before canals were also being used as a means of travel by the local people. Passage boats sailed regularly from Manchester to Altrincham, Lymm, Warrington, Preston Brook and Runcorn.

The Liverpool and Manchester Railway was opened in 1830 by Arthur Wellesley, Duke of Wellington and Prime Minister at this time. It was founded by two Liverpool merchants who wanted to transport produce from the Manchester textile mills to the port of Liverpool much quicker and for less than the canals or roads then cost. They faced strong opposition from canal companies and trustees, who had support from farming communities and landowners. When canal trustees were allowed to appoint three directors to the railway company and railway shares allocated, they finally started to believe the railways and canals could exist side by side and influenced many parliamentary bills to protect their interests. The railways quickly expanded and by 1841 trains were travelling from Manchester to Birmingham, London and Hull.

*

Now, let us take a brief look at other areas of interest around Manchester, relating to our story.

Today it is difficult to imagine that Moss Side was once rural and remote countryside scattered with black and white farmhouses and cottages: a place where the people of Manchester could take long walks during high days and holidays. Picnics were eaten beside ponds surrounded by bulrushes, reached by several public footpaths across farmers' fields. Moss Side can still be found two miles south of Manchester's old church, which we know today as Manchester Cathedral.

More than 300 years ago, most of the 420 acres of Moss Side was given to farming. There was no church, clergy or churchwarden in the area. There were no highways or highway surveyors. One could look south across the fields and see as far as Alderley Edge.

In 1821 Moss Side had a population of 172 residents. By 1831 there were 208 and every one of them, young and old, lived within the thirty-four houses there. As late as 1850 Moss Side was being described as 'an earthly paradise', very different from the Moss Side we know today.

A scattered group of farms made up a hamlet in this area more than 200 years ago. Two of these farms were named Greenhill and Pepperhill. Neither farm appeared to stand upon any significant rise in the ground, but it is said Pepperhill may have received its name from the wild peppermint which was once grown there.

Greenhill Farm at one time encompassed Pepperhill Farm, with land either side of Moss Lane East, situated between Claremont Road and Greenheys Lane.

Pepperhill Farm incorporated an old country cottage dating as far back as the early seventeenth century, and later a farmhouse was joined on to the cottage to make the original building semi-detached. There were also a number of outbuildings. A footpath led across the fields to the gabled black and white farmhouse made of oak quarter framing and oak pegs, its spaces filled with clay and bulrushes. A simple lane, from which only the cottage could be seen, led from

Moss Lane Grove to the farmyard. Once one arrived in the farmyard, the farmhouse could be viewed. Belonging to the cottage at one time were herb, flower and kitchen gardens, and the property also possessed a croquet lawn. This is believed to be the same farm described in the opening chapter of Elizabeth Gaskell's first novel, *Mary Barton*.

To the north of Moss Side was Hulme, a small village with one pub and a manor house. It remained chiefly farmland until the eighteenth century, by which time it had acquired the half-timbered Hulme Hall. This building was demolished in 1845 to make way for the railways. The railway, mills and smoking chimneys soon blotted out the sun and factories covered the Hulme landscape. In the first half of the nineteenth century Hulme saw its population expand by fifty times. This forced the hurried building of many houses in a limited amount of space. Living conditions were appalling, sanitary provisions did not exist, diseases were widespread and mortality rates very high.

The Manchester Ship Canal with its Pomona docks changed Hulme into an inland port for ocean-going vessels, enabling Manchester to become the headquarters for cotton manufacturing and a centre of trade and industry. Hulme developed southwards down Jackson's Lane (Great Jackson Street) and after 1832, when Stretford Road opened, Hulme became more widely known for its street of popular shops.

In 1838 Hulme became part of the Borough of Manchester. In 1844 Manchester Borough Council had to quickly pass new laws prohibiting the further building of back-to-back houses as conditions were so bad. Many of those that already existed were not demolished and remained in use until well into the twentieth century.

City Road opened in 1853 and ran past Hulme Calvary Barracks, where the Royal Horse Artillery and Army Service Corps were stationed. Henry Royce and Charles Rolls set up their Rolls-Royce motor car factory in Hulme in 1904.

During the Industrial Revolution, Manchester established new residential areas which spread some distance out from the main town, at the time separated by fields. Whalley Range was one of these first suburbs, created by Samuel Brooks and described as 'a desirable estate for gentlemen and their families'. In September 1834, Samuel Brooks bought more than eighty acres of land, where he built houses enabling people to escape the overcrowding in the growing industrial city.

Rusholme was once a country village, surrounded by fields and dominated by two large estates: Birch and Platt Hall. In 1885 Rusholme was incorporated into the city of Manchester.

The unpleasant effects of the Manchester factories prompted prosperous merchants to leave their town houses, and large villas were built on sites along Oxford Road to accommodate them. Two further schemes were built along Wilmslow Road. The earlier was the Brighton Grove estate, but the more successful, built in 1937, was the Victoria Park estate. Here, mansions with large gardens were laid out within an ornamental and gated park. By the beginning of the twentieth century some of these houses had been demolished and replaced by shops and terrace houses. Today, many are in use by Manchester University as student accommodation.

Rows of shops including tailors, furriers, milliners and bootmakers appeared along Wilmslow Road. In the early twentieth century, many of these shops advertised their services within a Rusholme Theatre programme.

The development of Bowdon, near Altrincham, as a residential area had begun in the 1840s, when landowners of the area sold off parcels of land. The opening of Bowdon railway station in 1849 allowed easy travel for the wealthy Manchester merchants. During the 1860s and 1870s many merchants moved into large houses here because of Bowdon's clean air and tranquillity. Kelly's Directory around this time described Bowdon as 'studded with handsome villas and mansions'.

Introduction

This story concerns five generations of the Bradshaw family, who established firm connections with the Manchester area. Across very different time periods we encounter five exceptional men and their families, whose lives together span more than 200 years, and discover how varied, yet similar, those lives could be. Theirs is a history filled with many twists and turns, changes and developments.

The Bradshaw family lived and worked in and around Manchester for many years. In the early days they worked hard to make a living, later generations benefiting from inherited wealth. Described throughout a number of generations as landed gentry, the family would exhibit great wealth, some airs and graces, a little influence, but no title. They made their fortune through good decisions and sound investments. They purchased land and property and rented these out, later selling land on to developers from whom they purchased more property, gaining further incomes from rent.

As with most families, some members achieved happier lives than others, some benefiting from adventure while others were associated with scandal. This is their story and the story of how the recent history of Manchester has played an important role in all of their lives.

We should, however, give mention to a man with whom the Bradshaw family have a strong connection. If not for him, their fortunes may never have come about.

Samuel Platt was born in Manchester in about 1718. He married Ann Partington on 1st August 1742. They were married at Manchester parish church, which we know today as Manchester Cathedral or, to give it its full title, the Cathedral and Collegiate Church of St Mary, St Denys and St George.

In 1743 their first child was born. Elizabeth (Betty) was baptised on 19th June, the first of Samuel's children to be baptised at Manchester's Collegiate Church. Samuel was recorded as a landowner on his daughter's baptism record. In 1745 he had a son, William, baptised on 14th July, but sadly this child died when he was only seven. A third child, Ann, was baptised on 23rd April 1749, and a fourth and final child, Samuel, on 1st April 1753.

The family appeared to be living on Shudehill in Manchester, an area which would soon become filled with dingy warehouses, factories and workshops. Samuel had his own pawnbroker business working from premises in Alport Street, which today we know as the Knott Mill end of Deansgate. The people of Manchester would pledge personal items in exchange for money, in the hope they could soon return to buy back their pledges. Many were unable to achieve this and Samuel would have regular auctions of these often valuable pledges. This was how he made his living.

PART I

1761–1797

———⌾⌾———

Platt and Bradshaw Union

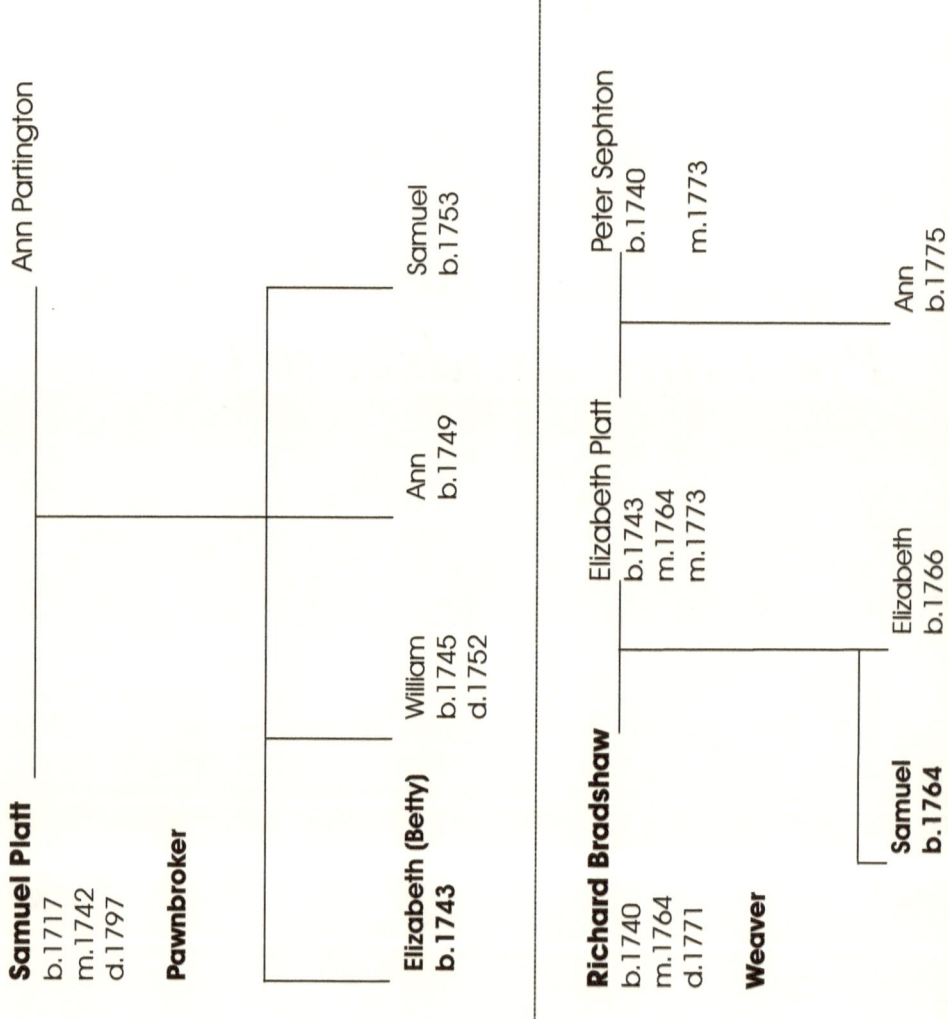

Samuel Platt
b.1717
m.1742
d.1797

Pawnbroker

Ann Partington

Elizabeth (Betty)
b.1743

William
b.1745
d.1752

Ann
b.1749

Samuel
b.1753

Richard Bradshaw
b.1740
m.1764
d.1771

Weaver

Elizabeth Platt
b.1743
m.1764
m.1773

Peter Sephton
b.1740

m.1773

Samuel
b.1764

Elizabeth
b.1766

Ann
b.1775

1

The 17th July 1761 was a muggy, airless summer's day. Many of the residents of Manchester had taken a general holiday to celebrate the opening of the first part of the Duke of Bridgewater's canal. Samuel Platt, along with his family, and Richard Bradshaw, a young, ambitious weaver, were among the many Manchester townsfolk who had gathered at Knott Mill to witness the first boat to be unloaded at the Duke's Wharf. Afterwards they enjoyed wandering between the many stallholders who had set up their wares in celebration of their town's special event.

Samuel's eighteen-year-old daughter, Betty, was preoccupied with the vibrant market stalls when she accidentally bumped into Richard Bradshaw approaching from the opposite direction. Samuel teased his daughter for not looking where she was going and shy Richard quietly apologised to Betty before continuing on his way.

Samuel Platt's family had lived in the Manchester area for quite some time, managing to purchase land and property. Married to Ann, Samuel had only three children, having lost his second child, a son, at the age of seven to smallpox. His eldest daughter was Betty. He had another daughter, Ann, and one son, Samuel.

Before he'd married, Samuel had worked as a chapman. He would invest in the raw materials of wool, cotton and silk, putting out the work to the Manchester spinners and weavers who worked from their homes and paying them for their results. Samuel would sell the finished cloths for profit, distributing them at markets and fairs. This was how he'd made enough money to purchase his current business. He had learnt to be shrewd and invest wisely. His work was both varied and profitable, enabling him to acquire some land and properties around Manchester, including his pawnbroker business on Alport Street and the comfortable family home on Shudehill.

Samuel had put everything into his pawnbroker business to make it successful. He kept indelible records and fully itemised all his forfeited pledges. He allocated a number to each pledge and noted the name and address of the pledger, the date of the pledge loan or the date of the last payment received, the date of any written notice and the date of forfeiture. He ran it as a family business. Samuel would value the pawn, his wife Ann made out a ticket, and their daughter Betty would put the article away in store. The Platt family were liked in the town and had a good reputation.

Richard Bradshaw was better known around the Hanging Ditch and Smithy Door areas of Manchester. Bradshaws had lived and worked in these areas since the early eighteenth century. But Richard Bradshaw's ancestry was a bit of a mystery to his friends and neighbours. Whenever the subject arose, Richard would try to avoid it. He only appeared to have one living relative, who was his brother, and he, like Richard, kept his family's origins to himself. The mystery surrounding the Bradshaw brothers only served to make them all the more appealing.

So it would appear that the Bradshaw and Platt families were destined to meet. They would not merge for a further three years, but nevertheless these two families would become one and over the next few generations would spread themselves out, firstly along Deansgate and later, as Manchester expanded, further away from its centre, spreading southwards into new towns.

Richard and Betty came to forget their first meeting, on the day the canal had opened, when Betty, excited by the market, had accidentally bumped into Richard. They had passed one another on many occasions since, as they lived very close, being situated at opposite ends of Withy Grove. It was Betty who had first noticed Richard as he walked past her family's home, laden down with garments he had made to sell at market. Following that occasion she had noticed him more and more. Eventually, they had met close to where Betty's father had his shop. Betty had said good afternoon, forgetting the handsome gentleman did not know her, and she had boldly offered to help him carry home the wool he had purchased for weaving. He had asked her how she knew where he lived and she had explained she had seen him walking past her house on a number of occasions, so they had walked home together along Deansgate, as though they had known each other since childhood. From that day on they had been inseparable.

It was now the spring of 1764, the very same year in which James Hargreaves invented the spinning jenny. The bustling market town of Manchester was, once again, bathed in pleasant sunshine. It was a fine Tuesday morning, the twenty-ninth day of May. The blossom trees were all but bare, due to a late May storm two nights earlier which represented the end of springtime. When the fast-approaching summer sun put in an unannounced appearance on this glorious morning to let everyone know summer was just around the corner, both the Platt and the Bradshaw families welcomed its sight. Today was the occasion of the marriage between Richard Bradshaw, a Manchester weaver, and his sweetheart, Betty Platt.

Theirs was a whirlwind romance: love at second sight, you might say. Nothing and no one was going to stop them or prevent the desire they felt for one another, although some had tried. Betty's father for one could see no good coming from his daughter's obsession with the weaver, and on more than one occasion had tried to prevent them from seeing one another. There was nothing in particular he had against the boy – in fact it could be true to say Richard reminded him very much of himself at that age – but he did think his eldest child could do better for herself. Samuel was a proud man with high standards. He had worked hard to acquire a good reputation; he was well respected within Manchester and wished to maintain this position. Samuel's wife, much like their daughter, had taken an instant liking to Richard, but Samuel held little interest in the boy. No matter what Richard did, he would never be able to match Samuel Platt's high expectations. Samuel wished his daughter's husband to be a man of property and lands, a man of great wealth.

So, when Betty had announced she was with child and was going to marry her sweetheart, her father had been both angry and disappointed with his daughter. He had instantly blamed her mother

5

for not educating their daughter in the ways of the world. He knew he should have spent more time with his daughter and, in hindsight, should have warned her about certain aspects of life, but he had thought that was the responsibility of her mother. He was too busy with his pawnbroker business to have constantly watched over Betty, validating appropriate suitors for her. It was his role to provide for his family; he couldn't be expected to do everything. When Betty had disclosed her condition to her father, explaining how Richard wished to marry her and how hopelessly in love they were, Samuel had muttered, 'No good will come from this, child. I can feel it in my bones.'

Richard seemed awfully mysterious about his family background and upbringing. Samuel had never met Richard's parents, who Richard claimed had died some years ago and was always vague about when questioned. Samuel had only met Richard's brother once and felt he too was hiding something. He had his suspicions, though. Samuel had considered whether Richard and his brother might in some way be related to the Bradshaws of Darcy Lever, near Bolton, and for some reason best known to themselves did not wish to make this common knowledge. Richard and James appeared to have little money between them, unlike the Bradshaws of Darcy Lever. A family scandal might explain why, thought Samuel. It didn't matter, though, as Richard was obviously unwilling to disclose any such information. Whatever the case, his reticence made it difficult for Samuel to trust him.

Unlike Richard, Samuel revelled in telling stories about his lineage. According to Betty, her father had invented a story about his own family history, for he was convinced he was connected to the Platt family who had owned much of the land in the Rusholme area for more than 400 years. He often told his family and friends of how the Platts had owned more than 300 acres of land in 1225 and in 1625 the Platt estate had been sold by Edmond Platt, his distant relative, to the Worsley family. Samuel would strongly maintain this belief right up until his death, and Betty believed this to be the reason why her father was obsessed with purchasing so much property and land around Manchester.

It truly bothered Samuel that his daughter could not have waited. 'A few months more and she would have reached twenty-one years of age. Things could have been very different, if only she had waited,' he repeated to his wife. He felt his daughter was now being rushed into a marriage that most likely would turn out unsuitable. But Betty was having none of it and Samuel quickly realised his feelings against the marriage were futile.

Betty and her mother soon had everything organised and under control. The day was arranged swiftly and, when it arrived, Samuel had to admit he had never seen his daughter so elated. She appeared more relaxed and content than she had in many weeks. Although a man of high principles, Samuel eventually relented and agreed to attend the parish church with the rest of his family. He was surprised to experience a profound feeling of pride towards his beautiful daughter as he gave her away on her wedding day to the man she so adored.

2

Richard should have been nervous on this, the morning of his wedding day, but he was quite relaxed as he read with interest a newspaper article about further problems the Duke of Bridgewater was experiencing with his canal building. The Duke had previously experienced problems with peat deposits which meant rerouting his canal. He had been forced to invent a new type of mortar to ensure embankments were made watertight, thus delaying work and resulting in many bills to Parliament having to be revised. And now it seemed he had been forced to purchase part of the nearby Hulme Hall estate at a cost of £9,000 because of disputes with landowners. The newspaper reported that the cost of constructing the waterways and of building wharves and warehouses meant the Duke's finances were spiralling out of control. He had been forced to borrow large sums of money and to reduce his personal outgoings, which meant losing many of his servants. *How the other half live,* Richard thought to himself.

Richard and Betty were married by the Reverend Maurice Griffiths, chaplain of the Manchester parish church. The ceremony was brief. Theirs was not the only wedding taking place that day. Betty's appearance was striking as she carried her bouquet of orchids and apple blossoms, gliding elegantly back along the aisle with her new husband. The small congregation followed the bride and groom outside the church, where they all gathered to offer their congratulations.

Richard had chosen his witnesses well. They were his two closest allies: his good friend William Bowers, a cloth merchant, whom he had known for many years and often confided in, and his brother, James Bradshaw.

*

During the afternoon of her wedding day Betty moved the few worldly goods she owned from her father's home into her husband's recently purchased house on Hanging Ditch. The couple's new home was one of nine new houses built during the first phase of Manchester's latest town planning. Hanging Ditch was one of the most ancient parts of medieval Manchester. More than 150 years earlier, Hanging Ditch was where the rivers Irk and Irwell had connected. A sandstone bridge of two arches had been built across the ditch and was locally known as Hanging Bridge. Hanging Bridge formed part of Manchester's medieval defences, when it was the main route from Manchester to the parish church. The ditch was soon condemned as an unsanitary open sewer when the people of Manchester disposed of all types of rubbish in it. In the following years the river was diverted and the ditch and bridge buried. Richard and Betty's new home had been built along the line of the bridge, which would remain forgotten for almost the next century.

Richard helped Betty carry her few belongings to their new house, where she cleaned, scrubbed and organised the small space they were to call home. It was a basic single room in which they had to sleep, eat and work. Richard had prospered enough over the years to purchase their new home, through hard work and diligence, but he was under no illusion. He knew he would never be a wealthy man, able to afford land. He was too much of a perfectionist for that.

Every week Richard and his fellow weavers would take their finished cloth to show the Manchester merchants in search of the best price for their goods. This had been where he'd met his good friend William Bowers, who had consistently been impressed with the quality of Richard's cloth. Richard's finished work was examined, measured and weighed. He was always paid a fair price for his work, but William would pay more as he recognised quality when he saw it. Deductions were taken from some weavers for bad work or short weight, but this had never applied to Richard. His high standards and persistence had paid off and he was financially quite comfortable by the time he married. He was secure in the knowledge he had some money put by, which he had received upon the death of his father. He kept this money safe and used it wisely. It was not enough to be able to invest in property but enough to sustain him and Betty for a few years.

The day after his marriage Richard returned to his work as weaver, but he was soon giving notice to quit. He had for many years worked alongside two other men in a well-lit attic room belonging to a fellow weaver, and this was where he had learnt his profession. Now that he was married, it made more sense for Betty to work alongside him at home. He had enough money saved to be able to afford to purchase a spinning wheel and handloom, which he soon installed in his new property, much to the frustration of his new wife.

Betty had much preferred the work in her father's pawn shop to being stuck at home all day. There was little space for the two of them, let alone an ugly handloom, and what were they to do once the baby was born? As Betty did not want her husband to notice her negative feelings, she kept quiet. She understood how passionate her husband was about his profession but had little desire to learn herself. However, she soon realised it was their only means of income. Because she loved him unconditionally, she was willing to do anything for him.

As Betty dealt with the spinning wheel, Richard and his friend William struggled to install the handloom contraption. Once it had been set up, Richard was eager to show his new bride how everything worked. 'I will operate the handloom as I have the strength required to batten, but I can show you how it works if you wish?'

'I'd like that,' replied Betty, trying to sound interested.

Betty was surprised at how noisy the contraption was but impressed by how easy her husband made the process look, and enquired if she could take a turn. Surprised by her enthusiasm, Richard allowed his wife to take over from him. It was quickly clear to all concerned that Betty did not have the skills or strength required to work the loom and Richard hastily took back the control. He commented, kindly, 'With a little more practice I'm sure you could soon get the better of it.'

Betty smiled at her husband's careful comment. 'Shall I try the spinning wheel now?' she asked apprehensively.

Using wool which had been carded and combed, Richard showed Betty how to loosen up the fibres in the thread by gently pulling at it and then demonstrated how to work the spinning wheel. Betty soon mastered the pedal which spun the wheel and how to join new wool to that already spun. After a few minutes she was able to spin an even thread and was quickly adding new thread to the bobbin. 'You're a natural,' her husband encouraged her. Having never experienced working with a spinning wheel before, Betty felt a huge sense of pride in what she had achieved.

Richard now knew he had made the right decision in moving his work into his home. His wife would be able to help spin the thread for his machine and attend to the finishing. He knew he would still need to purchase extra thread as he had done before, because it would take Betty about eight hours of spinning to produce enough thread for just one hour of Richard's weaving, but Richard could afford this. He had desperately wanted his wife to become accustomed to the craft he so adored and, now that she had, he was content. When his children were old enough he would also expect them to become involved in this fashionable profession.

3

Five months after her wedding, Betty gave birth to a son. She and Richard named their son Samuel, after Betty's father, and he was baptised on 14th October. For a short time after the baby was born and while Betty was still recuperating, Richard's output slowed down and he was forced to purchase more thread. It was then he realised how important a role his wife now played in his work.

As time went on and the child grew in size, his demands upon his mother and father's time also grew, which again had a knock-on effect on Richard's cloth production.

In Manchester at this time there were thousands of individual weavers, spinners and dyers and most textile production was done in private homes or in small workshops. Competition was tough. Richard knew this and was feeling the pressure to keep up with the demand from his regular clients.

However, all that was about to change. James Hargreaves had just invented the spinning jenny, which could spin a much larger number of threads at once, and before long this was followed by Richard Arkwright taking out his first patent for the making of mule yarn by means of rollers. Richard Bradshaw had the skills and the knowledge to see that there would be a huge impact on his profession. Soon good handloom weavers were being encouraged into full employment within a factory or mill and able to earn much higher wages.

In 1765 a new spinning mill was erected in Castlefield and a wharf was built where the Duke's Canal terminated. The Castlefield mill was set up with swivel looms driven by a waterwheel. The premises were filled with looms, the like of which Richard had never seen before. He'd gone along to enquire after work as he had heard the wages were far better than what he and Betty could earn together at home. He was briefly shown around by the factory manager, who was impressed by the ease with which Richard mastered the machines. Richard was instantly employed to superintend one of the power looms. He wasted no time in accepting the position and in deciding to sell his own handloom and spinning wheel, much to Betty's delight.

The deafening sound of these new contraptions didn't deter Richard. To him the noise was the sound of the machine's heart beating, rhythmically. He thrived under these new conditions. No one was happier than Richard to arrive home exhausted after a long day spent with the machines he quickly came to admire and respect.

With a better wage now coming into the house, Betty's news that she was expecting another child was welcomed by Richard. The couple could not have been more content. Life for them at this time was good. Betty's relationship with her father had improved enormously since the birth of her son, and her father had become very attached to the child. She would take her young son to visit his grandfather in his shop almost on a daily basis and Samuel would play with the boy on his lap, talking quietly to him about the people that entered his shop and their pledges, often holding up small shiny objects for the child to look at or grasp in his chubby little fingers.

When Betty shared the news that she was expecting another child with her father, he was thrilled for her. It did cross Samuel's mind at this time that he had been wrong in the negative feelings he had experienced over his daughter's marriage. Betty was obviously very content with her life. That was all he really wished for her.

Eighteen months after her marriage, Betty gave birth to a second child. This time she gave Richard a daughter and their family felt complete. The couple named their daughter Elizabeth when Richard commented that she had Betty's colouring and good looks, but she would quickly become fondly known as Lizzy.

Lizzy's baptism ceremony was held in the large chapel inside the family's parish church on 13th April 1766. The congregation was significantly greater than during previous visits. Sixteen other babies were baptised alongside her that day. This was far from unusual for the time. The town of Manchester was expanding rapidly as more and more families moved to the area in search of work and affordable housing. Immigrants also had flooded into the area via the port at Liverpool for some years now, and the locals at this time firmly believed that it was because of these immigrants that there had been an increase in the number of contagious diseases afflicting and even killing many of the residents of Manchester.

With the growth in population and in mortality there also came a need for more burial space. The parish church was able to acquire some extra land in 1767 situated just at the back of its building. That very same year Manchester suffered one of the worst floods on record and there was talk in Richard's mill of bodies being washed from their graves and swept through the streets, although no one appeared to have actually witnessed this event.

Soon it was announced another church was to be built in Manchester to ease the strain increasingly placed upon the parish church. St John's church was built at the Alport Street end of Deansgate during 1768 and consecrated the following year. Over the altar a beautiful stained-glass window was erected displaying figures of the apostles Peter, James and John. Gravestones soon began to be laid in the grounds surrounding St John's with a vault extending below the floor of the church, available for families to reserve space in for a fee. A steeple, housing a peal of eight bells and displaying four clock faces, completed the building. The first appointed rector to St John's was John Clowes, who would remain there for the next sixty-two years.

The church was founded by Edward Byrom. He had a handsome house on Quay Street, mainly due to the fact he had been instrumental many years earlier in paying for Manchester's first purpose-built quay on the River Irwell, situated at the bottom of

Quay Street. A great celebration was held at the Byrom house when the church of St John's was completed. Banners and flags were displayed, music played, and the ringing of bells and cannon fire could be heard from one end of Deansgate to the other.

Much of the land around Quay Street at this time was garden and allotments. The road was often a busy thoroughfare, but it had not lost its rural charm, and Samuel Platt commented to his family how he too desired to own a property on this street. 'I should like one which overlooks the new St John's church, as does Mr Byrom's,' he said. Samuel's family dismissed this ridiculous idea, assuming it was an impossible request.

Samuel's family made this new church their own, preferring to attend services at St John's rather than at their old parish church. Richard, on the other hand, after attending a service there with his wife and her family, quietly commented to her that he preferred the old church. 'There is something very special about the old church which is missing at St John's.'

'I like the newness of St John's,' Betty replied.

'I think that is the reason I don't like it,' said Richard. 'The old church has such a rich history. Did you know a church has stood on that spot for hundreds of years?'

'St John's will be that old, one day,' replied Betty.

'I'm not so sure it will,' replied Richard.

They thought it best they agree to differ.

Samuel Platt, on the other hand, could not have felt more at home in the new church and, when he discovered part of the vault had been reserved for Edward Byrom and his heirs, he too paid a deposit to reserve a space for himself and his family.

He became quite obsessed with the new church, paying a yearly fee for a family pew and encouraging his friends to join him, one of these being his good friend William Cooper. Samuel had known William and his wife for many years but could not recall how or when they had first met. William's wife was extremely amiable. The two women had always got along well, and this had made for a firm friendship between both couples. Samuel and William's families were soon regularly attending services held at St John's and often after a service would spend the rest of the day together.

4

Richard continued his work at the mill for the next couple of years, bringing home a regular income to support his growing family, while observing with great interest the numerous mills which were being constructed around the Manchester area, changing the familiar landscape forever. His family were comfortably well off in their small house and above all happy with their simple life. Betty continued to visit her father and mother at their pawnbroker's shop on Alport Street. It was important to Betty that her parents saw their grandchildren regularly. Samuel and Ann cherished the time they were able to spend with the children, playing an important part in their early lives, and, in turn, the children adored their grandparents.

The children considered their grandfather's shop a treasure trove, filled with interesting objects, each with their own story, and they saw their grandfather as the master of these tales, which he skilfully revealed, captivating their imaginations. Many a time, upon their return home, the children would relate a tale to their father about some object or other their grandfather had in his shop. Their father listened with interest to these stories, even though he found most of them difficult to believe. 'What tales your grandfather does tell,' Richard had commented on numerous occasions. He often turned to his wife for verification. Betty would always smile and reply, 'If my father says it is true, then it must be so.'

One winter's evening, such a story was being told to Richard by his children as Betty was preparing their evening meal. As she plated up the potatoes in their skins along with the hot stew, Betty enjoyed listening to the laughter of her children speaking with their father.

While the children bolted their meal down with enthusiasm, Betty noticed her husband appeared to be struggling to eat his. When she asked after his obvious discomfort Richard explained that over the last couple of days his throat had become terribly inflamed and sore. He was finding swallowing and talking increasingly difficult and painful.

'Would you let me take a look at your throat, husband?' asked Betty, once the children had left the table.

Richard reluctantly opened his mouth as he knew resisting his wife's request was futile. Upon inspection Betty noticed small white sores at the back of his throat. While forcing herself to hide her repulsion towards his pungent bad breath she said, 'I shall prepare you some chicken broth. It will be much easier for you to swallow. You will feel better in no time at all, I can promise you that.'

Betty kept her immediate concern to herself. Only last year there had been an outbreak of an ulcerous sore throat which had affected many in the town. Betty and her family had escaped it that time, but she was greatly concerned it may have returned. She blamed her husband's illness on the fact he came into contact with so many others at the mill. Who knew what horrors so many people in one enclosed space might be inflicting upon one another on a daily basis? The wellbeing of her two young children was paramount and only added to her anxiety as she prepared the broth.

Richard's reaction to his illness was very matter-of-fact. Although inwardly he felt rather drained, he explained to his wife that he knew of many men at work who were also suffering at this time. 'It is something and nothing, wife,' he said. 'I'm sure it will clear up as quickly as it appears to have arrived.'

*

Over the next couple of weeks Richard noticed most of the men at the mill who had contracted their sore throats at a similar time were fighting fit again, whereas his ailment was hanging around and clearly had no intention of receding. Betty checked her six-year-old son and four-year-old daughter regularly, for any signs that they had contracted the same sore throat as their father, and was relieved when they showed none. At every available opportunity she would take her children away from the increasingly stagnant town of Manchester for a walk across the nearby fields of Greenheys to the fresher, cleaner air, wrapping them up warmly if the wind was particularly bitter. She would air the house every day, throwing open the windows to allow the winter breeze to rush through, hoping it would take with it her husband's ailments. She made sure both she and her children ate well at this time to give them the strength to fight any malady they might come into contact with.

During the third week of his poor health, Richard was suddenly taken ill at work and had to be brought home. His face looked terribly sallow as he was supported in through their front door by one of his fellow mill workers. Betty thanked the man, then helped her husband to undress and climb into bed. Once she had her husband comfortable she threw a few belongings into a bag, helped her children on with their coats and made the ten-minute walk to her father's pawnbroker's shop, where she explained the situation to him. He was understandably concerned and agreed to look after his grandchildren until Richard recovered.

Betty rushed back to her husband as quickly as she could, aware that his condition had taken a turn for the worse, but not before calling upon her husband's best friend, William. He soon paid Richard a visit and listened with great concern as his delirious friend was unable to recall how he had managed to walk the short journey home from the mill. Richard's brother James was also informed, but there seemed little anyone could do for Richard.

Betty remained by her husband's bedside for the next three days, plying him with anything she thought would aid his recovery such as broth, a warm poultice of onion and garlic to his throat, the juice of oranges she squeezed directly into his mouth, and of course opening the windows and door regularly for access to fresh air. Whenever he tried to speak, Betty would urge him to conserve his energy. Whatever he wanted to say could wait until he was feeling better.

Richard's health deteriorated further and Betty's remedies were unable to cure him. Richard died during the early hours of a cold

March morning. His funeral took place on 8th March 1771 at the same church in which he had married Betty only six years earlier. The church for the funeral had been Betty's decision. Although she mostly attended St John's now along with her parents, she did live closer to the old church and felt it would have been her husband's first choice. Richard had never really taken to the differences in the teachings at St John's or warmed to the church itself. She believed this was what Richard would have wanted.

Their son, Samuel, was six years old at the time of his father's death. He had known something was seriously wrong from the moment his father had returned home early from work that day. He had enjoyed the few days he'd spent with his grandfather, helping in his shop to clean the shelves which were used to display his grandfather's many curious objects, but he had missed his parents and couldn't escape the feeling there was something terribly wrong at home. He had pestered his grandfather regularly for news of his father.

After her husband's death, Betty told her children their father had been ill and had become too weak to fight any more and was now at peace with the angels. Samuel and his sister, along with their mother, cried themselves to sleep that evening, huddled together in the same bed.

Two days later both children attended their father's funeral. It was a difficult service, especially for the children in unfamiliar surroundings. The Manchester church was a much larger church than they were used to and they both felt lost within it. Samuel recognised his mother's distress and sorrow that day but was too young to know how to cope with it or help her.

During the burial they all cried again, comforted only by the closeness of their relatives. Although the children were young, they were certainly aware that things would never be the same again, and Betty recognised her prospects, as a widow with two young children, were bleak, but for her children's sake she would have to try to remain positive.

5

Coming to terms with her husband's sudden death took its toll on Betty. She worried about her and her children's security. She had experienced some independence with Richard and did not want to go back to relying upon her father for financial support. The house in which she lived now belonged to Richard's brother according to common English law, but he had kindly agreed she and her children could remain in the property for a peppercorn rent. He had also agreed he would give her plenty of notice if he ever wanted to sell. Although her brother-in-law had been very kind to her, Betty was uncomfortable with the situation and needed to find an income to enable her to feed and clothe her children.

Samuel could see his daughter's distress at this time and wondered how he could ease this for her. After some discussion, he and his wife Ann agreed to purchase a number of properties which had just become available a little further up the street. Samuel had wanted to expand for some time and had been waiting for the right opportunity. Now he thought he had found it. Situated on Deansgate, on the north side, near where Peter Street and Quay Street crossed over one another and opposite the Quaker meeting house, several houses had become available to purchase, giving Samuel the extra room he needed in which to store the many pledges he seemed to be acquiring at this time. He wasted no time in making an offer and putting the family home on Shudehill up for sale.

When he told Betty of his plans, he made it sound as if without her assistance in the old shop, he would not be able to go ahead. For his plans to succeed he desperately needed her help. Of course, she was unable to refuse her father and realised this opportunity would allow her to keep the independence she had grown used to. They were doing each other a favour.

Betty moved out of her home on Hanging Ditch, enabling James to sell the property, and moved into her new home on Alport Street with the children. The property was small and the space above the shop had previously been used as a storeroom. When her father's pledges were removed to the new shop she was delighted to discover there was plenty of space for her and the children. She began to work downstairs with her father again in the old shop, while her mother, sister and brother worked at the family's new home and business premises on Deansgate.

Samuel mentioned to his son a further idea he had for one of his properties, as he had realised it had the potential to become a warehouse, should they need it in the future. Another property in the row was rented out to a Mr Washington, who shortly opened a public house.

Samuel's investment soon proved sound and he was eager to purchase more property. He read in the local newspaper about 395 square yards of land for sale along Brook Street, near to Garratt Hall in Manchester. At one time it had been part of Bank House Meadow and he knew he had to have it. Within days he had signed an agreement and purchased the land with the intent to build more houses. Already there were several houses close by and Samuel believed he could fit four or five more on the land he'd purchased.

As her father's prosperity grew Betty threw herself into her shop work. In working hard she allowed herself to become distracted from the grief she felt over the loss of her husband and for a time was more at peace with her life. However, eight months after her husband's death, she received news that her husband's brother, James, had succumbed to an illness. Betty did not know which way to turn as the feelings of grief returned and consumed her all over again. Once more she felt her life was in utter turmoil.

It was at this difficult time that Betty found some solace back at her old church. Since losing her husband she had regularly visited St John's, but lately, after the death of James, she had attended more services for morning and evening prayers back at her old parish church. She felt closer to Richard there. During evening prayers

Betty would leave the children in the capable hands of their grandparents.

It was after one of these Sunday evening services and through her grief that Betty connected with a fellow parishioner. She noticed a gentleman sitting alone at the back of the church and thought how sad he looked. The service had been over for some time and she liked to stay around afterwards to reflect upon her situation, light a candle for Richard and have a little private time with the Lord, speaking quietly to him about her husband. Being a compassionate person, she was moved to enquire as to the gentleman's wellbeing.

As he looked up to see who was speaking to him, for a split second the man thought an angel had appeared before him, for his eyes were full of tears and the light inside the church was playing tricks on him.

'I'm terribly sorry. I didn't mean to intrude upon your thoughts. I know how important time for quiet contemplation can be,' said Betty.

'That is quite all right. I have possibly been here far too long anyway,' he replied as he glanced around the empty church.

'The church has a way of making you feel quite peaceful about life's sadness, don't you think so?' Betty enquired presumptuously.

The gentleman smiled slightly, and then bowed his head once more. Betty did not know what to say then. She was about to leave when the man looked up and spoke again quietly. 'My wife died and was buried here last month. I am still trying to come to terms with my loss.'

'Oh, I see,' said Betty, knowing the feeling of loss only too well.

'And then ...' He paused, gulping back the tears. 'I buried my only daughter alongside her last week.'

At this point Betty decided to sit down in the pew next to the stranger, because she knew if she didn't she might just slump to the ground, overcome by sorrow. That cold stone church floor was not going to feel the warmth of her skirts today. Forwardly, she took the gentleman's hand and placed it inside the two of hers. 'I am so very sorry to hear of your loss. Smallpox, was it?' she asked knowingly.

He nodded, silent in his grief-stricken reply.

There was a minute more of silence between them, then Betty spoke up. 'I was widowed last year. I have two young children. This latest epidemic is a terrible worry.'

The man raised his head once more and spoke politely. 'I am sorry for your loss. It must be very difficult for you.'

Betty nodded and smiled courteously.

'My name is Peter Sefton. How do you do?' he said, removing his hand from between Betty's, holding it out for her to shake.

'Elizabeth Bradshaw, Betty to my friends,' she introduced herself while accepting the man's hand.

'I'm very pleased to meet you, Betty.'

The stranger's warm politeness made her relax a little and smile. As Betty's face lit up, something inside Peter was reawakened.

'Time to go, folks, please. I need to lock up now.' The sudden voice of the church warden jolted the pair and they jumped up like a couple of naughty children, quickly making their way out of the church. Once outside Peter and Betty politely said their goodbyes and made their way back to their very different, yet similar lives.

They met again inside the church on a number of occasions, both secretly hoping after each time to bump into each other again. Their prayers were answered and over the next few months they grew very close, sharing a particular sympathetic bond. Betty learnt that Peter Sefton was a pipe maker who came from a family of clay tobacco pipe makers originating in the London area and now spread across the north-west. He ran a small, yet successful business from premises in Manchester. He was not alone, as there were a number of clay pipe manufacturers in Manchester and competition could be tough at times. Peter was considered a gentleman by most, as he'd had a good upbringing and was comfortably well off. He lived at a fairly substantial property in the Salford area, owned property in and around Manchester and invested shares in a number of other businesses.

Betty found herself falling in love all over again, something she had, just a few months ago, thought would never again happen. She struggled with feelings of guilt over Richard but drew comfort from the knowledge that Peter was feeling the same. She smiled to herself as she recalled the battle she had endured with her father over her infatuation with Richard. His response when she introduced him to Peter was very different and he instantly approved of the gentleman who had been able to lift his daughter from her sombreness.

God can move in mysterious ways, thought Betty as she climbed into her empty bed on the evening before her marriage to Peter Sefton, one year after their first meeting in the church.

She had not been in bed long when she felt a gentle touch which startled her. Opening her eyes she could make out the outline of her nine-year-old son, Samuel. 'Samuel, whatever is it? You startled me.'

'I cannot sleep, Mother. I am too excited about tomorrow.'

Raising the bedcovers she told her son, 'Climb in next to me before we both catch our death. It is a chilly night for the end of April.'

As Samuel lay in the warmth and comfort of his mother's embrace, Betty said, 'Samuel, darling, you do realise this will be the last time you will be able to do this? I shall be sharing my bed with Peter after tomorrow.'

'I know, Mother. I like Peter very much.'

'That's good, dear. Now, off to sleep with you or we both will be no good for anything tomorrow.'

Samuel was soon sound asleep, quickly followed by his mother.

Betty married Peter Sefton the next day, 28th April 1773, in their comforting old Manchester parish church. A wedding party had never looked more elegant as they had strolled down the aisle. Peter looked handsome in his newly purchased frock coat, breeches, stockings and buckled shoes. Betty mirrored him in her beautiful silk gown purchased especially by her father. He had insisted upon it and upon purchasing new outfits for his two grandchildren. Samuel Platt was very proud of all of his family and wanted everyone to look their best. Betty's young daughter had been unable to count the petticoats under her mother's gown that morning, for there were so many of them. The child had attempted it four times and still not achieved satisfaction, and Betty had finally asked, 'Lizzy, dear, would you have your mother late for her own wedding?'

The chaplain, Humphrey Owen, performed the ceremony beside the richly carved choir stalls, and for Betty the service only seemed to last a brief moment. No sooner had Peter and Betty entered the church than they were leaving again as man and wife and the children, Samuel and Lizzy, of whom Peter had become very fond, were dancing around their feet wanting to congratulate them. Betty was very proud of her children as they had both sat silently, mesmerised, throughout the service. Once outside the church she was ready to swing her daughter, then her son, around and around in circles reflecting their excitement.

'Mother, look!' exclaimed Samuel, when his turn was over and Betty was feeling rather lightheaded. 'There's a chimney sweep!'

'Where, dear?' enquired Betty as she steadied herself, gasping for breath.

'Over there!' shouted the child, pointing furiously. He was correct. There was indeed a chimney sweep standing by the church wall, watching the proceedings.

'It is supposed to be lucky,' commented Peter, catching the conversation between Samuel and his mother.

In all the commotion Betty had not noticed her daughter skipping off across the graveyard. 'Where has Lizzy gone?' she asked, suddenly concerned.

Samuel and Peter turned together to look for her.

'Father, Mother, have you seen Lizzy?' Betty asked.

'She was here a moment ago,' replied her mother.

As a feeling of panic struck Betty, she heard her new husband begin to laugh. 'There she is,' he said, pointing. 'And just look what she has with her.'

Betty's seven-year-old daughter was making her way back across the graveyard with a very disgruntled-looking black cat firmly tucked under her right arm.

'Is that supposed to be lucky as well?' asked young Samuel.

'I believe it is,' answered his grandfather. 'Although perhaps not so lucky for the cat.' The whole family united in laughter at the sight of little Lizzy struggling to hang on to the wriggling cat.

'It would seem we have plenty of luck on our side today, darling,' said Peter.

'Yes, it would,' replied Betty, hoping in her heart their good luck would continue for many years to come.

*

After their marriage Betty and her children went to live with Peter at his house in Salford. It was only a short walk from where her parents lived and had their pawn shops, and Betty, after a short time of adjusting to married life again, insisted she continue to help her father. Thankfully, her new husband was more than happy with this arrangement.

6

Once again the premises above the shop on Alport Street had become empty. Betty's brother, Samuel, now twenty, well-educated and considered a gentleman like his father, manned the shop in Alport Street with his sister, Ann, and it was agreed he could move into the rooms above. Along with her mother, Betty assisted her father at the new shop. The Platt family and their pawnbroker business had never been so prosperous.

Betty would find herself making the short journey to Deansgate most days to work alongside her father. Her children, when allowed time off from their studies, delighted in visiting their grandparents. Their grandmother would regularly supply them with delights from her kitchen and their grandfather entertained them with tall tales from his shop.

Over the next couple of years, life for Betty's family remained settled. Her son Samuel attended a local Manchester school, the cost shared between his grandfather and stepfather, while Lizzy was schooled at home and learnt how to sew and cook. Peter worked hard at his factory during the week but at weekends enjoyed spending time with Betty and her children. The family would often take trips into the surrounding Manchester countryside, where they would enjoy warm summer walks and picnics.

In 1774 pleasure boats began to sail on the Bridgewater canal and the family enjoyed many of these day trips. They would set sail from the Duke's Quay early on a Saturday morning and head towards Barton Aqueduct or sometimes the opposite way, towards Altrincham. If they left the quay at 8 am, they could be in Altrincham by 10 am. Fares for the journeys were charged at two rates, the higher being if one chose to sit at the front of the boat. This, of course, was just what the children wanted to do each time. Samuel was often reprimanded by his mother for leaning too far over the edge as he tried to glance at the ripples in the water made by the boat. His sister, finding the whole thing amusing, giggled each time her brother got into trouble with their parents.

'This is such a sedate way to travel. Is it not, Peter?' asked Betty, trying her hardest to ignore her children's mischievous behaviour during one such trip.

'Some of the sights are truly breathtaking,' agreed Peter. 'It certainly helps one to relax and takes one's mind off things, especially after a difficult week at work.'

'Have things been difficult this week, dear?' Betty enquired.

'Let's not think about that now,' replied Peter. 'I want to enjoy this glorious weather and the countryside, and take pleasure from being here with you and the children.'

Betty could not have been more content.

*

In the spring of 1775 Betty gave birth to a daughter. She and Peter were thrilled as they had thought that having a child together was something God was not willing to give his blessing to. Samuel and Lizzy quickly became besotted with their new baby sister and the family were extremely content.

On 21st May, Peter and Betty had their baby daughter baptised. It was a beautiful but cool spring morning, so Betty had made sure everyone was wrapped up well. Crowds of parents, grandparents, godparents and children had gathered outside the Manchester parish church, for it was very common to have a multitude of baptisms taking place at the same time. Manchester was rapidly growing and it was clear that their beloved church was struggling to cope with the situation.

As the family approached the church, Betty turned to Peter with a look of concern. 'There must be more than fifty babies here, all to be baptised. Where will they put us all?'

'I doubt this is the first time the church has had such a large congregation,' replied Peter.

The look on Samuel Platt's face, when the sight of all those people met his eyes, needed no words. Betty could plainly tell what her father was thinking.

Outside and inside the church there was a complete mix of Manchester society. Dressed in their best clothes of varying degrees, parents were excited yet apprehensive about the church proceedings and all had one aim in common: to ensure the baptism of their child, so as to allow them a place in heaven. Everyone began to make their way into the church and the appropriate parties found a place close to the altar with only a little pushing and shoving when the crowd were instructed to kneel.

Betty and Peter found room not far from the altar, and just in time, as the reverend began the service without delay. Betty's parents, sister, brother and children managed to squeeze themselves into a pew, much to Lizzy's disgust, as she did not get to see or hear a single moment of her sister's baptism because of the bustling crowds around the altar. Babies yelled throughout the whole ceremony, but this seemed to little deter the proceedings. Mothers embraced their newborn babies close to their breasts and this seemed to quiet them down temporarily.

The couple gave 'Ann' as their choice of name when requested to do so and the whole thing was over very quickly. Betty found the whole experience quite exhausting.

On the way to Salford, Betty's father could contain himself no longer. 'I find it quite astounding that all of those babies did not become completely mixed up today. The speed they were held up, baptised and passed back to their parents was astonishing. Wouldn't you agree, Ann?'

'Oh, Samuel, really.'

'That would not happen, Father. Mothers know their own children. Isn't that right, Mother?'

'It certainly is, dear.'

'Well, it was all a bit of a shambles if you ask me,' replied Samuel.

'We didn't ask you, dear,' whispered his wife.

Peter remained quiet but quietly winked at Betty's son, Samuel, who was hanging on to every one of his grandfather's words.

The family arrived at Betty and Peter's Salford home, where they had a small celebratory luncheon in honour of Ann's baptism. During the family celebrations Betty's father was quite unable to empty his head of the sights he had witnessed earlier that morning at the old church. The whole experience had only gone to confirm his feelings about his beloved new church of St John's. Turning to his son-in-law he asked, 'Peter, after today, will you not consider leaving that overcrowded church and joining our smaller but more sophisticated congregation?'

'I will if that is what Betty wishes, but it is not completely up to me, Samuel. I have no strong desire either way.'

At that very moment Betty walked into the room carrying a plate of meats. Placing them on the table she enquired of her husband, 'What do you have no strong desire for, Peter?'

'Your father has some concerns over the old church and was asking if we would consider joining him and the congregation at St John's.'

Betty's reaction surprised everyone, especially her father. 'If you had asked me that question last week I would have declined to even consider such a thing, but after today I am prepared to give moving to St John's church some careful consideration.'

'Well, that is a surprise, Betty, although it shouldn't be, after the fiasco we all experienced this morning,' said her father. 'The ceremony more resembled a cattle market than a child's baptism.'

'Don't say another word, dear,' Ann warned him. 'Betty will come round in her own time.'

Samuel very sensibly decided to take his wife's advice, making no more mention of the subject.

By late afternoon, when the last guests had made their farewells, Peter and Betty both breathed a sigh of relief, for it had been a long and tiring day.

*

Betty did give careful thought to her father's suggestion, and the following Sunday Peter, Betty and the children joined the congregation of St John's church. All were pleasantly surprised when Betty commented afterwards how she had enjoyed the modern service, along with the calm atmosphere and friendly congregation. From that day on, St John's church became an extension of Betty's family.

Before Betty's youngest daughter had reached her second birthday, she became seriously ill. One January morning Ann become fractious and displayed signs of a rash and fever. Both of her parents feared the worst as measles and smallpox remained rife in the town. Betty, once again, sensibly sent her other two children to stay with their grandparents, and the couple did what they could for their youngest and most fragile child. They sent for the physician, desperate for a positive outcome, but none of his remedies seemed to help. Indeed, the child appeared to worsen within the hours after his visit.

Peter and Betty's worst fears were confirmed when, a few days later, flat, red spots began to appear, first on Ann's face, then her hands and forearms, and later her body. Within a day or two, many of these lesions had turned into small blisters filled with clear fluid, which then turned into pustules. There was nothing they or the doctor could do for the child. Ann died from smallpox aged one year and nine months old.

Distraught, Peter and Betty buried their daughter on 23rd January 1777 at St John's church, the ceremony led by the rector, John Clowes. It was a terribly distressing time for the family, bringing back many upsetting memories. It would take them a great many years to overcome the loss of their daughter, yet they knew their church and its congregation, now full of their many friends and of course their family, would help and support them through this impossible time.

Peter threw himself into his work. He had experienced so much sadness in his life. This was the only way he knew to take his mind off his loss. Betty recognised this was his way of coping but felt quite lonely at times, especially when her husband worked late into the night. This was the first time she had experienced the loss of a child, and her heart ached inside her chest so painfully it was sometimes difficult to breathe. It was her mother who helped Betty at this time. She had experienced the loss of a child when Betty's brother had died at the age of seven. Betty had only been nine at the time and could remember very little of her brother, William.

During one of her more despondent moments, Betty said, 'I just want to forget, Mother.'

Wisely her mother replied, 'You must never try to forget, dear. No matter what you do you will always remember, so don't try to fight those feelings. Embrace them, live with them, for it will become easier over time. I can promise you that, dear.'

Betty heard her mother's words and they began to ease her pain slightly. It gave her some comfort to know her mother understood how she was feeling.

Life had a way of continuing. Samuel's pawnbroker business went from strength to strength. He and his son Samuel were now running two successful businesses alongside one another, assisted by the female members of their family. The pair would hold regular auctions of forfeited pledges and this was how they made their living.

Betty and Peter found married life an effort. They worked long and hard to succeed in maintaining their relationship through their grief, in what often felt like impossible circumstances. They both threw themselves into long working days which gave them some focus away from their home life. They attempted to enjoy time with their family at home and within their church community, but they were never blessed with any more children: a bitter blow they both eventually came to accept and move on from, learning to enjoy the children they did have, for they were growing up with great haste.

7

Over the next decade Samuel Platt had the insight to make some investments in the local canals. In the spring of 1776 the Bridgewater Canal between Liverpool and Manchester was completed and Samuel invested a sizeable amount of money, profiting from dividends which then enabled him to re-invest. Samuel's investments went from strength to strength and soon he was able to purchase further lands and properties he desired.

At last in 1786 he was able to fulfil his dream of purchasing a property on Quay Street. The house did not overlook St John's church, but it was a stone's throw away. The Byrom family, living at number 19, had five windows across the front of their property; Samuel had only three. He had purchased number 47, a three-storey, brick-built house with cellars, set within a block of four other properties. For Samuel this was his greatest achievement. The day he, his wife and their daughter moved into their new property was a truly momentous occasion for him.

It had taken an age to move their belongings to their new home, even though their family and friends had helped. A number of carts had been used to transport their possessions the short distance from their Deansgate and Alport Street properties. Samuel oversaw the event, giving instructions as to which rooms his furniture should be placed inside. He watched in admiration as the younger men made the carrying of his larger furniture look easy. He looked on as his dining table and chairs, sideboard, bookcases, secretarial desk, chests of drawers, wardrobes and four-poster bed were all safely deposited in his new home. 'Be careful of that, my dears. I don't want to find it scratched,' he instructed Betty and his grandson Samuel as they struggled to carry his card table into the house.

When his precious eight-day clock with chimes, inside its mahogany case, was about to be lifted from the cart, Samuel had to look away. It was the one thing, if damaged, he knew he would be the most upset about. He had stopped the timepiece before it had been moved, which he had never had to do before. It had kept perfect time all its life and he prayed that when he wound it back up again, it would keep time just as well.

When the workers had departed, carpets laid, beds made, curtains fitted and dressing glasses in place, Samuel set about tackling his precious timepiece. Much to his relief he had the clock working again in no time, as if it had stood in that spot for centuries. 'Thank goodness for that,' he said to himself.

A moment later his daughter Ann called from the sitting room, 'Your supper is ready, Father.'

After supper was finished, she announced she was to retire early. 'I am quite exhausted by the day's events.'

Samuel slumped down into his armchair. At almost seventy, he had thought he might never see this day. Looking over to his wife, he said, 'I hope we have long enough left to enjoy this place.'

Ann looked at her husband and shook her head. 'You will feel differently tomorrow, my dear, after you have had a good night's sleep.'

'I hope so,' replied Samuel, distracted by the sudden thought he should get his affairs in order. He didn't know when his time would come, but he certainly knew it would be sooner rather than later. Now that he had land and much property, he really should make sure the people he loved would equally and fairly receive the legacy he was to leave behind.

On 15th March 1787, at the age of seventy, Samuel Platt the elder had a new will written to reflect his current fortune. He signed it in front of three witnesses. Many years earlier, when Betty's first husband had still been alive, Samuel had made Richard Bradshaw administrator of his first will, but much had changed since then. He was now a man of substantial property and wealth. His executors this time were named as Samuel Platt the younger (his son) and his good friend William Cooper.

Samuel made sure his wife Ann would be well cared for, leaving her an annuity of £40 each year, collected from rent charges from his other properties and payable on 25th December for his property on Quay Street. His son was to be left the sum of £1,500 and most of his other properties, including the Alport pawnbroker's which he was now running. Samuel's daughters, Betty and Ann, were to receive £500 each along with his granddaughter, Lizzy. He left his eldest grandson, Samuel Bradshaw, £1,000 and the promise of the pawnbroker business on Deansgate which he was now running for his grandfather.

Once his will had been signed, Samuel felt a great weight had been lifted from him. Now was the time to enjoy, to the fullest, whatever might remain of his life, as he had ensured his family would be well cared for after he was gone.

If his wife had thought he would cease to purchase any more lands or properties after the writing of his will, then she was to be sorely mistaken. On 24th June 1790 Samuel purchased a parcel of land measuring 1,876 square yards in Hulme, named Hurst Meadow. It was on the southerly side of the turnpike road from Manchester to Altrincham, just beyond Knott Mill and near to Mr Jackson's farm. At the time, land in the area was being snatched up quickly and Samuel had made his decision swiftly, quite sure that it was the right one. He planned to build two large houses, one of which he hoped his son would want for himself. Each would have a coach house, stables and gardens which would back onto the newly named Hulme Place, where others too were beginning to build.

Samuel's plan soon reached fruition and he was only too pleased when his son moved into one of the properties. Once again the whole family came together to help Samuel the younger move his few belongings into his new house.

'Well, my boy, do you think you shall be happy here?' enquired his father, grinning from ear to ear at his achievement.

33

'You are too generous, Father.'

'You might as well have it and begin to enjoy it now, rather than wait until I'm gone and it passes to you anyway.'

'Really, Samuel, must you always talk about death?' moaned Ann.

'It is inevitable, dear, there is little we can do about. We should meet it head-on and not be afraid of it.'

'Well, I for one would rather not think about it,' Ann insisted.

'I agree with Mother,' said Betty.

Samuel the younger extinguished his family's conflict when he asked, 'Do you think the place could do with some more furniture, Father?'

'I certainly do, my boy. It is as bare as a poor old woman's cupboard. I am sure your mother could find a few pieces she no longer wants or needs and you can take a look in the warehouse to see if anything there catches your eye.'

'Thank you, Father. That is very considerate.'

Ann smiled at her husband, as she approved of his generosity towards their son.

'I like to see my family happy,' Samuel said, cupping his wife's flushed cheeks as he kissed her on her forehead.

'Get off, you silly old devil,' shouted Ann as Samuel pulled her towards him to give her a cuddle.

Their children and grandchildren were entertained by their antics. Lizzy couldn't stop giggling, taking great pleasure from her grandparents' playfulness. There was never a dull moment when the family all came together.

They all spent the rest of the day together at Samuel's new house, the women fussing over the trivial aspects of the house such as bedside carpets and window curtains, tables, chairs and bed linen, while the men worried about where the card table might stand and where to keep the brewing equipment, barrels and wine bottles. When the family gathered for supper that evening, the house was welcoming and gay, as though it had stood there for many years.

8

Samuel's grandson had taken over most of the running of his shop on Deansgate. At first Samuel had found it difficult to stay away, but when he saw his grandson coping well it reassured him, and it wasn't long before he had managed to fill his time with other things, often jobs his wife had found for him to do. Samuel would usually call into the shop first thing on a Monday morning, to check his grandson had the help he needed for the week ahead, and again on a Friday to discuss what he called 'difficult items', which might prove tougher to move on. This was now his established routine and both men were happy with the arrangement.

When Samuel tried the door to his shop one Monday morning in the April of 1791, he was surprised to find it still locked with no one inside. Using his spare key, which he always kept about his person, he let himself in and began to set up for the day ahead, wondering what could possibly have happened to delay his grandson.

Young Samuel entered the shop later that morning, out of breath and as white as a ghost. He could hardly contain his emotions as he explained to his grandfather how Lizzy had been taken ill suddenly in the night.

'But she was in good spirits only yesterday. Whatever could have happened?' asked Samuel, pulling up a chair and indicating the lad should sit down to catch his breath.

Falling onto the chair the young Samuel replied, 'Mother sent her to bed early as she had complained of not feeling well, and when she checked upon her later, she had a dreadfully high temperature. I fear for her wellbeing, Grandfather. I don't know what to do.'

'I'm sure it will pass as quickly as it has arrived,' Samuel tried to reassure the boy. 'I'm sure your mother has everything in hand.'

'She's as anxious as I. I can see it in her eyes,' the boy said, wringing his hands together in great distress.

Before midday Samuel insisted his grandson leave for home, to see what news there was on Lizzy's condition. His grandson had been unable to concentrate on anything. Most of the pledges which had come through the door that morning had been scribed incorrectly into the ledger, and Samuel would have to go over all of them again. The lad was no use to anyone that day.

Young Samuel was reluctant to leave.

'I am quite capable of looking after the place on my own. I've done it for years, haven't I?' insisted Samuel, and the look of concern on his grandson's face subsided.

Upon his arrival home, Betty refused to allow her son to visit his sister. She said she did not want Lizzy to pass her mysterious illness on to him, so Samuel waited for news in the downstairs living area.

*

When his grandson did not return, Samuel Platt closed his pawn shop early, something he had rarely done, and walked over to his daughter's house in Salford. When his daughter opened the front door the news was not good. Lizzy had deteriorated further and Betty would not let her father inside the house as she feared he too might succumb to the fever.

'Would you take Samuel away with you?' she asked her father. 'He's no use here and I would not want him to catch it.'

'Of course, my dear. Send him straight out with his things.'

Betty and her son quickly threw a few clothes into a bag and the front door opened once more. This time Betty appeared with the younger Samuel, walking down the couple of steps with him to where her father was waiting on the pavement below. She hugged her son and said she'd be in touch when things improved.

'Give Lizzy my love, dear,' said her father, and she hugged him too. 'Tell her I wish her a speedy recovery.'

'I will, Father,' Betty called back, already climbing the steps up to her front door, eager to return to her daughter.

Grabbing her arm, her father said, 'Try not to worry, dear. She's a strong one, that one, and she's got youth on her side.'

'Yes, Father. I must get back to her now,' replied Betty, unable to share her father's optimism. Samuel left Salford with a heavy heart as he could see his daughter was distressed.

Lizzy's death came quickly later that day and it was a great shock to everyone, especially her brother, Samuel. They had become very close over the years, sometimes unintentionally shutting out everyone else. But it was Betty who would feel her daughter's loss the most, as she was forced to keep the true reason for her daughter's death a secret.

Just before Lizzy had died she had given birth to a stillborn child. The child had not reached full term and was terribly disfigured. It was a complete shock to Betty. Her daughter was in no fit state to explain herself and, within minutes of the child's death, Lizzy too had died.

Betty had spent no time dwelling on her predicament. Her family would never cope with this type of scandal. She knew what she had to do. As quickly and efficiently as she could, she had cleaned her daughter and removed the girl's nightclothes. Lizzy showed no physical signs of carrying a child except for the blood. Next she had stripped her daughter's bed, wrapped the child's body inside the sheets and removed the bundle to the garden, where she would bury it later. It wasn't until her dead daughter was redressed in clean nightwear and the bed remade that Betty began to sob uncontrollably.

Peter had stayed away at work, but upon his return around 7 pm that evening he discovered his wife sitting silently beside Lizzy's bed, gripping her daughter's hand. All the colour had been drained from Lizzy's face and he instantly knew she had gone. He rushed to Betty's side, pulled her up from her seat and embraced her, saying, 'There's nothing you can do for the poor child now. You must let her go.'

In each other's arms they cried, their shared memories flooding back from previous experiences, but Betty was forced to refrain from revealing her true feelings of despair. Her dear husband could never know the true circumstances of her daughter's death. Later that night, unheard and unseen, she crept downstairs and out into the garden, where she recovered the blood-soaked bedsheets still wrapped around the child's body and, after digging a deep enough hole, buried her secret forever.

Lizzy's funeral service took place on 6th April at St John's church, where her body was the first to be laid to rest inside the family vault. It was harrowing for all concerned, but especially Betty. She was keeping a terrible secret that no one could ever discover, a secret she had to take with her to her grave. She did not think it possible, but her heart ached even more than it had when her baby daughter Ann had died.

During the service she had wanted to read out one of Lizzy's favourite poems, 'Easter Holidays' by Samuel Taylor Coleridge, but she was in no fit state, so she asked her son Samuel if he would read it. Lizzy had known the poem by heart and often recited it while she and Samuel had been walking along the river or lying under a tree after a picnic together. Samuel knew the first few lines by heart himself, as he had heard it so often, but chose to read it off the pages of Lizzy's favourite book of poems. He did so with great calmness, his hands as steady as a rock. He read the words clearly so that the whole congregation could hear them, as if Lizzy herself were reading the poem aloud.

Hail! festal Easter that dost bring
Approach of sweetly-smiling spring,
When Nature's clad in green:
When feather'd songsters through the grove
With beasts confess the power of love
And brighten all the scene.
Now youths the breaking stages load
That swiftly rattling o'er the road
To Greenheys haste away:
While some with sounding oars divide
Of smoothly-flowing Irwell the tide
All sing the festive lay.

Lizzy had often replaced some of the poem's words with her own, such as *Irwell* instead of *Thames* and *Greenheys* in place of *Greenwich*. She enjoyed having fun with her favourite poem. Samuel did the same, allowing the congregation to learn something new of his sister. He continued to read until he reached the end of the poem's sixth verse. The poem was so appropriate, not just because it was almost Easter time in the calendar year but also because it summed up his sister so beautifully.

The months passed by as the family adjusted to life without Lizzy. Betty delighted only in caring for her husband and her remaining child, Samuel, who in her eyes could do no wrong. Her father coped by immersing himself in his business affairs and trying desperately to encourage his son, Samuel Platt the younger, to feel as passionate about Manchester land and property as he did.

Betty's son Samuel found friendship and compassion in one of Lizzy's friends and spent every available moment in her company. Their relationship would result in their having an illegitimate child, which brought them closer together and cemented their connection, although their families found it difficult to accept this situation at first. When Samuel's family found out they were disappointed in him and Ann Cross, a young girl whom they had grown to love as one of their own, who had slipped into the place where Lizzy no longer was.

Everyone in Samuel's family could see how happy he was with Ann and the situation and for this reason did not stand in his way. Ann's father, on the other hand, treated Samuel with distaste. His daughter was too young to marry without the consent of her parents and he refused to allow this to happen. Ann was forced to feel great shame by having to remain unmarried and live at her family's home after her child was born. However, in time, things would right themselves.

9

At the end of October 1792 and five years after writing his will, Samuel Platt the elder found himself able to make another investment when he acquired a plot of land, several houses and a stable around the Piccadilly area of Manchester from a John Smith for £400. The land, known as Standley Barn Close, was originally part of the Standley Barn Charity. This was the name initially given to the charity of Humphrey Booth the elder due to the fact that the lands purchased by the charity in Piccadilly originally belonged to William Standley.

The Booth charities were established in the first quarter of the seventeenth century when Humphrey Booth the elder, a rich fustian merchant of Manchester and Salford, granted lands which comprised five fields and a barn to trustees by a deed of transfer. This deed stated that the income from these lands should be used for the relief of the poor, aged or impotent persons dwelling in the town of Salford. In 1776 an Act of Parliament had enabled the Booth charity trustees to let their estates on building leases for terms up to ninety-nine years long. Houses were being built on the land around Piccadilly by 1790, and Samuel had seen an opportunity. He was right to invest and assume this land would significantly increase in value over the coming years. He signed an indenture, a legal contract, reflecting his obligation to purchase the land. He had the right to sell this land and property if he wished as well as the right to pass it on to his heirs as an inheritance. The deed stated that a percentage of the income from these lands should be used for the relief of the poor of Manchester.

Samuel Platt the younger had for many years observed the successful business dealings of his father and, early in 1793, decided he too should like to invest in land and property with his own accomplished wealth, mostly gained through hard work. His father had already given him the house on Hulme Place where he lived and he had run the pawnbroker's shop on Deansgate successfully now for a number of years. Samuel approached his father with a business opportunity which had come to his notice. A number of houses and a plot of land consisting of 1,289 square yards on Clarence Street in Hulme had become available. This land was situated close to Cornbrook. Samuel asked his father if he felt it was a good business prospect and if he should go ahead. His father was always willing to give his expert opinion and the younger Samuel welcomed his input.

At the same time both men were told of another plot of land, formerly part of Pitt Field, which was now Queen Street in Hulme. This land was half the size at 619 square yards, but they would be able to build two or three houses upon it.

Samuel the younger went ahead with his father's assistance and blessing, but purchased both plots for himself rather than with his father. His father had insisted upon this because his wife had stated very firmly the last time he had purchased land that she wanted it to be his last. She thought her husband was becoming overly infatuated with such transactions, far too late in life. 'All your business dealings will be the death of you,' she had complained. 'You are far too old to be worrying about these sorts of things. Can't you leave it to Samuel to take care of?'

Samuel the elder was delighted his son was finally following in his footsteps and congratulated him by throwing an impromptu celebration for the whole family at his home in Quay Street, much to the astonishment of his wife. Up until then, she had had no idea what the pair were up to, and Samuel the elder knew that she most likely would have tried to put a stop to it had she known. Ann had no option other than to celebrate with the rest of the family, which she did with dignity but also with a sense of pride for her son, as she could see this business transaction had made him very happy. It was also obvious her husband's spirits had been lifted by their son's business dealings.

Some months later the family were to celebrate further when Samuel's grandson announced he was to marry. Ann Cross's father had finally given his blessing to the pair, whose son was now more than half a year old.

'God works in mysterious ways,' declared Samuel Platt as he dressed in his finest outfit in May 1793. 'Out of something so very sad, it never ceases to amaze me that he can provide us with something to celebrate.'

'Whatever are you talking about, dear?' enquired his wife, rushing to avoid being late.

'I have always suspected that Lizzy's death hit Samuel harder than it did anyone else in the family, but today I intend to celebrate with my eldest grandchild as he marries a woman who has helped him through one of the saddest times in his young life. I know this girl will make him very happy.'

'I think so too, dear.'

'They've had a bumpy start. A child out of wedlock is never without its problems, but he has taken responsibility for his actions and shown Ann's family he is prepared to face up to his responsibilities. I do believe Ann's father knows that now.'

'I agree, but will you please hurry up? Stop your talking or we will miss the whole ceremony.'

Rushing to the old Manchester church, they arrived within seconds of the bride. 'I'm too old for this,' puffed Samuel, out of breath as he and Ann hurried down the aisle. Their family were all there to greet them and to see him and Ann into their seats.

As soon as Samuel's great-grandson saw the elderly gentleman, he reached out for him, and he spent the whole of the service seated quietly on his great-grandfather's lap, playing with a bunch of keys to Samuel's many properties. 'They could all belong to you one day, my boy,' Samuel whispered to the child, who looked up and smiled at him.

It was a great day of celebration and afterwards, at the home of the Cross family, one would never have known there was ever any discontent between Ann's father and her new husband. All could see the pair were very happy together and wished them much joy for the future.

Samuel Platt the elder had reached a time in his life when at last he felt complete. His family had been through much heartache over the years, but they had now made it through to better times. Their future looked bright and Samuel now felt it was time to take a back seat. He was after all, not as young as he used to be and it was time he slowed down. Life had become rather exhausting recently.

*

At the end of December 1796 Samuel began to feel quite unwell, suffering with a sore throat and runny nose which seemed to linger for far too long. Over the next few weeks his health deteriorated and when he developed a nasty cough, Ann finally persuaded him to see a physician. Samuel had hardly had a day's illness in his life and assumed, even at the age of seventy-nine, that he would regain his strength. He was an old man and his body was finding it impossible to recover from this particularly nasty attack of influenza. He was too weak to fight the infection which had taken a firm grip of him, and eventually his organs just gave up.

Sadly, because of his nonchalant attitude towards his illness, he gave his family little opportunity to say their goodbyes. Most were shocked by his death and regretted not having seen him in the days before. Secretly Samuel had wanted it this way. He detested any kind of fuss and did not want to worry his wife, who was also in poor health. He knew his will was in order and that his family would receive what was rightly theirs, and that was what he wished for them. He also knew he was loved and admired by his family and hoped they knew he loved them. For Samuel, there was little more to be said or done.

Samuel died in late January 1797 and was buried at St John's church, Manchester. His body was placed in the vault under the church which he had reserved all those years earlier, close to his granddaughter, Lizzy. Upon his death his executors saw to it that his will was executed. His wife and daughter remained at the Quay Street property. His son Samuel received monies and property on Brook St and took over the ownership of the Deansgate properties. His daughter Betty and her husband Peter were both left a sum of money. His grandson, Samuel Bradshaw, received full ownership of his pawnbroker's shop on Deansgate, which Samuel was only too happy to continue to run, along with the sum of £1,000, which he too would soon invest in more property.

PART II

1771–1817

Samuel Bradshaw

Told by Samuel himself

Samuel Bradshaw
b.1764
m.1793
d.1817

Gentleman/Pawnbroker

Ann Cross
b.1771

d.1804

Samuel
b.1792

Richard
b.1794

**William Platt
b.1796**

Elizabeth
b.1798

Ann
b.1800

Henrietta
b.1802

10

I had barely known my real father. He had died when I was six, so I could not remember him. A weaver by profession, he had owned no land and little property. He was a kind, hardworking man, my mother had once told me, and she also said I had inherited his good nature and unassuming manner. Whilst growing up I had not missed him as I had a grandfather of whom I was incredibly fond and a father in my mother's second husband, who cared for me as well as any father would. They had married when I was eight.

My mother was fortunate to have remarried a man with an impeccable reputation and property in the Manchester and Salford areas. A pipe maker by trade, Father ran a successful business from a small factory in Manchester, while we lived in an ample house in Salford. My sister and I wanted for nothing as children. Although we saw precious little of our father during the week, as he was a busy man with his pipe making business, we enjoyed days out at weekends and always felt accepted and loved by both parents.

When I was ten years old my mother had another child. During this time my sister and I were never made to feel excluded. My mother and father involved us in family celebrations and decision making. We even had a say in choosing the name of our new baby sister.

One might describe our family as comfortably well off, mostly due to the hard work and tenacity of my mother's father, who had at one time been a cloth merchant and later established a successful pawnbroker business. Whilst growing up, I had become extremely close to my grandfather. This was not because I was his first grandchild or because I had been named after him; it was much more. He was a gentleman in every sense of the word. He was the most honest man I would ever meet and he had a huge influence on my life. He was incredibly hardworking, whilst always finding the time to support anyone who needed it, emotionally and financially. He always had time for other people, listening respectfully to their stories of misfortune or achievement. He never judged but handed out sensible advice, which I undoubtedly believe will have secured him a place in heaven. I owe my grandfather a great deal for shaping me into the man I am today.

My sister and I had grown up in and around the Manchester area and we knew the place well. As we grew older we were allowed to visit our grandfather's pawnbroker shop whenever we wished and often did. His shop was a fifteen-minute walk from our home in Salford. There was never a dull moment in that shop, always some adventure to be had and story to be told.

Although it was a dark and crowded space, my grandfather's shop had a way of making everyone feel at home. Mostly lit by candles dotted upon shelves and cupboards, the shop gave up its secrets slowly, for everywhere I looked, a new item left behind surprised and excited my young imagination. To my sister and me, it was a treasure trove of lost and forgotten riches, each hiding a unique tale of its owner. Our grandfather was the keeper of these tales and would often stimulate our minds with stories of great wealth or sometimes human suffering, but mostly they were humorous stories he would tell through play-acting using a variety of props from his shop.

One chilly January day a great sadness took hold of our family, and it would remain for some time to come. I was thirteen years old and Lizzy was eleven. We had arrived home from our grandfather's shop, still laughing about the tale he had just told us and the silly impressions he had attempted, only to be greeted on the doorstep by our father, who was holding out two bags to us. 'Your baby sister is very ill and you must return to your grandfather's shop immediately.'

'Where's Mother?' I enquired.

'She's with baby Ann,' my father responded, gravely. 'The baby is not at all well and your mother is very worried.'

'Can we see them?' I asked.

'I'm afraid not, Samuel. Your mother has given me strict instructions not to let you or your sister inside. She fears you too may catch whatever it is the baby has. She wants you and your sister to take your things and go and stay with your grandfather for a few days, until it is safe enough for you to return home. Can you do that for her, Samuel?'

'Yes, Father, of course.'

'Give Mother and baby Ann our love, Father,' Lizzy said tearfully.

'I will, my dear. Now, be on your way with your brother. Look after your sister, Samuel.'

'I will,' I replied, and we made our way back to Grandfather's shop feeling very different to when we had left.

We didn't know it at the time but our baby sister had contracted smallpox, a disease which was prevalent in the town. Living in any densely populated town at this time brought with it disease and death, but you never think it can happen to you. We should have been more fortunate than most, living on the outskirts of the town, nearer to the countryside than the more populated areas. We should have been excluded from this type of affliction, yet it seemed we were not.

Three days later our grandfather was forced to share with us the sad news of our sister's death. Understandably everyone was very upset, not least Mother and Father.

Ann's funeral took place on 23rd January 1777 at St John's church. Poor little Ann had not even reached her second birthday and it was heartbreaking to see her tiny coffin being carried by Father into the church. The memories of that time will remain with me always. Until then, I had never witnessed my mother's overwhelming sadness. She looked like death itself on the day and for some time after. The day had stirred up many memories for my parents, who had both previously been forced to bury other loved ones.

After my sister's death, Father threw himself into his work more and more. He spent many more hours at his factory than he did at home with his family. I presume it was his way of dealing with his loss. Mother too spent more time working at Grandfather's shop and in the company of my grandmother. She appeared to gain comfort from her own mother.

After the death of my younger sister, my relationship with my other sister became more intense. From that day onwards we confided in each other more. We told each other everything, withholding nothing, enjoyed each other's company immensely and would go immediately to each other if we ever needed advice or reassurance about anything. In fact, as we grew older we rarely had time for other people. We took great pleasure in the time we shared alone together: walking along the canal towpath and observing the boat people, enjoying a pleasure boat trip on the Bridgewater or eating a picnic down by the pond on the Greenhill estate near Moss Side. Some might have called our behaviour unhealthy or inappropriate, but we saw nothing wrong in it. We were simply a great comfort to one another, nothing more and nothing less.

Do not misunderstand me, for we did converse with other people and were sociable towards others when it was required. Lizzy had her friends and I had mine, but together we shared a very easy relationship which took no effort and that was what made it so attractive to us both. Although this was a sad time for my family, I consider myself fortunate to have a great many fond memories of this time spent with Lizzy and growing up around Manchester.

Over the next decade I went through a great many changes in my life. While Lizzy received her education at home, I attended the grammar school, excelling in Latin, Greek and mathematics. It was at this school I would meet and make a great many friends; some would accompany me through to adulthood and we would remain trusted friends for the rest of our lives. William Gardner became a fustian and woollen cord manufacturer. James Chapman followed my grandfather and me into our profession and became a pawnbroker, first on Alport Street and later moving his premises into Thomas Street. John Harrison, with whom I probably spent more time than I did with anyone else, became a cotton merchant and did very well for himself when he opened Ancoats Mill. William Woolley, another good friend, became a fustian cutter and later lived a few doors away from me in Cumberland Street.

When I left school, I began to assist my grandfather full-time in his shop on Deansgate. I quickly acquired the knowledge and skills required to run such a business, mainly because I had a very good teacher in my grandfather. My uncle and grandmother ran my grandfather's other shop on Alport Street, sometimes helped by my aunt. My grandparents lived in one property and my uncle in the other. It was a family business in every sense of the word, except for the fact my uncle, as far as I was aware, had never set foot in this shop.

'Why does Uncle Samuel never come to this shop?' I asked my grandfather one day. 'You often go to the other one and Grandmother comes here when she is needed. So why not Uncle Samuel?'

'I think he much prefers it at the other end of the street,' Grandfather replied.

'Why?' I enquired.

'He has his own interests up that end and we must respect that, Samuel.'

I had no idea what my grandfather meant by this but felt I should not persist further in my questioning.

'Well, I for one prefer this shop, especially when it's just the two of us,' I said.

'So do I, dear boy, so do I,' replied my grandfather.

My uncle lived alone and had never married, and to this day I have no idea what it actually was that kept him away from this shop and at the other end of the street, but he seemed to much prefer the Hulme end of Manchester.

11

From a young age I was aware of my grandfather's dedication to his business affairs, knowing that he had the desire to buy up land and property and make money from renting out buildings. As I grew older he would often discuss his plans with me during our time together in his shop. I was fully aware he had striven all his life to achieve this aim and his hard work was now paying off as he had managed to accumulate a great fortune. He could become quite preoccupied when his dealings were about to reach fruition, and I struggled to understand why he was quite so obsessed.

It was a great day for my grandfather when in 1786 we helped him and my grandmother to move into a property on Quay Street. I don't think I had ever seen him as elated and excited as he was on that day. Going to live on Quay Street was a colossal achievement for my grandfather and meant a great deal to him.

Soon after his move to Quay Street, my grandfather was purchasing more land. This time it was in Hulme. His intention was to provide my uncle with a more desirable house in which to live and entertain. Soon he was able to bestow upon his only son one of two large houses he had built on the land. I believe my uncle was quite embarrassed by his father's generosity and it was this gesture which made my uncle re-evaluate his own life and future.

As my grandfather accumulated more and more land and property he was advised by his long-standing friend William Cooper to make a will, which he did in the March of 1787. Mr Cooper was well known in Manchester, possibly for being a little eccentric. He lived opposite St Peter's church, which was built around this time due to the increase in the local population.

I can recall visiting Mr Cooper's cottage on one occasion with my grandfather, when I was much younger. I forget why now; possibly the two men had some business to do together. As we walked around his ample walled gardens, which were planted with fruit trees and displayed a fish pond at the centre, I wondered why Mr Cooper should have a windmill on his land. Connected to this windmill were a stable for three horses, a cart house and a summerhouse, but it was the windmill which Mr Cooper so desperately wanted to show off. I'm sure my grandfather had seen it on many occasions before and was just humouring his friend, but Mr Cooper proudly showed us inside his windmill, explaining to me how it had four pairs of stones for grinding dye woods, two grindle stones, and two rasping mills. I'm afraid to say this tour held little interest for such a young boy. A field path led across the kitchen garden, away from the windmill and towards Castlefield, and I was more interested in following this path.

The two men had obviously spent much time in each other's company and appeared to get on very well. Mr Cooper insisted we return with him to his house for a drink. I must admit my clearest memory from the visit is of the excellent refreshments put on for us by Mrs Cooper.

I recall my grandfather's great relief when the whole process of writing his last will and testament was complete and he came to tell me in the shop. 'You will all be well cared for once I'm gone,' he said. 'I've seen to it that everything will be fairly split. There should be no reason for anyone to feel disadvantaged.'

I said very little as I did not know how to reply to such a statement. I didn't think my grandfather was looking for approval or reassurance. I suspected he just wished to express his relief at the conclusion of his will writing.

12

In the March of 1791, my whole life changed forever when our darling Lizzy fell terribly ill. It seemed that one moment everything was all right and the next all that had changed. Sunday after church we had enjoyed a stroll together along the canal path. We watched the goings-on of the boat people, laughing together about silly things, and later we visited Grandfather at his shop before returning home. But by early evening Lizzy was complaining she felt unwell and Mother sent her off to bed. Upon checking her some two hours later, Mother became very concerned as Lizzy was displaying a high temperature. We had no idea of the seriousness of my sister's complaint at this time as she had seemed so well earlier in the day. However, the following day my dear beloved sister was taken from us. My mother informed me, saying she had been too weak to fight the illness.

Lizzy had barely had the chance to grow into a woman. Recently she had discussed with me her newfound desire to seek a husband and even mentioned the idea of raising children. She should have had her whole life ahead of her, but that was not to be for poor Lizzy. Our home once again become a very solemn place.

We buried Lizzy on 6th April. I recall it was a Wednesday. The ceremony was brief and Mother asked me to read one of Lizzy's favourite poems. I know Lizzy would have appreciated this symbol of our love for her. My elderly grandfather was markedly shocked by her death and repeated over and over, 'It should have been me to go first, not our dear, beautiful Lizzy. The Lord has made a terrible mistake. The Lord has made a terrible mistake.'

I know my sister was looking down on me that day, for that was also the day her good friend Ann Cross came to visit us at the house. Ann had been to the house many times before, and Mother and I had spoken to her briefly outside the church after Lizzy's funeral. When she arrived at the house she soon become distressed, and my mother did what she could, but no amount of comforting seemed to console Ann. She was quite beside herself at losing her only confidant and did not know how she was to continue without my sister.

Ann did not outstay her welcome, but she was at the house for some hours. It was early evening when my mother suggested she should be heading home, as her parents would be wondering where she had got to.

'Samuel will walk you to your door, won't you, dear?' Mother asked, and I was willing to oblige. I knew exactly what the girl was going through. During our walk along the streets of Manchester to Ann's home, we both sensed Lizzy's spirit was walking beside us and trying to tell us something.

For the next few months I visited my grandfather often and saw a great deal of Ann. Both gave me great comfort. Ann managed to fill the void where my sister had once stood firm, and in return I was able to replace her dear friend. There were almost seven years between our ages, yet we did not allow this to prevent our friendship from developing.

By the end of the same year we had become more than just good friends. Our union was one brought about by a combined sorrow, which ultimately resulted in the birth of our first child in September 1792. Ann has often joked over the years how she remembers it well. The Manchester streets had never been brighter, as new oil lamps lit them up at night. She remembered their glow as they lit up the room in which she gave birth to our son, 'almost as if the Almighty was putting in an appearance and showing his approval,' she later said teasingly.

We were not married at the time of our son's birth. Neither one of us had known Ann was with child. It had come as a complete shock to us both. I recall Ann commenting on occasion how she thought she was putting on weight, but we had naively joked together that she would soon have to wear her mother's clothes if she became any bigger, for Ann's mother was a jolly, red-faced, rotund woman. Our families were understandably disappointed with us when they realised what had been going on. Ann's father, normally a tolerant, placid man, became angry and embarrassed about the whole affair.

Shortly after the birth of our son, Ann became quite ill. It was a trying time for all. I hardly saw her or the child for almost a month. Her parents kept her inside the house and wouldn't let me near, but thankfully her mother helped to nurse her back to good health.

I spent much of this time with my grandfather, working in his pawnbroker's shop and preferring his company to that of my mother and father. Grandfather did not seem to judge me, rather to accept the situation and move on.

It was at this time that my grandfather asked me to take over the day-to-day running of his shop. I suppose he thought it might take my mind off things. I now understand why he did this. I needed some stability in my life. I had responsibilities and needed a regular

income, and I had realised I should no longer rely upon my parents
for money.

'I think it's about time you stood on your own two feet, my boy,'
my grandfather said to me one day. 'Show them all what you're really
made of. I know you can do it.'

He was by now in his seventies, a fine age, but he explained the
work made him tire easily and he was due a rest. I couldn't argue
with that.

'I will make you proud, Grandfather.'

'I know you will, my boy. You will make us all proud.'

I split my time between working at the pawn shop, which I loved,
and visiting Ann and our son, Samuel. It was difficult to get the
balance right, but I had been given the opportunity to prove to
everyone I could do it and I was very determined. I was confident
Ann's father would soon realise I was a hard worker and could
provide for his daughter and grandson. Having to prove this was no
hardship for me, as everyone could see we were truly in love with
one another.

During this time my grandfather announced he was looking for
further property or land to invest in. Once again he asked my opinion
on various opportunities. I hope he valued my opinion when it was
given, although I'm not sure I was truly experienced enough at this
time to be asked. I suspect he was testing me in some way. He would
often disclose his business ideas and dealings to me before telling my
grandmother, and I knew I had to be very careful not to allow her or
my mother to learn of them. I was fully aware they did not approve of
the risks he sometimes took. I doubt my uncle would have approved
either at the time.

On one occasion around this time my grandfather returned very
pleased with himself. He had called into the shop having just signed
an indenture for land and property in the Piccadilly area of
Manchester. He was not ashamed to admit this land had cost him the
tidy sum of £400, yet claimed he would in no time have a decent
return on the properties through their rentable value, as the area in

question was much sought after. My uncle Samuel took an immediate liking to one of my grandfather's new properties, specifically 2 Back Piccadilly, which he soon claimed for himself.

Once Ann was feeling better, a baptism was arranged for our son on the 10th October at St Ann's, which was her family's church. Ann's father had eventually given permission for me to attend, although I didn't feel able to invite any of my family. I regretted that for many years, but Ann's family had organised the event and it had not been my decision to make.

Ann and I were in fact thrilled to have had a son together, although our families did not feel the same. My parents took some time to accept the situation and Ann's parents even longer. It was made difficult between us for quite some time as Ann's parents tried often to prevent us from seeing one another. I think they hoped our feelings for one another would subside, but we were determined and endured these difficulties. I promised Ann and her father that one day we would be married.

It was six months after our son's baptism before Ann's father eventually relented and accepted we still wanted to be together. Our wedding was planned by Ann's parents for 11th May 1793. My grandfather played a large part in their acceptance of our union, explaining that I was financially secure and confirming my adoration of Ann and the baby. He was very generous towards me and, with his help, Ann's family were eventually unable to think of any reason for us not to be married. I suspect Grandfather had also spoken with my mother, who was terribly excited once she discovered I was to marry. My grandfather had finally managed to bring our two families together, which was what should have happened months earlier.

Our wedding was nothing too exuberant; a simple affair was all Ann and I had wanted. The day was special because we could at last put behind us all the bad feeling between our families. This was the most important thing for us both. We were married in the parish church by the Reverend Brookes. My mother and stepfather had married there twenty years earlier, and the church was where most people in the town of Manchester wanted to get married.

Ann looked a picture as her father accompanied her down the aisle. Her mother held on tightly to our eight-month-old son, Samuel, but when he saw me after the service he grinned, wriggling and reaching out for me to hold him.

I had asked my good friend John Harrison, a cotton merchant by trade, to be my witness. We had first become acquainted during our school days and always stayed in touch even though both of us were often too busy to see one another. On the days we were able to spend some time in each other's company we would often meet at a local tavern; we would converse about events, exchange philosophies and almost always end up regretting the amount we had drunk the next morning.

After the ceremony my grandfather whispered to me quietly, so that no one else could hear. He said he wanted me to have his pawnbroker's shop as a wedding present.

'I couldn't possibly, Grandfather. It is much too generous of you.'

The expression on his face turned from one of excitement to rejection. I felt terrible.

'Would this small gesture on your wedding day not make you happy, son?' he asked.

'It would, Grandfather, but—'

He didn't let me finish. 'Then there is nothing more to be said. I want you to have it. I know I can trust you to run it in the same way as I have all these years. No one will notice the difference and I can retire peacefully to my residence in Quay Street.' He smiled, then grabbed my hand and shook it persuasively as if to bind the agreement.

After the ceremony everything fell into place. Ann, the baby and I moved into the premises above the pawn shop on Deansgate. I was by now almost thirty years old. I had my own home and a good income. I was regarded by many as a gentleman. I now legally owned and had taken over the running of my grandfather's shop, a decision accepted by my uncle. I was comfortably off, happy and finally had everything I wanted. My parents had accepted Ann and the baby. They had always had a soft spot for Ann and I believe they had finally realised they were missing out on their first grandchild. My marriage to Ann had felt like an age in its coming, but it was the first day of the rest of our lives and we were only looking forward.

Six months after our marriage Ann announced she was expecting our second child. We had thought this would happen quickly, as it had the first time, but when it did, Ann was apprehensive. She did not want to fall ill again afterwards, and this, I'm sure, was at the forefront of her mind throughout the whole time she was with child. During this time her moods were extreme and she often said she felt sad. Thankfully, once the child had been born, Ann was a different person. She suffered little discomfort and no illness.

We now had two sons, our second named after my real father, Richard. My mother was surprised yet delighted by the choice of name, and Richard was baptised on 2nd July at St Ann's church, where this time both families were able to join in with the celebrations.

Less than two years later we were back at St Ann's church to have our third son, William, baptised. This was in September 1796 and, although this should have been a happy occasion, I had been concerned for my grandfather's health of late. He was nearing eighty years old, and over the past month I had seen a great change in him. I worried he might not be with us much longer, and it was for this reason we decided to give our son William a second name: the surname of my grandfather. I was so fond of the old man and felt it a fitting tribute that the Platt name might continue for generations to come. He was thrilled when we announced our decision, as was my mother, who had also once held the name, albeit for a much shorter time.

'This is very generous of you, my boy. I don't know what to say.' My grandfather was overcome with emotion, his body quivering as he spoke.

'I never meant to upset you, Grandfather.'

'No, no, you haven't, my dear boy,' he replied, wiping a tear discreetly from his cheek with an unsteady hand. 'You have done quite the opposite. This is possibly the most respectful tribute anyone could have paid me. I thank you from the bottom of my heart. You have made me a very happy old man.' We hugged one another, and it was then I felt how frail he had become.

Within a month of William's baptism my grandfather was visiting the shop less and had taken to sitting most days with only my aunt and grandmother for company, or my uncle, if he found the time to visit. My grandmother was struggling to care for herself as well as her weak husband and much of the burden had fallen to my aunt.

My grandparents rarely ventured out. My mother would often make the journey from Salford to assist her sister in carrying out chores which their mother had become unable to complete. My wife did what she could, but it was difficult with the children.

I tried to discuss with my grandparents whether they should come and live with us or move to be with my mother, but they would not entertain such suggestions. They refused outright.

'We don't want to be a burden, my boy,' said Grandfather.

'We're sure you mean well, but we are happy here,' agreed my grandmother.

'We would get under everyone's feet, and that is no way to be remembered,' added Grandfather.

I didn't blame them. They were used to each other's company, and why should they have to give that up at their time of life? My grandfather had striven all his days to live in the house he finally owned. How could I expect him to be happy about leaving it?

13

During the winter months that followed the temperature fell dramatically, and January was a particularly severe month. My mother was visiting her parents more and more often and I had known her on occasion to insist on staying the night, against my grandfather's wishes. I tried to visit my grandparents most days and often I found them sat huddled close to a roaring fire; nevertheless their hands would be as cold as ice. Yet they remained content in each other's company.

My grandfather had always had a positive influence in my life. I had been very fond of the old man for as long as I could remember. When he passed away, in the early morning of 31st January 1797, my grandmother, mother and I were all beside him. I had not expected to become as emotional as I did, and my mother was strong for me, reassuring me, 'He wanted for nothing, Samuel. You are witness to the fact he died peacefully. He has enjoyed a long, fairly privileged and happy life and is now in an even better place. You have nothing to feel despondent about. Your grandfather will go to his grave a contented man.' Under these difficult circumstances my mother's words helped to soothe the absolute hopelessness I was feeling. My grandfather would be sorely missed by everyone who had ever known him.

Grandfather's funeral took place at his beloved St John's church on Byrom Street. He was laid to rest in the vault he had reserved years previously and beside my sister, Lizzy.

We all went to my grandparents' home in Quay Street after the funeral. Grandmother appeared lost. She kept looking over her shoulder as though she expected my grandfather to walk in at any time. Later that very same day, my mother suggested my grandmother and aunt go to live with her and my father. Grandmother seemed almost relieved when this suggestion was put to her. As my mother helped her to pack a small overnight bag, saying they would return the following day to collect everything else she would need, my uncle appeared in the doorway.

'I think it would be a far simpler solution for all concerned if I were to move in here, to be with Mother and Ann. It will cause much less upheaval for them. Don't you think so, Betty?'

'If you think that would be preferable, brother.'

My father agreed with my uncle. According to my mother, Grandmother was also happy with this solution and thanked my uncle for being so understanding.

'I really don't want to leave this house,' she told him. 'Your father and I have been very happy here and I feel as though part of him is still here with us.'

'I know just what you mean, Mother. Now, you're not to worry. I will go and fetch a few of my things and all will be settled in no time at all.'

My uncle's house at Hulme Place, the house my grandfather had built for him, was soon rented out. All the properties my grandfather had owned passed to my uncle, as well as £1,500. He now had responsibilities he had never had before and he rose to the occasion, becoming confident in business. My uncle would go on to purchase further property over the coming years, which my grandfather would have greatly approved of.

My grandfather had made sure everyone was looked after. My grandmother was to receive a £40 annuity per year, from the rent of other properties, to pay for the upkeep of her home on Quay Street. My mother, father and aunt were left £500 each.

In his will my grandfather left me £1,000. With this money and some savings I decided to purchase a property on Cumberland Street in Manchester. The house was of reasonable size for our growing family and there was a stable attached. We were able to employ a number of servants. We had paid a woman to cook and clean for us previously at our other house, but now we were able to employ a cook, housemaid and groom, all overseen by a butler. When necessary we would call upon the services of a gardener.

I had little to do with the day-to-day running of the house or the dealings with the servants; I left that to Ann. However, I enjoyed the assistance and companionship I received from my personal servant, John Shepley. Shepley had been a tenant of my grandfather's, residing for some years at a property on Garrett Lane, and came with excellent references. He saw to my every individual need, helping me to dress stylishly, accompanying me whenever and wherever I needed him, liaising with the other servants so that I didn't have to, and his extensive knowledge of alcoholic beverages could not be surpassed.

Our Cumberland Street home was in an ideal position as it was a short walk from my pawnbroker's shop and my grandfather's other properties along Deansgate, now in possession of my uncle. It was a pleasant walk for Ann and the children through the allotments sited on Gartside Street to my grandmother's home on Quay Street, a walk they took most days. Ann and I instantly fell in love with the place. It was a far less busy thoroughfare than Quay Street and ideal as the children had more space to explore.

I made more of an effort to visit my grandmother after my grandfather's death, yet I was unable to do this for very long. Four months later my grandmother also passed away. She joined my grandfather's side in the vault of St John's church on 27th May 1798. The death of a loved one has a habit of making one realise how little time we all have on this earth and how all of it is so very precious.

My aunt and uncle, for a time, remained living together in Quay Street, but it was quite obvious that neither was terribly happy with this arrangement. It wasn't long before my uncle moved out and went to live at 2 Back Piccadilly, where there was accommodation and a warehouse for storage. My poor aunt was left to rattle around in the big house, but she too would eventually leave, surprising us all by marrying. My uncle spent the next seven years toing and froing between one property and the other.

14

In the summer of 1798 Ann presented me with our fourth child, a daughter. We named her Elizabeth after my mother. She was a handsome child and all three of her brothers were very taken with her placid nature. We had Elizabeth baptised at St Ann's, as we had with all of our children. My wife's family had always attended this church and we were happy to join services at both St Ann's and St John's. Two years later another daughter was born. She was dark, like her mother, and so we named her Ann.

During this time I was trying to concentrate on my business, but my uncle appeared extremely agitated and I became concerned for his wellbeing. He made the decision to rent out the old shop on Alport Street and insisted he was investing the monies collected from the rent wisely, telling me he had 'bigger plans'. It would be some years before he would confide in me about what those plans were.

One might suspect my pawnbroking business of being established and run on the misfortune of others, yet I would argue with those who describe it this way. I believe I have always run my business in a sympathetic and caring manner, a lesson taught to me very early by my grandfather. His dealings with the people of Manchester on a day-to-day basis were always out of compassion. He taught me to be organised and efficient but, above all, honest. When a customer enters my pawnbroker's premises on Deansgate, carrying with them their tale of woe, often offering their most precious possessions, I ensure I make scrupulous records. I do this to ensure I know where the item has come from, who has pawned it, the date it was pawned and how much money was exchanged. This enables me to contact the customer when the time comes for them to buy back their possessions. Discretion is important to those customers who cannot afford to liberate their goods, as I am forced to sell on their belongings at regular auctions. I have never disclosed any personal details about individuals, as instructed by my grandfather.

My premises are often overcrowded with the precious assets which once belonged to the more unfortunate citizens of Manchester. These can include an assortment of furniture, linen, window curtains and printed hangings, dressing glasses, clocks, pocket watches, paintings, broaches, pins, crucifixes and other jewellery. Some have even described my shop as a treasure trove of objects which tell their own tales. I am only too aware I can be seen to profit from others' misery and I do my utmost to dispel this falsehood.

In 1802, the same year my youngest child, Henrietta, was born, my uncle took the decision to move back to 47 Quay Street. The house had become vacant and he admitted he had recently come to dislike the hustle and bustle of the Piccadilly area of Manchester. He told me he felt uneasy walking late at night, even though some years earlier the local council had employed night-watchmen to patrol our Manchester streets.

I conversed with him one evening at a local tavern, where he confided to me his thoughts and feelings. He was feeling particularly dispirited when I reminded him of a comment he had made to me some years earlier about having a 'bigger plan'. He reacted with surprise, as though he had forgotten our conversation, and I reminded him he had a station in life and reason he was more privileged than others. He appeared to have lost his way.

We discussed my grandfather, his father. We recalled the old man's words and deeds and soon we were discussing how my uncle could continue the crusade my grandfather had once begun. After a number of drinks, my uncle insisted on disclosing his financial situation to me, and together we discussed what would be his next course of action. We considered many options and our discussions went on afterwards for some months, but eventually, and in memory of my grandfather, my uncle managed to continue in investing for all of our futures.

It was that same evening in the tavern when I was to confide in my uncle about the concerns I had for my wife, Ann. Since the birth of our sixth child she had become quite unwell. She had, after all, had a child every alternate year for the past ten years. Some days she would feel stronger than others, but it had reminded us both of how she had felt after the birth of our first son. I did not know what I would do if I were to lose her. My uncle was very understanding and reassured me he had never known a stronger woman than Ann. 'I'm quite sure this melancholy will pass, given time,' he told me. 'You'll see. She will be improved in no time, mark my words.'

Over the next year Ann improved little, but great changes were taking place in my uncle's life. Uncle Samuel moved back to his property in Hulme Place, renting out the Quay Street property once more. He, as his father before him, was a gentleman who owned much land and property, and this was how he made his living. He continued to use the property at the back of Piccadilly as a warehouse, allowing me to store excess pledges made to my shop on Deansgate, but he had little interest in the pawnbroking business now. He had his heart set on acquiring more property and land, but finding the most advantageous exchange was proving more difficult than he had anticipated.

In March 1804 my wife took a turn for the worse. Her end came rapidly after a particularly bad fever, where she appeared to imagine all manner of creatures which most likely caused her to die of fright. Samuel wasn't yet twelve years old, Henrietta not quite two. What was I to do with six young children who all depended upon me alone, now that their dear mother was gone? At first I felt complete and utter despair, not knowing which way to turn.

We laid Ann to rest on 29th March 1804 in St John's vault, beside my grandparents. She had not seen out her thirty-third year. She had been taken from us too early and there was nothing I could have done about it.

Their mother's death had a profound effect on some of my children, none more so than Samuel, my eldest son. He became quite preoccupied with the church and its teachings, taking himself off to St John's and other churches within Manchester at every opportunity that was available to him.

Reverend Clowes soon wanted to speak with me about Samuel's affinity with the church. A discussion was held between us where the reverend asked if I had ever considered a career in the church for Samuel. Indeed, I said, I had not, but if it was something he wished to pursue I would not stand in his way. Reverend Clowes also asked if I had ever considered sending Samuel to university. I was now a gentleman with land and property and this appeared to make a difference. I had been able to give Samuel a good education so far, but the reverend had obviously seen a potential in Samuel which I had missed. A plan for the future was suggested, a path for Samuel to follow, and the rest of his life was suddenly mapped out for him. He was more than happy to follow this path, so I could do little more than support him.

Richard had always been a quiet boy, but it appeared his mother's death had affected him more than I had realised at first. He seemed to worry about unimportant things. I noticed he became quite malnourished as he chose to eat far less than everyone else. He would come to me and ask about his mother, saying, 'I can't remember what Mother looked like,' or 'Father, I've forgotten the sound of Mother's voice.' These things seemed to upset him terribly and I was forced to seek my mother's advice.

'Give him time to heal, my dear. We all need time. It's been a terrible shock for us all.'

Her words were of little comfort to Richard but always helped me.

On occasion I might find Richard huddled alone in a corner somewhere in the house, silent tears trickling down his face. I did not know how to respond during these times and attempted to rally the boy with a story from my shop, as my grandfather had on so many occasions with my sister and me. This seemed to do the trick and I found myself thinking about the boy's future. I decided to get Richard more involved with my pawnbroker business, with the thought in mind that he might one day wish to take over from me when I was ready to retire. 'Take up the baton', you might say, as my grandfather had passed it on to me. I know my other children all missed their mother very much, but they were young enough to have the time required to adjust, as I had when I'd lost my father. For my youngest daughter, Henrietta, it was worst at night. Sometimes there was just no consoling the child and for a time my mother took her in.

A week after Ann's funeral my uncle came to see me at my home in

Cumberland Street. We talked again, mostly about my grandfather and what he would do if he were in my position. We both knew that he believed family came above all else and I had to be strong for my children and their futures. 'Invest, my boy, invest,' my uncle joked as he attempted to sound like my grandfather. We both knew he meant every word of it, yet finding a good deal for my uncle was proving difficult. Finding one for myself would also prove to be a challenge.

Before the year was out I had moved my family from our home on Cumberland Street to enable myself to purchase a large property next door to my shop on Deansgate. This property was situated on the corner of Cupid's Alley and Deansgate. At the time a widow named Ann Schofield was living there. She had lost her husband some four years earlier but now wanted to move away from Manchester. She had been in my shop on occasion, but I didn't know her well. It was by chance she happened to mention wanting to leave the area, if only she could sell her property. I was able to purchase the property for a good price and quickly. After making some changes to the premises, I managed to convert it into a warehouse, enabling me to store my pledges in a more orderly fashion. The building was large enough inside to be able to hold my auctions there. This in turn freed up space inside the property at 62 Deansgate, allowing us to live there and run the shop from Cupid's Alley. There was no stopping me after my purchase of 1 Cupid's Alley. I now had a taste for the property business and I was keen to purchase more.

A plot of land consisting of several dwelling houses became available on Little Quay Street. They were smaller houses than my uncle's on Quay Street, yet they would bring in a substantial rent when occupied. They were my next acquisition.

At the same time my uncle began to buy many more properties around Manchester. He already had two properties which fronted the main Altrincham highway out of Manchester and which backed onto Hulme Place, but he was keen to purchase more property in Hulme. In September 1805 he purchased a plot of land consisting of

619 square yards, formerly known as Pit Field. He was soon the landlord of four houses which stood in Queen Street, Hulme. Some months later in April 1806 he purchased several more houses on Back Quay Street.

A further opportunity was made available to my uncle when a parcel of land on Garrett Lane became available, near to where my grandfather had previously purchased land on Brook Street and where my uncle was now proprietor. The land consisted of 440 square yards with several dwelling houses, coach house, stables, cottage and gardens. The annual chief rent from these properties was substantial. Uncle Samuel was extremely pleased with this purchase. 'I shall finally make myself a fortune,' he proudly announced. 'There is no stopping me now.'

15

In the September of 1807, my life changed once more. I do not know all of what occurred, but I know my uncle had a meeting arranged to discuss the possible purchase of a substantial piece of land and properties in the Greenheys area, south-east of Hulme. He had told me little of his interest in this area, but he briefly mentioned his meeting the day before when he called into my shop to ask if he could speak with me after it. 'I have a business proposition I wish to discuss with you,' he announced. 'I should be able to tell you more tomorrow.'

I was intrigued. My uncle appeared slightly agitated, but I thought very little of it at the time, as I put his emotional state down to excitement.

The story told by the men who observed my uncle's rapid demise was one of harrowing circumstance. They explained my uncle had become fervent whilst discussing the piece of land and its value. When, after some toing and froing, the men selling were unable to reach an agreement, my uncle had apparently become exasperated with the situation, asking for a few moments to collect his thoughts. I was informed he had turned away from the men, presumably to think about his offer, when he dropped to the floor like a stone, his body suddenly shuddering in spasm. It appeared he could not breathe. Saliva was running from his mouth as his body tremored for more than a minute. When he eventually lay still, the men went to him, but he was already dead. I have since discovered this affliction is known as a fit and is thought to have something to do with brain malfunction. The doctor who was sent for informed me that there could be a number of reasons for my uncle's sudden death and that there would have been nothing anyone could have done. His death had come quickly and was a terrible shock to me.

We held my uncle's funeral on 25th September 1807 at St John's church, where his body joined the rest of our family in the vault. It was a sombre day for the whole family. A huge sense of responsibility now rested on my shoulders and I did not want to let anyone down.

Coming to terms with the wealth I had suddenly inherited was challenging. My uncle's home in Hulme was quickly rented, but I now had the mammoth task of ensuring the rents from all of his and my other various properties across Manchester were also collected in full and on time. Mother, although now in her sixties, took it upon herself to help me with this.

Following my uncle's death I felt terribly restless and did not understand why; then one day a thought entered my head about the business deal my uncle had been forced to leave unfinished near Greenheys. I made some enquiries into the nature of his dealings and discovered the land in question had once been part of a manor in Hulme belonging to Sir John Bland, former owner of Hulme Hall. The farm property, consisting of a number of buildings and thirty-eight and a half statute acres of land, had recently been in the possession of the Wyatt family and had belonged to the Barber family of Moss Side when my uncle had made enquiries. I discovered the last of the Barbers had died recently and this was why the land was again up for sale. When I made this discovery the hairs on the back of my neck stood proud and I was sure I could feel my uncle's presence beside me. I knew immediately what I had to do. I put forward a proposal for the land and it was accepted. I paid £5,775 for the farm known locally as Pepperhill. This was in 1809.

Within a week of this purchase we had left our home in Cumberland Street, moving our servants and possessions into my uncle's house at Hulme Place. The property had become vacant and thankfully had been kept in good condition. I was able to sell our home on Cumberland Street quickly, freeing up the necessary capital for our move.

I went on to purchase a number of other properties over the next few years, some in Ladd Lane and Peter Street, Manchester, and a number in Bradshaw Street, Hulme. To enable myself to do this, I needed to hold regular auctions to sell pledges left by my customers which had remained unclaimed, as well as use monies from the rent of some of my properties.

It was around this time I remember having a difficult talk with my third and youngest son, William. He must have been about fifteen at the time and about to leave school. I had been putting it off for weeks. I had wished, since the death of my uncle, to have a legal declaration written in case of my death. I could wait no longer. It was essential to discuss with William the path he was to follow as he approached adulthood, for at this time he had shown a desire for very little.

My eldest son, Samuel, had chosen a life committed to the church. My son Richard was to follow me into my profession as pawnbroker and succeed me when my time came to leave this world. Richard was an agreeable son and always willing to please. He had no difficulty in complying with my request. William, on the other hand, was a very rare kettle of fish. I explained to him that I wanted to treat him as fairly as my other children in what I bequeathed to him, yet I was unsure as to his allegiance to me and our family name. Not once had he particularly given me concern over anything specific, but neither had he expressed any opinions or strong feelings about anything.

We sat for quite some time together, in discussion on various topics, and I was pleasantly surprised to discover he was of a very similar opinion on most matters to mine. He agreed to use his inheritance wisely and invest in property, expressing a keen interest in building or investing in a mill. I cannot say I was deeply excited by this particular prospect but realised there could be money to be made by such a venture, and we were able to end our conversation positively and part on good terms.

I was assisted in the writing of my last will and testament, a thirteen-page document, by attorneys William Sergeant and James Appleby. Will Sergeant, an acquaintance from my school days, now a practising solicitor, lived just along the road from me at Cornbrook Bank in Hulme. He and Mr Appleby were present on 29th January 1811 to observe as I and my witnesses signed the legal document. I drew comfort in the knowledge that I was leaving an equal and fair inheritance to all of my six children, as my grandfather had done before me, and I had no doubt my trusted friends James Chapman and John Harrison would be there to carry out my wishes when I was no longer able to do so.

I now had many assets, including a number of recently purchased properties in Longford which had previously belonged to Thomas Walker, and the land and farm properties in Moss Side. In Manchester I owned property near Brook Street, on Quay Street, Peter Street, Ladd Lane and Cupid's Alley. In Hulme I owned houses on Bradshaw Street and Hulme Place. Then there were the properties which had been in the family for many years, certain lands and buildings including a warehouse in Cotton Court and a number of properties on Deansgate purchased from the will of Sir Aston Lever.

I divided up my assets as equally as possible between my three sons, using extra monies where necessary to raise each son's legacy to the value of £4,000. To my son Samuel I left my Moss Side properties, to my son Richard my properties in Longford, and to William certain lands and buildings in Cotton Court. As my mother was in good health and it seemed she would outlive us all, I left to her my properties in and near Deansgate, Peter Street, Ladd Lane and

Bradshaw Street. My daughters were also to receive the sum of £4,000 each. For each of my friends, William Gardner, William Woolley, James Chapman, John Harrison and William Sergeant, I left £5 to pay for mourning rings. To my loyal servant, John Shepley, I bequeathed £50, as long as he should remain in my service at the time of my death. To my other servants who should be living with me at the time of my decease, a full mourning suit.

Once my will had been signed and witnessed, I believe I felt the same kind of relief my grandfather had experienced when he too had completed the same task.

16

By 1815 Samuel had become a clergyman: a member of the established church. Our family had attended services regularly at St John's church in Manchester for many years. My mother had always been a strict, devout churchgoer and insisted her children and grandchildren uphold the same values, so no one was more delighted to discover Samuel had turned to the church in search of a career.

He began to practice his calling as curate and assistant to the Reverend John Gatliff, who was rector at St Mary's Parsonage in Manchester. On the 14th October he took his first marriage service, which was followed later that same day by a burial. Over the next two months he would perform many baptisms, marriages and burials. We were all very proud of his achievements.

In 1816 Samuel was admitted to Brasenose College, Oxford, where he achieved a master's degree in art and the sciences and studied English, history and geography. He was ordained a priest on 29th September at a cost of £90. After this he returned to St Mary's parsonage, where he performed many more ceremonies over the next year.

Richard was now running the pawnbroker's shop on Cupid's Alley. I would visit on occasion or assist him if he needed me to, but the business was very much more his now than mine. It was a weight off my mind that he appeared to enjoy it so much.

William had recently shown a greater interest in business, and the desire to expand his knowledge in this area would doubtlessly stand him in good stead for the future.

My main concerns now were my daughters' futures. I asked my eldest son, Samuel, to promise he would take care of them if anything were to happen to me. I needed to know he would find them suitable husbands and ensure their future happiness. He reassured me he would do everything he could.

One fresh, sun-filled morning in early December, William and I decided to visit my properties in Brook Street, Chorlton Street and Major Street, to collect the rent from the tenants who resided there. We chose to stroll back at our leisure along the banks of the River Medlock as the day was a dry one. While crossing the canal we had been discussing one particular tenant who had been reluctant to give up his rent. As we turned into Great Bridgewater Street, a great many mill workers began to run out from the Albion Mills site, shouting in distress. Smoke had started to pour from one of the buildings and the scene soon turned into complete pandemonium. Men, women and children scattered in all directions, many frightened, some verging on becoming hysterical, many of the children and women crying. Some had minor cuts and bruises, but one man staggered out with his hands black and burnt, his face displaying the pain and shock he felt. Sadly this was not an uncommon occurrence in the town, for many factories and mills had burnt down over recent years.

'We should see if there is anything we can do,' William said to me bravely.

'Don't you go in there, boy!' I commanded. 'It's too dangerous!'

'I just want to get closer, Father, to see if there is anything we can do.'

Together we rushed forward, dodging the crowds as they pushed past us, fleeing in the opposite direction. The spectacle which met our eyes as we entered through the gates of the mill buildings was one of horror. We could feel the heat coming from the building and the smoke began to choke our lungs. Many blackened, soot-covered bodies of both sexes and all ages lay, coughing and spluttering, gasping for air in the yard outside. Many others were leaning over, attempting to assist them. Shouts could be heard from outside and inside the building and one man, presumably the manager, was shouting, 'Get these people away from here!'

William went up to this man and asked, 'Is there anyone left inside?'

'Just my foreman, sir. He went in to check that everyone was out. Look, here he is now!' shouted the man, pointing at a soot-blackened man who was bent double in an effort to catch his breath.

'Is there anything we can do to help?' William asked.

'Yes, sir. That is most kind. You can help move these people away from the building. My fear is that it may soon collapse.'

William and I began to help move the workers, most of whom had been overcome by smoke. As together we grabbed an arm each of one man and lifted him to his feet, we heard the hysterical screams of a woman.

'Martha! Martha Bostock! Where are you, Martha?'

We heard the manager shout, 'She'll be out there in the street somewhere, woman. You will have missed her.' He turned to his foreman for reassurance and clarity. 'Everyone's out, aren't they, George?'

His man gave the thumbs up as he was coughing and still unable to catch his breath.

'There you go, nothing to worry about,' said the manager.

The woman left as quickly as she had appeared, shouting again for Martha, presumably her daughter's name.

William and I spent the next few minutes moving as many workers as we could away from the building and into the street, to where word had got out. Most women were being comforted by relatives and a large number of men had begun to form a line beginning at the Rochdale Canal, where they were collecting water to pass down the line to the mill. Water was reaching the building, and William and I joined the line to help.

It took more than two hours for the men to get the fire under control, and by that time the inside of the building had been completely destroyed, but it was still standing. As we turned to leave, eager to get out of our smoke-filled and sweat-stained clothes, we spotted the same woman we had seen previously, apparently still searching for her daughter. At that very moment she let out a great cry of despair and pain, dropping to her knees on the cobblestones. We turned back to see what she had seen. A man, exiting through the gates of the mill, carried what was obviously a young girl's body in his arms, her dirty auburn hair swinging from side to side, her clothes and skin blackened from the smoke. The woman knew instantly it was her child. Two women rushed forward to put their arms around her. As they cradled her, the man gently placed the child's body on the floor in front of the woman and she sobbed hysterically.

'Let's go home, Father,' said William quietly.

The two of us never spoke of the incident afterwards. William appeared to get on with his life as usual, but I could not get those terrible scenes out of my head. Did my son really still wish to have anything to do with one of those places? I feared for his safety and for the sum of money he wished to invest, for it appeared most likely it too could go up in smoke. That would be a terrible waste.

Some days later, I read in my newspaper that the girl, Martha Bostock, had worked twelve-hour days at the mill and had been nine years old. The report also stated that damage to the mill buildings were estimated at a cost of £25,000. This was an enormous amount of money. I feared my son did not know what he might be getting himself into, should he wish to invest in such a mill. Yet I could not bring myself to mention the subject, for it brought back to me all those shocking scenes of human suffering.

At night I found it difficult to sleep. I suffered terrifying dreams where members of my family were burnt to death, screaming in agonising pain as they tried to escape the flames. These images would not leave my head, even after I had woken in my sweat-soaked bed. My life deteriorated after that event, as the sights I had seen stayed with me every day. Soon, I was unable to distinguish between the nightmares and reality and took to my bed, exhausted yet unable to sleep. By the end of the year I had become so unwell, I was admitted to the Manchester infirmary. I knew my time left was to be short.

PART III

1817–1874

William Platt Bradshaw

William Platt Bradshaw
b.1796
m.1830
d.1874

Gentleman/Landowner

Catharine Ann Allott
b.1806

Catharine Ann
b.1831

Henry P
b.1832

Richard
b.1834

George W
b.1836

Mary
b.1837

Edward A
b.1839

Ellen
b.1841

Frances
b.1843

Rupert
b.1844

Frank
b.1847

Agnes
b.1849

Lucy
b.1851

Philip W
b.1854

17

William had been on the cusp of becoming a man when his father passed away. It was merely a matter of months before his twenty-first birthday, when at last he would be seen by the world as an independent adult in charge of his own destiny. The third son of a wealthy landowner, William very much appeared to have been born to a life of privilege.

William's eldest brother, Reverend Samuel Bradshaw, had taken over the day-to-day running of their father's house. He was a busy man, going daily between Hulme and St Mary's parsonage. His brother Richard threw himself into his work as pawnbroker on Cupid's Alley. He was the more genteel of William's brothers and kept himself to himself. After the death of their father William's three sisters clung to one another for support. Henrietta, the youngest, found it the most difficult to come to terms with her father's sudden demise.

William's father had never been the same since the two of them had witnessed a fire at a local mill. A few weeks after the fire, he had been admitted to the Manchester infirmary, displaying irrational behaviour which he seemed unable to control. He looked dreadful, as though he hadn't slept for weeks. He had stopped eating and become extremely thin. His three sons had had no idea what to do for him and, together with a doctor, had agreed he should be admitted to the hospital. A week later he was dead.

William and his siblings buried their father at St John's church on 7th January 1817. St John's was the family church, a place they all had spent much time in and knew well. Their father had half-yearly paid for a family pew and secured a place in the vault beneath the church. William was surprised to see so many people attend his father's funeral. He had done little towards the preparation. It had been his brothers Samuel and Richard who had taken charge.

Before his father had entered the hospital, Samuel had been granted a leave of absence by the church and remained at his father's side, saying prayers most days. He had also been the one to speak with fellow members of the clergy at St John's about his father's burial service. Richard had organised the procession of mourners who had walked behind their father's coffin as it was transported by a horse-drawn hearse the short distance to the church from the family home in Hulme.

Mourners included their father's good friends William Gardener, William Woolley, and his executors James Chapman and John Harrison. William Sergeant and James Appleby also attended. Samuel's long-standing and loyal servant, John Shepley, to whom his master had left the sum of £50 in his will, wore a newly purchased mourning suit, paid for by his deceased employer.

The Reverend John Clowes was there to oversee the events of the day. Later it was just he and the immediate family who went below the church to witness Samuel's body being placed into the vault, laid to rest next to his dear wife.

After the service, mourners were invited back to Hulme Place, where William's sisters, with help from Cook, had prepared some cold meats, potatoes, pickles, pies and biscuits for the guests. No one outstayed their welcome and, apart from the sisters remaining in their mourning clothes and solemn mood for some weeks after their father's death, the house was quickly restored to normality.

Left with no parents to influence him, William relied greatly upon his brothers for guidance. Samuel quickly returned to his work at St Mary's parsonage, while Richard worked only a few streets away at his pawnbroker's shop. Richard and William had always got along well and William knew he could go to Richard for advice. As for his clergyman brother, Samuel was extremely busy attending to his parishioners' many needs and had little time for his own family.

William's three sisters, all as yet unmarried, remained living in Hulme Place. Elizabeth was eighteen, Ann sixteen and Henrietta fourteen. The three girls had adored and worshipped their father, especially as they had lost their mother at such a young age. Since the death of their father the family home had changed and could appear, at times, rather a solemn place. The atmosphere did improve eventually, although not for some time after their father's will had been read.

From their father's will, each of the siblings received considerable amounts of property or money, some of which was to be held in trust until they reached their twenty-first birthdays. The family home, Hulme Place, automatically passed to Samuel. Their father had also left Samuel all his property in Moss Side, including Pepperhill Farm, worth around £4,000. Richard was left property and land in Longford worth £3,000, plus the sum of £1,000, and of course he already had the pawnbroker's shop on Cupid's Alley. William was left certain lands and buildings in and near Cotton Court in Manchester to the value of £3,892, plus £108. Therefore each of Samuel's sons had been bequeathed an equal amount. However, frustratingly, William was unable to do anything about his inheritance for another eight months, before he attained the age of twenty-one. His three sisters were also to receive the same amount of money, left in trust until they too reached twenty-one.

The year his father died, Samuel began a subscription to Manchester Infirmary. He did this with the blessing of his brothers and in thanks for the care the hospital had shown their dying father. Through making this subscription he met another man, Thomas Gough, who was doing the same. The Gough family were cotton spinners and becoming well known across Manchester at this time. They owned many factories and mills across the region. The two men soon became acquainted and it wasn't long before Samuel introduced his new friend to his brother William. Thomas Gough encouraged William's desire to purchase his own mill, and over the next few years the two engaged themselves in business which would suffice William's yearning.

Upon his twenty-first birthday William inherited his father's properties near Cotton Court with a rented value estimated at £194 and twelve shillings per annum. One of these buildings was a small warehouse situated close to Smithy Door. This property, like the others, was rented out and the rent collected regularly for him. It wasn't long before William decided to sell these properties and invest the money in a mill. Everyone with means was doing the same at this time, thought William. He knew his father would approve, as they had discussed it shortly before his death.

William was determined that nothing would keep him from fulfilling this wish. However, he required advice and additional financial investment and he knew this could take time. When Samuel had introduced him to Thomas Gough, William had known it was Thomas who would be able to help him reach his goal. The next few years would prove to be a frustrating time for William, but he was determined to see his venture through.

On 8th November 1819, and shortly after her twenty-first birthday, Elizabeth married the Reverend William Stewart at St John's church. Her new husband was some fourteen years her senior and had been the perpetual curate of St Mary's church in Hale, Liverpool, since 1813. It had been her brother Samuel who had introduced them. The two men had gone to the same school in Manchester and had both attended Brasenose College in Oxford, where they were ordained. They had later been reacquainted through the church and had become firm friends. The difference in age between Elizabeth and the Reverend Stewart did not seem to matter to Samuel and he greatly encouraged their relationship. Elizabeth enjoyed the attentions of an older man and their affection for one another grew rapidly.

William could see his sister was very fond of the Reverend Stewart. The man had managed to lift his sister out of her solemn mood and she was now positively glowing with the adoration she felt for him. Elizabeth's sisters had also appeared happier since the announcement of her marriage. Busying themselves with helping her to plan for her wedding had taken their minds off their father's recent death.

Shortly before her marriage to the Reverend Stewart, Elizabeth was asked to act as witness to the signing of a document drawn up on behalf of her three brothers. Samuel was far too busy to be dealing with property matters and had recently heard he might be leaving for London. He had agreed to convey his freehold properties and land to his brothers for a year for a nominal fee of five shillings. Upon the one-year lease period expiring the properties would revert to him. This would enable his brothers to invest in further property if they should choose.

Immediately after her wedding Elizabeth moved out of the family home and went to live with her new husband in Hale. Their first child was born one year later and her brother, the Reverend Samuel, was invited to be godparent.

18

William's wish to own a cotton mill finally reached fruition when he invested in the construction of a building on Great Bridgewater Street in 1820. Many changes were taking place around Manchester at this time. A water company supplied piped water through iron pipes to those who could afford to be connected and there was great excitement about the gas lights being installed along the Manchester streets.

The site of William's new venture was known as the Albion Mills and ideal for firms wishing to rent space to expand their cotton manufacture. These new buildings were close to the spot where he and his father had witnessed the fire, some three years previously. William entered this venture along with a number of other investors, one being Thomas Gough, who would influence and encourage William in ways he never would have thought. The Gough family were well regarded and influential. They appeared to have their fingers in many pies in the Lancashire area.

Even before William's birth the demand for cotton had increased. With the development of the port at Liverpool and completion of the Bridgewater Canal, transporting raw cotton from plantations in the USA had never been easier.

These new mill buildings which were now springing up all over Manchester had to be substantial enough to house the workers and the increasingly large machinery needed to produce the various yarns. William's new mill consisted of three floors, housing dozens of groups of powered machines, each performing a different stage of production. From the outside it resembled a giant brick box with rows upon rows of windows. Although the surrounding area was quickly being eaten up by similar constructions, whose billowing chimneys stood taller than church spires and could be seen for miles around, William believed, like many others, that his mill would only go to improve the township of Manchester. He did not consider for a moment that this might not be the case.

Streets upon streets of back-to-back houses had been hastily built with little care to house the many workers of these mills, yet William was not required to take an interest in the living conditions of his mill's workers. They were not his problem. As long as the rent for his mill was paid on time by the mill manager, nothing else concerned him and William was able to get on with his life.

At the same time, William's brother Samuel had decided to leave Manchester for good. He had accepted a call to a church in the Pentonville area of London. He caused a terrible amount of distress to the other occupants of Hulme Place when he announced he would be holding an auction of the family's household furniture to raise funds for his move. He advertised the auction in the *Manchester Mercury* shortly before he moved away, leaving the house almost bare. His sisters were understandably upset at seeing most of their father's furniture being carted off by complete strangers.

Richard and William were less than impressed by the callous way in which their older brother had handled the situation. They suspected the house would feel very different once their brother had left, and they were right. They hoped things might return to normal, but it was soon obvious that their remaining sisters no longer felt the place was their home and, in short succession, both had begun to talk about leaving the family home.

Henrietta was the next to fly the nest. She met Manchester merchant Peter Newham, falling for his charms immediately, and their marriage was planned for the moment she turned twenty-one. The pair were married on 11th September 1823 at St John's church. Given Peter's trade, it made sense for them to live near to the port of Liverpool. They ended up living next door to Elizabeth, in Hale. Peter also had property on the Isle of Bute, in Scotland, where the couple would spend many summers.

Ann was the last of the sisters to leave the family home. It made sense for her to join her other sisters in Liverpool, yet she remained unmarried for some time to come.

During this period William was witness to his family slowly splintering. In December 1824 his grandfather Peter Sefton died, and his grandmother followed some short seventeen months later. His grandfather was buried at St Mary's, the old Manchester church, but his grandmother had a place waiting for her in the Bradshaw family vault beneath St John's.

William felt most despondent at this time. He was losing too many family members far too quickly for his liking. He accepted his grandparents had both lived to a good age, but the family had lost their eldest member and matriarch. Life appeared to be changing rapidly for William, so he was thankful his brother Richard was settled and had no plans to leave the area.

Richard kept himself busy running his pawnbroker's business on Cupid's Alley. He kept his head down and made a good turnover, as his father and grandfather had done before him. He was content with his lot. He collected monies from the rent of his properties in Longford, and this gave him the means to live well, but he was as yet unmarried.

William inherited a sum of money after the death of his grandparents and decided he should invest in more property. He used this and some money he had made from investing in the mill, and was able to purchase a number of new properties in Hulme which had been built mainly for the mill workers. He acquired five houses on Little Quay Street, eight houses on Sykes Street, five houses on Queen Street and twelve houses on Bradshaw Street. He was extremely pleased with these investments.

Samuel had not returned to Manchester for either of his grandparents' funerals, even though his grandmother's properties in Deansgate, Peter Street and Ladd Lane had automatically passed to him upon her death. He had written to Richard to say he was much too busy in London to be able to return to Manchester, but shortly after this he did return briefly, to invest in more property, as his father had taught him. He secretly purchased a number of houses on King Street and Back King Street. Both Richard and William were completely unaware of their brother's visit, as he slipped in and out of Manchester under the cover of darkness, merely to sign the necessary paperwork. He made no attempt to inform or visit them.

The next time William and Richard heard from their brother was in 1828, when Samuel announced in a letter that he had married. He was now living at 14 York Place, Pentonville, close to his work. He described the woman he had married as pleasant, recently widowed and fallen on hard times, although not of her own making. Both Richard and William found it difficult to imagine their brother with a wife but immediately sent their best wishes to the couple by return post.

19

Recently, William had started to feel quite weary. His good friend and business associate Thomas Gough noticed the change in his friend and invited him to stay with him in Cumberland at his lakeshore holiday home. This venture would prove to do William the world of good. He was able to experience a completely different world to the one he was used to. He learnt how to relax, spending time reading and fishing from boats upon the lake. He enjoyed walking excursions up the side of mountains and began to appreciate the countryside and fresh air much more: so much so that when it was time for him to return to Manchester, he was in two minds whether to do so. He made a promise to himself and to Thomas that he would return the following year.

Life in Cumberland had revived William. In no time he had felt like a different man and he had found himself so at home beside the lakes, he soon took the easy decision to rent a cottage near Coniston and to live more permanently in that area. To enable himself to do this he was obliged to sell his shares in the mill and relinquish his business dealings with Thomas, but William was so sure he was doing the right thing that this mattered little. He was sure he and Thomas could maintain their friendship without being in business together.

During the following year William became acquainted with members of the Allott family. They too were enjoying the joys of a Cumberland summer, escaping the limitations of their home town. The Allott family were established in the sixteenth century as gentleman farmers, near Wakefield in West Yorkshire. A descendant, the Reverend George Allott of Hague Hall, his wife, Mary, and their seven children had travelled more than a hundred miles from their home in South Kirkby and were introduced to William during a garden party one Saturday afternoon, given by the reverend of St Michael and All Angels church, Hawkshead.

William took an immediate shine to their eldest daughter, twenty-year-old Catharine. In return the reverend took a shine to William, all the more so after discovering his brother was a member of the clergy. The two men had plenty to discuss and when William was eventually left alone with Catharine, he found her company both stimulating and satisfying. She was mature and greatly educated for her age. Amongst their many conversations, William mentioned that he had never seen the name Catherine spelt with two 'a's before. She explained that it was because her father had attended St Catharine's College, Cambridge.

As Catharine's father had seen his daughter's increased happiness in the presence of William, he was only too pleased to invite William to visit their home in South Kirkby. William was more than willing to accept his invitation.

Things moved swiftly for William and Catharine, mainly due to Catharine's parents, who were quick to take William under their wing, especially after discovering he had lost his own parents so early. The reverend instantly assumed the role of William's father, wishing to advise him on business matters and the like, and the two men soon came to hold each other in high esteem. William was quite overwhelmed by the family's acceptance of him, noting their importance in the village. He had forgotten what it had felt like to feel part of a family and found himself quite overwhelmed as those feelings flooded back.

On 12th May 1830 William Platt Bradshaw and Catharine Ann Allott were married at All Saints church in Catharine's home town of South Kirkby, where her father was the vicar. William had attended more than one service at the church before his wedding day and had noticed the monuments and plaques placed around the church in memory of some of Catharine's family members, noting their lengthy connection to Hague Hall. He was not to know just how many more of these tributes would adorn the church over the coming years.

All of the Allott family and, it seemed, the whole of the village of South Kirkby had turned out to help celebrate their wedding day, filling the church to the brim in prayer and song. No one took more pleasure from the day than Catharine's father, as he led the ceremony and married his eldest daughter. It was the happiest day in William's life, especially as his sisters and brothers were there to join in with the celebrations.

By this time William had taken up full-time residency at Coniston Bank near Hawkshead, where he rented a substantial cottage. This was where the couple were to live after their marriage.

William only journeyed back to Manchester as and when it was required of him, as travel between these two places could take most of the day by stagecoach. He might be forced to stay in a Manchester inn for a number of nights, if his business there required it, but hoped that soon he might travel this route by train.

The first railway, the Stockton to Darlington line, had opened five years earlier, and there had immediately been talk of more lines being built across the country. By now a more substantial project was near completion, and that was a railway line from Liverpool to Manchester, which had taken a great deal of time and money to build. A first bill presented to Parliament was rejected, but later in the May of 1826 it was passed. When it opened some four months after William's marriage, in the September of 1830, many people from the Liverpool and Manchester area, some even from London, took shares in the railway. William was one of the many Manchester businessmen who swapped their money for shares. He was wise to do so, as the railway was a financial success, paying its investors an average annual dividend of 9.5% over the next fifteen years.

However, as there was as yet no railway from Manchester to his home in Cumberland, William would have to make do with travelling by the Carlisle stagecoach from Kendal to Manchester. The Royal Invincible left Kendal around 10.30 am, arriving some ten and a half hours later in Manchester. It was always a long day, having to leave home around 6.30 am for the four-mile hike to Hawkshead, followed by anything up to three hours by horse and cart to Kendal, where he then caught the stagecoach. On occasions William would stay at the inn in Kendal the night before to ease this journey.

It would be another decade before there would be a huge boom in building more railways, which would link most towns in Britain, speeding up travel times. By then, he might not need the line.

20

William's first child was born on 9th April 1831 at the family home in Coniston Bank. She was baptised Catharine Ann (after her mother) firstly on 12th May at St Michael and All Angels in Hawkshead and again one week later by her grandfather at All Saints in South Kirby.

Catharine's sister Sarah was delighted when asked to be godmother. She was instantly enchanted by the child, forming a special bond with her goddaughter that would remain strong between them for the duration of her life.

The Allott family held a great gathering afterwards at the rectory, in celebration of the baptism. William was overwhelmed by the number of people who turned up to welcome his child into the church. The rectory was filled to the rafters. There was standing room only. The whole village had turned out to witness the event, just as they had previously on his wedding day.

After the formalities, William and Catharine stood chatting with Catharine's parents. The two women fussed over the child while the reverend offered a few words of wisdom to William, making his son-in-law feel most uncomfortable.

'I do believe you have turned a paler shade, my dear boy,' the reverend said with a laugh, patting William on the back.

Catharine looked up and, after a glance at William, asked her father, 'What in heaven's name have you said to him?'

'All I said was, I shouldn't expect it to be too long before we are all here again with the next one.'

'Father, really. No wonder William looks so pale.' Catharine took her husband's hand sympathetically.

'Really, George,' agreed Mary. 'Must you?'

Turning to his daughter, the reverend said, 'I'll just say this. I can remember your mother doing exactly that to me.' He looked back at William. 'Once they get started there's no stopping them.'

At which point Mary handed the child back to her daughter and the reverend was masterfully manoeuvred away from William, Catharine and the baby, past the hordes of well-wishers and off into another room.

Catherine cast an apologetic look at William. 'I am so sorry about Father. I suspect he's had a little too much to drink. He's not that used to it, you see.'

'Catharine, I admit I was a little surprised when I realised just what it was your father was trying to say, but he means no harm. In actual fact, he has rather amused me.'

'Well, I'm not amused,' replied Catharine, at which point William knew it was time to turn their attention back to their daughter and guests.

*

While William and Catharine relished their new role as parents and the experiences and challenges that family life presented, Samuel was experiencing something very different. Things appeared to have gone astray for the Reverend Samuel, now living and working in Marylebone. He had married in 1828, but married life for him had not quite worked out the way he had thought it would. He might have been accused of rushing into his marriage with a widowed woman because he had wanted a wife who would cook, clean and care for his every need. She might have been accused of marrying because of her knowledge of his inherited wealth. Whatever the reasons and whoever might be at fault, the marriage was not to be a success and wife Eliza had soon had enough of her husband's difficult ways. The problem was made all the more pressing when Samuel started to drink heavily. His ministerial duties had taken their toll on this man of God. His congregation in Marylebone, often poor and in need of a great deal of support, tested his faith to the limit.

Samuel became unable to meet the needs of his congregation and the difficulties in his personal life consumed him. Soon he was unable to perform even the most basic of his ministerial duties. Worse for the drink, he would be slurring his words and swaying during many services. Complaints were made by his parishioners, resulting in his temporary removal from his ministry, until such a time as he could be considered fit to resume.

Samuel was unsure as to what had triggered his behaviour, but the situation escalated further on Sunday 11th March 1832, when he was arrested and taken before a magistrate. Having no Sunday service to oversee, Samuel had visited a local drinking establishment on New Road and spent many hours drinking himself into a stupor. Upon leaving the establishment he had accosted a passer-by. Grabbing hold of the arm of the respectably dressed woman, he had insisted upon her accompanying him back to his house. She had refused and begun to shout for assistance. A crowd had gathered and a policeman had soon approached, demanding to know what was happening.

Samuel spent that night in a police cell and went before the magistrate the following day. He had no recollection of what he had done. The magistrate listened as the policeman described how Samuel had threatened to stab anyone who attempted to touch him. When asked by the magistrate Samuel professed he had given up his orders.

The magistrate looked at Samuel with disappointment. 'I sorely regret that a man of your rank should have conducted himself in this way, and on the Sabbath, and I order you to find bail.'

Samuel nodded in agreement.

The magistrate concluded, 'Sir, I do not wish to see you in my court again.'

The first time that Samuel's family suspected anything was wrong was when he wrote to his brother Richard asking him to put the house on Hulme Place up for sale. Richard immediately contacted William in Cumberland, explaining in a letter that Samuel had declared he was experiencing financial difficulties and that an amount of money from the sale of this property would greatly ease his troubles. With the house at Hulme Place not being used any more by the family, the three brothers had agreed some months earlier that it made sense to rent it out. A Mr Meyer had rented the property from them and so far this had been a good arrangement.

Reluctantly, and after much discussion between them, William and Richard agreed it was their brother's property to do with as he saw fit and Richard agreed he would sell the property on behalf of Samuel. He advertised it in the *Manchester Guardian* on 21st April, describing the property as 'an excellent house situated at the bottom of Jackson's Lane, Hulme, fronting the Chester Road, now in the occupation of a Mr Meyer, with stables, coach house and four cottages at the back and a large plot of ground, free from chief rent'. Richard asked for all enquiries to apply to 1 Cupid's Alley.

William's suspicions were aroused by Samuel's strange behaviour and via his father-in-law's contacts he was able to discover his brother's secrets. With the sale of the house already complete, William and Richard wasted no time in writing to their disgraced brother informing him of their wish to disassociate themselves from him until a time when he had redressed his recent behaviour. They were hoping this action would encourage their brother to change his ways. Their letter went straight to the point, as both brothers believed Samuel's behaviour could ruin both their business and their personal reputations.

Not long after the sale of Hulme Place, Catharine gave birth to a second child. Henry Platt was born on 6th October in Coniston Bank. Like his sister he too was baptised at St Michael and All Angels, but it would be more than a year before the family were able to return to Yorkshire to have him baptised by Catharine's father. When the family did travel back to Catharine's home town of South Kirkby in the summer of 1834, it was to have two children baptised. Another son, Richard, had been born in February that same year, so the two boys had a joint ceremony performed by their grandfather in July.

It was during this visit that the Reverend Allott engaged in a brief discussion with William regarding his brother. Grasping William's arm, the reverend steered him away from their guests to a room at the back of the rectory which he used for his parish work.

'My dear boy, take a seat. I need to have a quiet word with you.'

William was immediately concerned, but could not have predicted what his father-in-law was about to tell him.

'It's about your brother, Samuel.'

William realised the situation must not have improved.

Reverend Allott explained he had been informed that Samuel, for a brief period, had been welcomed back into the church, as he had appeared of sober character once more. However, more recently

Samuel had started to drink heavily again and there was a growing feeling of agitation among his fellow clergy in that area of London.

'What am I to do?' asked William. 'I am not my brother's keeper. I shouldn't think he would listen to my suggestions anyway.'

'I doubt there is anything any of us can do or say, my dear boy. I just thought you should be aware of the facts,' replied the reverend.

'Yes, right. Thank you, sir,' replied William.

There was silence between the two men for a number of seconds, then William spoke again. 'You will inform me if you hear any more?'

'Of course, my dear boy, of course.'

Two months later William received a letter from his father-in-law, written to both him and Richard, with an enclosed cutting taken from a London newspaper. The letter included the words, 'How sorry I am to have to break this news to you,' and 'I wonder if I might intervene, with you and your brother's approval, of course.'

The cutting told of how the Reverend Samuel Bradshaw had once again been brought before the magistrate. This time he was described as being 'blind drunk' and 'totally incapable of taking care of himself'. He had been discovered by a policeman in Regent Street, a short distance from his home, around six o'clock in the evening, sitting in a doorway, 'overcome by the potency of his spirituous devotions' and having mislaid his coat and waistcoat. He was taken to the Vine Street station house, where it was decided he was so incapable of giving an account of himself to the bench that evening that he should sleep it off and his hearing should be deferred until the following day. When stood before the magistrate the next morning and asked as to his station in life, Samuel had replied, 'Gentleman.' When William reached this point in the newspaper cutting he tutted and shook his head in dismay. *Mother and Grandfather must be spinning in their graves,* he thought. The report concluded, 'The charge of drunkenness was not denied, he paid the customary fine of five shillings and walked away.'

William sent a letter of reply to his father-in-law by return post. He thanked him for his interest and concern and desperately hoped the church could make Samuel see sense. William explained he was willing to offer any support his father-in-law thought necessary. He said he would write immediately to his brother–in-law, the Reverend William Stewart of Hale, a good friend of his brother, to inform him of the dire situation and to see if he could be of any assistance. William's embarrassment and shame could be sensed throughout his letter.

Richard was a little less understanding and made it quite clear, in his letter back to William, that he wanted nothing more to do with his older brother.

The following month William received further news of Samuel. It appeared that together, his father-in-law and Reverend Stewart had managed to perform a miracle. Colluding with fellow members of the clergy, they had been able to convince Samuel to adopt a life without the demon drink, eradicating it completely from his day-to-day existence. With the help of his wife, who had decided to give her husband another chance, Samuel said he felt positive he would be able to continue down a path of righteousness.

William was pleased to discover that, after serious discussions, his brother was willing to assure the church he would work cooperatively with others and obediently accept the directions of the church authorities. Samuel now wanted to prove once again that he believed firmly in his own calling and abilities and wished to demonstrate his desire to serve the church. William was also informed that Samuel was now undergoing instruction to become a deacon. No one was more relieved than William to hear that his brother had turned a corner.

21

William was spending more and more time away from the family home in Coniston because of his business commitments. He was no longer able to achieve the tranquil life he had once enjoyed, whiling away the hours on walks and fishing on the lake, as he was rarely at home. When he was able to be with his family, it felt as though it had been a mere moment before he had to make his way back to Liverpool for a meeting about the railways or to Manchester to collect his rents. Travel between the two towns had been made much easier since the construction of the Liverpool and Manchester railway line, but travel from those places to his home in Coniston remained arduous.

After a great deal of discussion with Catharine, William concluded that if they were ever to see anything of each other, they would have to move their family closer to where William did his business.

William was forced to relinquish the lease on his Coniston property in 1835. The family would spend only their holidays together in Coniston that coming year. He reluctantly moved his family to the port of Liverpool. This made sense because his three sisters lived there, and he knew they would be good company for Catharine and the children when he was away on business in Manchester.

Elizabeth and the Reverend Stewart now had six children. Elizabeth was grateful her sister Ann lived with them at the vicarage and was on hand to help with her growing brood. She knew this would all change when Ann found herself a husband. Henrietta and Peter Newham lived in the house next door. Although married for more than twelve years they had no children. The three sisters remained close and were excited when William and Catharine announced they would soon be moving to the area with their family.

Once settled in Liverpool, William was able to travel between there and Manchester much more quickly. It would now only take him around two and a half hours to travel the distance between work and home, enabling him to spend much more time with his family. The Bradshaw women liked nothing more than getting their families together and preparing a feast in which everyone could partake. The sounds of their children's laughter as they mixed with their cousins made a delightful scene and they relished these times, as they could never be sure how long they might last.

On Sunday 5th July, William, along with Reverend Allott and

Reverend Stewart, attended Samuel's ordination to become a deacon at the cathedral in Lichfield. They travelled the one hundred miles to Lichfield the day before, staying overnight at an inn on the outskirts of the town. They arrived at the venue in good time and were impressed by the sandstone building. It was even more overwhelming once they went inside. The three men took to their seats, along with the many other guests, including a fair number of other clergy who were also there to be ordained. It was a day of great celebration for the men and a huge relief for William.

Afterwards, the men enjoyed a meal together in a nearby tavern. Samuel's wife was conspicuous by her absence, but Samuel gave the excuse his wife didn't like to travel.

'I was looking forward to meeting her again,' said William. 'The last time was very brief.'

'Shortly after your wedding, wasn't it, Samuel? We met up to sign your will,' recalled the Reverend Stewart.

When Samuel had married in 1828 he'd had the forethought to make a will. His wife, William and the Reverend Stewart had been named as executors and had visited him in London when the will was complete and needed to be signed.

'Yes, I remember it well. You shall meet her again, brother, just not today,' came Samuel's brief reply, as he tucked into the plate of food prepared for him by the tavern owner's wife.

The conversations that William was able to initiate with his brother, before his departure for home, were stunted. But at least Samuel seemed well and at last appeared to be more settled with his life in London.

'We will come and visit you soon,' were William's parting words to his brother.

It therefore came as a terrible shock when, one month later, William was informed that Samuel had died. He had secretly started drinking again and died from heart failure, having consumed a large amount of spirits one evening after a disagreement with his wife. William was genuinely shocked by his brother's sudden demise.

Catharine was unable to console her husband. She and her sisters-in-law were at a loss for what to do. It was the Reverend Stewart who managed to pull William back up and out of his feelings of hopelessness with kind words and reassurance.

Richard appeared to be unaffected when informed about his older brother. He almost seemed to show a sense of relief at the news. He was in no doubt that he would not be attending Samuel's funeral. He made his feelings quite clear to William. He wanted nothing to do with the day.

Once again, William did not see Samuel's wife. It appeared Richard was not the only one who wished to have as little as possible to do with Samuel's funeral. His widow had Samuel's body sent from London to Manchester by train, so that he could be laid to rest alongside his father in the vault at St John's, as had been his wish. She had also arranged payment for the Bradshaw funeral pew in the nave, for which the family were grateful.

After his death, Samuel's widow received a sum of money from the rents of his Manchester freehold properties on Deansgate, Peter Street and Ladd Lane, the interest of which was payable to Peter Newham. She was also able to keep the London house she was now living in, on Judd Street. Upon her death these properties would revert to William.

In his will, Samuel had expressed a wish that all three executors share the rent received from his houses in Hulme, but both of these had been sold four years previously when, as was now clear, he had needed the money for drink.

Samuel's godson, Elizabeth's eldest child, was left, in trust, houses in King Street and Back King Street, along with a legacy of £100. Samuel had £5,000 vested in three-percent stocks from which he left each of his sisters a sum of money. The remainder was to go to his brother William. Richard, although not mentioned in his brother's will, did benefit from it, as the Moss Side properties left to Samuel in his father's will reverted to him.

Lastly, Samuel had requested a plain and simple funeral at St John's church. He wished for little ceremony or expense, but to be placed into the family vault under the nave.

22

Richard couldn't help feeling that his family had forgotten about him. They all seemed to be getting on with their lives and he was now the only one left in Manchester. His pawnbroking business earned him more than enough to live on, but things had changed. He no longer held the same passion for this occupation that he once had.

Manchester was of recent times a very different place to when his father and grandfather had run their shops. His shop, on more than one occasion, had attracted the wrong kind of person. His premises had endured a number of visits from the police. During the Christmas of 1831 a robbery had taken place at the house of Mr Towmow of Wellington Place, Campfield, while the family had been at tea. A large coat, a cloak and an umbrella had been stolen. Later that afternoon, the cloak had been pledged at Richard's shop by a young boy named Edmund Watson. Richard had handed money over for the item, which he had not realised had been stolen. The boy had later been arrested at his father's house and committed for trial.

More recently, in the April of 1835, a man named John Leese, who worked for Mr Brown, the watchmaker on Bridge Street, had taken five watches and two clocks entrusted to him by Mr Brown and under false pretences pledged them at Richard's shop. After this incident Richard had become very concerned about his reputation.

Manchester's population had exploded, its boundaries expanded, and now there was talk of the town becoming incorporated. Everything was changing and Richard didn't much care for the area any more. Everyone seemed to have little care for anyone else, poverty was everywhere you looked and most recently he had even seen a couple of undesirable women hanging around on the corner of Cupid's Alley. They could only do his business harm. Richard was getting itchy feet.

Richard had never in his adult life, especially after the death of his father, found any solace in the church, but that was about to change. He needed to return to his shop one evening, around dusk. As he approached Cupid's Alley he noticed a women whom he had previously seen hanging around the street. He ignored her and went to unlock his premises.

Suddenly she was behind him, her hands wrapping themselves around his waist. 'What can I interest you in this evening, sir?'

Richard was shocked by her brazen behaviour and could feel his cheeks redden. 'I think you have me confused with another man,' he spluttered, pulling away from her grasp, tripping through his shop doorway and slamming the door behind him. 'The nerve of the woman,' he muttered to himself. For a moment he quite forgot why he had returned to his shop that evening.

Richard managed to compose himself and fetch the records he had returned for, and, when he was ready to leave, he glanced out of the window to see if the woman was still there. She was. What was he to do? He waited for a moment and observed the creature desperately searching the streets with her eyes for her prey. After a minute or two another woman, much younger, joined her, and for the next few minutes they were locked together in deep conversation. The second woman was dressed very differently and seemed to be reading off a piece of paper to the first woman, who appeared to be nodding in agreement. Richard dare not move for fear of being spotted. Eventually the first woman, the one who had accosted him, left with the bit of paper in her hand, but the other woman stayed behind, searching inside her shoulder bag for another piece of paper. Richard thought, *Now's my chance.*

Just as Richard left his shop the woman looked up and spotted him. 'Can I give you one of these, sir?'

'I don't wish to have anything from you, my girl,' replied Richard.

Realising the gentleman's mistake and rather embarrassed, the girl held out the piece of paper to him. 'I am from St Peter's Presbyterian church, sir. Please will you take a look at this?

At this point Richard also realised his mistake and gently took the paper he was being offered.

'My name is Suzanna. We do not close our eyes to Manchester's social problems, sir. Not at our church.'

'That is very commendable. However, I'm not sure you should be walking these streets alone at this time of night, my dear. Will you allow me to walk with you and get you safely to where you are going?'

'That is a very kind offer, sir.'

'My name is Richard. Richard Bradshaw, at your service, miss.'

'Well, Richard, I am on my way back to St Peter's. You may accompany me and join us for our evening meeting if you wish.'

'I'm not sure it's my kind of thing,' replied Richard, trying to be tactful.

'You will never know if you don't give it a try,' Suzanna encouraged him.

Making the decision to join Suzanna for the evening service at St Peter's would prove to be a turning point in Richard's life.

23

On 7th January 1836 William and Catharine welcomed another son into their family. George William Bradshaw would be the only child of theirs to be born in Liverpool. At this time they could never have expected their son would later return to the port of Liverpool to become a merchant seaman.

Through his connections with the railways William made a new acquaintance. A young Warrington gentleman, Thomas Bolton, whose family had connections to the Penketh area of Warrington, was doing business in Manchester on behalf of his sister. She had asked him to purchase shares in the railways for her.

Thomas and William met when Thomas stopped for refreshments at the Royal Hotel on the corner of Market Street. The two men introduced themselves and found they enjoyed each other's company. Thomas was a refreshing change from most of William's middle-aged associates and the two discussed business together. William invited Thomas to his son's baptism the following week in Liverpool and introduced him to his family. His sister Ann, although some twelve years his senior, took an instant shine to Thomas, and he to her.

One year later, in March 1837, Thomas Bolton applied for a licence to marry Ann. It was granted and they married on 6th April. Because Ann was still living with her sister in Liverpool, this was where she chose to be married. The ceremony took place at St Mary's church and was led by her brother-in-law, the Reverend Stewart. Richard made the trip especially, from Manchester to Liverpool by train, to give his sister away. This was his first proper journey by rail and he was so impressed by the experience, he wanted to share it with absolutely everyone. His excitement convinced William to suggest a business venture to him.

'You really should invest,' advised William.

Thomas was in agreement. 'You'd be a fool not to. Both your brother and I, so far, have had a good return on our investments.'

Richard proved difficult to convince. He secretly had other plans for his money. This was not a bad thing, for soon the value of investments in the railways would plummet.

Ann and her sisters were all delighted to have their family together once more to share in Ann's special day. The women had rarely seen their husbands and brothers so animated, especially Richard. They were almost able to forget their brother Samuel was missing from the festivities.

After their marriage Thomas and Ann moved to Penketh. Here they at first shared the family home with Thomas's mother and later purchased their own nearby. It would take the couple more than ten years before they were able to enjoy the company of a son, the one and only child they would be blessed with.

William and Catharine had lived in Liverpool now for more than a year, but Catharine was not happy. She had moved from her peaceful village in Yorkshire to Coniston, but Liverpool was very different from both of these places. While her children delighted in watching the boats come and go along the River Mersey, Catharine longed to return to Coniston. It was here their fifth child, Mary, was born on 4th October 1837. After returning to Coniston during the summer months William and Catharine had decided to stay, at least until the child was born.

When Mary was six months old another decision was made, as her mother persuaded her father to move to South Kirkby. Catharine missed her family immensely. She had enjoyed spending time with William's sisters in Liverpool, but now, more than anything, she desired the company of her own sisters, Sarah, Mary and Frances.

William took the difficult decision to sell the house at Coniston and temporarily rented a property in Tickhill for his family. This property was eighteen miles away from Catharine's family and a temporary measure, until they were able to find something closer. They arrived back in Yorkshire as Catharine's sister Sarah announced she was to be married.

Sarah Allott married Joshua Hepworth on 4th June 1838. It was another grand occasion. Joshua Hepworth had played an important part in Badsworth parish affairs, being a trustee of the Badsworth church estate in his early twenties. Now in his thirties, he owned a great deal of land and property in the area and had just purchased Rogerthorpe Hall, situated between Badsworth and Thorpe Audlin, near Pontefract. 'A most suitable companion for Sarah,' her father could be heard saying to numerous members of his congregation throughout the day.

Catharine felt proud when her eldest daughter, Catharine Ann, was asked by her aunt and godmother to be a flower girl, leading the procession into church and up the aisle. The child scattered fresh petals from a basket ahead of the procession and wore a wreath of fresh flowers and sweet-scented rosemary in her hair. Sarah had seen to it that her niece felt as important and special as she herself did on the day. She presented Catharine Ann with a silver bracelet in appreciation, a small token of love which Catharine Ann would always treasure. The child delighted in her important role, fussing over her aunt, fetching, carrying and seeing she wanted for nothing all day.

'Doesn't our daughter look a picture?' said William proudly to his wife as the crowds all clapped their hands with delight.

'She does. I am so proud of her. She looks so grown-up.'

'Yes. It makes me think about how fast time seems to be passing us by. It won't be long before we are watching her go down the aisle.'

Catharine laughed. 'Oh, William, don't wish me that age too soon. She's still only a child of seven.'

Later that same year, in the November, William and Catharine's two youngest children, George and Mary, were jointly baptised at All Saints by their grandfather. It had been a busy year for the Reverend Allott and that cold November day was the first time when his whole family had been able to come together since Sarah's wedding. Once again it was a joyous occasion to see other family members and catch up with their news. Catharine had news of her own to share with William that day. She was with child again.

Their next child was born in May 1839 and again the family made the journey to South Kirkby with one-month-old Edward for him to be baptised by his grandfather. This time the family occasion was bathed in warm sunshine and summer flowers.

'The church always looks so beautiful at this time of year,' Catharine commented to her father, after the service.

'Yes, my dear. That is true. I do hope it looks as beautiful on Mary's wedding day,' replied her father.

'I had no idea,' Catharine almost shouted in alarm. 'Why has she said nothing to me?'

'Quiet yourself, my dear; nothing has been announced as yet. We should not get too excited.' But it was quite obvious her father already was.

'I had no idea Mary was even seeing anyone.'

'Oh yes, for some time now, but I shall gossip no more. I'm sure she will announce it to us soon. I suspect she may even marry before the year is over.'

Her father was right. Another family celebration was held in the September.

24

In 1840 the Manchester and Leeds Railway opened a station near Wakefield at last and named it Kirkgate. William and Catharine moved their family once more, this time to a place called Moor Top in Ackworth. Catharine was delighted that their new home was only five miles from her father's church. Kirkgate station was only eight miles from their new home and made travelling back to Manchester much more bearable for William.

In October 1838 Manchester had been incorporated as a municipal borough. The first election of councillors to the new borough had taken place on 14th December. William had wanted to be part of the council but family commitments had not allowed this at the time. Since then he had regularly attended meetings of the council.

More recently William had been able to get more involved with Manchester Borough Council. Having property and lands in the Manchester area, it was in his interest to do so, for many changes to the area were happening at this time and much land was being sold off for development. Manchester's population was growing rapidly and so were its industries. William needed to stay in touch with all of these developments to ensure his investments paid off. He worked hard over the coming months to establish a good relationship with the elected Manchester councillors.

William's seventh child was born in the June of 1841. In the July, baby Ellen was christened by her grandfather at All Saints church.

During this time William travelled regularly back and forth between Manchester and Yorkshire. He persisted with his interest in becoming a member of the Manchester council and in December the following year, William P Bradshaw was proposed and seconded as a candidate for the position of council treasurer. William finally felt as though he might get his feet under the table. There were many candidates put forward for this post and competition was tough. It was eventually voted upon but, much to William's disappointment, he was unsuccessful. He strongly suspected he had lost this position due to the fact that he lived outside the Manchester area. His disappointment was obvious when he returned home to Yorkshire that evening.

'What do I have to do to prove my commitment to the place?' exclaimed William in frustration to his wife.

'I'm sure I don't know, dear,' replied Catharine. 'You spend so much time in Manchester.'

'Generations of my family have lived and worked in that town. My brother and I, between us, own a decent amount of land and property there. We both have invested a great deal into the place over the years, helping to improve it. What more do they want?'

'I'm sorry you weren't elected, dear, but you mustn't give up. You were so close this time. Give it a few days and you will feel differently, I'm sure,' Catharine assured him, but William was not convinced.

Frances was born in February 1843 and, as tradition dictated, was baptised by her grandfather. When Rupert was born in the November of the following year, he was baptised by his uncle. Catharine's father had been taken ill, suddenly. He was now sixty-seven years old and leaning more and more upon his son, James Allot, curate of All Saints. The reverend was very proud of his three sons, all of whom had followed him into the church. James, his eldest son, worked alongside him at All Saints, while John was vicar at a church by the same name in Maltby le Marsh, Lincolnshire. His son George had been ordained as deacon two years ago and more recently had become a priest in a nearby village.

Catharine visited her father at his bedside on the day of Rupert's baptism. The concern she held for her father's welfare was evident. She thought he looked terribly frail.

'Did the ceremony go well?' he asked her, reaching out his hand to her as she approached his bedside.

'Yes, Father. James did you proud,' replied Catharine, accepting her father's weakened grip.

'Oh, good. I am pleased. I can relax now.'

'How are you, Father?'

George could see the concern in his daughter's eyes. 'It's a mere chill, my dear. I will be well again in no time. You'll see.'

'Is there anything I can get for you, Father?'

'No. Your mother has everything under control. She's made enough soup to feed an army. She'll have my strength improved in a few days. Now, you are not to worry.'

But Catharine left with a heavy heart and found it difficult not to worry about her father. She had never seen him look so unwell.

A few weeks later her concerns appeared to have been unfounded, as her father was back in his church resuming his responsibilities as though he had never been away.

The following year, when the rent was due on their house in Ackworth, the owner decided he did not want to renew and William and Catharine found themselves searching for another home. Thankfully, this time they were able to quickly find another property near Wakefield, not far from Catharine's parents. Catharine was relieved. She had not felt able to move further away, because she worried about her father's health.

The house was beautiful, situated in Woodthorpe, a hamlet of Sandal, and close enough to the railway station at Kirkgate. Catharine adored their new home. There was an ample garden for the children to play in and the village had an array of shops, able to supply all that her family required. They settled quickly, employing a number of servants and a tutor for the children.

In January 1847, the tenth of William's children was born. Frank was first to be born at the family home in Woodthorpe. He was taken to South Kirkby for a baptism at All Saints, performed by his grandfather. Although Catharine thought her father looked much older, he seemed to be taking care of himself. She was relieved he appeared happy and well. Once again the ever-growing family celebrated the day together, enjoying each other's company.

25

After Richard's first meeting with Suzanna on the corner of Cupid's Alley, he joined her for the evening service at St Peter's Presbyterian church. The elders of the church welcomed Richard with a great warmth and he immediately felt he belonged. Soon that group of strangers had become his new family.

There were more than twenty years between Richard and Suzanna; in fact he was much closer in age to Suzanna's father than to her, and the two men had immediately formed a strong friendship on that first night, when Richard had delivered Suzanna safely back to the church.

'She's far too strong-willed. Just like her mother,' Suzanna's father had told Richard. 'She insisted she go alone. Wouldn't have it any other way. She knows her own mind all right, does Suzanna.'

After meeting Suzanna and her family and attending St Peter's evening service, Richard's outlook on life began to change. He suddenly made the decision to leave his shop, renting out his pawnbroker business and home to a Mr John Cuff.

For the next few years Richard went to live intermittently in one of his properties on Ladd Lane and played a big part in the church's sessions and in decision-making, alongside Suzanna's father. The two men were invited to travel to Quebec, Canada, and assisted in building more Presbyterian churches over there. During a visit they discovered the small town of Lachute. This rural area was sparsely populated, but held much beauty and charm. Richard immediately fell in love with the place and began to think about living there and purchasing a working farm.

When Richard was first introduced to this new way of life, neither he nor Suzanna had any way of knowing how their lives would change. They would never have believed they would end up as husband and wife, but as time went by their friendship altered and, with the blessing of Suzanna's family, the two were eventually married. They married in 1848 after Richard, along with Suzanna's family, emigrated to Canada.

In June, the same year, the Reverend Allott died. He was seventy-one years old. He had been unwell again, but Catharine had been no more concerned than she had been previously. He had looked poorly when she had visited, but she had assumed he would recover as he had before. So his death came as a great shock to both her and William.

A funeral, led jointly by his sons, was held in June, when the whole town showed their reverence. The crowd was so vast that many people were forced to stand outside the church. After the service a more private burial for the immediate family was held in the graveyard. A number of onlookers silently lined the stone boundary walls, not content with only being allowed to attend the service before. The graveyard was covered with an array of brightly coloured floral tributes; only small patches of green grass were visible through the multi-coloured carpet of flowers.

Later that day, when the family at last were able to achieve some quiet prayer in private at the rectory, Catharine and her sisters reflected upon the service their father had given his community. With their mother, they concluded they should have a stained-glass window designed for the church in memory of their father, a man who had dedicated his whole life to his church. It took them quite some time to agree upon a design and a great deal of money to commission it. All family members were at the church when the finished glass was installed in the south wall window of the nave, and all were more than pleased with the end result.

'A fitting tribute,' remarked William to Catharine, kissing her lovingly on her cheek. 'Your father lives on in his church.'

Less than five months later, the family were forced to bury another loved one. This time it was Catharine's brother James, who had been

111

struck down by a mystery illness, not dissimilar to that of his father. The family were understandably devastated at the loss of James, who was thirty-eight years old.

The day was very different from when they had buried Catharine's father. It was bitterly cold for November, and William was fussing over his wife as he had not long discovered she was with child again.

'I don't think Mother will ever get over this,' sobbed Catharine as William attempted to console his poor wife. 'This should never have happened.'

It was a trying time for Catharine, forcing her briefly to question her faith. William endeavoured to support her as best he could, but it was mostly her two brothers' strength and faith which saw her through that difficult time.

In March 1849 William and Catharine's eleventh child was born. The following month the family travelled the nine miles from Woodthorpe to South Kirkby, arriving at the rectory late morning for the baptism. Agnes was baptised by her uncle, George Allott, who had recently been appointed vicar of All Saints.

Many family members were now married and had moved away, but Sarah and her husband Joshua attended the baptism. They lived only four miles away at Rogerthorpe Hall. Here, Joshua employed nine labouring men to work on his 270 acres of land. Within the house they employed a groom, cook, housemaid and dairymaid. Sarah often had Catharine or her mother to visit. The house felt so empty when it was just her and her husband there.

Sarah also welcomed visits from her goddaughter. Catharine Ann was a young woman now and a breath of fresh air whenever she came to stay. Her energy and enthusiasm for life always had a positive effect on the whole household. Sarah had told her sister on more than one occasion how she felt the house wake up when Catharine Ann came to visit.

As Catharine struggled to come to terms with the loss of both her father and her brother, William threw himself headlong into his work. His business life was as busy as ever, something he was grateful for at the time, as it allowed him to escape the sense of loss his wife so evidently felt.

Shares in the railways were at an all-time low and causing many businessmen a considerable amount of concern. William was one of these when, on the afternoon of 8th December 1849, a Tuesday, he was asked to chair a meeting of shareholders of the Manchester, Sheffield and Lincolnshire Railway company. The meeting was held at the Star Inn, Manchester, and approximately fifty gentlemen were present. He opened the meeting by explaining that seven shareholders had met at the Royal Hotel the previous Wednesday, anxious about the threatening aspect of the affairs of the company, the problem being the continuing depression of stock.

'It appears, gentlemen, that the vast majority of us now consider the railway company to be in a disastrous position.'

Mutterings of agreement could be heard around the room.

'We want a thorough investigation into these affairs,' shouted one gentleman from the back of the room.

'Of past and present policy and of the management involved,' shouted another.

William, as well as all the other gentlemen in the room, was fully aware that a £100 share was now worth a mere £16 compared with £38 the previous year and the problem needed investigating.

Mr Harrison Blair rose to his feet and spoke clearly. 'Gentlemen, at one time shares were changing hands for £151. My concern sits firmly with the present management of the line and the policy of the directors.'

'I am in total agreement,' concurred Mr Morton of Wakefield. 'I feel it necessary for an inquiry into these points.' And so the discussion continued for some time.

William would often return home to Yorkshire exhausted from his business dealings. This enabled him to move through the grieving process far quicker than his wife ever could have.

26

Now married and living in Canada, Richard had recently moved into a two-storey, stone-built property and was running a farm. Back in England he would have been known as a gentleman farmer, owning land and property. He lived in Lachute, in the parish of Saint-Jérusalem-d'Argenteuil, where he and his wife Suzanna attended the Presbyterian church run by minister Thomas Henry.

Their first son was born in April 1848. Not long after his baptism, the child became ill and died; he was buried in February 1849. It was the Reverend Thomas Henry and his wife who helped Richard and Suzanna to cope with their loss. The reverend had five children of his own, one also having died in infancy, so he was able to show great compassion, understanding the grief the couple were going through. Richard and Suzanna went on to have three more children over the coming years, keeping William up to date with all of these developments in letters.

With Richard living abroad, it fell to William to ensure the rents for both his and his brother's many properties in Manchester were collected on time. This had always proved a challenge, and recently, with his other business commitments to the railways and the council, and travelling back and forth to Yorkshire, William had been under a great deal of pressure. Due to the nature of these business affairs, William soon realised he needed to spend more time in Manchester.

Before long, William found himself only travelling back to Yorkshire during weekends, choosing to stay for the rest of the time in Manchester. He had countless early starts and numerous meetings that went on late into most evenings, and his spending more and more time away from his family soon started to have a detrimental effect on his marriage. Most of the time he felt tired and irritable when he eventually arrived home to his family on a Friday evening, and often he felt quite despondent about the whole situation.

One evening, after another tiring week, William attempted to unwind with a drink and his newspaper in one of Manchester's many public houses. An advert in his newspaper caught his eye. He began to read a notice about the sale of a farmhouse called Barton Grange in Eccles, and his whole demeanour changed. As well as a substantial number of acres, the farmhouse had eleven rooms with an additional cottage of six rooms next door. *I could rent that out to a wagoner or farmhand,* he thought to himself. He had received regular letters from Richard over the past couple of years, telling him how wonderful his life in Canada was, how he enjoyed farming the land and how he wished he'd done it years ago. William instantly knew Barton Grange was the answer he had been looking for. He made enquiries the following day.

In the summer of 1850 William moved his family for a fifth and final time, to the town where he had strong foundations, good connections and plenty of land and property. Catharine reluctantly left her home of Yorkshire and everything she had ever really known from childhood to move into the farmhouse on the outskirts of Manchester.

Catharine Ann, their eldest daughter, was nineteen at this time and finding the upheaval difficult. She asked on more than one occasion if she could stay with her aunt at Rogerthorpe Hall, but William was having none of it.

'Not this again,' William replied, exhausted from repeating himself. 'Your mother and I have decided you are coming with us, my dear. There is nothing more to discuss.'

'But Aunt Sarah wouldn't mind, Father. I know she wouldn't.'

'Your aunt is a very busy woman. She does not need you following her everywhere she goes. Besides, your uncle would never agree to it. Now, there's an end to it.'

'I'm sure he would agree, if you would allow me to talk with him,' insisted Catharine Ann.

An infuriated William turned to his wife for support. 'Will you speak to the girl? She seems to be completely deaf to my words.'

'I know you are used to getting your own way with your father, Catharine, but he has made his decision. You must respect that or face the consequences,' his wife said, at which point Catharine Ann stormed from the room.

'Thank you, dear, I think. But what did you mean by "she always gets her own way"?'

'You know exactly what I mean, William. You spoil that child. You always have done.'

It was futile for William to attempt to respond, as he knew his wife was right.

*

Soon after the family moved, William discovered his wife was with child again. In March 1851 William's twelfth child was born. Although the family were now living in Lancashire, they still made the trip back to Yorkshire to have Lucy baptised by Catharine's brother. No one was happier during this visit than Catharine Ann. To be returning to Yorkshire and visiting her aunt again filled her with joy.

27

On 6th June 1851 a census of the country's occupants was taken. The enumerator knocked at William's door and was welcomed inside. Catharine offered him a drink, but he declined, saying he still had many more properties to visit that evening. When asked his occupation, William described himself as 'proprietor of lands' and Catharine as 'a lady'. He painstakingly helped to record details of eleven of his twelve children, along with their general servant and nurse.

Nineteen-year-old Catharine Ann, recorded as the 'daughter of the proprietor', felt she was more of a mother's help, constantly having to assist her mother with the younger children. When she was allowed days off, and these were few, she enjoyed travelling back to Yorkshire to visit her aunt.

Eighteen-year-old Henry was recorded as an 'architect's pupil'. After being homeschooled by a number of different teachers in Yorkshire, he had attended classes at the Mechanics' Institute in

Manchester's Cooper Street. He now worked for an architect in offices on King Street.

Richard was seventeen and a 'mechanics pupil'. He too had been homeschooled in Yorkshire and now attended Manchester's Mechanics' Institute. Here he was learning the principles of science, which would enable him to apply what he had learnt to his trade of choice.

William was proud of both Richard and Henry as he recognised they worked hard, but it was Henry who showed a stronger desire to learn and achieve. William hoped both boys would become architects but had greater aspirations for Henry. Henry would often share his knowledge of newly opened or completed buildings across the world with his father. Since its early publication Henry had collected volumes of *The Builder*, and enjoyed discussing its illustrations in detail with his father. William could remember that, when Henry was a young boy, he always had a pencil in his hand, drawing and designing. He was influenced by the buildings in and around Manchester but later by French and American architects. Henry and Richard were both inspired by George Gilbert Scott, an English architect who used Gothic styles of architecture and had been appointed architect to Westminster Abbey.

William's son George did not appear on the census. Against his father's advice, he had left home some months previously in search of a job. Aged fifteen he was drawn back to the place of his birth, where he joined a ship as an apprentice merchant seamen. This was to be the beginning of a life at sea for George. He would spend two years and eighteen days on board this first ship, writing only once to let his family know that he had boarded. William was furious with his son when he discovered what he had done. In William's opinion, George was wasting his life.

William recorded his next six children as Mary (thirteen), Edward (eleven), Ellen (nine), Fanny (eight), Rupert (six) and Frank (four). All of these children were being 'schooled at home'. William was paying for private tutors to visit his home daily, to teach the children the basic reading and writing skills they would need in life. Last were his two youngest daughters, Agnes (two) and Lucy (three months), recorded as 'infants'. They were being cared for by their mother and a nurse. Once William's servants were noted, the enumerator was free to leave.

William was now fifty-four years old and his pace of life had started to slow down, which was curious considering he had recently moved his family to Manchester. He was not as actively involved in the affairs of the town as he once had been. He told Catharine he thought the younger generation should have more of a say and so he tended to take a back seat during the fewer meetings he did attend. In part he spoke the truth, but there were some changes which were taking place around Manchester that William did not agree with and he felt he was better off staying out of these affairs.

At least once a week, William would have his groom get the horse and carriage ready and he would make the nine-mile journey into Manchester. He might attend a meeting, collect some rents or visit a friend, but on these occasions he usually spent most of the day in Manchester. William continued to collect the rents from his many properties, but he had not purchased any further property for quite some time.

Although William managed his farm labourers rather than working the land himself, he had recently discovered he enjoyed gardening. He asked one of his workers to cultivate a small patch of land for him, where he began to grow a few vegetables.

Family life could be chaotic and, on occasion, William felt he was getting in the way. 'You're always getting under my feet,' Catharine so eloquently put it one day. Gardening seemed the perfect solution. It got him out of the farmhouse and allowed him some time for quiet contemplation. It was a weather-dependent activity, though, and Manchester weather could turn quickly. On those occasions he might go for a walk, crossing the Liverpool to Manchester railway line, over the fields to Worsley, where he would enjoy a drink beside a warm fire in one of its many hostelries before making his way back home for supper.

28

In April 1853 George's ship arrived in Boston, Massachusetts. Some of the men were allowed to leave the ship for a number of hours but instructed to return by a certain time, in readiness for the ship's departure the following day. George was enjoying his newfound freedom and being back on dry land. After a number of drinks on American soil he quite forgot to return to the ship and spent most of the night drinking and socialising. When he woke the following morning he found himself slumped in a doorway of a street he didn't recognise. When he was eventually able to find his way back to the dock, he had missed his ship's departure.

George had failed to return to his ship on time and was recorded as having deserted. Realising the penalty for this could be imprisonment, he boarded another ship and went to sea for another two months. He never repeated this behaviour, nor did he write to inform his mother of his recklessness.

*

William's thirteenth and final child was born in February 1854. He was named Philip Webster after Sarah Webster, who had married Philip's uncle, George Allott, in the June of 1851. Catharine had taken an instant liking to her sister-in-law and asked her to be godparent to her son when he was baptised in September. The family made the journey back to Yorkshire for this one final baptism.

It was during the 1850s that William's sons Henry and Richard both moved to Kentucky in the United States of America. At this time, Kentucky saw an increase in the arrival of English immigrant architects. It was an exciting time for architects, as the progress in building expertise brought about many changes in construction methods, making the need for architects increasingly apparent. The Italianate architectural style became popular in Kentucky at this time. Building features included gently sloping roofs, deep overhanging eaves supported by a row of decorative brackets, and tall, rounded windows.

Henry Platt Bradshaw arrived in Louisville in 1859, shortly followed by his brother Richard. Henry soon became involved with the designing of both the Louisville city hall and the Louisville steam and power company buildings. Later he set up a company with a number of other architects, and they called themselves Bradshaw, Stancliff and Vodges. They regularly advertised their services in the local papers and Henry went on to design many other buildings in this area. Henry and Richard lived well in the USA, but not for as long as they might have expected.

*

In May 1860 George arrived in Liverpool after spending the last six months at sea. He headed home for the first time in almost a decade. He had on a number of occasions written to his mother while away but was anxious about meeting his family again after so long.

The meeting with his father did not go well. William could not help feeling betrayed by his son. He had wanted more for George than a life at sea. He made a weak attempt to welcome his son home, but it was obvious George was greatly changed for his experience and the two men had little in common that they felt able to discuss or share.

Catharine was delighted to see her son, although, when he had walked in through the scullery door, she had hardly recognised this man as the boy who had left all those years previously. She politely introduced him to his sisters Mary, Ellen, Fanny and Agnes, who all had grown and whom George could scarcely remember. When he had left the family home, all those years ago, his mother had just given birth to Lucy, and he was astonished to discover she had gone on to have another child while he had been away. He was also surprised to see his mother looking so old.

George stayed longer than he had planned as his mother insisted on making him something to eat before he left. While George was enjoying the plate of food she had prepared, his two brothers Rupert and Frank arrived home from a day's fishing trip down at the River Brock. Rupert had little interest in the stranger who sat at his family's table; he was more interested to show off his catch, but Frank was

120

different. Frank wanted to know everything there was to know about his brother's life at sea. His sisters and Rupert soon lost interest and left George, Frank and their mother to their discussion.

Frank and his mother listened intently as George shared some of his more personal experiences with them. Some of George's experiences concerned Catharine, but most made her and Frank laugh out loud. Later, Catharine began to clear up around her sons, then disappeared to help Cook prepare for supper. George and Frank remained seated at the table, Frank asking many questions about his brother's life at sea and what it had been like when George had first left home. George was honest with his brother and told him it hadn't been easy, playing skivvy to the rest of the crew, but also explained that there was nothing like going to sea and the freedom it gave one.

It was getting late when their father walked in. Amazed to see George still at the farmhouse, he said, 'I hope you're not filling young Frank's head with any of your daft ideas, boy.'

George jumped to his feet. 'No, Father. Frank and I have just been catching up on things, but now I think it's time I really should be going.'

'Yes, I think so too,' remarked his father, as Catharine entered the room.

'Do you have to go?' asked Frank.

'I'm afraid so, little brother,' replied George, ruffling Frank's hair.

'Where will you stay, George?' enquired his mother.

'I have a place I rent in Bromley.'

'Are you heading there this evening, dear?' she asked with concern.

'I shall most likely find somewhere to stay in Manchester tonight and head to Kent tomorrow.'

William threw a glare towards his wife, willing her to remain quiet and not invite the boy to stay the night. Catharine assumed correctly that George would refuse her anyway and didn't bother.

'What will you do next?' enquired Frank.

'I shall go to London to be examined, and when I have received my second mate's certificate I shall head off back to sea.'

For a moment the room fell silent. Then George reached out to shake Frank's hand. 'Goodbye, Frank.'

Frank willingly took his brother's hand and shook it with enthusiasm. The same gesture was offered to his father, who reluctantly accepted, shaking George's hand just once.

'Goodbye, Mother, and thank you for the food. I'll write soon.'

His mother flung her arms around him. 'Take care of yourself, my boy. We will miss you.'

George exited the farmhouse as quickly as possible, without glancing back. He hadn't realised he would feel this much emotion when coming back to visit. He would think twice about returning another time. He had clearly upset his mother. But life after George's visit quickly returned to normal for the household of Barton Grange. That is, with the exception of Frank.

29

In 1861 the next census was taken. The family remained at their home in Barton Grange, yet they were somewhat depleted. The house appeared far quieter and felt empty at times. Only seven of William and Catharine's thirteen children now lived at home.

Catharine Ann was away, visiting her aunt in Yorkshire. She travelled with her uncle and aunt as they embarked on a trip across the border and into Scotland. While there, thirty-year-old Catharine Ann was introduced to a Yorkshire man who owned a sufficient acreage of farmland in the Castleton area. With her parents' blessing, her uncle and aunt encouraged her to spend much time in this gentleman's company while in the area.

Henry and Richard still lived and worked in Kentucky. Their work as architects kept them too busy for a social life and neither had married. They had visited England only once over the last decade, and that was to see their parents. No one was more pleased by this visit than their father, eager to hear all their news. Excited, they informed their father of their plans to set up in business together in

Louisville. They explained their architectural firm would be operated equally by them both and was to be called Bradshaw and Brother. They hoped to attract several of Louisville's leading architects to pass through their offices.

Over the coming years, the brothers would be instrumental in designing a number of Italianate schools, churches including St John's evangelical church on East Market Street and the first of Kentucky's synagogues, named the Adath Israel building, on Broadway. The brothers would stamp their mark across Louisville, their buildings standing for many decades.

Edward was no longer residing at the family home. As he had approached his twenty-first birthday, he had expressed the desire to travel abroad. After some correspondence between his father and his uncle Richard, Edward was invited to visit Canada. Edward stayed with his uncle in Quebec and helped on his farm but soon became restless and wanted to explore further. At the time of the census, Edward had travelled more than 500 miles from Quebec to Ontario in search of work. Here, he had met Ann Hunter, who he was to discover had been born in Yorkshire, some fifty miles from his place of birth. Within the year she would become his wife.

George by the time of the census had spent more than seven years out on the sea, but in the previous May he had arrived in Liverpool and decided to pay one last visit home before making a new journey. When his mother had seen him walking up the path towards the house she had gone running out to meet him, flinging her arms around him. George had been embarrassed and looked about to see if anyone had seen his mother's display of affection.

He felt very little had changed at home. His family's lives appeared to have stood still in this part of the world. Some of his other brothers clearly felt the same way, as Henry, Richard and Edward were all now living abroad. Two of his younger brothers remained at home, but George suspected that was only because of their ages. *Give them time and they'll be heading off for pastures new as well,* he thought.

Before his father arrived home, George quickly discussed his plans for the future with his mother, over a swiftly prepared meal. He told her how much he enjoyed his life at sea and how he was getting to experience the world. He'd travelled to America but was hoping to see more of the world and the people in it.

'You will be careful, dear? You know how much I worry about you,' fussed his mother.

'I will, Mother. You have nothing to worry about.'

'And you will write to me? I do so like to receive your letters and know that you are safe.'

'I will always write to you, Mother, and let you know where I am.'

Catharine looked at her son with a deep longing in her eyes. 'One day I hope you will write to tell me you have settled down and have a family of your own,' she said.

'Well, I can't promise you that. We shall just have to wait and see.'

As George left Manchester, he was completely unaware that the path he was about to take would change his future forever.

Frank's name did not appear on the 1861 census. He had been furious when he had discovered in the previous May that his brother George had paid the family a visit and he had missed him. He made his mother recall every little detail of his brother's visit: what he looked like, where he'd been and where he was going to next. He would not allow her to miss out a thing. She promised she had given him every little detail, but he insisted she go over it all over again.

Everything seemed to change for Frank after this. He became very restless and early one morning, before the rest of the house was awake, he packed a small bag, holding some of his belongings and some money he had managed to save, and left. He bought a ticket and caught a train to Liverpool, where he boarded a boat named the *Trivoli*. On board for the next four months he worked as pantry boy. He was fourteen. His mother was devastated when she discovered he had slipped away in the night. His father was furious that he had wasted school fees upon the boy, and that history had repeated itself, but there was very little he could do about it. William wanted nothing more to do with Frank. He hoped he would soon come to his senses and return home.

The rest of William's children were included in the census. Mary, Ellen, Fanny, Rupert, Agnes, Lucy and Philip were all receiving schooling at home. William also employed two servants in his house at this time.

30

In Canada, in January 1861, Quebec also held a census. Richard was living in Argenteuil as a farmer with Suzanna and their three children. His nephew Edward had recently visited them from England, but he only stayed a matter of months before he expressed a desire to explore the country further.

Richard was not a well man at this time. He had been suffering, quietly, unable to share his painful secret with his wife. She could never know the pain he was in. It would be far too distressing for her. He chose to keep his illness from her and everyone else.

Therefore Suzanna was shocked when Richard died later that year, very suddenly and in excruciating pain. There was little warning that anything was wrong with her husband. He woke one morning at the usual time, sat at the table for his breakfast and the next minute was lying lifeless on the cold stone floor. The doctor explained to Suzanna that it was typhoid fever that had killed her husband. Suzanna buried Richard in Lachute's Presbyterian cemetery on a bleak November day, her young children at her side, struggling to come to terms with the loss of their father.

Suzanna wrote to William, but it was one of the hardest things she had ever had to do. She turned to the Reverend Henry and his wife, Helen, for help. 'The good Father will not forsake you in this hour of sad bereavement, if you put your trust in him,' the reverend tried to reassure her.

When Suzanna's grief became too much, it was Helen who was there to support her with the farm and the children. Her ten-year-old son Alfred was forced to grow up quickly and within a few more years had taken on much of the farm work from his mother.

Suzanna would never marry again. She stayed in Lachute, along with her children, and remained a widow for a further thirty years until her death.

When William received news of his brother's sudden death, he was understandably upset. He sent his condolences by return post to the sister-in-law he had never met, thanking her for informing him promptly and succinctly. He informed her he would immediately be taking the appropriate steps to see Richard's business investments were in order and that she and her children would be provided for.

It was a few days after this news that exactly what his brother's death meant suddenly hit William. William was now the only remaining Bradshaw son and sole heir to the Bradshaw lands and properties in and around the Manchester area. Collecting the rents for these properties had never particularly been an issue for William. He had seen to this anyway since his brother had moved to Canada. However, it had suddenly become his responsibility to ensure these lands and properties continued to increase in value, and this weighed heavily on his mind.

When their brother Samuel had passed away, William and Richard had inherited the share given to Samuel by their father. Now William was to inherit a second share, and in doing so would come to own the entire fortune his father had amassed, and more, purchased later by himself and his brothers. From Richard's estate, William was to inherit the land and buildings at Pepperhill, his houses on Ladd Lane and his properties in Longford. Richard had, of course, previously sold his properties on Deansgate and his pawn shop to enable himself to move to Canada.

The responsibility William now had to his children's futures, and the question of how to distribute his wealth between them fairly, seemed to take over his every waking hour for the next six months. He had seven sons and six daughters, many more children than his father had considered when writing his last will and testament. His daughters were fairly easy to manage. They could be left a sum of money from his estate as a dowry. He trusted they would marry well.

Providing for his sons was a little more complicated. George appeared to have left the family for good and in doing so had turned his back on his inheritance. He would receive no financial assistance from William. Frank seemed to have followed in his brother's footsteps. However, William felt it was still early days and Frank was young enough to turn his life around. William would allow Frank further time to prove he was more sensible than his brother and decided he would include Frank in his will at this time.

Henry, Richard and Edward were all living abroad. Although they seemed to be financially comfortable, William would make sure they all received their fair share. Rupert and Philip were good boys and, although Philip was only seven years old, he was showing great progress in his schooling. William had been a little concerned at one time that Rupert might attempt to join his two brothers and run away to sea, but at sixteen he and his father had begun to discuss the options for his future. Rupert was mature enough to understand the importance of travel and education for a young gentleman if he was to 'get on in life', as his father had put it. Rupert had assured his father that he understood and would never run away from the privileged life he had been born into. William was greatly relieved.

When his will was finally signed and witnessed, he at last felt able to get on with his own life.

The next decision William was to make was to sell his farm at Barton Grange. Now fifty-five years of age, he was determined he and Catharine should do less and enjoy the rest of their lives to the full. William had worked hard, making business decisions almost every day of his adult life, and now he wanted some repayment.

William and Catharine took the decision to sell their home and began to rent a property in Burnage, south of Manchester, some seven miles away. Their new home was known as Burnage Lodge, a beautiful house, cottage and gardens in idyllic surroundings, close to Burnage Hall. The hall had been built around 1840 by John Watts, whose father had founded the Watts warehouse on Portland Street in Manchester. Burnage Hall was built of brick and stone, with ornamental gardens, orchards and glasshouses, set back from Burnage Lane and approached by a magnificent avenue of lime trees. Burnage Lodge and Cringle Brook Lodge were to the north of it, the only two other buildings on the estate, which was surrounded by thirty-six acres of fields. Both William and Catharine fell in love with Burnage Lodge instantly.

31

In March 1862 Edward wrote to his parents informing them of his marriage to Ann Hunter. He said he understood they could not be there and that the occasion would be very small.

Ann had been born in Yorkshire, north of Kingston upon Hull. Her mother had died after giving birth to her. Her father, a farm labourer, had remarried when Ann was around nine months old. Her life had altered dramatically in 1854 when her family had endured the arduous thirty-five-day journey on a ship from Liverpool, over more than 3,000 miles, to their new life in Ontario, Canada.

Ann's childhood had mostly been spent exploring the surrounding farmlands, where her father worked as a labourer, so making the transition to a similar area in Ontario came easy. But not all of her family had left together. Ann's eldest sister had chosen to remain in England as she was due to be married. She joined the rest of the family a few months later, her first child being born in Canada in March 1855. One brother had chosen to stay and work in Lincolnshire as a slater. Another remained in England for a time, married and began a family, but by 1860 they too had moved to Canada.

Ann's parents desired a better life for their family and believed they could achieve this in Canada. Her father had heard talk of great opportunities, cheap or free land, better-paid jobs and a healthier way of life, away from a country which was becoming more and more industrialised. Attracted by the possibility of a higher standard of living, the family left England with high hopes. They survived a difficult journey, suffering only from terrible sea sickness.

The family settled in Whitevale, Ontario, ten miles from where Edward worked in Whitchurch-Stouffville. Six years later, Edward and Ann met, to be married on 27th February the next year. Within the year Edward's first child had been born and again he wrote to his parents giving them the news.

'They have named the child Emma Amelia,' Catharine read aloud to William. 'Such a beautiful name, don't you think so, William?'

'Yes, my dear.'

'Edward says she is the prettiest little thing he's ever seen. She has enormous round eyes and when she smiles, little dimples appear at either side of her mouth. He sounds quite taken with the child, doesn't he?'

'He certainly does,' replied William. 'Does he happen to say what he's doing for work these days?'

'Not really,' lied Catharine, knowing her son remained a lumberman. 'He mostly talks about Ann and the baby. He does mention that Ann would like a large family.'

'He'd better make sure he gets himself a well-paid job, then,' muttered William.

'That's a little unfair, dear. He's never been out of work,' said Catharine.

'No, but he's only ever had a job which requires little skill and pays accordingly.'

'They are the types of jobs he enjoys,' said Catharine, in defence of her son. 'He prefers manual work.'

'Well, he will never be able to do much with his life, then, will he?'

'It seems having a wife and a family is enough for him. It is for some men.'

'Not this one,' muttered William under his breath, but the moment those words had escaped from his lips, he regretted them. Catharine folded away her son's letter, choosing not to read any more of it to her husband. Sometimes he could be so infuriating.

*

A great family celebration was held on 3rd March in 1864 when William and Catharine's eldest daughter, Catharine Ann, was married at St Paul's church in Withington to William Brakenridge of Liddel Bank, Roxburghshire. The church had recently reopened after the completion of construction work to enlarge it. A new choir vestry had been added, along with a clock inside the tower.

Catharine Ann left her parents' home that morning to travel the two miles to where her future husband, her favourite aunt and the rest of her family waited. She looked striking as she entered the church, linking arms with her proud father.

'I was beginning to wonder if this day would ever come,' her father jested as they started down the aisle.

Catharine knew he was only toying with her and jostled his arm in retaliation. 'You know me, Father. I don't like to be rushed into things. I like to take my time.'

It was a spectacular day with no expense spared by William for his beautiful daughter. The church was awash with ribbons and flowers, their colour and scent encircling the arched entrance. A large gathering was held afterwards with celebrations that went long into the night.

During the reception, Catharine Ann's mother and aunt sat and reminisced about the day Catharine was flower girl at Sarah's wedding. The pair recalled that poignant moment as Catharine Ann had led the procession, and how everyone had begun to clap at the spectacle.

'What are you two so deeply locked in conversation about?' Catharine Ann enquired, snatching a few minutes to sneak away from socialising with her many guests.

'We were remembering all those years ago when your aunt Sarah was married and you were her flower girl,' confessed her mother.

'You were so little back then, just seven years old. Do you remember that day, my dear?' asked her aunt.

'I can remember it as if it were yesterday,' replied Catharine Ann. 'I can still remember feeling grown-up and terribly important. Just like today, I suppose.'

'Do you remember your aunt gave you a silver bracelet as a thank-you on the day?' asked her mother.

'Of course I do, Mother. Look!' Catharine Ann lifted the top layer of her wedding gown to reveal a hidden pocket sewn into one of the underskirts of her dress. She took out the tiny bracelet. 'It's too small for me to wear now, so I had a pocket made for it. It's my something old.'

'Oh, you dear child, you kept it,' exclaimed her aunt.

'Of course I did. It means a great deal to me. You mean a lot to me.'

Her mother's eyes were beginning to fill with tears.

'You both mean a great deal to me,' continued Catharine Ann, and she moved forward to embrace both her mother and her aunt. As she did so her husband William came up beside her and politely asked her mother and aunt if they would mind if he whisked her off to introduce her to some of his guests.

'Not at all, dear. She's avoided her duty for too long as it is,' said her mother.

'We'll see you a little later, dear,' Sarah reassured her. Then Catharine Ann was whisked away.

When Catharine Ann laid her head on the pillow in the guest house in which she spent her first night of marriage, she still had a big smile all over her face. William lay next to his new wife and stared at her for a time before saying, 'Are your jaws not aching yet, wife?'

Catharine was unsure as to what he meant.

'You haven't stopped smiling all day,' he said with a laugh.

'I shall have this smile on my face for the rest of my life,' announced Catharine Ann. 'I am so happy.'

'Me too,' agreed William.

The following day Catharine Ann was only slightly subdued as she said goodbye to her parents before leaving with her husband for Scotland. As they set off, her husband announced they would be stopping off en route and spending a week beside Coniston Water for their honeymoon. He had planned it weeks ago.

Catharine Ann was both surprised and excited. 'Do Father and Mother know?' she asked.

'They do. Your father helped me pick a very nice hotel. You will love it.'

'I can't wait,' whispered Catharine Ann.

*

The following year William and Catharine Bradshaw expected to receive news from their daughter announcing she was going to have a child. Instead that news came from Canada. Edward's wife had given him a second child, this time a son. Edward's excitement was as clear as day in his letter to his parents. He explained how he and Ann had decided to name the child Henry, after Edward's brother.

Catharine was in constant contact with all of her sons, even though they were living abroad, and she would write and tell them all about what their brothers were doing. She felt it made for more interesting reading than just telling them about home. Edward had always looked up to his eldest brother and was suitably impressed by what his mother had told him in her letters. It had only seemed right to name his first son Henry.

Remembering their conversation after Edward's previous letter had arrived, Catharine chose not to discuss Edward's news with William in any great detail. Instead, she mentioned he had written, then took the letter off to another room, where she read it through a further three times before picking up a pen to reply. She had just begun when William shouted, 'I'm off for a walk. See you later.' He didn't wait for a reply. She heard the door close, then continued with her letter writing.

*

In July 1866 William received an upsetting letter from his brother-in-law, Thomas Bolton, informing him of his sister's death. Ann would be the first of William's sisters to die. She had been taken ill whilst staying with her mother-in-law in Penketh, Warrington, and that was where her husband had decided to have her buried.

William had heard very little from Ann over the years. It was rare for them to visit one another, even though they lived fairly close. After her marriage, she and Thomas had spent most of their time travelling between Warrington and Southport. Thomas did much of his conveyancing and insurance business in Southport and often they would travel to visit his widowed mother in Warrington.

When Ann was forty-seven years old and ten years into her marriage, she had ruled out ever having children. She and Thomas had both been shocked to discover Ann was expecting a child. They named their only son Edward, after Thomas's father, who had died some seven years before. Ann had written shortly afterwards to inform William of her son's birth. That had been nineteen years ago.

William could only recall seeing his sister once or twice in the time after, the last time being at Catharine Ann's wedding. Although that had been just three years ago, they had said very little to one another at the time and Ann had not brought her son along with her. Thomas had accompanied her, but both had been somewhat distant with William and Catharine, exchanging the necessary pleasantries, but nothing more.

There was an obvious sorrow in the letter written by Thomas Bolton, but William couldn't help feeling he was only doing his duty in letting him know.

'What am I supposed to do with this?' William asked Catharine, brandishing the letter. 'He's already had the funeral. No doubt he couldn't face having us there.'

'That's a little unfair, dear,' said Catharine.

'And to think it was me who introduced them to each other all those years ago,' muttered William. 'I'd like to think that counted for something.'

'I'm sure it does, dear. But people change.'

32

In early 1867 William and Catharine received another letter from Edward in Canada. They were still hoping for news from Catharine Ann, but her brother had beaten her to it again. Edward had news of a third child, named Agnes, but, more importantly, he wanted to share some news about his work. Catharine read the letter, then shared her son's news with her husband.

'Edward explains in his letter that he wishes to set himself up as a lumber merchant. He is wondering if we could help him out financially to purchase a saw mill.'

'At last!' exclaimed William, the most animated Catharine had seen him in a long time.

'You're willing to help him, then?' asked Catharine.

'Of course, my dear. I have waited a long time for this moment.'

Catharine's relief was clear. She read on. 'He goes on to describe an incredible sight he has recently witnessed. Thousands of logs were placed together to make a raft upon the river, and between twenty and thirty-five men stood upon the logs, propelling the raft downriver using numerous oars. He says it really is a sight to be seen.'

'Oh, yes! I have read about this Canadian spectacle in my newspaper. It was discussing the Ottawa River timber trade. It's a major industry over there, you know. There is definitely plenty of money to be made.'

Catharine tutted. 'Is that all you think about?'

William refrained from replying to his wife's comment, knowing it would only cause another disagreement and he didn't feel like one today. At last he had received good news from Edward and he wanted to savour the moment.

More good news was to follow in March when Catharine Ann's first child was born in Scotland.

'At last!' cried Catharine Bradshaw when she read her daughter's letter. 'I thought this day might never come.'

Catharine Ann had known the previous year she was with child, but had chosen to tell no one, not even her husband. It had not been the first time she had found herself in this position. She had lost a baby once before, early on in her pregnancy, and had never told a soul. That experience had devastated her and she still had not really been able to put it behind her or share it with anyone, not even her mother. This time she had chosen to wait it out and her patience had paid off. Her letter was filled with excitement and trepidation.

'I'm sure she would like it if we paid them a visit,' suggested Catharine to her husband.

William surprised Catharine with his response. She had been sure he was going to find a reason for them not to travel.

'I don't see why not. When would you like to go?' he replied.

'As soon as possible?' Catharine was concerned she might be pushing her luck.

'Then you had better write back to the girl promptly and warn her,' came William's reply. Catharine did just that and the following day William purchased their train tickets to Carlisle.

33

1867 looked like it was going to be a year filled with celebrations. Catharine could not have been happier in her role of grandmother. Her family was growing quickly. Catharine now had four grandchildren scattered across the world and she was terribly proud, informing all of her friends and neighbours. William was less enthusiastic to share this information. He saw it as nothing more and nothing less than a fact of life.

At the beginning of May, William and Catharine received more good news, this time from Kentucky. Richard had married. He was clearly content with his new wife and mentioned his business was going well, so the brevity of his letter bothered Catharine very little.

'Not more grandchildren on the way,' complained William, jesting with his wife's emotions.

'You old misery,' Catharine said, accusatory.

'You know I don't mean it,' replied William.

Do I? thought Catharine.

William always looked forward to receiving news of his sons in America. He was very proud of both of them. They had worked hard and succeeded in life, and he enjoyed reading about the latest drawings and plans they were working on and the difficulties they had to overcome in order to get their plans to fruition. So, when William received another letter, so soon after the last, he refrained from opening it straight away. He set about finishing some paperwork and then helped Catharine with a job she had asked for assistance with in the garden, before sitting down quietly to enjoy his son's letter.

From the moment he began to read, he could tell something was wrong. Henry was trying to warn his father that all was not well with Richard. There had been some sort of incident, which he went into in very little detail, and Richard had become unwell. William was sure this incident was the reason for his son's sudden illness, or why would Henry have mentioned it? His concern was great, but he was so far away from his sons there seemed very little he could do. William decided he would not mention anything to Catharine at this time. She would only worry. He would wait until he had further news from Henry.

Two weeks passed and William received another letter from Canada. He made himself comfortable in his chair before opening it, eager to hear his son's news. As he began to read the letter, William's hands slumped into his lap and it was a few minutes before he could muster up the courage to read on.

Dear Father and Mother,
It saddens me to have to inform you of some very terrible news.
There is no easy way to tell you about poor Richard. His lovely
wife, Mary, tells me she woke up on the morning of 24th July to
find Richard lying next to her, his face a peculiar colour and

not a breath leaving or entering his body. She is understandably terribly distressed for they had only been married a few months.

My dear brother, so it seems, had suffered a failure of the heart whilst he slept. The doctor said nervous exhaustion was the most probable cause. The only good to come from this is knowing he will have experienced no pain.

I know this will come as a terrible shock to you both, as it has to myself, but we must hold some comfort in the knowledge that he did not suffer.

This is a devastating blow for me. I do not know what to do with myself at the office each day. Everything has changed. It will take me some time to adjust, but please be assured Richard will receive the funeral he deserves and a monumental memorial stone, fitting to his achievements.

I am so very sorry to have to deliver this news in this way. I hope my letter does not leave you feeling most terribly desperate.

Your beloved son, Henry Platt Bradshaw.

William felt as though he had been kicked in the stomach. Richard was thirty-three years old. It was no age at all. How on earth was he going to tell Catharine? By now the funeral would have taken place; there would be nothing she could do. For a split second it crossed his mind to say nothing, but that soon passed. William and Catharine had always had an honest relationship. They did not keep secrets, they shared the important things. He could not keep this from her. He wanted to protect her from this news, but he knew that was going to prove impossible.

When Catharine walked into the room, William instructed her to sit down. The moment she did and looked at her husband's face, she knew he was about to give her bad news. Nothing could have prepared her for what he had to say, and when he had finished she sobbed and sobbed. In all the years they had been together, everything they had been through, the many children they had brought up together, there had never been anything as devastating as losing a child, whatever their age.

It took Catharine some weeks to bring herself to write the numerous letters to her other children and family to inform them of Richard's death. She hoped no one would feel Richard's loss as deeply as she did.

Catharine received letters of condolence from everyone she had written to except for Frank. She had written to him at the last address he had given her. He had been very good at keeping his mother informed of an address where she could contact him. The last time she had heard from Frank was more than a year ago. He had written to her from an address in London. She could only assume he was still using this address but was away at sea, and she would just have to wait until he contacted her.

It was May 1869 before she heard from Frank. As soon as Catharine began to read his letter it was obvious he had no idea his brother had died. He was writing from an address in Upper Hill Street, Liverpool, which he said he rented from a jolly old widow who liked a drink, and whose husband used to be a dock worker.

Frank's letter was a surprise for Catharine as he had written that he was to marry. In her naivety she wondered how he had found the time to make any woman's acquaintance, for it seemed to her he was always away at sea. Catharine knew from Frank's previous correspondence that he was usually only in port for a couple of weeks. How on earth was this enough time to get to know anyone properly?

In reality his mother was right. Frank did not know his future wife very well. More importantly, she did not know him. Frank did not explain how they had met, only that she was called Alice Greaves and that she was a little older than he. Alice lived with her widowed father and four brothers, keeping house for them all since the death of her mother.

Frank informed his mother that he and Alice were to be married on 15th May, while he was home on leave, and after that date she could write to him at Alice's address on Warwick Street, Liverpool. It would be a very quiet affair, he continued, held at St Mary's church in Edge Hill. He said he did not expect her to travel to Liverpool for the wedding and mentioned he would be returning to sea the following week.

When Catharine addressed her return letter, she wrote it to Mr and Mrs F Bradshaw, secretly anticipating Alice would open it first and read about Frank's brother. Catharine hoped the news might be less of a shock if Frank's wife delivered it to him in person. Then she went to find William in the garden and give him Frank's news.

'Getting married! Well, you do surprise me. I certainly didn't see that one coming,' commented William as he wrapped his runner bean plants around the string frame he'd made for them to grow up.

'I must admit I was surprised also,' agreed Catharine. 'How does a merchant seaman find the time to meet a woman and get married?'

'You are probably better off not knowing those details, dear.'

'What do you mean by that?' she asked.

'Oh, nothing. You never know, getting married might make Frank see some sense. Hopefully he will soon have had enough of the sea and start to realise the importance of getting on with some proper work.'

'I hope you're right, dear. It would make me very happy if he were to visit soon. We might even have some more grandchildren in the next year or two.'

'I don't doubt that,' replied William, much less enthusiastic about that prospect than his wife.

A month or so later, William and Catharine received a letter from Edward. He was writing to inform his parents that he and Ann now had a fourth child and that they had decided to name her Elizabeth Ann, after her mother.

'He mentions a little about how the rest of his family are, but the greater content of his letter concerns how well his business is doing,' said Catharine, a little disappointed.

'Hand it over, then, woman. Let me read it,' insisted William, reaching across the table for the letter.

Edward had managed to set up a successful business in Stouffville, Ontario, where he was a lumber merchant and saw mill proprietor. He had made money quickly and, to William's surprise, was now able to pay back almost in full the sum of money his father had sent out for him, enclosing this payment in his letter. William had not expected Edward to do this quite so quickly, but by achieving this success Edward had gained great admiration from his father, who'd become more interested each time one of Edward's letters had arrived.

Edward explained that there was talk of a railway being built at Stouffville soon, which would make the supply and distribution of his logs far quicker and easier, and he was planning on investing in this railway. This pleased William.

'Business is good and will soon be even better for our son, Catharine,' said William, smiling. 'Will you be writing to Edward by return post?'

'Yes, dear.'

'Please will you inform him I consider it a wise decision to invest in the railways?'

'I will, dear. I will let him know.'

'And tell him he should consider his debt paid in full. I don't wish to receive any further monies from him.'

'Yes, dear.'

News from Catharine Ann about the imminent arrival of her second child was next to reach William and Catharine in 1870. Catharine Ann and her husband were living in Scotland. They rented a large farm at Liddel Bank, near Castleton, where they employed ten men to work the land as well as a number of servants to assist inside the house. Although Catharine Ann loved the property and the area she did sometimes wish her parents lived closer. She had not seen any of her family for quite some time and on occasion had felt quite isolated. It was her mother's regular letter writing which saw her through the more difficult days.

In her letter, Catharine Ann asked her mother if her sister Ellen might like to visit, to help once the baby was born. Her mother felt this would be a good opportunity for the sisters to see one another again and for Ellen to experience spending some time away from home. If Catharine wasn't careful she would end up with two spinster daughters on her hands. She already had Mary, who was over thirty and never shown any interest in finding a husband. She didn't want Ellen heading in the same direction. She shouldn't complain, really, as Mary was a godsend, especially now that she and William were getting on in years. She would prefer it, however, if Ellen were to find herself a suitable partner.

Catharine Ann also informed her parents that if her second child were to be a son, she and William had decided to name him Henry, after, her successful architect brother whom her mother was always writing to her about. Her mother agreed with her daughter's choice of name, although her father had other ideas.

'Surely that could become a little confusing, dear. We already have one grandson with that name.'

'How can it be confusing? Edward's Henry is in Canada and five years older,' replied Catharine.

'I just think there are plenty of other names to choose from. What's the matter with William?' asked William.

Catharine stared at her husband in disbelief.

'I don't mean name the child after me!'

'Well, what do you mean?' asked Catharine, watching her husband squirm.

'William, after his own father,' replied William, quickly realising he had a legitimate argument.

'Let them name their children what they choose,' said Catharine. 'We didn't have anyone telling us what to name our children. That was our decision.'

William knew he had lost this argument and gave up as gracefully as he could manage, but not without muttering under his breath, 'I still think William is a good, strong name for a boy.'

In her next letter to Catharine Ann, Catharine mentioned that she liked her choice of Henry as a name and that her brother would be thrilled to hear of it. She also told her that Ellen would be delighted to visit Scotland and help after the birth of her baby.

Catharine had previously informed her daughter of Richard's death and now was able to describe how Henry was coping without him. Henry had recently written to his mother explaining how he had thrown himself completely into his work to overcome the sadness he felt and his hard work had paid off. He had been commissioned to design two new churches in Louisville, one being St Louis Bertrand, a Roman Catholic church on South Sixth Street, the other the First Unitarian church on South Fourth Street. Catharine wrote to her daughter, 'By all accounts when these buildings are completed they will be quite a spectacle. Your brother is a very clever man.'

Catharine Ann wrote again soon, to inform her mother she now had a son called Henry. Her mother promptly saw to it that Ellen was put on a train bound for Carlisle, arranging for her to be collected at the station. It was at times like this that Catharine Ann missed her mother the most, as her mother had always been extremely organised and Catharine Ann was not. The two women became prolific letter writers, writing to one another almost weekly. There was always something for Catharine Ann to ask or tell her mother.

34

William was seventy-four years old when the 1871 census was taken. This time he recorded himself as a landowner. He and Catharine remained at Burnage Lodge. Three of their daughters continued to live with them: Mary (thirty), Agnes (twenty-one) and Lucy (twenty), all unmarried. Their youngest son, Philip, had recently taken lodgings in Clapham, Yorkshire, and was training as an estate agent.

Catharine Ann and William Brakenridge remained in Scotland along with Ellen, who was helping with Catharine's baby. Ellen and Mary had travelled together to Scotland, then Mary had returned to

Manchester with her four-year-old niece, Catharine Brakenridge. Mary had agreed to return the child to Scotland when the time came, and accompany Ellen home when she was no longer required.

Catharine and William Bradshaw were delighted to have their granddaughter stay with them for a couple of months. It pleased William to educate his granddaughter in how to cultivate the vegetables in his garden, and Catharine attempted to teach her the Latin names of the plants and flowers she had grown. Catharine was impressed by her granddaughter's ability. The child was able to copy the long Latin names, her writing extremely tidy for such a young age. Her mother had taught her well. She was polite and helpful; not a minute went by when she was any trouble. Her ability to listen carefully and follow instructions did her credit and her inquisitiveness would stand her in good stead for the future.

William found her a delight to be around. In the evenings they sat together while he read her stories. Her favourite book was one she had brought from home called *Alice's Adventures in Wonderland*, which William too found he enjoyed. On more than one occasion Catharine had been forced to interrupt their reading as it was past the child's bedtime. William and Catharine would undoubtedly miss the child when it was time for her to return home.

Henry had grown used to not having his brother beside him any longer, although there were still times when he found this very difficult and could become quite despondent. Still, he had no intention of leaving Louisville and returning to Manchester. His business was good; assignments came through his office doors all the time. Work had recently begun, using his designs for a new sanctuary for the Church of the Messiah on Fourth and York Street. This building was just a few streets away from where he was now living in West Walnut Street. He remained unmarried but had many friends. At almost forty years old he was only now beginning to think about finding himself a wife. Before, he had hardly had any time to even consider this possibility.

At the time of the census Frances and Rupert had been

encouraged by their father to visit Henry in Kentucky. They travelled together by ship and spent a number of enjoyable months sightseeing and discovering the numerous buildings which Henry and Richard had designed. Whilst there, they paid their respects to their brother's memory when they visited Richard's graveside. They had been forced to find it themselves as Henry had used the excuse he was too busy to accompany them, but they understood the trip was too difficult for him to bear. They were impressed by the large stone monument Henry had designed, commissioned and had erected in memory of their brother. It was indeed a fitting tribute to Richard.

Frances and Rupert had noticed a remarkable difference in their brother Henry since they'd last seen him in England. He was not the same man who, all those years before, had shown so many great aspirations. He had aged terribly, looking much older than his years. His hair was now almost white and his face displayed many lines of worry. He was a troubled soul. His whole demeanour gave him away.

Henry was of course very happy to see his younger brother and sister, treating them to many day trips around the local area. The pair were quite spoilt whilst staying with him. Henry's two servants also took a shine to their master's relatives and saw they wanted for nothing. Frances and Rupert enjoyed their brother's hospitality, admiring his house and furnishings. It seemed to them that Henry owned many desirable and collectable objects, but they knew he had worked hard to gain them. There would be many stories to share with their parents upon their return to England.

George had worked his way up through the various ranks of seaman. He had started his career helping out the able seamen with tasks such as standing lookout and general cleaning duties. At this time he did not possess a certificate of competence and was only allowed to do the more unskilled jobs, such as cleaning the ship and its hold and repairing broken lines and ropes. These were physically challenging jobs and had to be done regardless of the weather.

He regularly wrote to his mother informing her of his ascent through the ranks. Once an able seaman, he worked under the boatswain, mooring lines, operating deck gear and acting as a general lookout. When promoted to boatswain George was classed as more highly skilled in the deck department. He carried out tasks as instructed by the first mate, which involved directing the able and ordinary seaman.

When he'd acquired his third mate certificate, George learnt how to manoeuvre a vessel, keeping it safe and on track. It was his responsibility to inspect all the equipment on board, ensuring it was safe and operational, and to train and instruct the newer crew members.

As second mate George had to navigate the ship, which included updating the charts and making passage plans. As first mate he was the head of the deck department and second-in-command, after the ship's master. Here George's primary responsibilities were the vessel's cargo, its stability and supervising the deck crew. He was responsible for the safety of the ship as well as the welfare of the crew on board. On occasion he was able to experience command of the whole ship in the absence of the master.

In his most recent letter home, George had explained how he was now working towards gaining the highest responsibility he could: that of captain. As captain he would be legally responsible for the day-to-day affairs of the ship in his command. It would be his responsibility to ensure that all the departments under him performed to the requirements of the ship's owner. As captain he would represent the owner and be called 'Master'. George's ultimate goal was to become master of a ship. Catharine was very proud of her son as she read in his letter about his latest achievements.

George had done a lot of work in and around the port of Auckland, New Zealand, a centre for coastal and overseas shipping. Boat building and marine engineering were becoming important industries in this area and George had been drawn here on a number of occasions. He was in Auckland at the time the census was being taken in England. He liked the place. While the city of Auckland grew as a commercial centre, the rural lands around remained undeveloped. George would soon decide to make this place his home.

Frank and Alice were having very serious troubles at this time, but Frank's parents knew nothing of these.

Edward was running a very successful business in Stouffville, working as a lumber merchant. He supplied logs to many contractors. He had also invested in the railways, with his father's approval, and the station at Stouffville was all but complete in 1871. This would make his business even more efficient, delivering his logs faster, further and cheaper. His business would soon go from strength to strength.

When Edward wrote to his parents in 1873 to tell them he and his wife had a fifth child, a son, his mother wrote back with less happy news. Catharine's letter contained a great many concerns for her husband's health, as she felt it only fair to inform her children of her worries.

35

By the end of April 1874 William had become seriously ill. One of the first signs that all was not right with William was when he began to experience difficulty sleeping at night. At first Catharine would feel him get up out of their bed and listen to him go into the kitchen, where he would bang around for a while in search of a cup for a drink. A few minutes later he would be climbing back into bed. As the weeks went on, the time he spent out of bed lengthened until eventually, after some months, he had stopped going to bed altogether. William had taken to sitting in his chair every night and Catharine was unsure as to whether he had slept or not.

Catharine had put her husband's irritability down to him being tired, at first. One minute he would snap at her, or criticise her for the smallest of matters; the next minute she was unable to get any kind of reaction from him at all, for example if she needed an answer to a question.

William was finding it harder and harder to sit for long periods of time, and these periods soon became mere moments before he would have to get up and walk around. He had become so easily distracted he would leave his meal partway through to go out into the garden and then forget what he had gone out there to do.

William's emotions were up and down. One moment he might experience elation as he picked his vegetables in his garden, the next his mood seemed to spiral out of control and he might become anxious or depressed over finding a snail amongst his lettuce. Something so simple could drag him down to a low point from where it felt like he might never recover.

Catharine had contacted the local doctor, who had been to see William on a number of occasions. He had prescribed many tonics but none ever seemed to work. Catharine and her daughters were at a loss for what to do. They sought further expert medical advice and William was admitted to the lunatic asylum at Wye House in Buxton, suffering from mania. It was with great reluctance and apprehension that they made this decision. Catharine could see no other way to keep her husband safe and longed for him to make a speedy recovery.

The establishment advertised its premises 'for the care and treatment of the insane of the higher and middle classes'. Catharine and her daughters hoped Wye House, its surroundings and the available fresh spring water would have the healing powers required to cure William.

Catharine and her daughters visited William regularly after he was admitted, but, one month into his stay, when they were all eager to see an improvement in him, they experienced terrible disappointment.

William had been allowed to stroll through the grounds of the imposing building along with the other patients. The house had beautiful gardens which were well cared for, and Catharine believed William would enjoy the opportunity to take in the fresh air. As she and her daughters approached him, William appeared to be talking to himself. When he spotted them he began waving his arms frantically and shouting hysterically, uttering all manner of rubbish. His daughters became terribly upset, seeing their father behave in such a way, and Catharine was left having to comfort them while her husband was carted off by a couple of doctors. It appeared William had lost all contact with reality and Catharine and her daughters had only aggravated the situation. They never returned for another visit.

One month later, on 5th July, William Platt Bradshaw died of exhaustion, from which he had been suffering for three weeks. This, in turn, had been caused by the mania he had experienced for at least the last two months. He was seventy-seven years old. This was a terrible and sad end for such a well-liked and respected gentleman.

Catharine had to deal with the difficult task of informing her husband's closest friends and associates of his demise. She received a great deal of support from family and friends at this time, for which she was very grateful.

William was buried in the vault at St John's church, Byrom Street, Manchester, on 9th July 1874. Eight of his twelve children attended their father's funeral, the majority of his sons being too far away from England to travel at this time. The church was full, mostly of William and Catharine's closest friends and acquaintances.

Catharine later arranged and paid for a stained-glass window to be made and erected inside the church to commemorate her dear husband's memory, in the same manner she had when her father had died. She commissioned a Mr Taylor of Berners Street in London to design and build the window. It would be one year before her own death in 1882 when the window was erected in the north aisle of the church, depicting 'faith, hope and charity'. Faith was depicted by Abraham offering up his son Isaac, hope was represented by the brazen serpent in the wilderness, and charity, which occupied the central panel of the window, was depicted by the crucifixion.

The window was added as a companion to the window erected to John Owen, a philanthropist who bequeathed a large fortune to trustees for the foundation of a college known later as Owens College.

In the lowest division of the window were the arms of the Bradshaw family. Underneath, Catharine also had a monumental brass engraved with the inscription, 'To the glory of God and in the memory of William Platt Bradshaw, who departed this life July 5th 1874 aged 77 yrs.'

PART IV

1867–1913

———⌒⌒———

Frank Bradshaw

Told by Alice Bradshaw, his wife

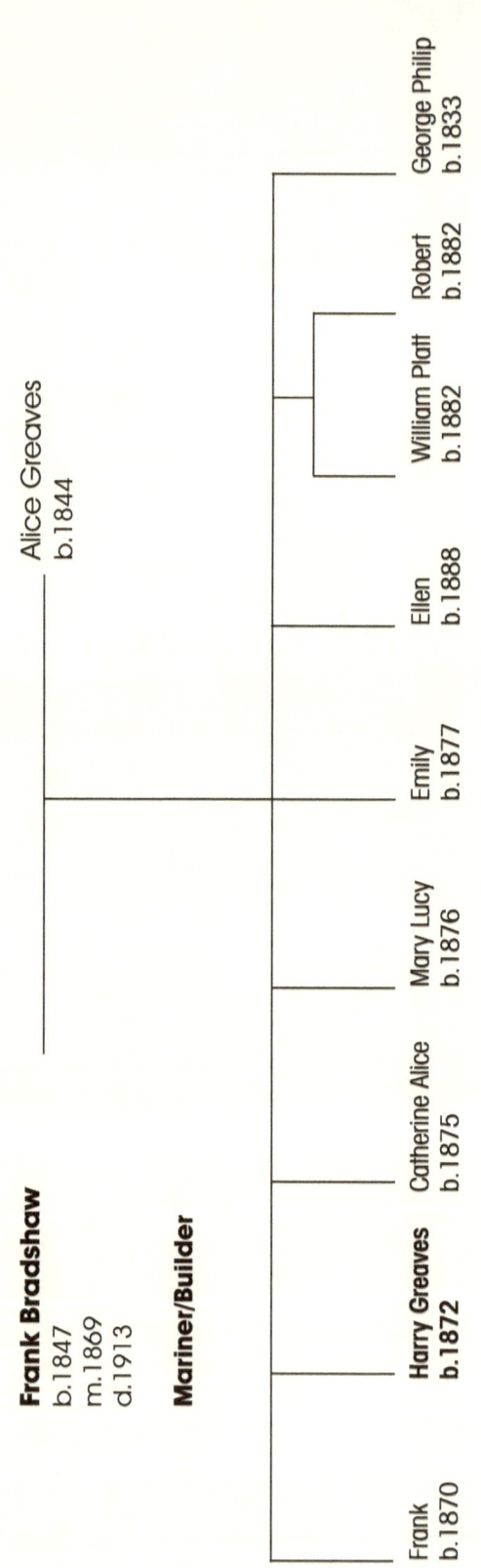

Frank Bradshaw
b.1847
m.1869
d.1913

Mariner/Builder

Alice Greaves
b.1844

Frank
b.1870

Harry Greaves
b.1872

Catherine Alice
b.1875

Mary Lucy
b.1876

Emily
b.1877

Ellen
b.1888

William Platt
b.1882

Robert
b.1882

George Philip
b.1833

36

My father, Robert Greaves, had been born in 1820 in Carrington, near Manchester. My mother, Mary Christian, had always lived in Liverpool. They had married at St Bride's in Liverpool in 1844 and my mother had informed me on more than one occasion that I had been the product of their wedding night. I only came to understand this comment as I grew older. My mother went on to have seven more children while my father worked as a brass finisher at the brass foundry on Pleasant Hill Street. We all lived together in a small house on Warwick Street. Tightly packed back-to-back terraces lined the street and many of those adjoining. We were not well off, but we were happy enough. 'If you've never had it, how can you miss it?' was one of my mother's favourite sayings.

As a young child I would often enjoy the ten-minute walk along the Liverpool streets, which were all the same, to meet my father from work. I would witness a mix of Liverpool residents from all walks of life going about their daily business and often stopped to chat to the ladies, who might be scrubbing their doorsteps or polishing their windows. As I left Mother would often say, 'Don't dawdle, dear. I don't want your father having more than one drink before you fetch him home.' What she meant was that she didn't want him squandering his money away on drink or there would be nothing left for food. Money was the cause of most arguments in our house, but on the whole Father was not too difficult to retrieve from the pub. I would make sure I could see him through the window as I waited outside and would nip in as he took his last mouthful, before he could purchase another. Father would always drink in the same pub near the docks, and this was where I would meet Frank for the first time.

I met Frank in 1868. I was twenty-three at the time and he a little younger. It was a difficult time for me back then. Some five years earlier everything had changed when we had suddenly lost my dear mother, my two youngest sisters and my baby brother. There had been no epidemic that year; they had all died for different reasons. Whooping cough, scarlatina and smallpox had killed the children, and my mother had suffered from terrible diarrhoea.

Understandably my father had changed after these events. His moods varied from day to day and they were often difficult to predict. It was not unusual for me to quietly cry myself to sleep at night. I suddenly had to look after and cook for my father and four younger brothers, and keep the house clean and tidy. My eldest brother, Walter, worked with my father, James was a joiner, Robert an engine fitter, and Henry was just fourteen. Money was coming into the house and there were fewer mouths to feed, but Father was spending more and more money down the pub and I was struggling to put enough food on the table each day.

On this particular day I had been standing outside the pub, waiting for my father and brother to finish their drinks: a chore I seemed to be having to do more and more just recently. Walter had promised me he would make sure Father did not order any more to drink and they'd be right out. We would then walk home together to have supper. They had already had more than their usual.

Frank had approached the pub and acknowledged me waiting outside with a tip of his cap and a charming smile. It was immediately obvious to me he was a seaman, returning to the docks of Liverpool between trips, and I wondered which exotic country he had just visited. I had seen many seamen around the Liverpool area in my lifetime and could always spot them. They usually had rough hands and weather-beaten faces, yet they often had a most contented look. Frank appeared exactly like this.

As he pushed open the door to the pub my father and brother pushed past him and fell out into the street. 'Sorry, mate!' shouted Walter from down on the pavement. 'Can you give us a hand, sis?'

I stepped forward as Walter was struggling to help my father up and, although I tried, I was no help to him either. That was when Frank stepped in. He asked Walter if he could help and Walter accepted. Together the two men helped my father to his feet, but it was soon clear that Walter and I had little chance of being able to bring Father home on our own.

'You look as though you could do with some extra help to get him home. Do you live far?' enquired Frank.

'No, not far at all, really,' I replied.

'Off we go, then,' Frank insisted as he threw my father's right arm across his shoulder and supported him on one side, while Walter struggled on the other. I led the way.

It was obvious both men were exhausted by the time we reached the house and I felt it only right to invite this kind stranger in to join us for supper. At first Frank was reluctant to accept.

'Father will have to go straight to bed without his,' I said. 'He's in no fit state to eat what I have prepared, and I'd rather not see it go to waste.'

'Well, if you insist, I will graciously accept.' It struck me how well-spoken Frank was compared with the average Liverpool seaman and that he didn't have a Liverpool accent.

My other brothers were not surprised to see their father in such a state and immediately complained to me that they were hungry. Walter and Frank eventually introduced themselves with a shake of hands and Walter thanked Frank for his help. Frank was introduced to my other three brothers and given a drink while I saw to Father. When I returned we all sat down to the supper I had prepared. We listened as Frank told us about how he had just returned from more than a year at sea. He had travelled around the islands of the East Indies with a varied cargo and he was full of stories about his adventure. He was very entertaining and my brothers all took an immediate liking to him.

Frank explained he was renting rooms from a widow not far away on Upper Hill Street, and as he left I heard him ask Walter if it would be all right to call again soon.

'Someone's got an admirer,' Walter commented after Frank had left. I ignored his teasing and went to bed, trying to hide the silly smile I had permanently painted upon my face.

Frank visited the house many more times before he left for sea again some three months later, but by then he had asked my father if we could marry upon his return. The time had flown by and I had discovered very little about Frank's life or family. He had especially said very little about his father. It appeared they did not see eye to eye on many things, although his mother sounded as though she was a very refined lady. It would be much later before I discovered the truth about Frank's upbringing and inherited wealth.

It was obvious to me from the very beginning how important it was to Frank that he make something of his life and that he do this alone, with no interference or help from anyone else. He was a very proud man who seemed to have something to prove and he could also be quite secretive at times. I didn't know it then, but he would surprise me constantly throughout our lives together and at times I would wonder if anyone, including himself, ever really got to know the real Frank.

Frank returned to Liverpool after being at sea for one year and five months. He knocked on my father's door on Saturday 24th April 1869, looking tired and smelling of drink. I forgave him the drink, as to be honest I had often considered whether I would ever see him again. I had no idea what a man like him saw in a girl such as me. I had nothing to offer him.

The past year and a half had dragged so slowly and although I had received a number of letters from Frank during that time, he was not the best at letter writing. They were very matter-of-fact, he gave very little away if he was missing me and not once in his letters had he mentioned our impending wedding. When I saw him standing on the doorstep I was shocked, excited and relieved all at once. We didn't talk much that night; he was tired. I fed him, he asked if I had booked the church and then he left to catch up on his sleep.

The following day, before the morning service, Father and I spoke to the vicar to arrange a date for the wedding. That was the first time our banns were read out in church. It was then that Frank wrote to his parents to inform them he was to be married. He told me he had written to them but did not disclose what he had said.

Over the next two weeks the banns were read twice more and on the afternoon of 15th May I was married to Frank Bradshaw. My father gave me away and afterwards we had a small family celebration at my father's favourite pub near the docks, where the landlord supplied a steady flow of food and drink into the late hours.

Frank was quite drunk and needed some assistance in reaching the house that night. He insisted upon consummating our marriage although he was all but incapable of completing the act, and my first experience of lovemaking was a painful one. I had expected a little more romance from my new husband, but as soon as his lovemaking was finished he turned over and was snoring loudly for the rest of the night. I cried myself to sleep, as he had not been the gentlest or most considerate of husbands.

37

A week after our wedding Frank went back to sea and for a short time life went back to normal. Then a letter arrived addressed to 'Mr and Mrs F Bradshaw'. As Frank was away at sea and it looked important I decided to open it. The letter was from his mother. It was a very sad letter informing Frank of the death of one of his brothers. I wished at first I'd not opened it, but later I thought it would be better for him to hear this news from me upon his return, rather than having to read it in a letter. It did occur to me to wonder whether this was the intention of Frank's mother in addressing the letter to both of us.

This would not be the only news I would have to share with Frank upon his return for I was soon to discover, as my mother had before me, I had fallen pregnant on the eve of my wedding day. Father went into an immediate panic and confessed he was already struggling to pay for the house. With another mouth soon to feed, he would be forced to find another home which would cost less. He quickly did and moved our few belongings into an even smaller terraced house on Exe Street, about a mile away from the foundry. Frank was due to return in a couple of months and we had left a forwarding address with the new tenants at Warwick Street.

Although it was only a matter of twelve weeks this time, it felt like Frank had been away for much longer. He was genuinely surprised to discover we had been forced to move house and there were obvious tensions as soon as he arrived. Frank had not left me any money and I think my father resented this, although neither of them had ever spoken about it. It hadn't helped that as soon as Frank walked through the door, Father announced I was to have a child. Frank hadn't even had time to take off his coat. Unsure as how to respond, Frank turned to me and asked, 'Is that a good thing?'

'Well, I think it is,' I replied.

'That's all right, then.'

'Another mouth to feed!' added my father, unhelpfully.

'That's not a problem, Robert. I have some money put by. I'll not see you out of pocket.'

'I shall see to it you don't, my boy.'

I helped Frank off with his coat and told him I needed to talk to him about something else.

'Can I get a wash before there are any more revelations?' he joked.

'Of course. I'll show you through to our room and fetch you some warm water.'

When I had done that I made Frank something to eat and poured him a drink. Returning to our room at the back of the house, I sat on the bed and waited while Frank had a wash and changed his clothes. After he'd washed he took a large gulp from his glass of beer, closely followed by a mouthful of bread and chicken.

'So what do you so urgently want to talk to me about that you can't leave my side?' Frank asked, almost spitting his food out at me.

'We've had a letter from your mother. It arrived not long after you'd left. I'm afraid it's not good news.' I was trying to cushion the blow but failing terribly.

'The old man dead, is he?'

I was shocked by Frank's flippant response and it took me a few seconds to compose my thoughts. 'No, Frank. It's your brother, Richard.'

Frank's face changed and he looked more serious.

'Your mother says she received the news from your other brother, Henry?'

'Yes, they both work and live in America. They're very successful architects over there. They have their own business out there, you know?'

'No, I didn't know.' *Because you've never told me this before,* I thought to myself.

'What's happened, then? Don't keep me in suspense. Where's the letter?'

'I can fetch you the letter in a moment. Your mother said he did not suffer. It seems he just died in his sleep. His wife found him.'

'What?' Frank looked confused. 'I didn't know he had married.'

'He hadn't been for very long. Just a few months, I think, according to your mother.'

'Where's the letter, Alice? I want to read it,' demanded Frank. 'And why are you opening my letters?'

'It was addressed to us both,' I replied. 'I just thought it would be better if this news came from me, rather than you having to read it.'

'Well, you had no right. Don't you ever again open any letter that is addressed to me! Do you understand?'

I nodded. I understood, all right. I hadn't ever seen him so angry. I quickly fetched the letter and left him alone to read it in private.

A couple of days later I felt brave enough to broach the subject again.

'Frank, are you going to write back to your mother?' I enquired meekly.

'Not that it's any of your business, but I've decided not to.'

I was shocked. How could he do that to his mother? She must have been terribly distressed to lose a son and with him being so far away in another country, the agony must have been unbearable. I couldn't let it go. I had to try a different approach.

'I could write back to her on your behalf and offer our condolences.'

I wished I'd never opened my mouth. Frank flew at me like something possessed. He was beyond anger. He never laid a hand on me, but his nose was almost touching mine as he spat out random and hurtful words at me. This was a side to my husband I was afraid of. I ran from the house into the street and kept going for some ten minutes before I could gather my thoughts. I was shaking with both fear and anger at being treated in such a way. I walked and walked around the streets of Liverpool for the next hour before returning to the house. We had both needed time to calm down and think about what had just happened.

Upon my return, I found Frank had gone out. That night he arrived home, rather the worse for drink, after I had gone to bed. He climbed into bed next to me, turned me to him and said, 'I'm sorry about losing my temper this afternoon. It won't happen again. I promise.' Then he kissed me and, although he made every effort to make love to me, he was not capable that evening and had soon fallen asleep.

About a week later Frank went back to sea. He told me not to worry as he would be back in plenty of time before the baby arrived. In the meantime I should start looking for somewhere for us to live. But he left me with no means to acquire this. My father and brothers couldn't afford to help. As my pregnancy progressed I realised I was pleased to have my family around me, as Frank was always away. I would have hated to have been on my own in another house during this time.

As my time got closer and closer and Frank had still not returned, I was becoming more and more distressed. A thought kept going through my head that he might never return, and then what would I do?

38

My first experience of childbirth was a traumatic one. It went on for hours and hours and I actually thought I might die from the pain. By the time our son finally made an appearance, I was utterly exhausted, but the child appeared healthy and he and I both slept for hours.

The following day I was able to get a proper look at him. My baby's head appeared larger than it should have been, in comparison with the rest of his body, but he seemed content enough. Nobody else commented on this, so I accepted the child as God had made him.

A week later, and with Frank still not returned from sea, we had the baby baptised. I decided to name him Frank, hoping this would please his father. When Frank finally returned some three weeks after our son's birth, he seemed unmoved by this gesture.

Frank had little time for me or the baby and seemed to prefer to spend most of it down the pub. When he returned to sea two weeks later he had spent hardly any time in our company. At home, he had seemed very distant and I did not understand why he was treating us in this way. After he had left, I could only recall the one time when Frank had held his son. That had been the day he had arrived home, and after that he had barely glanced at the child.

Over the coming weeks and months I had to overcome problems with feeding my baby, as he would often vomit after the breast. He had also become quite irritable. I had to stop myself from saying out loud, 'Well, you're your father's son, aren't you?' I had secretly told myself, *If this is what motherhood is like, then I am never having any more babies.* I was given little help from my father or brothers, whose attitude was 'you made your own bed, now you have to lie in it.' At this time I can remember feeling terribly unhappy and wishing my mother were still alive. She would have known what to do.

Frank did not make the situation any better, for when he did return from sea he went straight to the nearest pub and drank until the early hours, then stumbled in and woke the baby as he fell over getting into bed.

When our child had reached his first birthday his health began to deteriorate. His father was always away at sea, and my father and brothers were working long hours at the brass foundry to make ends meet. I was left at home to cope with a child who was becoming sicker by the day, as well as having to manage the everyday chores of running a household. My job soon became impossible. My child was fractious most of the time. He had made attempts to walk, but his balance was quite unsteady and he would often fall over. He was always being sick and appeared to be in a lot of pain around his neck and head. His health was a constant worry for me.

My son's head appeared to be growing at a much faster rate than the rest of his body and he now looked completely out of proportion. When I took him out people stared and pointed at my child, and made upsetting comments. I would have found myself confined to the house if it hadn't been for one kind elderly neighbour who agreed to sit with my son while he slept, so that I could nip out to the shops.

In desperation, in April 1871 I arranged for the doctor to visit our home at 34 Exe Street. It had taken me weeks to scrape enough money together to pay for his services. After he had examined poor Frank, the doctor told me my son had hydrocephalus. I had no idea what this was or how serious it would prove to be. The doctor explained this was a condition where a blockage in the ventricles does not allow fluid from the brain to filter out into the blood vessels and that this was the reason why Frank's head had become so large.

'How long will it take to clear, doctor?' I naively enquired.

'I'm afraid it won't, my dear. There is very little I can do for the child now.'

'There must be something you can do,' I pleaded.

'I'm very sorry to have to tell you this, but I don't think your boy has much longer to live. He is very poorly and in a great deal of discomfort.'

I was distraught. A week later and with my father by my side, I watched as young Frank slipped away, a couple of days before his father was due home.

Frank made it home in time for our son's funeral but spent most of his leave drinking. Nothing I said seemed to make a difference. Drinking heavily was the only way Frank was able to deal with the situation. I threw myself into the housework, scrubbing and cleaning the house from one end to the other, clearing away every reminder of my lost baby.

As far as I was aware Frank had never written to his family informing them of his son's birth. Now he wouldn't have to. It was as though his firstborn son had never existed and he was glad to forget him. I, on the other hand, would never forget. My baby had grown inside me for nine months. I had fed, cleaned and cared for him for more than a year and been witness to his terrible suffering. My memories of my boy would never die. He would remain in my heart for the rest of my life.

While Frank could return to his other life at sea, able to forget our troubles, I was forced to deal with the realisation that I was carrying another child inside me. The first time I had become pregnant was on my wedding night. The second time was the evening of my first son's funeral. Two very different occasions with the same outcome. I hoped more than anything this time would be different, but that didn't stop me from worrying every single moment.

When our second son was born, everything was different. Frank was at home on leave and the baby was born within a couple of hours of labour starting. I had very little pain and the child was perfect. My brother Henry was tasked with retrieving Frank, my father and my other brothers from the pub and, by the time they all returned, I had half-prepared a meal and the baby was fast asleep in its crib. The vision of domestic bliss which met their eyes as they entered the house that evening had a profound effect upon them all. When we all sat down together for supper, civilised conversation was mixed with mutual appreciation and respect.

'So, what do you want to call him, Alice?' whispered Frank as he leant quietly over the baby's crib beside the open fire.

'What do you think of Harry?' I asked thoughtfully.

163

'Henry's better,' piped up my youngest brother, who promptly felt my father's hand across the back of his head.

We all looked back at Frank, who was still staring down into the crib. Eventually he answered. 'I think Harry will do just fine.'

'That's settled, then,' agreed my father.

'I also have a middle name in mind,' I added quickly.

'Oh, yes?' said Frank, as he returned to sit at the table.

I hesitated as I was unsure of how Frank would react.

'Well, child, don't keep us in suspense,' said my father.

I looked at Frank for approval. 'How about Harry Greaves Bradshaw?'

Slowly a broad smile appeared across my father's face. 'I like it,' he said.

'It'll do, I suppose,' teased Frank.

Five weeks later our son, Harry, was baptised at St Clement's church surrounded by his family. He was as good as gold and slept throughout the whole ceremony, even when his head was soaked beside the font.

My father had asked if he could bring along a friend to his grandson's christening and I had no objections when I realised to whom he was referring. Very recently he had on occasion mentioned a lady by the name of Maria. He had met her while drinking in his favourite pub as she had been employed to clean the premises. 'We got talking and enjoyed each other's company,' was how my father described their early acquaintance. I finally got to meet her when he asked her to help out around the house, when I was about to have Harry. At that time I was very grateful for her help and we got on well, but I had no idea how fond my father was of her. Only after Harry's baptism did I realise, when I saw them laughing together, how very relaxed they obviously were in one another's company. I was pleased for my father. It had been more than nine years since the death of my mother and it appeared Maria was good for my father. Two months after Harry's baptism, my father remarried.

39

Living arrangements obviously had to change. Father's house was just too small, but none of us felt as though we were being pushed out. The time was definitely right for us all to move on. Walter, James and Robert all found houses and soon had wives of their own. This just left Henry with my father and Maria, as Frank and I had moved to nearby Fernhill Street. Henry too would soon marry.

Over the next couple of years life remained similar. While Frank was away at sea, I spent most days visiting my father and Maria, and when Frank was in Liverpool, we enjoyed days out together with Harry. Frank and I enjoyed taking him to the new Sefton Park, where there were beautiful walks, a lake and small streams. Frank would sail a small yacht for his son and Harry would run along the grassy bank trying to keep up with it. Those times now seem precious. Frank would be back off to sea again before we knew it, and when he returned Harry would have to get used to his father being at home all over again.

It was during these times Frank occasionally confided in me about his own childhood and his relationship with his father. I discovered Frank had been born in Yorkshire, in a place called Woodthorpe, and was number ten of a family of thirteen children. It was immediately clear to me that Frank had always felt unsure as to where he fit in within his family. I had never experienced this, being the eldest child. I believed this was his greatest problem and the reason he'd left home so young for a life at sea. Frank believed he could never match his father, who it turned out was a man of great wealth through clever investment in property, so why should he even try?

Frank had told me he was closest to his brother George, who was more than ten years older. George had also run away to sea for a similar reason: that he could not compete with his brothers, who had moved abroad and made very successful lives for themselves. Frank explained how, during a visit home, George had told him great stories about his adventures at sea, and since then Frank had felt a pull in the same direction. History had repeated itself when Frank, aged fourteen, had disappeared early one morning, leaving his family and home. He had been cross to have missed a visit from George the previous year and from then on had begun to save up enough money to follow in his brother's footsteps. He said he had never regretted his decision, even having to start at the bottom as pantry boy. He had seen it all as a challenge. He told me he was still thrilled by the start of every new journey.

'But what about your parents?' I asked. 'How did they react when you left?'

'I have often written to my mother and enclosed an address where she can write back to me. I know she worries and she must have been upset when I left. She said in her letters that my father pretended he was unperturbed, but she and I both know he is still angry with me, as he still is with George. I think he is mainly irritated over the money he thinks he wasted on our tuition fees. Getting an education was important to my father. But he could be cruel. If he saw any of us getting too close to our tutors he would replace them with another, and this was upsetting for us when we were so young. If Father did not see an instant improvement in his children's abilities then he would discharge a tutor without giving a reason and replace them with a much sterner one. We didn't understand why he was being so unkind.' He paused for a moment. 'My mother's letters made it sound as though Father would come round to my decision. I knew he wouldn't. He had never accepted what George had done, so why would he with me? I suspect she was trying to spare my feelings, but I know I will never be able to return home while my father is still alive. He wants nothing more to do with me. Of this I am sure.'

'Have you never been back? Not even to see your mother?' I asked, surprised.

'Never.'

Frank described to me how his life had changed overnight, from always feeling trapped to one of absolute freedom. His father had expected great things from him and his siblings, insisting they do

166

things his way. Frank had felt stifled and restricted, unable to compete, and had craved more freedom, often disappearing from home for hours at a time and always getting into trouble for it. He remembered endless conversations about how his father had made important decisions when he'd invested in a mill and then the railways, and how these conversations had bored him. His father had always said it was vital to ensure one received a good education and invested well in property. 'This is your ticket for life, boy,' he would often say.

I was sure Frank must have broken his mother's heart, but I did not voice these thoughts. Having a son of one's own, and having lost one as well, can change your outlook on life. Family suddenly becomes very important and not just something you take for granted. This was also how I wanted Frank to feel, and why I would encourage him to accompany me and Harry to the park when he was at home on leave. After all, this was what most other families were doing at this time.

For a short time, my and Frank's relationship was improved. He confided in me some of his most personal feelings, and at last I knew something of his family and childhood. Frank had not stopped drinking and the pub was still his first port of call when reaching dry land, but he didn't always arrive home completely intoxicated. He might only have one or two drinks before coming home to see me and Harry. Frank was changing, but he would never have admitted to that.

In May 1874, while Frank was away at sea, we received another letter from his mother. I instantly recognised her handwriting but chose not to open it as I did not want to give Frank an excuse to reprimand me or to start drinking more. I concluded that, if the letter held bad news within it, that wouldn't change before he was due home in July and there was nothing I could do about it anyway.

The day before Frank arrived home, a second letter reached us. The writing had changed, but I could still recognise it as being Frank's mother's. I could tell something was wrong when I compared the two envelopes. The first had been written calmly and precisely. The second seemed rushed and frantic. I handed them both to Frank as soon as he arrived home and left the house with Harry, making the excuse that I had forgotten to take some groceries around to my father's house. I thought Frank might be glad of some privacy while he read his mother's letters and hoped he would later confide in me.

I returned about an hour later to find the house empty and the letters gone. Frank had left his bag where he had dropped it upon entering the house and most likely returned to the pub.

I could not sleep that night, as he had not returned home before I went to bed. Around midnight he came crashing into the house and made so much noise he could have woken the dead. Sadly, it was Harry he woke. I was forced to lie in bed listening to my son crying out for comfort while my drunk of a husband forced himself upon me once more. All I could think was that something terrible must have been written within the pages of those letters for Frank to react in this way. He had not been this bad since the death of our first son.

The following day Frank did not get up until almost lunchtime. When he finally did, he looked a terrible colour. I fetched him a drink and asked if he wanted something to eat. He nodded and I heated up the meal I had prepared for him the night before. I said nothing, just waited, hoping he would give me his news in his own good time.

After he had finished his meal, he pushed his plate to one side and stared across the silent room to where I sat, sewing up the hem which had come down on one of my skirts.

'Are you all right?' he asked.

'Yes.' I replied, unsure of why he was asking me this question.

'I don't remember much about last night,' he said. 'Did I hurt you?'

I was shocked and embarrassed by his concern and could only manage a shake of my head. I wasn't about to admit he had left me bruised and bleeding.

Silence took over the room again, but courage got the better of me and I finally asked, 'Are you all right?'

That was when he told me his father had died. He'd been taken ill back in April and sent to a hospital to recover, according to his mother, but he never did. He had died within a few months of his arrival. Frank's mother was understandably upset and in her second letter had told Frank when and where his father's funeral was to be held. Frank had missed it all. He had come home to Liverpool one week after his father's funeral in Manchester, and this news had obviously tipped Frank over the edge.

Frank would never be able to show his father what he had done with his life or be able to prove he was successful at something. He would never have the opportunity to introduce his father to his grandson. His father would never tell Frank how proud he was of him, and this mattered to Frank, more than he would ever admit.

I remained quiet as Frank spoke and when he had finished he said, 'I want us to go and visit.'

'Your mother?'

'Yes. Would you be able to leave tomorrow?'

'Of course. Would you like me to see if Maria and my father can have Harry?'

'No. I would like Harry to come with us. He'll love it on the train. I'd like my mother to meet you and him.'

'The train? Won't that be expensive?' I had never travelled on a train before.

'I have enough money, don't worry.'

'Then I'll let my father know we are going. How long do you think we will be gone for?'

'Just for one night, I imagine. That should be enough.'

Enough for what? I wondered.

I informed my father and then packed a bag of overnight things, most of which were for Harry.

'Best clothes,' insisted Frank when he saw me putting things into a bag. Impressions were so important to Frank and I couldn't help wondering if he was possibly more like his father than he cared to admit.

40

I could tell Frank was nervous about meeting his family again. He talked almost nonstop throughout the entire train journey.

'My father would be unable to accuse me of not having a ticket for life now, wouldn't he? I've worked my way up through the ranks and gained many qualifications.'

'I'm sure if we were seeing him today he would be very proud of you, Frank,' was my reply, but Frank continued as though he had not heard me.

Frank described how at the young age of fourteen his first position on board ship was that of pantry boy. He was the lowest ranking of all on board his vessel and he said his jobs for the rest of the crew were endless.

'Occasionally I would be asked to carry a message for the captain, running from one end of the ship to the other. Mostly I would be expected to help the cook in the galley prepare the meals and carry buckets of food from the galley to the forecastle, where the ordinary seamen ate.' But it seemed Frank was also expected to become familiar with the workings of the ship's sails, ropes and lines and be able to handle these in all weathers. Frank recalled how he enjoyed having to scramble up the rigging into the yards whenever the sails had to be trimmed and how he would do this job for a mere few shillings a month.

'There was no formal training, we learnt as we went. I was one of the lucky ones who picked things up quickly. If you got things wrong, you'd receive a clout round the ear and soon learnt to get it right. Some lads were regularly bashed when they got it wrong.'

Although he was young, Frank considered the job he was doing to be one done by men. This seemed an important reason for why he had chosen the job. Even at fourteen he wanted to be taken seriously and respected by his fellow seamen, which was why he preferred the title of 'ordinary seaman' to that of 'boy'. Frank explained how he hated to be called 'boy'. For the first few years of his life on board, he remained at this lowest rank of the ship's crew. He was given instructions by many individuals who ranked above him, such as mates or able seamen, but, according to Frank, he was immediately liked and, because he was a hard worker, was able to follow orders and showed promise, he was soon respected.

By the end of 1864, after three years at sea, Frank had acquired enough experience and was now the right age to become an able seaman. Frank was an experienced sailor who could carry out any job required of him on board. He explained to me that this would be as far as many men would ever get, but he was determined to achieve much more.

During 1866, Frank kept himself very busy. He sat his third, second and first mate's exams, and was able to pass each one. This was probably the only time he was grateful to his father, as his formal schooling as a child had allowed him to master the necessary mathematical skills to attempt the exams. Frank explained how during this time he had set sail on four different journeys, on the last of which he was away for just over a year.

As Frank continued, Harry switched between listening to his father's tales and watching through the train window with fascination, mesmerised as the world passed by at great speed.

Frank talked about how he had passed exams in navigation, seamanship and commercial code signals. He had worked his way up the chain of command, carrying out duties such as watchkeeping, maintaining signalling equipment and navigating.

'It wasn't long after this that we met,' he added with a smile on his face, 'and the rest is history, as they say.'

'Does your mother know anything of your life at sea?' I enquired.

'I wrote and told her of most of my achievements. I hoped she would pass them on to my father and that he might be proud of me, but it didn't work out quite like that.'

As we talked, from time to time, I too glanced out of the window. All around, the land was so luscious and green. Small hamlets were scattered haphazardly across the landscape, farmhouses and buildings added intermittently for good measure.

'We're nearly there,' announced Frank as he appeared to recognise a landmark.

From the railway station we travelled a further five miles away from Manchester in a two-horse omnibus, having then to walk a short distance further to where Frank's mother lived in Levenshulme. Frank had never been to the house before, so we stopped to ask an elderly gentleman where to find Burnage Lodge. He explained we needed to look for Burnage Hall.

Burnage Hall and its grounds were to the east of Burnage Hall Lane, set well back from the road. Immediately to the north of here were two lodges, Cringle Brook Lodge and Burnage Lodge. A mausoleum called Dyers Tower stood across the road. The estate was surrounded by fields and displayed formal gardens to the west and a tree-lined drive through a park to the east and south. I had never seen anywhere so beautiful and as we approached the cottage-like house, I was suddenly overcome with the thought, *What if they don't like me?*

Sensing my reluctance, Frank caught hold of my arm. 'We've come all this way. It would be silly to turn around again.'

I nodded, realising the situation was most likely far more difficult for him than it was for me.

I should never have worried. We all were immediately made to feel very welcome and it was obvious Frank's mother was greatly relieved, after all this time, to see her son again. She kept quietly thanking me for visiting, when Frank wasn't listening, to the extent it became quite embarrassing.

Frank's sisters, Mary, Frances, Agnes and Lucy, were delightful and played with a very contented Harry endlessly, leaving me feeling quite redundant. They had managed to find him a little wooden toy horse and cart and another toy which whistled while spinning, and these kept him occupied for quite some time.

Frank's mother was polite and asked about my family and our life back in Liverpool, but the conversation would always find its way back to Frank and what he was doing. There was ever so much for them all to catch up on and by nine o'clock that evening I was exhausted and forced to give my apologies and retire, leaving Frank in deep discussion with his mother and sisters.

It had passed midnight before Frank joined me in bed. Without a single word spoken between us, we made love, the way we should have done on our wedding night, gently, passionately and with a great desire and respect for each other.

In the morning it was obvious much had been discussed the previous evening in my absence. Frank's mother had brought him up to date with what his brothers and sisters were doing and where they were living now. He had been informed of his numerous nieces and nephews, but admitted he didn't think he would be able to remember all their names. 'I should have got Mother to write them all down,' he later commented.

His mother had also discussed with him some plans of her own. She was thinking about leaving the lodge. It held too many memories for her. She said the rent was high and she was certain she and her three daughters could find something a little less extravagant.

'Mother has asked if, when she does move away, I will consider overseeing the rent collection for Father's many properties in Manchester,' said Frank. 'I understand that since my father became too ill to collect these rents, she has employed someone to do this for her. She has asked if I will manage this person. It will mean visiting Manchester each time I am home from sea, but I'm sure I can handle that. Mother has also mentioned returning one day to the place of her birth, to Yorkshire. I suspect she has always missed the area.'

On our journey home, Frank and I discussed these conversations in more detail. He then announced that his mother had also informed him that his father had left him a sum of money. Frank had been surprised by this news, as he had assumed his father had written him out of his will, as he had with his brother George. His mother had apparently assured him that this was not the case and that his father had never wished to deny Frank his rightful inheritance. However, there was a condition to his father's will, and I could see this had made Frank quite angry. If Frank was to accept his inheritance, he would have to invest whatever sum of money he received from his father in property or land around the Manchester area.

'So the old man will have his way after all,' muttered Frank.

'You don't have to accept the money, Frank.'

'No, but I know I will. But in my own time, when I'm good and ready.'

I was surprised to hear him say this. After visiting his mother, Frank seemed to have changed.

'It will mean a fresh start for us, Alice,' he said.

'Would it mean moving away from Liverpool and my family?' I asked naively.

'Harry and I are your family now. Wouldn't you like him to grow up somewhere away from the docks, with cleaner air, and to be able to give him the opportunities your brothers never had? If I do as my father requests, we could buy a much larger property to live in. Harry could get a good education and I wouldn't need to be away all the time.' Frank seemed to have it all worked out.

'You would give up your life at sea?' I enquired.

'I am seriously considering it.'

I was shocked. A life at sea was all Frank had ever known.

In one day everything had altered. Although I didn't completely dislike what Frank was suggesting and it made great sense for Harry's future, I couldn't help thinking that over the course of one night Frank had turned into everything he disliked about his father. He was now suggesting we do all the things his father had wanted him to do all those years ago, and wasn't that the reason he had run away to sea in the first place?

'Are you sure this is what you want, Frank? It seems an awfully big step.'

'If we don't try, then we shall never know, shall we?'

'That is true enough, I suppose.'

'Please don't panic, Alice. Nothing is going to happen overnight. We can take our time and make the right decisions. I will need plenty of time to think and plan. I can't do anything until the money is released, and Mother said that alone could take quite some time.'

'Did she say how long?' I enquired, as I wanted to know how long I had before I would have to move away from my family.

'She wasn't sure. She seemed to think the will might be quite complicated. She thought Father had both sold and purchased properties since making it. She also said he had added a codicil to his will, just before he became ill, but she was unsure as to its contents. It could take years, Alice. We will just have to be patient.'

A big part of me was very much relieved by this information. 'So, in the meantime, are you planning on going back to sea?'

'Oh, yes. I'm not ready to give that up just yet.'

41

Nine months after visiting Frank's mother at her home in Manchester, I gave birth to our first daughter. It was April 1875. She had been conceived under very different circumstances to those of her brother. So, when Frank suggested we name our daughter Catharine Alice, I agreed and thought it most fitting. We remained quite happy during this time, even though Frank was often away at sea for months at a time and when he returned would always visit the pub first, before coming home to his family.

Frank's mother had written to us earlier in the year to inform us of her change of address. She and her three daughters had moved to a place called Congleton, some twenty miles away from where they had been living. They had found a property named Vale House which, from its description, sounded charming. Frank's mother and three sisters had settled into the area well and were very content with their new home.

It was to their new address I wrote to inform my mother-in-law of her latest grandchild and the name we had chosen for her. She wrote back immediately, terribly excited we should name our daughter Catharine, after her. She enclosed a number of small gifts for the baby from her and her daughters, saying they were all looking forward to meeting the child. She hoped we would all attend the marriage of her daughter Frances on 18th August, in Congleton. Frances was to marry Frederick Earle, a preparatory school teacher. After their marriage the couple were to live in Roxborough Park in Harrow as Frederick had secured a new job there. Before I was able to accept this invitation, we received some news which would devastate Frank.

Frank had just returned from a trip to Manchester to check upon the rent for the many properties his family still owned. He walked through the door bursting with ideas, for he had found Manchester to be a place full of promise and couldn't wait to share his findings with me. I had no idea of the contents of the letter which I placed beside him as he sat down to his meal. The letter contained news of Frank's favourite brother, George, whom he had looked up to and aspired to be like for all these years. Frank turned pale as he read that George had been reported missing, feared dead.

George had been living in Auckland, New Zealand, for quite some time. He had married and had one child. He and Frank had always kept in touch. The news he was missing had come from George's wife and had deeply shocked Frank. In her letter, Margaret explained that on 3rd June George, captain of a fifty-one-ton schooner named *Pacific*, had left Timaru in the south, heading for Onehunga in the north. There were nine people on board, including a mate, cook, steward and four seamen. There was also a full cargo of wheat bound for a Mr Bycroft of Onehunga. Twenty-four hours later, when they must have been in the neighbourhood of Cape Campbell, disaster had stuck. George and his crew must have been hit by excessive weather conditions when a fierce gale of wind came at them from the south-east. Margaret went on to explain that a New Zealand newspaper had speculated that either 'the cargo had shifted in the squall and she had capsized' or 'in running for shelter she had struck one of the reefs off Cape Campbell and gone to pieces'. All she knew was that her husband and his crew were all lost, along with their vessel and its cargo.

Margaret ended her letter with a request: she wanted nothing more to do with the family. She stated she was not in any need of financial or emotional assistance.

Frank was devastated by news of his brother's likely death and immediately began to drink more and more on the occasions when he was at home. During these drunken episodes he would tell me about his father and how he had been very strict with his children, expecting complete and utter conformity from them. There were times when I worried for Harry, but he was usually asleep in his bed when his father came home, the worse for drink. Frank would often rant on for days, retelling me time and again what his father had been like when his brother had left for sea and how George had never been forgiven.

Then one night, Frank arrived home earlier than usual and I had only just put Harry to bed. Frank was not as drunk as he could have been and it was obvious he had much on his mind. 'My older brothers conformed and Father was proud of them,' he began, only slightly slurring his words. 'They were successful in life.'

'You're successful, Frank. Just look at what you have achieved.'

'I know that, woman,' he yelled back at me. 'But I used to feel the same as George and desire adventure. Now losing him is making me question everything I have ever achieved in my life.'

Frank was obviously very confused and distressed. He had lost someone very dear to him. But at times it was hard for me to be sympathetic, especially when he would take his drink-fuelled emotions out on me.

That night appeared to be a turning point for Frank. He came to a decision that he should do something other than work at sea. He wanted to do something with the money his father had left him.

While on leave, Frank visited his mother in Congleton and told her about George. He had not wanted to inform her by letter, but took the one he had been sent by George's wife, in case she wished to read it. Frank's mother was understandably very upset, along with his sisters. He later told me that what disturbed her the most was the fact she did not know where her son's body was. 'His body will never be buried,' she had cried. 'He will never have a grave.'

'There were no words to console her,' explained Frank. 'She begged me not to go back to sea.'

'What did you say?'

'I promised her I would give it up very soon and told her of some of my plans.'

'Was she pleased?'

'Very relieved.'

When we visited his family one month later, to attend Frances's wedding, it allowed Frank further time to discuss some ideas with his mother.

'Whatever it is you decide to do, Frank, know that I have always been very proud of you,' his mother told him. 'Invest wisely, as I'm sure you will, and you can set yourself and your family up for life.'

The atmosphere that day was bursting with promise and fuelled with happiness. His mother's words had given Frank a boost. We left the celebrations feeling excited about what the future could hold for us.

The following October we had another daughter, whom we named Mary Lucy after two of Frank's sisters. I wrote again with our news to Frank's family. A short time later we received a letter from Frank's mother. Her news was not so happy.

Frank's aunt, Sarah, who by all accounts had married a very wealthy Yorkshireman, had died, just short of her seventieth year. Frank's sister Catharine Ann was devastated, according to his mother's letter. She had been very close to her aunt. Having lived in Scotland these past years, Catharine Ann had not been able to visit her aunt in Yorkshire as often as she would have liked. She now felt very guilty about this.

Frank's mother went on to explain how Sarah's husband Joshua was making adjustments to his will, so that his home at Rogerthorpe

Hall near Pontefract would pass to Catharine Ann upon his death. It appeared his sons had no interest in their father's property and this had been something his wife had requested upon her deathbed. Frank's mother knew how fond her daughter was of the house and of that particular area of Yorkshire.

'It sounds as though Catharine Ann will do all right out of this,' commented Frank impassively, as he folded his mother's letter and put it back inside its envelope. It never ceased to amaze me that he could be so indifferent to his family's wealth. Having never even dreamt of such riches, it astounded me that someone should take such things for granted.

It wasn't long after this, just as I discovered I was with child again, that Frank's family were forced to deal with more devastating news. Frank's brother Philip was at this time staying in Mercara, India. I understand that Frank's father had encouraged all his sons to travel the world as soon as they reached the age of twenty-one, often giving them the means to do so. Philip had reached this age six months after his father's death and had every intention of carrying out his father's wish.

Frank's mother had received a number of letters from Philip over the last couple of years and he had kept her well informed as to his whereabouts. He had covered a great distance and told his mother of the many incredible sights he had witnessed during his travels. Frank's mother had last received news of her youngest son in the April of this year. She had been concerned, as his final letter had described the terrible famine which had struck the area where he was visiting. Philip had described in his letter how many people had already succumbed to the famine, and how the Madras authorities had only recently increased their meagre rations. He told his mother he had seen some terrible sights but refrained from giving her too many distressing details. He was determined to stay there and try to help in some way. The next she knew was when the authorities contacted her to inform her of her son's death. Philip had died from the effects of cholera on 28th May 1877.

179

Frank's mother was distraught. We visited her in Congleton and I thought she looked quite unwell. Sadly she had little time to recover before she received further devastating news.

At the end of July, Frank's mother received another letter, this time from the USA. Her eldest son, Henry, who worked as an architect and lived in Kentucky, had unexpectedly died. Like his brother Richard, ten years before, his death had come quickly and was a shock to everyone. His mother received the news from Henry's wife. I don't think they had been married long and they didn't have any children. Frank rushed to visit his mother again.

Frank told me his mother had been so proud of her eldest son. Throughout his visit, Frank said she kept repeating herself: 'My poor, dear boy. He was very talented, you know. He will be remembered for his very many designs. He was very talented, you know.'

When our fifth child, Emily, made an appearance in the October of 1877, Frank was still coming to terms with losing two more of his brothers. In total he had lost four of his six brothers. On bad days, when he would return home the worse for drink, he would say things like, 'I guess that is what comes with having large families,' and, 'Oh, well, more inheritance to come to me.' His comments could be cruel and I was often relieved that it was only I who heard them. However, I knew Frank was hurting. He had always been unable to cope with bad news and saw the only way out through the bottom of a glass. I had first discovered this some years ago when we had lost our firstborn son.

On the occasions when he arrived home ranting in the way he often did, upsetting the children with his carrying on, I could easily have packed our bags and left him. But I remained ever hopeful that one day he might give up the drink and we could settle into a life filled with only happiness.

42

The next few years were occupied with Frank splitting his time between his work at sea and visiting Manchester to collect rents. The time he spent at home was limited.

On the occasions when Frank visited Manchester, he stayed in a small apartment on Jenkinson Street, in a place called Chorlton-upon-Medlock, just outside Manchester. He rented this property, but it was not large enough for the children and me to accompany him. I had to make do with the information he shared with me upon his return, unable to get to know the area in the intimate way that Frank appeared to have. Frank attempted to describe the villages around Manchester. He had become quite obsessed with one particular area called Moss Side. His enthusiasm for this area gave me hope.

Frank shared stories with me about how his family had once owned much of the land in Moss Side. 'The fields of Moss Side surrounded two properties my family once owned called Greenhill Farm and Pepperhill Farm. It used to be a popular area for picnics during holiday times.' Frank's description of these places was idyllic. Moss Side had at one time been described as 'an earthly paradise' by one resident who had lived there some thirty years ago, he claimed.

Today, the area was fast becoming full of narrow streets and terraced houses built for the workers of Manchester. It appeared that most of the land that Frank's family had once owned had been sold and houses had begun to spring up everywhere. Building plots were being sold to individuals or larger companies, and it was here that Frank saw his opportunity.

Many changes were taking place around this time for Frank's family. His uncle, Joshua Hepworth, had died the previous year and left Catharine Ann his manor house in Yorkshire. She had recently made the move there with her family from Scotland, although her sister Ellen, who had been living with her, had decided she was unhappy with this arrangement. She had contacted Frank and asked if she could stay with us, temporarily. I was unsure of this arrangement at first, but soon found Ellen to be a blessing, especially as my pregnancy neared its conclusion.

Frank's mother decided to move to Yorkshire to live. I am sure this had everything to do with Catharine Ann's move there. Mary, Agnes and Lucy all accompanied their mother and set up home together on Church Lane in Hemsworth, four miles away from Catharine Ann.

In August 1880, our sixth child was born. We named her Ellen after her aunt, as she had been such a help to me during this time and we had become very close. Ellen was a great comfort to me as Frank was always going away, more and more frequently visiting Manchester. Ellen was also a great help with the children and took a particular shine to Harry, now almost ten years old. He and his aunt were inseparable, always off on walks together and exploring, leaving me with my less demanding daughters.

One evening Frank returned from Manchester, full of enthusiasm, and announced, 'I'm thinking of going into the building trade.'

'Really?' I was genuinely surprised.

'I also think I have found us the perfect place to live.'

'Hold on a moment, Frank. You are running away with yourself.'

'I can't help it, Alice. I think this is just what I've been waiting for.'

I had never seen Frank so excited.

'Tell me about where you think we might live,' I said anxiously.

'There is a park, named Alexandra Park, which opened just a few years ago. It is beautiful, Alice. You and the children will love it. There are ornamental gardens and a boating lake, a pavilion and a bandstand for Sunday afternoon concerts. You can walk for two whole miles around the park, if you wish. Just imagine, you could be one of those elegantly dressed ladies who are accompanied by their wealthy husbands for a pleasant Sunday afternoon stroll through the park.'

'Pleasant stroll! With our horrors?'

Frank laughed. I couldn't remember the last time he had laughed like that. 'Just opposite the park, along a road named Claremont,

182

they have built some new houses. They are terraced houses, larger than what we are used to, with small gardens to the front, so that you don't have to step out onto the road. Ideally, I would like to purchase a number of those. But for now, I am in the process of securing a property on Derby Street in Moss Side.'

'How many houses do you want to buy?' I enquired.

'Eventually I was hoping to buy up a row of six on Claremont Road; probably live in one and rent out the rest.'

'Six!'

'Yes, and that is just the start. I can afford to buy many smaller terraces.'

I had no idea how much this would cost and it was only then I realised Frank had more money than I could ever imagine having.

It appeared Frank had it all worked out. He said he had spoken to a solicitor and was working on finding himself a team of builders to employ. He wanted to sell off some more of his family's land and build houses for the workers of Manchester. With the rent from these properties he could then afford to buy the larger properties, of which more were soon to be built along Claremont Road.

43

By 1881 we had left Liverpool and were living at 84 Derby Street, Moss Side, along with our five children and Frank's sister Ellen, who had insisted upon accompanying us. The house was larger than our previous and I quite liked it, but Frank insisted it was only temporary and we were not to get too used to it. Frank also insisted we employ a general servant girl. At seventeen, Lizzy was eager and willing to help with most things. She assisted Ellen with much of the food preparation and with shopping for supplies. She kept the house spotless and, although I did occasionally help with certain household chores, I was very pleased to have Lizzy's contribution.

Frank's new occupation was that of builder. This did not mean he went out and got his hands dirty building houses. Frank was by no means afraid of hard work and I'm sure he would have relished helping with the heavy lifting and bricklaying, but since we had moved, Frank had behaved more like a gentleman than a labourer. This transformation was undoubtedly due to Frank gaining access to his inheritance. Adjusting to this different style of living was going to take me longer than Frank, it appeared.

I recall Frank insisting the family accompany him on a walk one day, not long after we had moved into the area. We walked along Claremont Road in Moss Side, where he showed us the houses he was so fond of, opposite Alexandra Park. A little further along this road, opposite Chorlton Lodge, which had been built for the park's superintendent, he stopped at a piece of waste land.

'I have my eye on this. It is where I would like to build us a new house,' he whispered, careful that no one should hear him and have the same idea.

Ellen, the children and I admired the view of the park for a moment, then Frank said he wanted to show us something else.

We happily followed Frank as he explained he wanted to show us a small piece of what remained of his family's history. As we reached the end of Claremont Road we turned left into Princess Road, then turned right onto a narrow dirt track. This roadway took us to what remained of Pepperhill Farm. As we approached, Frank told us about the farmer, Peter Botham, who had once rented the farm and its many acres of land from Frank's family. He had now retired and moved into a house on Claremont Road. The farm buildings were now rented by another farmer, but there were only six acres of land remaining. Many of the existing buildings appeared unused and shabby. Frank was given to understand they had recently been purchased by the Moss Side Board of Health.

It was clear these black and white timbered buildings had once been striking in appearance, but now they looked tired and unloved. The children had great fun exploring the derelict properties, throwing sticks into the stagnant pond, climbing trees and running across the fields which still surrounded the property at this time.

'It won't be long before everything you see before you will be gone,' said Frank.

I was unable to tell if he felt this to be a good or bad thing. I hoped a small part of him felt it would be a bad thing, to lose this piece of history.

Almost as if he knew what I was thinking he said, 'They call it progress. Things never stay the same for very long.'

'That's very true, brother,' agreed Ellen. 'That is very true.'

*

Once I began to get to know the area, I discovered that Manchester town was quite similar to Liverpool. It was large and busy, giving the impression it was affluent, although some areas, as with Liverpool, were obviously impoverished. Its centre held no great appeal for me, but neither had Liverpool's. These were places I infrequently visited. I much preferred the smaller, more accessible shopping areas of Hulme and Moss Side, where I found I could purchase everything I needed.

During the day, when Frank was busy with business, I might find time to enjoy a stroll through Hullard, Whitworth or Alexandra Park with the children and Ellen. Soon, there would no longer be fields or surrounding countryside to wander through and these parks would be all we had left.

The population of Manchester was increasing all the time, mostly due to a migration of low-paid workers from the land, who had moved into the town in search of better-paid jobs. With this came the necessity for more houses to be built. Frank was now part of this process. What had once been farmland was rapidly being eaten up and used as major building plots.

Frank purchased a piece of land, which soon had rows of terraced houses built upon it, and before I knew it he owned and collected rent for about sixty properties. These houses were situated on both sides of Bedford Street, a road positioned at right angles to where he wanted us to live on Claremont Road. Frank had also purchased a couple of other properties on Egerton Road and Darncombe Street, including two corner shops where he was able to ask for a greater rent. He was already discussing plans to increase these numbers, building more houses upon space not yet used in adjoining streets. I had never seen him more motivated or passionate about anything.

Frank saw that his terraced houses were built to comply with the 1875 Public Health Act. A building act of 1878 defined certain specifications for the common house such as the thickness of walls, ceiling heights, space between dwellings and the size of windows.

'If I am going to do this, I need to do it properly,' Frank had insisted. 'No cutting any corners.'

Frank spent many hours overseeing the work of his builders, never allowing shoddy work to go unnoticed and often making his men complete jobs again if he was unhappy with the standard. He certainly seemed to have done his homework and read many books on building methods.

Most of the houses Frank had built had a front parlour, a middle living room and a reasonably sized kitchen to the rear. Beyond the kitchen would be a coal store and a water closet, and there would be two or three bedrooms upstairs. Most of the people who lived in these houses worked at the mills and factories in and around Manchester. Whenever new tenants moved into one of Frank's houses, he went to personally meet them and made sure they were happy with the arrangements.

'If you are good tenants, then I am a good landlord,' he would often say. 'Any trouble, though, and you will be straight out, no negotiating.' Frank was tough but fair. He made it clear he was not a man to be messed with. He liked things done his way.

It appeared Frank was content with his new business. His work appeared to mostly keep him away from his drinking. This wasn't to say he never visited a public house, as he sometimes used them for meetings and secured some great business opportunities whilst there. On occasion he might also enjoy the odd drink with his team of builders, which he said enabled him to sustain a good working relationship with his men.

*

In the summer of 1881 I discovered I was to have another baby. My pregnancy this time was not without its challenges and I was grateful to have Ellen living with us and helping with the children. To complicate things further, Frank had just managed to purchase a row of six houses on Claremont Road and insisted we move in during the last month of my pregnancy. I was enormous by this stage and only just able to manoeuvre myself up the steps and into the new property. I was too exhausted to be of any help and poor Ellen and Lizzy ended up doing most of the work.

On 8th February 1882 we all had a huge shock as I unexpectedly delivered twin boys at our new home. I delivered the first baby at 1.20 pm and the second an hour and a half later, much to everyone's surprise.

Frank was more astonished than anyone. 'How on earth did that happen?' he asked me, as if I should know the answer. When he had got over the initial surprise he said, 'Oh well, I suppose this evens things out a little. Now we have four girls and three boys. Shall we have one more boy, Alice and then stop at that?' He was smiling as he said it, but, after two births in quick succession, I was happy to make this my final time.

Frank suggested we name our twin sons after both our fathers, William Platt and Robert. Ellen and I both agreed the names were an excellent choice.

It took me some weeks to recover, which was why once again Ellen was a godsend and why the twins' baptism was delayed. I could not have done any of it without Ellen's help, but what followed would make her blame herself, unnecessarily, for the rest of her life.

While Ellen and I were concentrating on the twins and my youngest three daughters, my eldest two children were receiving some tutoring at home. We had been told that Harry had great potential and, because he was eager to learn, would go far in this world. Frank was a little sceptical, though, and gave the boy a hard time. Left mostly to do as they pleased after their lessons, Harry, now ten years old, and Catharine Alice, six, would be encouraged to join their father to witness him at work: that of overseeing the building of houses and rent collecting. These trips brought the children into contact with many diverse Moss Side residents and proved to be the cause of much heartache.

I had seen very little of Catharine Alice over the six weeks since the birth of my twin sons, as I was confined to my bed to recover. The first I knew anything was wrong was when she had an attack of the fever and Ellen offered to stay with her throughout the night. The following morning Catharine Alice appeared to have recovered, but the day after that she had a cough and sore throat and was complaining of a headache. She had always been a delicate child and had very little strength in her. As she worsened we arranged for a doctor to call. He diagnosed typhoid and within days we lost poor, dear Catharine Alice. We were all completely devastated.

Frank immediately took to drinking again. He and Ellen had jointly nursed Catharine Alice and it had been Frank who had sat with our daughter as she had slipped away. There was no consoling him at this time. Ellen tried numerous times to speak to him, as she was desperate to help. She blamed herself for not recognising the signs earlier and, no matter how much I told her it was no one's fault, she could never forgive herself.

Ellen was unable to get through to her brother, no matter how hard she tried. Frank rapidly declined, drinking most nights, arriving home looking for an argument with anyone. That 'anyone' was usually me and, during this time, Harry took an obvious dislike to his father. More than once he challenged his father for the way he was treating me, but he was too young for Frank to take seriously. On one occasion Frank lashed out at Harry, who the following day had a bruise on the side of his face. I could see the hate for his father growing and there was very little I could do to stop it.

As the weeks passed, Frank was again able to reduce the amount he drank and took back control of his temper, at least enough to attend St Mary's church in Hulme on 24th September, to have the twins baptised. Ellen informed her mother of our daughter's death and of the date of our sons' baptism and hoped for her brother's sake she would attend. I don't know how much of Frank's behaviour Ellen disclosed to her mother, but the letters she sent obviously did the trick, for their mother arrived the day before the baptism, along with Frank's sister Mary. Agnes, having married some four months earlier in the May, did not accompany them. She was now living in Wales with her husband, Francis Bishop: 'a fine gentleman of great wealth', according to Frank's mother. Agnes was with child, it seemed, and both Frank's mother and Mary were very excited at the prospect. The news just kept coming from the two of them; Frank's sister Lucy was by all accounts doing well for herself and living in Paris. She had recently announced she was to marry, in November, a French gentleman of good social position named Charles Mansuy. It was obvious Frank's mother was very proud of all her daughters' achievements and that was all she seemed to want to discuss.

The baptism went well and both boys behaved. The same could not be said for their father. The names Frank had chosen for his sons had gone down extremely well with his mother and, in her eyes, Frank could do no wrong. So when he took himself off to bed early, once again the worse for drink, his mother's only comment was, 'If a man cannot enjoy a drink on the day of his sons' baptisms, when can he?' I remained silent, as did Ellen.

Before leaving the area to return home, Frank's mother informed us she was to visit the church of St John's, off Deansgate. She had organised a stained-glass window to be erected in memory of her late husband. Frank made no offer to accompany her on this trip and showed no interest in her generous and emotional gesture. She in return made no attempt to insist he accompany her. I thought it best not to interfere.

It was a relief when it was time for Frank's mother and sister to return to Yorkshire. I had enjoyed seeing them both, but it was a strain, especially as his mother had not once mentioned Catharine Alice.

As she left our house and climbed into the carriage which was waiting for her, I noticed my mother-in-law looked quite frail. I hadn't really spotted it before now. She must be in her late seventies, I thought, a good age for a woman. It crossed my mind, in that split second, to wonder if I might ever see her again.

44

The next decade in our lives was to be filled with constant ups and downs which one moment threw the family into grief and turmoil and the next, excitement and euphoria. Frank invested more and more into building houses and by the middle of 1883 he had more than doubled the number of properties he owned. He had been able to purchase six more houses on the next block along from us on Claremont Street, as well as countless smaller terraced houses on Wellington and Russell Street. It was around this time that Frank began to refer to himself as a gentleman rather than a builder.

Our final child was born in August 1883. Frank insisted we name him George Philip, after Frank's brothers who had died the previous decade. We delayed our son's baptism in the hope that Frank's mother and Mary might attend, but sadly this was not to be. What should have been a joyous occasion for our family soon turned very sombre. Seven weeks after our son's birth, Frank's mother was taken ill. Mary called upon Catharine Ann for help, but Catharine Ann was also unwell, so her husband William made the ten-mile journey and agreed he would sit with his wife's mother, in an attempt to reassure Mary. Whilst he was at White Hall in Hemsworth, she took a turn for the worse.

Mary wrote to Frank, explaining that their mother Catharine had been feeling unwell for the last couple of days and, after a visit from their doctor, had taken to her bed. While Mary and her brother-in-law had been sitting with her, Catharine suddenly and without warning had lost consciousness. Mary said she had checked to see if her mother was breathing, and she was, so Mary had raced to fetch the doctor again. By the time they had returned, her mother had passed away. The doctor said it was serious apoplexy and exhaustion which had killed her.

A huge cloud descended over our family that day.

Frank's mother was to be buried at All Saints church in South Kirkby, but Frank refused to attend the funeral, saying it sounded as though Mary and the Brakenridge family had everything organised and didn't need him. I insisted he at least organise a wreath for his mother, which he did with only a little resistance. His mother's death, although not necessarily unexpected because of her age, hit Frank hard, but his drinking became no worse this time than it had been after the death of our daughter.

Frank threw himself into concentrating on his many properties and on encouraging Harry in his education. Harry at this time was attending the commercial school on Stretford New Road, not far from where we lived. This building was very handsome, designed in 1845 in the Tudor style, and Harry often commented on its appearance. The school had a good reputation and attracted boys from similar backgrounds. It housed a library and museum, and specimens of natural history were also available for the use of those pupils who wished to study in this area. Frank was keen to invest in our son's future and often donated money to assist with equipping the school. Harry was excelling in most subjects, including science and art, and we were told he was extremely gifted in mathematics.

Harry appeared to have become very interested in architecture. He would spend hours walking the streets of Manchester, admiring the work of British architect Alfred Waterhouse. He and his father often discussed this man's many achievements, such as the town hall, Assize Courts and Strangeways Prison, and Frank would tease Harry, saying he must get his love of architecture from his American uncles.

There was one phrase I'd heard Frank say to Harry on many occasions. *You must acquire yourself a ticket, my boy. It will set you up for life.* Frank was quite right; a gentleman needed a skill. Finally it appeared to be sinking in, as Harry had recently become more and more interested in becoming a civil engineer. Frank fiercely encouraged our son into this profession.

Six months after his mother's death, we were shocked to receive news that Frank's sister Mary had also died. Aged forty-six, she had contracted meningitis and become very poorly extremely quickly. She had sent word to Catharine Ann, at Rogerthorpe Hall, to pay her a visit urgently. By the time Catharine Ann had arrived, Mary had deteriorated further and was confined to her bed. She was suffering with terrible headaches and was sensitive to light, insisting her sister keep the curtains to her bedroom window closed at all times. Mary slept for many days and Catharine Ann prayed that her sister's condition would improve. Catharine Ann stayed with her overnight and, on the morning of 20th March, Mary had a seizure and slipped into a coma. She died ten hours later.

Catharine Ann organised her sister's funeral and informed Frank. Once again Frank made no attempt to attend the funeral, even though he had been recorded as her next of kin and Mary had left him almost £5,000 in her will. Frank soon put this money to good use investing in more properties on Wellington and Russell Street in Moss Side.

In July 1885, Harry received the results of the science and art examinations he had taken the month before. In drawing he achieved a second grade for his freehand model, which he was extremely pleased with. It was then that Harry told us he would definitely like to become a civil engineer. Frank was both excited and proud of our son, but his happiness was short-lived.

In October we received some terrible news about Frank's brother Edward, who lived in Canada. According to the correspondence, Edward had been struck by a train while unloading logs. He was a saw mill proprietor and lumber merchant, running a very successful business in Stouffville. He supplied logs to many contractors and apparently was a very strong, fit man, according to his wife, Ann. She had been unable to get to the hospital before he had died two hours after the accident. From her letter, it was clear she was finding it difficult to come to terms with her loss.

Frank took the news of his brother's death badly and began to drink heavily once more. There were times when he would return home and look for anyone to pick a fight with. Harry was fourteen now and almost as tall as his father, although not as strong. If Harry was at home when his father returned from *one of his sessions*, as Harry had named them, Harry would make sure all the girls were together in one room at the top of the house and have Ellen take care of his three younger brothers, and he and I would contend with Frank. On most occasions this arrangement worked well. Frank would soon run out of steam and Harry would help him up to bed, or Frank would fall asleep in his chair and remain there until the morning.

One evening Frank returned home late, entered our bedroom and begun to shout about the difficult day he had endured. Apparently, one of his tenants from Palmerston Street had argued with him about the rent charges going up. It was past midnight and Harry woke to hear his father shouting. Thinking the worst, he stormed into our bedroom, half terrified for my wellbeing and half dazed with sleep, brandishing his cricket bat from school. Frank took one look at the boy, grabbed the bat out of his hand and attempted to hit him across the head with it. Thankfully, Harry had the foresight to move swiftly and dodged the bat, but a scuffle ensued.

'Stop it! Both of you,' I screamed, 'before someone gets hurt!'

Thankfully this brought them both to their senses and Frank fell on the bed, quite exhausted from the struggle.

'I thought he was hurting you, Mother,' Harry said.

Frank tutted.

'No, dear, I'm quite well, thank you,' I said. 'Go back to bed now.'

'If you are sure.'

'She's sure!' shouted Frank, sprawled across the bed.

The following day, after Frank had left the house, Harry asked me again if I was all right.

'I have made a decision, Mother. I am never going to swallow a drop of alchohol, not even when I am a grown man. I promise you now. I will never, in the whole of my lifetime, ever touch that poison. Do you believe me, Mother?'

'I do, Harry. I think you would be very wise not to,' I agreed.

45

Our youngest son, George, had always been a sickly boy. If there was a cough or cold to be had, it would be George who caught it. It always took him longer than the others to get better and, during the times when he was ill, life in the same household was a challenge. I admit I had little time for sickness myself and, if I ever did feel unwell, would spend the day in bed and feel fully recovered the following day. I therefore expected everyone else to be like this, even young George, and so I blame myself for what happened next.

I had never known a child to have so many colds in one year. Both Ellen and I made sure all of the children were wrapped up well whenever they ventured outside, especially during the colder months, and that they all received plenty of fresh air and regular walks, so we could not explain why, at the beginning of June, George was again suffering from the symptoms of a cold. I was tired of seeing him with a runny nose, and soon an irritating cough had developed also, which kept most of us awake each night. His illness progressed further and soon he gained a fever. I did not call for a doctor. Ellen suggested it, but I was convinced that in a couple of days the cold and fever would both have subsided. I could not have been more wrong.

George's illness began around the time we were due to move house. In the summer of 1887 Frank decided we could do better for ourselves than the house we had on Claremont Road. He had always admired the much larger houses we saw during our Sunday walks through Alexandra Park. Our favourite walk led us around a garden area named 'the terrace', which had a clock tower at its centre, and then past the bowling green, where we would stop and watch for a time if there was a match being played. We would then continue past the gymnasiums and the bandstand, which brought us around to the opposite side of the park and alongside Demesne Road. Frank had often commented upon the houses in this road and had recently seen the area described as 'a desirable estate for gentlemen and their families'. When he finished staring out across Demesne Road and admiring its grand properties, we would return home following the path which ran alongside Alexandra Road. I must admit, I too had admired the houses along these roads, with their huge gardens, but had never believed that one day I might be moving into one.

The move itself went exceptionally smoothly as Frank had organised everything, but it was a difficult time for me, as Ellen had decided not to move with us. Frank offered to set his sister up in her own home and compelled her to accept his proposal. I was unhappy with this prospect at first, as I knew I would miss her terribly, but I came around to the idea when Ellen assured me she would only be a matter of streets away.

Ellen moved into her new home, a large semi-detached property on Arnold Road, a few days before we moved. I helped her move some of her things and later timed the walk between our two new properties. I was relieved to discover she was only a ten-minute walk away.

Even before we had moved all our furniture into our new home, Frank insisted on fixing a plaque to the outside wall, beside the front entrance, which he'd had made especially. It read 'Woodthorpe'.

'A fitting tribute to my place of birth, don't you agree?' asked Frank, who had indeed been born in Woodthorpe, near Sandal, but had kept the idea of naming our new house completely to himself. I shouldn't have been surprised, for he often did things without consulting me. I couldn't help wondering if he was trying to compete with his much older sister, who at this time was renting out her Yorkshire property named Rogerthorpe Hall, preferring to live near the sea in Weymouth.

Ellen was there to help me with the children the day we moved to our much larger, detached property on Demesne Road. The children were all very excited, running around the new house, shouting and screaming at the tops of their voices. Three-year-old George was desperate to keep up with his siblings, but it was impossible for him to do so. I found him at the bottom of the stairs, coughing and terribly short of breath. Ellen made him up a bed and he was happy to lie in it and rest.

Over the next couple of days George's illness progressed to the point where he was coughing up a thick mucus. I cannot go on to describe his further symptoms, as it is too upsetting, but by the time I realised things were serious and called for the doctor, it was too late. My darling George died in his father's arms, as I watched on, helpless, some six days after we moved into the house. The doctor diagnosed pneumonia. I had no idea that he had been so seriously ill. I have never really got over any of my children's deaths, yet I blame myself for George's. We buried our dear son at Southern Cemetery on 17th June.

*

We were both in our mid-forties and had lived in Demesne Road for about four years when the 1891 census was recorded in April. I recall Frank insisted he be recorded as a 'retired master mariner'. He had finished with building houses. He now employed someone to collect his rents for him and he spent most of his time mixing with other gentlemen from the area. He had joined many gentlemen's clubs and regularly visited Manchester's Free Trade Hall, concert halls, theatres and art galleries. Although Frank no longer built houses, he still owned many and our income from their rents allowed us a very comfortable and privileged life.

When I was able to escape the confines of my home and motherhood, I would endeavour to support the underprivileged of our society, attempting to offer help and advice which often was not well received. I joined a small group of ladies who met regularly, donating unwanted items of clothing, making up food parcels and visiting the local poorer communities. I enjoyed this work and gained some satisfaction from it, but it was short-lived as Frank did not approve.

All six of our children remained living with us at this time. Harry was a student, training to become a civil engineer. He worked hard and was becoming skilled in this area. All of the other children were attending local schools. We employed a young girl from Hulme named Mary Hughes as live-in kitchen maid and domestic help, but she didn't stay for long. Around this time, we went through a quick succession of hired help, usually due to William and Robert taking advantage of these girls' inexperience and playing pranks on them. One time I arrived home to a terrible commotion and a kitchen full of toads. The boys had caught them earlier that day and decided to let them go in the house. Our young maid was screaming, standing terrified and shaking on top of the kitchen table. Thankfully we managed to collect up all of the toads before Frank arrived home and I had to make up some plausible story as to why we had lost yet another one of our servants. Sadly, I became quite good at inventing such stories over the years.

Frank's family had significantly depleted over recent years. He had lost five of his six brothers and a sister, together with three of our own children. Frank had one brother left, with whom his sister Ellen was in regular correspondence. Rupert had moved to live on the Isle of Man around 1880, so Ellen had informed us around the time we moved to Moss Side. He had settled in a place called Maughold, near Ramsey, in the north of the island. Living on means left to him by his father, he rented a property and like me tried to do some good within the local community. When I had begun to visit the poor, Ellen had told me of the works her brother was doing. He often donated to the Ramsey charities, providing coal for the poor and ingredients for the soup kitchen, funding breakfasts and dinners for poor children. His latest donation had been forty pounds of beef to the soup kitchen when he had written to Ellen around the time of the census.

Ellen told me of other letters she had been sent, some three years later, when Rupert had become very excited about a property he wanted to acquire. He had attended an auction for the sale of this property, known locally as the Ramsey Palace, which had gone into liquidation. He had wanted to develop the land and build a number of houses there. Ellen had, of course, written and told him of Frank's success, and she believed this had sparked a desire in Rupert also. Rupert explained the bidding had started at £2,000 but rose only to £2,400 and the lack of interest from the other bidders put him off. He surmised there to be a problem with the land. The lot was soon withdrawn and Rupert returned home empty-handed.

It was during this time Frank had written to his brother to give him some advice on purchasing land and property. Frank genuinely wanted to help his brother; it seemed to him that Rupert was inexperienced in this field and might gain from his knowledge. Rupert had written back to Frank, thanking him considerably for his advice, saying it was most useful.

We were surprised then to learn from Ellen some years later, in January 1896, that Rupert had passed away. According to Ellen he had been unwell for some time but had not wanted her to share this knowledge with anyone. Rupert had left his wealth, which amounted to just over £6,000, to Frank. We were all very sad to learn of Rupert's death, but Frank had never been particularly close to him and focused his thoughts on what to do with his unexpected inheritance.

46

Ellen had always been a prolific letter writer, but the following year she was forced to share a dreadful scandal with me and Frank, which she gained knowledge of through her correspondence with her sister Lucy. Ellen had rushed round to our house on a freezing cold December morning, clutching in her hand a letter she had just received.

Although there were almost ten years between them, Ellen and Lucy had always been close. Ellen had helped her mother when Lucy was a baby, she had occasionally assisted Lucy with her schoolwork and, after Ellen had left home, the two sisters had remained in constant contact via letters.

In the early 1880s Lucy had travelled to Paris, where she had met a gentleman of good social position with whom she had fallen head over heels in love. He had swept her off her feet, wining and dining her in the top restaurants, accompanying her to the most popular theatres and buying her the most fashionable garments Paris had to offer. She wrote to Ellen, terribly excited to share her feelings with her sister and ask her advice. Ellen was honest with Lucy. She had never experienced the same emotion and was unsure as how to advise her younger sister. She could tell this man made her sister terribly happy and advised Lucy to follow her heart. Lucy did and married Charles Mansuy in November 1882.

For the first few years, Lucy had seemed very content with her husband. They lived in Chatenay, near Montmorency, where Charles owned a handsome villa. He was a sports writer who attended race meetings most days in Paris, contributing to several newspapers.

Lucy had never been happier, although she had confided in her sister that she longed for a child. Her husband had made it quite clear to Lucy that he did not wish to have children too early and Lucy had, at first, been happy to accommodate his wishes. But as time went on her husband became more and more distant, especially when she broached this subject.

The years passed and nothing changed, until one day Lucy found a receipt for a meal for two at a restaurant in Paris, on a day when her husband had told her he had been somewhere else. Lucy wrote to Ellen, asking again for her advice. Ellen suggested she confront her husband, to put her mind at rest. 'There is most likely some reasonable explanation for the receipt,' she wrote. Lucy followed her sister's advice, and it was then that she discovered her husband's secret.

Charles confessed to Lucy that while travelling to the city of Paris most days for work, he had become a regular visitor to an English dressmaker on Rue de Rivoli. It soon became apparent to Lucy that her husband was seeing another woman and that he had become quite obsessed with her. At this time, Charles was also deputy mayor and could not afford for a scandal to break, so he asked Lucy to forgive him and promised he would cease to visit the dressmaker.

As I have said, it was a cold December morning in 1896 when Ellen burst in through the front door of our house on Demesne Road, all of a panic. I invited her in to sit down and poured her out a small amount of Frank's brandy, as I knew where he kept it hidden. 'This is for medicinal reasons only, my dear. You look as though you've had a shock.'

She accepted the glass and sipped from it. She then told me how Lucy had discovered her husband's affair. After confronting her husband, Lucy had believed he had stopped seeing the woman and for a time things had improved.

'I have not heard from Lucy for the past few months,' Ellen said. 'I assumed everything was all right. That was until today.' She handed me a letter.

I sat down in the chair opposite where I had seated Ellen and began to read. The letter was difficult to understand at first as Lucy's emotions were clearly all over the place, but I eventually managed to decipher it.

Lucy explained her husband Charles had seemed uneasy for a day or two and had appeared to be in rather a dejected condition when he had arrived home on the Thursday evening. He had not gone into work on the Friday and she had been unable to get to the bottom of his sadness, but respected his wish to be left alone in his study, where he spent most of the weekend.

On the Monday morning, Lucy was given a telegram for her husband by one of her servants. She took it up to him as he had remained in his bedroom, not having appeared for breakfast. Getting no response to her knock, she entered the room. He was still in bed. Lucy handed her husband the telegram, which he took from her, opened and read. She watched on as the colour drained from her husband's face. He climbed out of bed, pressed the telegram into her hand and hurried downstairs. He went into his study and closed the door behind him.

Lucy went on to explain in her letter that the telegram was from an investigating magistrate. He was summoning Lucy's husband to his office for questioning in relation to the sudden death of an English woman named Georgie Thompson.

What Lucy described next was truly devastating. She went into the study to confront her husband, who was busily writing a letter. He placed it inside an envelope addressed to a friend in Paris and handed it to Lucy, to give to the servant for posting. He then asked if she would mind fetching him a particular book from the other room. Lucy left the room to fetch the book as her husband had requested and had been gone for only a matter of seconds when she heard a loud bang. When she and her servants rushed back to the room they discovered Charles had shot himself with a revolver through the heart and was clearly dead.

I was deeply shocked and saddened for Lucy and for poor Ellen, who I think in some way blamed herself.

As the weeks passed, we learned more about why Lucy's husband had done what he'd done. The scandal was soon reported in the French newspapers and over in England as well. Poor Ellen was beside herself with the sadness she felt for her sister and was desperate to travel to France to support her. Frank was adamant that would be the wrong thing to do and insisted she remain in England. Ellen sent a telegram to Lucy explaining Frank's unreasonable demands, saying she was willing to defy him if Lucy wished for her to travel. Lucy sent word back. 'I have no wish to further upset the family. I suggest you remain at home. I am saddened and shocked by what has happened but accept my situation. I will write soon.'

It seems the chain of events, once begun, could not be prevented. Lucy's husband had never stopped seeing the English dressmaker in Paris. As the affair went on, the dressmaker had discovered she was pregnant. Letters had been found at her lodgings from Lucy's husband, complaining that 'the birth of a child would be intolerable'.

He had arranged for his mistress to have a private operation at a house near Madeleine. Charles had no idea he was sending his mistress to her death. Georgie Thompson had died from the effects of an abortion operation on the Thursday, the day Charles had returned home depressed. Upon learning the following Monday that he had been summoned to the investigating magistrate's office, he had committed suicide. The scandal had obviously been too much for him to bear. In the letter he had written to his friend just before he had died, he explained he was deeply in love with Miss Thompson and asked that her body be buried at Chatenay, in the same plot as he.

When Frank discovered the truth from his newspaper, he was disgusted with Charles. 'And he called himself a gentleman, indeed. What was the man thinking? Did he have no feelings at all for his wife?'

What made the whole thing so much worse was that later it was discovered the two doctors involved in the operation had lost many other patients under similar circumstances. They themselves were now to be investigated. We were unable to draw a line under matters for quite some time and it was forever being reported in the newspapers.

In March 1897, a trial of the doctors was begun and poor Lucy was called to the Seine Assize court to give her account of the events, forcing her to relive it all over again. Many other witnesses were called, mainly men who had paid large amounts of money for the doctors to perform illegal surgical operations, which had accidentally killed their wives. As there were many witnesses, the trial went on for some time. At the end of the trial the jury took only fifteen minutes to deliberate their guilty verdict. The two doctors were each sentenced to five years' imprisonment for the crime of abortion.

This was not the end of the story, though. We were to read in newspapers some two months later that one of the doctors had become insane and been transferred from Malas prison to an asylum. It would seem this scandal was never to go away.

Thankfully, Lucy was able to recover from this terrible event and rebuild her life. She remained in Paris and four years later, in 1901, married again.

47

We must have been at Demesne Road for about ten years when Frank announced he was arranging to have a brand new boiler fitted. When we had moved into the house it had been almost new. It had been fitted with modern gas lighting and a coal-fired furnace in the cellar, which allowed hot air to rise up through vents in the floor and heat the house. We also had fireplaces in each of the main rooms, which could be lit as and when we needed them.

We had an indoor bathroom situated on the first floor at the back of the house, with hot running water, but it did take a long time to fill the bathtub. There was a large water tank in the attic and one water pipe ran down to a boiler in the kitchen where the water was heated, albeit slowly.

Frank informed me he and Harry had visited the offices of the British Engine, Boiler and Insurance Company situated on King Street. There they had met assistant engineer John Gow and together they had discussed installing a new hot water system for the house.

'They are fitting it next week,' Frank announced at the end of our short conversation. My mind went into panic, as all I could think about was the mess it would create, but I needn't have worried. I was pleasantly surprised by how professional the company were during fitting and the results once they had got everything working.

A couple of days later John Gow visited the house, to inspect his men's workmanship and to get Frank to sign the necessary paperwork to have the boiler insured against loss of life or damage caused by an explosion. Harry was also at home and I listened as he chatted to John Gow, while his father read through the lengthy paperwork.

'What exactly does your job entail?' asked an interested Harry.

'Well, now, if I get called out to breakdowns, I need to decide what is to be done and give instructions for doing it. Or in smaller consulting jobs, like this one,' (at which point Frank looked up as if to say, 'It's a pretty big job to me, son,' but thankfully managed to stop himself), 'I visit the place, get particulars, make out a scheme, and submit it for approval and any alterations. Except in this case you and your father saved me the initial visit.'

'I see. Do you do anything else?' enquired Harry.

'Sometimes I'm needed to assist in engine and boiler trials. Otherwise I report to the engine department and they're always able to find me something to do.'

'That all sounds very interesting,' said Harry, quickly following this up with more questions.

Harry and John Gow appeared to have much in common. It turned out they worked minutes away from one another, both having offices in Manchester. They had both completed civil engineering exams and seemed to have similar interests. It was obvious this was to be the start of a long friendship.

*

In 1898 Harry seemed to have gained a new lease of life. I thought at first it was because of his friendship with John Gow. The pair, despite having four years' difference in their ages, seemed to thrive in each other's company. But a mother's intuition told me there was more to it and that it might have something to do with a woman.

Harry was now twenty-six years old and a man of independent means. He had completed his education, the results of which were excellent, and was now working as a surveyor in Manchester. He operated from premises within the four-storey Barton Arcade. Some years earlier, when Harry had secured an office there on the second floor, he had taken both his father and me to visit. The building was situated between Deansgate and St Ann's Square. We entered via the Deansgate entrance. I found the cast iron and glass structure very striking, its glass domes finishing it off handsomely. The building also displayed an attractive decorative floor.

We took the stairs to the second floor, where Harry had his office, and admired the views from the balustraded balcony. There was glass everywhere, which allowed light to flood into the building.

'That's rather a lot of glass,' commented Frank, looking up towards the roof. 'I'd wager it was a swine to construct.'

'Yes, Father. I understand it was brought here all the way from a factory in Glasgow.'

'Was it indeed?'

'It's quite beautiful,' I said. 'I should think you will be very happy working from here, darling.'

'I expect the rent is rather steep, though,' complained Frank.

'It's not cheap, Father, but I have enough work coming in to more than cover it.'

'Hmm,' said Frank incredulously.

Both Frank and I were very proud of our son's success, although his father rarely told him so. Harry had become a qualified civil engineer. He was used to drawing up plans for possible building sites around the Manchester area and submitting them to developers. He liked to see a project through from beginning to end and was building up a good reputation in his line of work. Although Harry and his father at times could have a strained relationship, he would occasionally seek his father's opinion about certain plots of land in the area. Through his work he came into contact with surveyors, clerks, accountants, estate agents and builders. It was through one of these acquaintances he would meet his future wife.

Harry met Mr Brown, a commercial clerk, when Mr Brown turned up at his office one day to deliver some paperwork, having completed a job for one of Harry's clients. As Harry made polite conversation with this middle-aged gentleman, he became distracted by a young, dark-haired girl who was standing just outside his office, looking up at the glass ceiling and admiring the view. She was the clerk's daughter.

Mr Brown noticed Harry was distracted and decided to introduce the pair. He explained he had been railroaded into allowing his daughter to accompany him into the town, so that she could do some shopping.

From that day onwards she and Harry had been inseparable, according to Harry. He had fallen deeply and desperately in love with this beauty, who would later be introduced to me as Ethel Darnley Brown.

At this time Harry had been working on plans and securing a piece of land for house building between Ayres Road and Upper Chorlton Road. He had been successful and building work had started. By the end of 1898 Harry had reserved for himself the best house on this new street, which he was able to name Darnley Street especially for Ethel. It was plain that he adored her. Needless to say they were soon married and once again he proved his love for her by marrying her on St Valentine's Day. I had never known my son was such a romantic. This girl had stirred something inside Harry which even he had not known he possessed. He certainly didn't get this characteristic from his father.

Their wedding day was truly a special time for us all, and afterwards Harry and Ethel moved into their new home together. It was a large double-fronted end terrace house, the only one on a street which was otherwise filled with much smaller terraced houses. Well situated at number one, it was close to the shops which lined Ayres Road. Harry had done well for himself and his new wife.

During the summer, Harry and Ethel shared with us some very exciting news. We were to become grandparents. At this time Ethel's parents, a pleasant couple, were living on Clarendon Road. Nearer to her time, Ethel informed me she wanted to be at her parents' house when she had our first grandchild. I knew she was close to her mother and younger sister, Marion, and she said they would be a great support to her. I suspect she was terribly nervous about the whole thing.

Ethel's family were devout churchgoers and had behaved impeccably on the occasions we had met them. Her parents had brought her up well, and the whole family seemed extremely close. I could not have asked for a more desirable wife for my son. It was therefore a little unfortunate that Ethel's family were not as financially comfortable as we were. Although it did not concern Harry or me, there had been occasions when Ethel's parents had clearly felt uneasy about this detail, especially when Frank made mention of his many properties and investments. I, on the other hand, had never forgotten my humble beginnings and got on very well with Ethel's mother, Mary.

Mary had taught her daughter well about the ways a wife should perform her duties. This was confirmed the day I discovered what was inside a small black book Ethel appeared to always have in her possession. I had noticed her, on a number of occasions, flicking through this pocket book and had been intrigued for some time to know its nature. Unable to stifle my curiosity any longer, I enquired as to its use. Thankfully, Ethel was keen to explain.

'It was my mother's idea,' she explained. 'When I was nineteen, Mother purchased the book for me and suggested I note down recipes for cookery, laundry and anything else which might help me in the future, when I married and was in charge of my own house.'

'What a clever idea,' I replied, wishing my mother had presented me with one before her death or that I had thought of the idea for my own daughters.

'Would you like to take a look inside?' Proudly, Ethel handed me her black pocket book.

'Thank you, my dear.'

Ethel had begun the book in October 1896 with a recipe for making cold starch. 'My mother insisted I write the first recipe down, as she said she was fed up of repeating herself about how to wash clothes properly. "You will thank me one day," she used to say, every time I added a new recipe. She was right. This little book is almost as precious to me now as my mother's Bible is.'

Later on in the book Ethel had added a recipe for making melted soap, but the majority of her recipes were for cakes and puddings, such as queen cakes, scones, parkin, Manchester pudding and shortbread. Ethel's mother had insisted she note down recipes for Christmas cake and Christmas pudding. I noted she also had recipes for jams and preserves.

'I'm very impressed,' I told Ethel. 'Now I understand why Harry is looking so well cared for.'

Ethel gave me one of her shy smiles.

*

On 7th February 1900, at ten to seven in the morning, assisted by Ethel's mother, my first grandchild, Katherine Alice, was born. There was great excitement. Mary and I fussed over mother and child. Ethel and the baby wanted for nothing.

Katherine Alice was a beautiful child. She had a thick head of dark brown hair, almost as dark as her mother's, and the biggest brown eyes I had ever seen. She was as good as gold and Ethel appeared to be a natural mother, seeing to her daughter's every need.

Ethel said Harry was completely lost for words and quite emotional when he returned from work that evening to discover he had a daughter. He later rushed in through our front door calling out, 'Mother, Father, have you heard the news?'

Frank was down the pub, of course, wetting the baby's head. I had just started to make my way upstairs for an early night. The excitement of the day had quite taken it out of me. I turned and made my way back downstairs. 'Yes, dear. Isn't she a beauty?'

'She certainly is, Mother. I don't mind admitting I am quite overwhelmed by it all.'

'I'm very pleased to hear it, my boy. And so you should be. You have many responsibilities now.'

'Yes, I know. Those responsibilities make me feel as though I have aged ten years already in the last few hours.'

'You'll get used to it,' I tried to reassure him. 'Is Ethel still at her mother's?'

'Yes. She's going to stay there for this evening and I'll go and collect her and the baby tomorrow. I shall go into work a little later tomorrow, wait until Ethel and the baby are settled at home. It will be strange not having her at the house tonight. I've become quite used to it.'

I laughed. Sometimes Harry said the funniest things. 'I'll pay them a visit tomorrow afternoon. I'll take something nice with me. We have a new girl, Agnes, who's a great help in the kitchen. I'm sure she wouldn't mind baking us up a treat.'

'Thank you, Mother. Ethel would like that.'

'You'd better go and get some sleep, my boy. You may be in for some sleepless nights pretty soon.'

'Not me, Mother. I sleep like a log.'

'We'll see.' I smiled knowingly.

We embraced one another. Harry kissed me on my cheek, then left for home. I went up to bed thinking about when my first child had been born and how I was grateful that for Harry the experience had been very different. I didn't hear Frank arrive home that night, but I don't think it was too late.

Harry and Ethel visited regularly with baby Kate, and in the October of that same year I was able to share a recipe of my own with Ethel. When Harry and Ethel arrived with the baby on Sunday afternoon, Kate was rather unsettled. 'It's just not like her,' worried Ethel. 'She's usually so happy and content. I've tried everything.'

Kate was suffering from wind and it was obviously making her feel very uncomfortable.

'I have the perfect cure for that, my dear. Do you have your little book with you?'

Ethel smiled and produced it from her skirt pocket. I found her a pencil and she noted down the ingredients I listed, taking care to underline the heading, which read 'Baby Medicine'.

'Do you have all of that, dear?' I asked.

'I think so. Loaf sugar, magnesia, turkey rhubarb, oil of aniseed, boiled water – oh, and peppermint essence.'

'That's correct, dear. Don't forget the peppermint. Just mix it together and baby should be right as rain in no time.'

They didn't stay long that afternoon as Kate was fractious, but I was pleased to see a couple of days later she was back to her normal self.

*

When the 1901 census was taken in April, Mary, Emily and Ellen were all in their twenties and none of them, as yet, had married. William and Robert were both nineteen and had been able to secure themselves good jobs. Both worked in Manchester, William as an insurance clerk and Robert, a clerk in a bank. We also had our domestic servant Agnes at this time, who stayed with us for about a year, then left to marry a man named Frank Hind, a clerk who worked for a road contractor. My husband had on occasion come across this man and found him very pleasant. Agnes kindly invited us to her wedding, but Frank had made sure he was too busy that day to attend.

At the time of the census, Frank was no longer working, but we were able to live off the income from his many properties. He had inherited a large sum of money from his sister Mary and brother Rupert, in excess of £10,000. He had of course invested this money into property but had spent some of it on installing a large billiard room in our house, where he would go to 'get away from it all' and, of course, enjoy a drink. Harry would occasionally come over to enjoy a game with Robert or William, and on these occasions it was great to have all my children under one roof. The house would come alive with laughter and noise again.

48

In February 1902, Ethel gave birth for a second time. This time she gave Harry a son. He was thrilled and it was quickly decided they would name their son after his paternal grandfather. Frank was overwhelmed and said very little at the time. I nudged him gently to respond and he eventually said, 'That sounds perfect.'

A baptism was arranged and, although Ethel was experiencing some problems with the child's feeding, everything was normal for

210

the first five months. The child appeared to be growing and was fairly healthy. None of us had any great cause for concern. Then, one morning in July, Ethel hammered on our front door, Frank squealing in her arms and she in a terrible state. 'My mother's not in and I didn't know what to do. He just won't stop crying.'

I tried to reassure her. 'All right, dear, I'm sure it's something and nothing. Babies can be up one minute and down the next. Let me have a look at him.'

Ethel handed her son to me and I laid him on the table, unwrapping him from his blanket. He had started to calm down but all of a sudden, without warning, he let out a cry like I'd never heard before and at the same time drew his knees up to his chest. This action was closely followed by a pungent smell.

'He appears to be in some discomfort and I think he needs a change, my dear.'

'That's the fifth time this morning. I have left our poor domestic washing through piles of napkins.'

'I don't wish to concern you, my dear, but I do think we should send for the doctor. It is better to be on the safe side.'

Poor Ethel. She looked panic-stricken. I advised her to return home, said I would organise for the doctor to call and that I would be with her as soon as I had done that. Ethel wrapped up the shrieking bundle, lifted him up from the table and did as I advised.

The doctor and I arrived at the house together, less than an hour later. Ethel was not there. She had gone next door to the shop on the corner of Ayres Road, where she knew the owner well. We knew this because we could hear the baby's cries.

The doctor wasted no time in examining Frank. Then he asked Ethel some questions about the child's bowel movements, whether he had vomited and how long he had been displaying these symptoms. Eventually he said, 'I do have a suspicion about what it could be, but I would like a second opinion. Would you mind if I arranged for another doctor to call tomorrow?'

'I suppose not,' agreed Ethel. What else could she do?

211

'In the meantime try to get as many fluids into him as possible.'

'I will, doctor, thank you.'

'I'll show you out,' I said.

As he went back through the door of the shop I caught his arm. 'What do you think is the matter, doctor?'

'I'd rather not say at this stage, Mrs Bradshaw, but if my suspicions are correct, I'm afraid it doesn't look good.'

The doctor's suspicions were correct and confirmed by his colleague the following day. Harry did not go into work, so that he could be with Ethel when the doctor arrived. Ethel's parents were there also. Harry and Ethel looked dreadful and it was obvious neither of them had got any sleep that night.

It had been less than twenty-four hours since I'd last seen my grandson, yet it was clear his health had greatly deteriorated. He had developed a fever and was very weak. After another few hours his tiny body went into shock, haemorrhaging, and he died. On his death certificate the doctor wrote 'intussusception of the bowel'. Harry bravely tried to explain to me that this was something to do with his intestines becoming twisted, but I was too upset to take it all in.

All poor Ethel could say was, 'I don't understand. What could have caused it? Did I do something wrong?' Mary tried tirelessly to comfort her daughter. It was a very distressing time for us all and it brought back memories of my own son, Frank, who had died more than thirty years earlier.

Frank and Harry organised and paid for a family burial plot at Southern Cemetery on Barlow Moor Road. My grandson's funeral was held on 2nd August, two days after his death. He had lived for a short five months.

Harry was amazing. He was a tower of strength for Ethel and I knew that in time they would recover from their sad loss. The death of a child can bring you closer together, but it can also tear you apart. Thankfully it did the former in this case.

The following week I went out and purchased Harry a gift. 'I want you to have this,' I said to him the next time I saw him.

His face was a picture as I handed him a copy of the Holy Bible. He had never been a great lover of the church.

'You don't have to read it if you don't wish, but I thought you could write down inside it the births and marriages of all the children you and Ethel will go on to have. It's the fashionable thing to do these days, apparently.'

'Thank you, Mother. It is very thoughtful of you. I know Ethel will see it as a thoughtful gesture also.'

He took his gift home and wrote his name and the date on the first page. Then on the next page he made a note of both his daughter and his son's dates of birth. I was sure the pages would soon fill, and a couple of months later Ethel was indeed expecting another child.

It had been shortly after his daughter's birth that Harry had treated himself to a 'hand and stand' Sanderson camera. He said he needed it for work and was keen to show off this gadget. In 1902, after the death of his son, he swapped the camera for a more refined version. Sanderson cameras were designed by F H Sanderson, a cabinet maker with an interest in architectural photography. Harry said many professionals in his line of work were purchasing them as tools of their trade, and updating them when better lenses and shutters become available.

According to Harry his new camera incorporated improvements to reduce distortion, which undoubtedly was useful in Harry's line of business. He was quite excited by it at the time, pointing out its key features, which, I'm sorry to say, I did not fully understand. 'Mother, look here. These are called the lens board support struts. They allow the camera to make a variety of movements. Watch.'

'It sounds very complicated, Harry.'

'No, not really, not once you know what you're doing. Look,' he said, moving the lens. 'They allow the lens to move on its axis, letting me gain the correct perspective when I want to photograph something. Do you see?'

Poor Harry, he was desperate to share the machine with me and show me all the amazing things his new camera could do. I looked over to Ethel for support, but she looked exhausted from the early stages of her pregnancy and just shrugged her shoulders. She was as baffled as I was.

'Your father should be home soon. I'm sure he would like to see it.'

Thankfully, Frank arrived a few minutes later.

49

In May 1903 Ethel gave birth to a healthy baby girl and she and Harry named her Frances Mary. She soon became known as Molly. Her older sister, Katherine, doted on the child. Ethel put on a brave face, attempting to take motherhood in her stride, but I think she found it a bit of a strain. Harry threw himself into his work, but, unlike his father, he always made time for his wife and daughters.

Harry was not the only one to treat himself to the latest of modern contraptions around this time. I knew that Frank typically liked to do things on a much grander scale, but it still surprised me when he started to show a great interest in purchasing a motor vehicle.

John Skinner and William Temple Edwards had established a business together in Ashford, Kent, as coachbuilders. By the end of 1900 the firm had been dissolved, but by 1904 Edwards had set himself up as coachbuilder for Renault Frères.

Renault had come to England in 1902 and had soon imported 250 cars through their sole supplier, Roadway Autocar Co. Ltd. Frank had read about these sales in his newspaper and from that moment had been determined to own one. I had little liking for these new contraptions. I thought they looked dreadfully dangerous, but, no matter what I said, I was unable to convince Frank not to purchase one.

In 1904 sales had risen to 450 cars when the supplier had changed its name to Renault Frères. It was during this time that Frank purchased a four-seater car from William Temple Edwards. His car had been assembled at the Edwards factory in Kent, then delivered to the goods station on London Road, Manchester, where Frank was to collect it one winter's afternoon in the January of 1904.

Frank had summoned Harry and Ethel to our home earlier in the day, with an instruction for Harry to bring along his camera. They also brought John Gow, who had called on Harry just as they were leaving. John had shown an interest in witnessing the car's arrival, so Harry had invited him along. He knew his father wouldn't mind as Frank had taken a liking to Harry's good friend and would delight in sharing his purchase with him.

While I chatted with Ethel, keeping her and the children company in the back room, Harry and John joined Frank at the front of the house. Aged fifty-seven years, Frank was behaving like an overexcited child as he waited for the time to depart. He had been constantly checking his pocket watch for most of the morning. Each time I had entered the room he had quickly found something else to occupy himself, reaching for his newspaper or suddenly joining in with Harry and John's conversation again.

Finally, it was time for Frank to leave to catch the tram for the station. Once on the platform, he signed the necessary paperwork and was able to return home with his new purchase. We were in no doubt of his arrival; he sounded the noisy horn far too many times as he entered the street and it brought all our neighbours to their windows. No sooner had he arrived than he insisted we all go outside and climb into the contraption for a photograph.

'Harry! Fetch your camera! Quickly now,' he shouted. 'I want everyone outside in their hats and coats as quickly as possible!'

Frank became quite impatient, as it took the girls a few moments to put on their coats and organise the children. 'Hurry now, hurry now,' he insisted. We all piled outside and into the car as instructed.

Frank's car was green in colour with buttoned brown leather upholstery. Along with its De Dion-Bouton engine, it displayed two impressive side oil lanterns and a double-twist brass bulb horn. The registration number for Frank's car was issued in Manchester and one of the first issued that year. Displayed in a prime position on the front of the car, it read, 'N246'.

Frank sat behind the wheel, I was in the passenger seat and our granddaughter, Katherine Alice, sat between us in the front. Our daughters, Mary, Emily and Ellen, climbed into the back via the rear entrance, followed by Ethel carrying baby Molly. It was a bit of a squash and I'm sure I heard the machine give a groan as we all settled ourselves for the photograph to be taken. Harry stood handsomely on the road beside me, and John Gow was instructed by Frank to position himself at the front of the vehicle.

'Wouldn't you rather have Robert in the picture, sir?' asked John, awkwardly.

'I'm quite happy this side of the camera, thank you,' called Robert.

Harry had entrusted his latest Sanderson camera to Robert to take the photograph. As Robert had for some time been accompanying Harry to work and shown great interest in what his brother was achieving, he knew how to work the camera. I had recently discovered the pair had briefly discussed the possibility of going into business together, but they had not made mention of this to their father as yet.

We all kept as still as we could, for as long as we could; that is, except for baby Molly, who wriggled constantly and consequently appeared blurred once the photograph had been developed. Frank sat with his head held high, facing forward in his seat, the only person not looking at the camera. When it was all over, Frank invited John and Harry to join him for a test drive. The men all disappeared for an hour, exiting in a cloud of dust, leaving the rest of us to enjoy a warm drink and something to eat back inside the house.

Frank was thrilled to discover he'd purchased his Renault before John Roberts of nearby Hulme had provided the bodywork for the first Royce petrol engine car. That car, completed in the Cooke Street factory, was taken on its first test drive around Manchester on 1 April 1904, but Frank had beaten them to it. He delighted in this and in the fact that he had been the first person on our street, and indeed one of the first men in Manchester, to have purchased a car. He could not have been more content when one year later the King followed in his footsteps and purchased a landaulette from the same Renault factory.

John Gow had been a friend of Harry's and an acquaintance of the family for some six or seven years now, but it had not been until he'd turned up at the house on the day of the car's arrival that I had noticed Mary's interest in him. Mary was now twenty-seven years old and had never really taken the prospect of finding herself a husband seriously, but I wondered if this might all be about to change. Although there were eight years between Mary and John's ages, I sensed he had stirred something inside her that day. It wasn't long before they started to see a lot more of each other.

Most weekends during the warmer months, Frank and I would climb into the car, along with either Harry and Ethel or Mary and John, and enjoy a few hours away from home. Many times we travelled the ten miles to Altrincham where we visited Thomas Simcock, Ethel's elderly uncle, who lived on St Margaret's Road. We became very fond of Mr Simcock, with whom Frank got along very well. The journey would take us around an hour and it was mostly enjoyable, although I disliked it intensely when Frank drove quickly. I'm sure he went faster on purpose, just to upset me.

'The car has a speedometer that goes up to thirty miles per hour, Alice. I'd like to be able to use it one day.'

'Not when I am with you in the car, thank you. It frightens me to do this speed.'

'We are only doing ten miles per hour, Alice. We are allowed by law to do fifteen.'

'Then it is a ridiculous law and if you speed up I'm afraid I might just scream.'

'Impossible woman,' I heard him mutter, just loud enough for me to hear over the noise of the engine.

On the whole these trips were pleasurable and it was good to breathe in the fresh air. I always felt invigorated after one of our trips out. I was not the only one, for Mary always took a great deal of pleasure in the company of Mr Gow, but it seemed the pair were in no hurry to rush things and I would have to wait another seven years before they tied the knot.

During 1904, Frank received news from America, from his brother-in-law, Frederick Earle. He and Frank's sister Frances had married in 1875, and she had moved with her husband from Congleton to Harrow. There, they had lived in a beautiful house on Roxborough Park. Frederick had a good job and was master in a preparatory school, but I understand they had never had any children of their own. I had heard Frank say on more than one occasion she had left it too late. Then suddenly they had moved abroad to live in California, and we had heard very little of them since.

Frederick was writing from their home in Haywards, California, informing Frank of his wife's death. Apparently Frances had been admitted to the Alameda County Hospital, where she had died.

Frank sat for a few moments digesting the news and obviously working out his sister's age, as eventually he said, 'She must have been sixty-one years old.'

'Not such a bad age,' I said, realising I was less than two years younger than Frances.

'There's not many of us left now,' said Frank, rather morbidly. I chose to ignore this comment, hoping Frank would cheer up. Thankfully his sister's death had no lasting effect upon his mood.

Closer to home changes were also taking place. William was making noises about travelling abroad and Robert had decided to leave his job at the bank and work alongside his brother Harry as an estate agent. The pair had always got on well and were excited at the prospect. There was already talk of purchasing more land and property. Together with their father, they would sit for hours in the front room discussing the best investments to be made around the area.

50

On the 17th March 1906 Harry and Ethel gave us another grandchild. They named their daughter Ethel Nora, after her mother, but she soon became known as Nora. Harry and Ethel now had three daughters. Ethel's parents moved to Claremont Road and her mother was always on hand to help with her growing family. It was not until after Ethel had Nora that she seemed to relax completely into her role of mother.

During this time Harry had been working hard to get some new properties passed through the planning department and built along Wilmslow Road. The plans were submitted and finally approved by Manchester Corporation in March 1906. In the April Harry and Robert went to sign a memorandum agreement with the Victoria Park Trust relating to the shops that were going to be built, with frontages onto Wilmslow Road and the Victoria Park entrance. The Victoria Park Trust had been formed by residents back in 1845 when there had been just a dozen or so houses on the site. The trust had not got the recognition they deserved until Rusholme was incorporated into Manchester County Borough in 1885, around the same time Frank had been building in Moss Side.

The park remained a private estate, extremely grand according to Robert and Harry, and could only be entered by paying a toll at the entrance gates. The Crescent Gate entrance off Wilmslow Road was demolished to make way for the shops Harry wanted to build. I was also given to understand a number of prominent people lived on this estate.

While in Rusholme, finalising plans for the build, Harry noticed some unrest within the local community. It appeared that Platt Hall, a six-acre estate, had become vacant and there was talk of Manchester council selling off the land to allow for a garden city to be built in its place. This was not pleasing the Rusholme community. Harry heard rumours from the locals that the hall was to be demolished and all the trees cut down. They were saying that the bricks from the house were to be used to build new housing and probably his shops. These rumours were spreading like wildfire and according to Harry there was great discontent in the area.

Harry had heard his father, on a number of occasions, mention there was a connection between our family and Platt Hall, but Frank had never found any solid proof of this claim. All Harry knew was that his grandfather had been given 'Platt' as his middle name, most probably handed down through his family, just as Frank and I had given it to William.

Soon, a local historian named William Royle formed a petition, which Harry, Robert and Frank all signed, and the house and grounds were eventually saved. This was when the land was renamed and became known as Platt Fields.

Harry's plan eventually reached fruition in late 1906. Two buildings of five properties each, three storeys high, which at ground level would become shops, were built along Wilmslow Road, one at either corner of the Park Crescent entrance to Victoria Park. Within the agreement it was stipulated that at all times the Victoria Park entrance should be free from obstruction and that this space of land, measuring at least twenty-two yards in width, should not be built upon. The size of the bay windows Harry could build within the entrance was restricted and no goods for sale were allowed to be displayed in these windows. It appeared most important that the area keep its splendour.

Harry and Robert accompanied me and Frank to see these two buildings once they were finished. Harry had by then sold the majority of these properties, retaining the two at each corner of Park Crescent, which he was now renting out. I noticed an ornate stone plaque upon one of the buildings, which read, 'Crescent Gate 1906'. Harry said it was so it would not be forgotten that at one time there had been gates here to Victoria Park.

Both buildings were already attracting a great deal of trade. All the shops were open for business. I could see a boot dealer, tobacconist, confectioner, ladies' outfitter, butcher and baker. Harry and Robert were certainly pleased by the success of their recent business transactions. I was very proud of them both.

Less than a year after having Nora, Ethel gave Harry another daughter. Lucy Marion was born on the 28th February 1907, much to Frank's annoyance. He had been convinced Ethel would have a boy this time. Outside the church on the day of Lucy's baptism, as the rest of the family fussed over the new arrival, Frank leant over to me and said, 'Whatever is the matter with them? Isn't it about time they managed a grandson for us? Don't you think so, Alice?'

I tutted at him and walked away quickly, as I was afraid I might say something I would regret. He had obviously forgotten that Harry had lost a son and that we'd had four daughters, one after another, after Harry had been born, but I wasn't about to remind him.

Frank went down to the pub straight after the ceremony, wetting the baby's head, so it appeared that having another granddaughter didn't put him off celebrating.

*

It was the beginning of August when a telegram arrived, delivered to the house by a young boy who cheekily waited for a tip until Frank sent him off with a flea in his ear. The telegram was from Frank's sister, Agnes, who lived in Berkshire. Her message was brief and didn't tell us much. She would be paying us a visit next week and would explain in more detail then. Frank was to meet her at the station as she had given details of her train times. She would only impose upon us for one night and then head home again.

'Sounds rather serious,' commented Frank.

'I wonder what has happened. We don't very often hear from Agnes, do we, Frank?'

'No,' was his only reply, but I could see there was concern on his face.

'Well, there is no point in trying to second-guess these things. We shall just have to wait until she arrives. I shall make sure a room is made up ready for her to stay overnight.'

'What? Oh, yes. Thank you, dear.'

It seemed an age before Agnes arrived and when she finally did, the house quickly became a very solemn place. She looked terrible. All the colour had drained from her face and it was obvious she had been crying during her train journey. We all sat down. Agnes and I had a cup of tea and Frank helped himself to something stronger. As her story unfolded I felt I should have joined Frank in a brandy.

Agnes explained that her husband had been extremely poorly for quite some time, suffering dreadfully with the most terrible headaches. They had been quite unbearable for him. He had seen various doctors, but nothing they had prescribed had been of any great help. On Saturday 3rd August the poor man, who undoubtedly must have been suffering tremendously, took himself off to Paddington station and jumped in front of an oncoming train. He died almost instantly from shock and collapse injuries.

Agnes's son, Orlando, whom we had never met, had accompanied his mother to his father's inquest, held on 7th August.

'My poor boy. He's supposed to be looking forward to his wedding in a couple of weeks' time. It just isn't going to be the same without his father there.' Agnes wiped away a tear with her handkerchief. 'Orlando explained to the coroner that his father had been suffering with gout in the head and the coroner, a Mr George Danford Thomas, concluded he had committed suicide while of unsound mind. It's going to be all over the newspapers and I wanted to warn you. I'm so sorry, Frank. I know how you hate scandal.'

I held my breath as I waited for Frank's response. Surely he could see how distraught his sister was.

'None of this is any of your doing, Agnes. I can see that you have done nothing wrong. It is all just so terribly unfortunate. A truly miserable situation. We are genuinely shocked and saddened by your news.'

'Thank you, Frank.'

I was surprised by my husband's kindly response. 'You must stay with us for as long as you need, Agnes.'

'That is very kind of you, Alice, but I shall be leaving tomorrow. I have Francis's funeral to arrange.'

'Of course.'

I am ashamed to admit I was relieved once she had left.

*

Our son William had been experiencing some restlessness for some time now, and who could blame him with everything that had happened? On a number of occasions he had confided in me about his feelings, but he had also spoken privately with his father. Frank had said to me afterwards, when I had made enquiries into our son's unhappiness, 'I'm sure he'll let you know when he has decided what he wants to do.' This hadn't helped, and as the days and weeks passed I found myself becoming more and more anxious. I knew William was unhappy and I couldn't help feeling he was more like his father than he would care to admit. It was as though he no longer wanted to be here. He longed for new horizons.

Frank, of course, had every sympathy for his son, saying, 'There really is nothing to worry about, dear. I can relate to just what he's going through. I have been through it myself. He just needs to get away from here for a while and explore the world.'

I had gathered that much all by myself, but I couldn't bear the thought of him leaving. Although many of my children were leaving home, settling down into their own lives, they had all remained local and I saw them all regularly.

Then it happened. William and Frank decided they would tell me together. William had decided he wanted to travel abroad.

'Where will you go? And when?' I asked, not letting him answer the first question before I fired the second at him.

The pair of them had conspired and William had already purchased a ticket for a steam liner to Paraguay, leaving Liverpool in the next couple of days. I was devastated.

'We knew you would try to talk the boy out of it if he mentioned it to you first,' Frank said, cruelly. 'It was I who suggested he sort things out first and then we could tell you together.'

William could see how he had upset me. 'I'm truly sorry, Mother, but this is something I really must do.'

'Don't apologise,' said Frank. 'This is your decision, boy.'

But I couldn't help feeling Frank had pushed him into it.

Later, once I had calmed down and slowly begun to come to terms with William's decision, I realised that I was being selfish and apologised to him.

'I promise to write regularly and tell you everything,' William assured me.

'It will help put my mind at rest, if you can.'

'I will, Mother, I promise.'

I hoped he would.

Some weeks later we received a package from Paraguay. Inside was a gift for each of us and a letter from William. He wrote, 'My journey by steam liner was terribly long but just about bearable. The roads here are terrible, mere dirt tracks, and transport is difficult and costly, but I have now found my feet and have finally settled into a reasonable-sized property.'

He went on to explain how the government there had been overthrown in July 1908 and that there remained a great deal of unrest. His letter was quite long and described his new home in some detail, more for his father's benefit than mine, I suspect. 'The country is divided into twenty-three counties governed by chiefs and justices of the peace, who are assisted by municipal councils. There is an ongoing unsettled boundary dispute with Bolivia. The population is a mix of Argentines, Italians, Brazilians, Spanish, German, French and Uruguayans. The English are in the minority here, Father, so you would hate it. I myself rather like it. I am certainly getting to experience many different cultures, all in the one place. Grazing land here is abundant and taken up by cattle-raisers with horses, mules, asses, sheep, horned cattle, goats and pigs. Most of the animal products produced here are exported. Tea and tobacco are grown in large quantities and I enclose a sample of each for you to try.'

'I hope he's not expecting me to try the tobacco,' I joked. But

Frank thought I was serious and said, 'I suspect the tea is for you, dear, and the tobacco is mine.'

William went on to say, 'The other main industries here produce timber, fruit and beans. The oranges here are especially good. Paraguay's main imports are textiles, haberdashery, ironwork and spirits, which it imports from England, but our exports back to you are rather insignificant and not worth a mention.'

Much later in his correspondence he explained how he had made many new friends and acquaintances, one of these being a family who lived close by. He mostly mentioned the daughter of the household, a girl by the name of Rosa, who it was obvious had sparked his interest. Frank kept quiet. I could tell he wasn't sure if he should approve of his son with a foreigner, but William was too far away for Frank to do anything about it, and whose fault was that?

51

Over the next few years our lives would be filled with happier times, spent at weddings and with grandchildren. Harry and Ethel finally produced a son in the October of 1908, much to Frank's approval. They named him Rupert Darnley, giving him Ethel's family name. Frank, of course, used this excuse to visit the pub and show off to his likeminded acquaintances. How relieved he was to at last be able to announce he had a grandson.

Harry presented me with a framed photograph of his family, taken the summer after Rupert's birth in their garden. Harry and Ethel are sitting on deck chairs, surrounded by their five delightful children. It is a charming depiction of the family and now takes pride of place upon my sitting room wall.

When Harry and Ethel visited with their children, it would always be Rupert with whom Frank spent all his time. Harry's daughters, with whom Harry was besotted, held no interest for Frank. Frank and his grandson were like two peas in a pod. Poor Harry was quite left out.

As Rupert grew older, he realised his grandfather would let him do almost anything and often took advantage of the situation. There were many times when Frank overruled Harry about some matter to do with Rupert. I found myself, on occasion, experiencing strong feelings of dislike towards Harry's son, which frightened me. He could often be spiteful towards his older sisters. Frank would laugh at this behaviour, which served only to make the child worse. As Rupert grew older, visits from him became more and more dreaded by everyone, except Frank.

William married Rosa shortly after arriving in Paraguay and wrote to us regularly with updates on the farming business he had set up out there. He and Rosa soon started a family and went on to have five children over the next couple of decades. He visited England a few times, but it was clear when he did that his home was now in Paraguay. I missed him terribly, but knowing he was happy eased my pain.

Ellen was the next of our children to marry. In July 1910 we celebrated her marriage to Mr John Coates. John was an architect's clerk and he and Harry had worked together on more than one occasion. It was Harry who had introduced John to Ellen. Harry was obviously a good judge of character, as Ellen and John struck up an immediate friendship. After their marriage they moved five miles away to a five-bedroomed semi-detached property on Belgrave Crescent in Eccles.

Ellen had her first child in 1911 and named her Alice Greaves, after me. I recall she was disappointed she had not been able to include her daughter on the census that year as Alice had been born four days after it had been taken.

At the time of the census, Frank and I had been married for forty-two years and lived in Demesne Road for twenty-four of those years. Recently we had started to feel our ages, suffering from silly little complaints that most people in their sixties might experience. Mary, Emily and Robert were still living at home. Robert and Mary had weddings planned for later the same year, which left Emily, who had always told us, in no uncertain terms, she would never marry. It was fast becoming an expensive time, but both Frank and I were pleased to have something good to look forward to. We were lucky to still be able to afford two domestic servants who also lived with us at the house, and between them were able to accomplish all domestic duties in the many rooms of our comfortable home.

On 1st June, Robert married a local girl named Eveline Coupe. She had been born in Birmingham, which was where she told us her father had once sold linen baby clothes and later manufactured underwear, much to Frank's disapproval. It appeared her father was able to turn his hand to almost anything. She had lived in the Withington area since childhood and recently moved with her parents to Demesne Road. Her father was at present an iron merchant.

'He must be earning a fair bit, if he can afford one of these houses,' Frank had said to Robert one day.

Robert's reply to his father was brief. 'That's none of our business, Father.'

The girl was sweet enough, but Frank made it quite obvious he felt our son could do better for himself. After their marriage Robert and Eveline moved a mile away to an attractive semi-detached house in Westfield Road, Chorlton-cum-Hardy.

Mary's marriage to John Gow followed Robert's and was held on 10th August. Frank and I had thought we would never see this day. The pair had courted on and off for over seven years. Mary was thirty-five years old and it was now or never.

John's mother had recently become rather frail. I understand she was eighty years old at this time. John and Mary visited her frequently in Yorkshire and I believe John had realised she would not last much longer. He knew his mother would leave him a substantial sum of money when she died, which would enable him and Mary to live quite comfortably. I wouldn't be surprised if his mother had said to him that she wished to see him happily married before she departed this life, as there was little time between the announcement and their marriage. According to Mary, John and his mother were extremely close. Mary had had many years in which to discover this.

Frank jokingly said to me, the morning of Mary's wedding, 'Should I just go and ask Mary if she is definitely sure she wants to go through with it?'

'Don't you dare,' I threatened him. 'She might change her mind, then what would you do?'

'Good point. Maybe I shouldn't joke about these things.'

'No, you shouldn't. I'll go and see how she's getting on.'

On my way out of the room, I picked up my favourite lace handkerchief. I thought Mary might need something borrowed for her special day.

'Make sure she's not changed her mind,' I heard Frank shout, as I left the room.

I found the day quite exhausting, but I did enjoy it. Mary looked so happy, she positively overflowed with joy. All the family were there to give the bride and groom a good send-off. Harry's daughters looked like little angels in their new outfits and Rupert managed to behave for most of the day. Frank, on the other hand, had far too much to drink again. Harry helped me to get him upstairs to bed that evening and I didn't hear anything from him until almost lunchtime the following day.

A couple of months later Harry and Ethel told us they were to have another child. In the May of the following year, Janet Greaves was born and once again a family name was passed down.

As Harry completed his family, his brother Robert was just beginning his. In March 1913, Robert's first child was born. What a joyous occasion this was for the family, and another excuse for Frank to drink far too much. I paid mother and child a visit the following day and both were doing well. Robert and Eveline announced they would be naming their daughter after her mother. But they wanted to make the spelling of their daughter's name different: Evelyn.

'What do you think, Mother,' asked Robert. 'Do you like it?'

'I like it, darling, but it's not my decision. You could call her Cyril and I'd be just as pleased.'

I'm not sure Robert realised I was joking, but I made Eveline laugh.

Three days later Robert turned up on the doorstep with some devastating news. Baby Evelyn had died. There had been no warning. She had shown no sign of being ill; if anything, quite the opposite. She had been a happy and content baby. My poor boy sobbed in my arms for over an hour, which I think did him good and enabled him to return to his wife to give her the support she must have needed.

When Robert and Eveline had adjusted to their tragedy they told me what had happened. Robert had left early that morning for work. Eveline said she had spent far too long over the last couple of days watching her daughter sleeping, mesmerised by her beauty. She had told herself she must try to get dressed and leave her alone to sleep. She had fed her baby and the child had gone back to sleep. Eveline had dressed quietly, so as not to disturb her peaceful daughter, and had gone downstairs into the kitchen to see the cook and make herself a drink.

'Cook insisted I sit down while she made me a drink and we chatted for a short time before I said, "I shall just nip back upstairs and check on the baby."' At this point Eveline could continue her story no longer and it was left to Robert to finish.

'As poor Eveline entered the room she could immediately see all was not well. Our baby's body was shaking uncontrollably, her muscles contracting involuntarily.'

Eveline was clearly left distraught by her husband's account, as she was forced to relive the experience. 'I didn't know what to do,' she sobbed.

'The doctor said there was nothing you could have done, my dear. He said it would have been over in a matter of seconds,' Robert attempted to reassure his young wife. He looked over to me. 'The doctor said Evelyn had experienced a convulsion.'

'I am so very sorry, my dears, so very sorry for your loss.'

52

On the afternoon of Wednesday 30th April 1913, Frank was to meet Harry in Manchester. Harry had a bit of business he wanted to discuss with his father and they had agreed to meet at Harry's office around 4 pm.

Ellen called in that morning, heavily pregnant, along with little Alice, who had just started to walk and was into everything. John had accompanied them, leaving them with us while he saw to some business in Manchester.

'I hope you don't mind, Mother,' Ellen said. 'I just had to get out of the house. I will go mad if I have to stare at those four walls for much longer.'

'Don't be silly, darling. You know you're always welcome. It won't be long now, will it?'

'Should be very soon. John says he thinks I'm much bigger this time. He thinks it might come early.'

I laughed. 'Men. They think they know it all. Your baby will arrive when it's ready and not before.'

Frank lasted five minutes in our daughter and granddaughter's company before he went and hid at the back of the house in his billiard room. Miraculously, he reappeared moments after they had been collected, wondering when his lunch would be ready. I was glad to see him leave after his lunch and finally get the house to myself for a while.

Frank took the tramcar into Manchester, and some time later a severe thunderstorm began, causing torrential rain like nothing I had ever witnessed before. It seemed to engulf the whole area. At its height, around 5.30 pm, the servants were frantic as the rainwater poured in through the cellar windows. It was around this time that Harry and Frank were leaving Manchester to catch a tramcar home.

Harry explained later that as they had left his office the heavens had opened. As his father had stepped into the tramcar along

Deansgate, he had lost his footing in the wet weather and fallen onto the granite paving, cutting his head and injuring his leg. As Harry helped him up, Frank was adamant that he was all right and Harry should stop fussing.

'You're bleeding, Father.'

'What?'

'Your face is bleeding, just above your eye. Here,' and Harry produced a handkerchief from his pocket to wipe up the blood.

'Give that here,' demanded Frank, snatching the makeshift dressing from Harry's hand. 'I can do it myself.' All the time the pair of them were getting more and more soaked.

'You getting on, gents?' asked the ticket collector, just as another flash of lightning preceded a thundering roar. At which point Frank clambered onto the tramcar, followed by Harry and a small crowd, pushing and shoving so as to get out of the rain. Frank and Harry managed to find themselves the last two seats on the crowded tramcar, just as it pulled away.

They travelled along Deansgate, turning into Great Jackson Street, Warwick Street, Bradshaw Street and finally Princess Road, where they got off and walked through Alexandra Park, home. The pair were completely soaked through when they arrived, as it was still pouring down outside. Harry had insisted he wanted to accompany his father home, and I'm so glad he did, for I would not have known what to do next if he had not been there.

Frank looked dreadful as he entered the house. He was very quiet and it was obvious he wanted to be left alone.

'Go and get out of those wet things before you catch your death,' I fussed.

Frank disappeared to change, and Harry told me what had happened as I helped him off with his jacket and found him a towel.

'How does he seem to you?' I asked.

'He was rather quiet on the way home. I'm sure he's just embarrassed, nothing more serious, I shouldn't think,' and we couldn't help giggling together like a couple of schoolchildren.

I'd asked the servant to make two hot drinks and she appeared with them some minutes later.

'Go and see if your father has sorted himself out yet, and tell him there is a hot drink down here for him.'

'Will do,' agreed Harry, disappearing up the stairs. Seconds later he was back down in a terrible state. 'I'm going to fetch the doctor, Father's not well. I'll be as quick as I can,' and he was gone.

I raced upstairs as swiftly as a sixty-eight-year-old can, to find Frank lying on the bed beside a pool of vomit. His face was a terrible colour. He was mumbling but not making any sense. It was difficult to understand what he was trying to say and he didn't seem able to move. The lightning was still occasionally flashing outside the window and seemed to be distressing him, so I closed the curtains. I sat with him and held his hand as our domestic cleared away my husband's vomit. I didn't know what else to do.

After what felt like an age but in reality was minutes, Harry returned with the doctor. Harry and I left the room so that he could examine Frank in private.

A quarter of an hour later, when the doctor appeared downstairs, he looked very serious. 'I am terribly sorry, Mrs Bradshaw.'

I couldn't bring myself to speak. Harry spoke first. 'What is it, doctor? What's the matter with my father?'

'There is no easy way to say this, Mr Bradshaw. Your father passed away a few moments ago. There was nothing I could do for him. I'm so terribly sorry.'

'What happened to him? He slipped about an hour ago and cut his head, but that shouldn't kill you!' Harry was almost shouting at the doctor.

'Shall we discuss this somewhere else?' asked the doctor. 'I can see your mother is quite distressed.'

'No, I'm all right,' I managed to say. 'What do you think has happened to Frank?'

'I suspect he has experienced a cerebral haemorrhage.'

Both Harry and I obviously looked blank.

'That is when there is a bleed in the brain, and I suspect in turn this has caused Mr Bradshaw to endure a stroke. There was nothing I could do. I am very sorry for your loss.'

'Was it the bang to his head which caused it?' asked Harry.

'It's too difficult to say, I'm afraid. We may never know.'

The room fell silent and I didn't see the doctor leave. Harry must have shown him out.

The next few days were a blur. Harry and Robert saw to all the arrangements and I was very well looked after by my daughters, Mary and Emily.

On 3rd May we laid Frank to rest in the Southern Cemetery, in the family grave alongside Catharine Alice, George Philip, baby Frank and baby Evelyn. Poor Ellen was beside herself and John had to take her home early as she was so upset. Three days later she gave me a grandson. It went without saying he was named after his grandfather.

Frank left me more than £35,000 in his will. I honestly had no idea that he had accumulated this much money. Emily and I were now rattling around in the house on Demesne Road, but I had no intention of moving.

PART V

1912–1960

⁓

Harry Greaves Bradshaw

Told by Janet Greaves Bradshaw, his daughter

Harry Greaves Bradshaw
b.1872
m.1899
d.1960

Easte Agent and Surveyor

Ethel Darnley Brown
b.1877
m.1899
d.1933

Katherine Alice (Kate)
b.1900

Frank
b.1902

Frances Mary (Molly)
b.1903

Ethel Nora (Nora)
b.1906

Lucy Marion
b.1907

Rupert Darnley
b.1908

Janet Greaves
b.1912

53

I was born in May 1912. My parents had married on 14th February 1899 at St James, Moss Side, many years before I had been born. Every Valentine's Day, without fail, my father would produce a beautiful bouquet of flowers for my mother and she would become embarrassed as Father reminisced about their wedding day. As children we all found it very amusing, but I now look back on these times with fond memories and a desire that my marriage might have been half as happy as theirs.

When I was born, my parents Harry and Ethel already had five other children: Kate, Molly, Nora, Lucy and Rupert. I remained the youngest child of the family, which I didn't mind, as I was often spoilt by my parents and especially by Kate.

My childhood was a happy one. We moved to Church Bank, Richmond Road, in Bowdon when I was two. It was shortly before the start of the First World War. I am pleased to say I have no significant memories of this war, as I was too young to remember it, but I have heard some stories from my sisters. This first war appears not to have affected us too much at Church Bank, although I understand we lost most of our servants during this time, as they were able to find better-paid jobs outside the home. The Second World War was another matter.

I am fast approaching my fiftieth year. My home remains important to me, but over the years it has also proved to be a bit of a burden. My father purchased the property in late 1913, not long after his father had died. My parents had often visited the area when they had previously lived in Manchester, calling in on relatives.

My father told me he had witnessed many dramatic changes to the Manchester area in the decade before he had left. As time went on, his wish to move his family away from the ever-increasing town, to a more desirable neighbourhood, became far greater. Over the years both my parents had commented on numerous occasions how they had admired the area of Altrincham from the moment they had first visited, promising themselves that one day they would move here.

The house my father found for us was a three-storey semi-detached property, with a cellar and shared driveway, in a beautiful village just outside Altrincham called Bowdon. According to my mother, Father was like an excited child when he first came across this property, which was unusual, really, considering the business he was in.

My father had trained as a civil engineer after leaving school, securing himself offices in Manchester. My mother once told me they had first met when she had accompanied her father to the Barton Arcade on business.

'It was love at first sight, wasn't it, my darling?' my father teased her. I recall that was the only time I had seen my mother blush.

Over the years my father had overseen many housing developments to fruition in the Manchester area and had owned much property there also. Some of these properties had been passed down through my father's family, and some my father was able to purchase for himself.

During my childhood my father's job was that of estate agent and surveyor. He was hardworking, frugal and extremely proud. He would get up early every morning, leaving the house smartly dressed, briefcase in hand, to catch the train into Manchester. His office for a time was on Princess Street in Rusholme; that was when he was in partnership with my uncle. HG and R Bradshaw, Estate Agents and Surveyors, lasted for more than ten years. My father said he enjoyed working alongside his younger brother. Business must have been good for them as both my father and my uncle were able to afford a number of expensive properties during that time.

From the 1930s my father's office was on King Street in Manchester. He shared it with a number of business partners, who would run it for him while he was abroad. Double doors took you through to a dark and gloomy inside, which drew you up the stairs and into a musty-smelling office, scantily furnished with desk, chair and leather couch. It was a cold, damp place, in which I never really wanted to spend any length of time. Later, when visiting family abroad, it would be this address my father recorded as being his permanent residence.

As the youngest child of the family, I was well looked after. When my parents weren't around, there was always someone to take care of me. This was usually the servants or my sisters, Kate and Molly. I can especially recall Kate on many occasions playing hide and seek with me in our large garden and spending hours in the sun on the front lawn, making daisy chains and reading me stories. I often wish I could go back to those times, when none of us had a care in the world.

Every Sunday morning, without fail, Mother expected us all to attend church with her. Dressed in our Sunday best we'd walk to St John's church on Ashley Road. The journey was less than a mile and should have taken us around a quarter of an hour, but Mother always made us leave in plenty of time, as she knew how we dawdled and she hated us to be late.

'Today is my day for resting and, while you are out, that is just what I intend to do,' my father would announce whenever he was asked if he would like to accompany us to church. This was never questioned and he was never expected to attend. As children we were told in no uncertain terms that we would attend every Sunday without exception, until the time when we had been confirmed. After that we were free to choose whether to continue with our religion.

My mother was very religious. Throughout my childhood I'd never known her to miss a Sunday service. She would attend church meetings during the week and joined the Mothers' Union, helping with fundraising whenever she could.

One particular day, my mother looked rather melancholy. Gazing out of the front room window, she seemed to be in her own world. She appeared not to hear me enter the room. I asked if she was all right and she replied, 'When you move from one area to another you are forced to leave things behind, and I hoped we would find replacements for some of those things here.'

'Do you mean people, like Aunt Marion?' I asked, concerned, as my mother seemed quite sad. I knew she was very close to her sister and hadn't seen her for some time.

'No, I don't mean your aunt, although family is important. We are not so far away that we cannot visit her or your grandfather if we desire, are we?'

I wondered if she was thinking about her mother, as my grandmother had recently passed away.

'What do you mean, then?' I ventured, feeling more brave than usual, as my mother could often suddenly shut down a conversation, especially if it wasn't going her way.

'I'm talking about the church.'

'Oh,' I replied, a little confused. 'Are you unhappy with St John's?'

'No, not at all. I admit I was a little surprised we ended up there rather than at St Mary's, but I am more than happy with St John's.'

'Why have we never attended St Mary's?'

'When we first moved here, I found St Mary's rather overcrowded and unfriendly, so I tried St John's. My uncle Thomas had joined St John's when he had moved to the area. Your father has little interest in the church, of course, so the choice was mine rather than his. At St John's I was made to feel very welcome from my first visit. I took all of you with me each time. You must have been about two years old when you attended your first service there. All of my children have enjoyed Sunday school at St John's and all will be confirmed there.'

With that she turned from the window and left the room. The conversation was over and she had obviously said all she needed to say, leaving me a little confused. There were often times like these when I didn't understand my mother. She could frequently seem very complicated to me as I was growing up.

However, I was very fond of both of my parents. They were strict but usually fair. They had rules and we were expected to stick to them. Manners were very important to both my parents, but it would usually be my mother who enforced these. Mealtimes were the worst. I learnt from a very early age to remember to say 'please' and 'thank you', to eat everything that was placed in front of me, whether I liked it or not, and never to recoil or show distaste at any meal. I had seen my sisters disciplined too many times over the dinner table. It was far simpler to shut up and eat up.

54

Being the youngest, I often was allowed to do things that perhaps my brother and sisters had not been allowed to do, and I suspect this may have caused some ill feeling at times. Mother used to take me everywhere with her when I was little, when previously she had left my brother and sisters with the servants. I enjoyed the special attention she would give to me and often arrived home with something my mother had purchased for me: a new item of clothing or small toy such as a skipping rope.

On special occasions when other adults were invited to the house, things were different. Rupert and I were briefly introduced but then whisked away by one of the servants, while my older sisters were encouraged to socialise. Nora especially hated these times and would try to sneak away using the excuse she was just going to see if Rupert and I were all right. Mother would soon send Kate to fetch her and she would moan all the way back to the guests.

Rupert was just as spoilt as me on occasion, if not more so, especially by my mother. I suspect that was because he was her only son. Father was a little firmer with him, but Rupert had a way of getting what he wanted. In the end, his conceitedness would contribute to his demise.

My mother was a devout royalist. She was born when Queen Victoria was on the throne, married my father just before Edward VII become king and died while George V was ruling. She followed, supported, admired and celebrated every occasion with the royal family. Any news regarding the royal family, and Mother seemed to know all about it before anyone else did. Father used to tease her, asking, 'Have you been sent the news directly from the palace by carrier pigeon?' Of course, she never found this funny.

She once explained to me how the British public associated the royal house's German name of Saxe-Coburg and Gotha with the horrors of the First World War, and so George V had changed the name to Windsor. Her stories and facts fascinated me and I became just as obsessed with the royals as my mother.

The one royal occasion which particularly sticks in my mind, as Mother was so excited about it, was in 1932 when King George delivered a Christmas speech over the wireless. Mother smiled as the King broadcast, 'Your loyalty and your confidence in me has been my abundant reward.' She firmly admired him for overcoming his fear of public speaking and for controlling his stammer. When his speech was ended she raised her glass to him, saying, 'God bless you,' and wished the royal family a happy Christmas. Father was sound asleep throughout the whole broadcast, most likely due to the large lunch and bottle of wine he had consumed. He had little interest in the royal family and couldn't understand what all the fuss was about.

I have lived here now for more than forty years and cannot imagine living anywhere else. The house has seen many changes over the years, not just structurally but as people come and go. My home, number four Church Bank, is a large semi-detached house, presenting on three floors, and has further rooms in the cellar. A substantial driveway invites you warmly up towards the two joined houses, numbers three and four, through gardens to both sides. Our garden, on the left, displays circular rose beds and neatly kept lawns. My neighbour's garden, to the right, is usually a little unkempt. Established trees and shrubs create a boundary to both properties, making them feel quite private.

From the front our property appears smaller than next door's, but this is an illusion. The properties' floor plans form two interlocking L shapes, making the actual size of the houses and number of rooms identical. Our house has a pillared porch entrance with steps up to the front door and one large window to the left of it, which leads to our sitting room. Next door's entrance is similar but has a large window to both sides, a sitting room to the left and a dining room to the right. We have two first-floor windows looking out over the front of the property, while next door has three.

One can walk around the left-hand side of our property, along a path which passes a detached veranda. Access from here to the house is via the sitting room. The veranda, which my father added to the house shortly after he purchased it, is open to the elements but has a south-facing aspect and is a delight to sit under as long as it is a sunny day. Following this path, lined either side with grass, will take you around to the back of the property, where there are a smaller garden and outbuildings.

At one time the property had much more land behind it. Here, there used to be a tennis court where I remember my sisters would throw tennis parties. Alas, I was too young to be allowed to join in. When they outgrew their interest in tennis and started to move away, my father sold off this part of our land, reducing the garden substantially.

Upon entering through the front door, the first room you come to is the sitting room, where we have a number of comfortable chairs and more recently a television, acquired in 1959. I was first introduced to the delights of television in 1952 when we visited friends to watch the Queen's coronation on their newly purchased set. Most of the other furniture within the house used to belong to my mother and father. In the sitting room is my mother and father's mahogany bookcase set above a bureau, along with an octagonal occasional table, decorated with marquetry.

Mother and Father's extending mahogany dining table and chairs are in the dining room at the back of the house, purchased around the time of their marriage and therefore older than me. They were purchased through Joseph Fitter of Cheapside, Birmingham, and the table uses a winding mechanism displaying his badge. Along the wall sits a mahogany sideboard which contains plates, glasses and cutlery.

A Jacobean card table, which I am given to understand has been passed down through my father's family, sits neglected in a corner.

Behind the dining room is another room, fondly remembered as the butler's pantry. At the moment this room is being used for storage. Next door to this, a bathroom and a toilet. On the opposite side is my kitchen, complete with many original features and scullery. I now live on this floor.

Next to the dining room, a stairway takes you to the first-floor landing with arch window overlooking the back garden. A self-contained flat, complete with its own front door, has a landing which turns on itself to reveal a number of doors which lead you into four separate rooms. This is where the Smith family used to live, but now it belongs to my daughter and her family.

Up the final flight of stairs you will reach a further three good-sized rooms and one smaller. I rent out this top floor to an elderly lady named Mrs Mather. She has her own sitting room, kitchen and bedroom, with the use of the bathroom on the first floor. Before her, this floor was used by a number of female teachers who worked at Altrincham High School.

55

When I was five years old I started at Culcheth Hall boarding and day school for girls. I did not board; I went home. The school was a large house with garden, tennis courts, field and gymnasium. I spent the next ten years at this school and have fond memories of it and the staff who worked there.

My sisters had all started school in Manchester. Kate continued her education in Manchester after we moved to Bowdon, my father paying for her to board at the school, so as not to disrupt the last two years of her education. Getting us all a good education had always been extremely important to my father. Even more important to my father was that we found ourselves a 'ticket'. By this, Father meant gaining a qualification and ultimately a respectable profession.

When Kate was boarding in Manchester, my mother and father would try to visit her as often as possible. They would often take me with them, as Kate was very fond of me, but I was too little to remember those times. Kate had told Mother how much she missed me, so when we were on holiday in Colwyn Bay in October 1913, Mother took me to a local photographer, Alfred Haley on the Penrhyn Road, near to the railway station. There I had my photograph taken, standing next to a chair upon which Mother had placed a toy animal in an attempt to distract me. I was holding on to a small ball the photographer had thrown for me and I appeared extremely content. Mother said Kate was thrilled with the picture.

Mother had a postcard especially printed of this photograph and sent it to her sister Marion, who lived off Burnage Lane in Levenshulme. On the reverse it reads, 'Isn't this a jolly photo of baby? I have had it taken for Katherine. We are going to see her on Saturday. I shall be in Manchester over the weekend. Hope you are all well. We are all A1. R included. Love from Ethel.' I know this because the postcard is now in my possession. 'R included' refers to my brother, Rupert. According to Mother he had just recovered from a nasty bout of measles which he had contracted a matter of weeks after starting school in Bowdon.

Kate left school with few achievements and, it could be said, was a disappointment to my parents. By the time she was twenty, my mother had more or less disowned her after she became pregnant.

Molly completed her schooling at Culcheth Hall, having transferred there when we had moved to Bowdon. Molly had brains, or that is what I remember my father saying on numerous occasions. She left school and trained as a primary school teacher.

Nora also went to Culcheth Hall, but because she was the 'plain Jane' of the family she was not required by Mother and Father to further her education. It was expected she would remain a spinster, stay at home and care for our parents when they became elderly.

After Lucy finished her schooling, she trained as a dance teacher. She is tall and elegant. For many years now, before and after her marriage, she has taken classes of children and taught them how to ballroom dance.

My only brother, Rupert, had always been a lazy child, and this trait followed him into his adult life. He left school with few prospects, assuming he could live off my father's money. He managed it for a time, able only to find part-time farm work, and before he could secure himself a permanent job he decided to travel abroad. I recall him saying on more than one occasion that he was a free spirit. He did later train briefly to become a mechanic.

Having such a large age gap between me, Kate and Molly caused problems on occasion. When I was about seven or eight, Kate and Molly both entertained friends at our home. Some of these friends were boys. I lost count of how many times my sisters screeched for Mother when all I had done was walk into the sitting room or dining room. It wasn't long before door knockers were fitted to the hall side of these doors and I was told in no uncertain terms by Mother that I had to knock upon them loudly before entering. Of course, once I realised why, it turned into a great game, as I found every excuse there was to enter those rooms when I knew my sisters were 'entertaining' a boy.

Most of the time, the reception I got from these boys and my sisters was cool. Then, one day, Kate brought home a boy I had not seen before. I watched from the staircase as they entered the front room and pondered over an excuse for knocking on the door and entering. I tried to give them enough time alone for them to think they were not going to be disturbed, then knocked loudly on the door and entered quickly. Both shot up from their seats, trying to look innocent, but both were rather red in the face.

'Janet! What is it? What do you want?' asked Kate, obviously rather annoyed and embarrassed.

'Hello,' I said, boldly going up to this new boy. 'I'm Janet.'

Normally the boys just grunted something under their breath or shuffled uncomfortably in their seat, waiting for me to leave again, but this one spoke. 'Hello, Janet. My name is Frank. It's very nice to meet you.'

Kate's face was a picture. She was quite taken aback that her friend should want to make conversation with me.

'What are you doing with yourself today?' he asked.

He had caught me a little off guard. 'Oh, nothing special,' I replied. 'Cook said I could do some baking with her. We're going to make jam tarts.'

'They're my favourite. How did you know?' asked Frank.

'I didn't,' I replied innocently. 'Would you like me to save you one?'

'I shall look forward to it.'

Frank seemed very friendly and was smiling at me all the time. Kate, on the other hand, gave me one of her warning looks. I left the room as quickly as I had arrived. I heard them both laugh quietly as I went. I chose not to stand outside with my ear to the door, as I normally did, but to go and find Cook.

When the tarts I'd helped to make were cool enough to eat, Cook let me take some on a plate for Kate's guest. When I knocked on the door and got no answer, I thought Frank must have already left. But then he opened the door.

'I thought you'd forgotten about me,' he said, smiling.

'Oh, no. It took a little longer than Cook thought it would,' I replied in my very grown-up voice.

'I find that hard to believe, having such an expert as yourself in the kitchen to help her.'

I walked into the room, blushing, and placed the plate of tarts on an occasional table near to where Kate was sitting.

'Would you like to join us?' she asked.

I was surprised, but accepted and pulled up another chair. Between the three of us, we finished the jam tarts quickly. I felt very grown up because Kate and Frank had allowed me to join in with their conversation.

When Frank had left, I told my sister, 'I like Frank.'

'So do I,' replied Kate. 'Very much.'

After that Frank became a regular visitor to the house, and Kate and I always made sure we did some baking together before he was due. After a time the two of them began to spend more time together away from the house at dances or shows and I got to see less of Frank.

When my school broke up for the summer holidays in July 1920, I arrived home excited about the prospect of being free to do as I pleased for the rest of the summer. As I entered the house a terrible argument was in progress between Kate and my mother. My father was still at work and I could hear Mother shouting, 'You stupid, stupid girl! What were you thinking? Your father will disown you for this. You will be lucky if he ever speaks to you again. You have brought such shame upon this family.'

I could hear Kate sobbing, 'I'm so sorry, Mother, I'm so sorry.'

'It's too late for being sorry. The damage is done!' screamed Mother.

Kate flew out of the sitting room, rushed past me and disappeared upstairs. Mother was the next to meet me in the hallway. She stopped dead when she saw me.

I attempted a smile. 'What's happened?' I asked as politely as I could.

'Go to your room and don't come down until you are called,' was her reply.

I did as I was told. Even though I had no idea what had happened, I sensed it was not good. When Father arrived home the shouting began again, although it was only Mother's voice I could hear. Mother and Kate's relationship changed after that.

One month later, in September, Kate left home. She married Frank Wainwright in a registry office in a very small, quick ceremony which I was told about after the event. Then they went to live with Frank's family in Crewe.

It was during this time my father purchased the house next door. I think he had hoped Kate and Frank might move in to it, but this was not to be. Mother was furious with Father when she discovered what he'd done. It must have seemed to him that no matter what he did, he was unable to please any of the women in his life.

Looking more on the positive side, my father explained that at least now he had the opportunity to move the £6 per annum chief rent from our house onto next door's, before he sold it again. Having worked in the property business all his life, he knew about loopholes, but this issue had secretly irritated him for a long time and before now there had seemed no easy solution. So, for a very short time, he owned both properties. Fortunately he was able to resell next door quickly, to a Mr Jones and his family, who accepted their double chief rent of £12 per annum, leaving our house a freehold property. Little reward, considering my father's original intention.

When Kate's baby, Elaine, was born at the end of March the following year, it was only my father who showed any interest. This was his first grandchild and he was determined not to miss out. Before Elaine's first birthday, Kate, Frank and the baby moved into a house on Hazel Road in Altrincham. On the rare occasions Mother would accompany us there, the atmosphere was tense. Mother made life very difficult for Kate. She did not welcome her or the baby at Church Bank and Kate was often shunned from attending family functions. I really felt for my sister.

56

I had always been fascinated by an old-looking book which sat upon a shelf inside the cabinet in the sitting room. I was never allowed to touch it or remove it from the cabinet, even under supervision. I was told it belonged to my father and he would be very cross if I ever touched it. This only served to fuel my inquisitive mind. Why was he so protective of this book? It was a Bible. He never went to church and I had never seen him reading it. I could not understand why it was so important I shouldn't touch it.

I recall feeling brave one day. I must have been about six and Father and I were enjoying some time together, alone in the house. Mother had gone to visit a sick friend, Cook was shopping and the rest of the family were at school. Father was in good spirits as it was the year after the war had ended. We were playing a game of hide and seek in the downstairs rooms and he had just found me hiding behind the full-length velvet curtains. I recall the book catching my eye and I asked if I could take it out and have a look at it with him. 'Not today, darling,' was his brief reply and he instantly left the room. I was not brave enough to help myself.

As I got older, the need to touch that book and turn its pages grew stronger within me. When I was around nine or ten, I found myself, one Saturday morning, left at home with only Cook for company. She had gone off into the kitchen to get on with the dinner and had left me instructions to play quietly in the front room. Now was my chance!

The key to the cabinet was always left inside the lock, so it was easy enough to open. I carefully lifted the Bible from its shelf and set it down on the table. It was bound in black leather. The gold writing on the spine simply read, 'Holy Bible', and it smelt musty. I gently opened the book at the first page, instantly recognising my father's writing, which read, 'HG Bradshaw, August 1902'. Strange, I thought; that was not my father's birthday. Come to think of it, no one in my family had an August birthday.

I cautiously turned over to the next page. This page was covered in my father's writing and along the top of the page was the word 'Births'. Below it were listed my and my siblings' names, alongside the dates and times we were born. Then I noticed there appeared to be too many names. The second name down I did not recognise. The line read, 'Frank Bradshaw, February 18th 1902, 1.35 pm'. I had no idea who Frank was.

I heard Cook coming back along the hall and closed the book quickly. I replaced it on the shelf, locked the cabinet and sat back down with my toys.

Cook walked in and asked if I was all right. 'Would you like to come and help me in the kitchen, now?'

I reluctantly got up and went with Cook, and for a time forgot about what I had seen.

Some time later, I have a memory of my older sisters huddled together, whispering to one another. I overheard them discussing my mother and the birth of a baby boy who had died. They shut up when they realised I was trying to listen to what they were saying. I'd never heard my mother discussing this subject and assumed I'd misunderstood my sisters.

The family Bible now belongs to me and I am able to open it and turn its pages as freely and as often as I like. There is no mystery any longer about Frank, the baby my mother lost and the brother I never knew.

*

As mentioned before, my father worked for many years alongside my uncle Robert. Their business was registered as HG and R Bradshaw, Estate Agents and Surveyors, at 115 Princess Road, Rusholme. This office was situated in the area between Claremont Road and Moss Lane, where my father's family had once owned much land and where until recently my father still owned many houses. I understand he and my uncle inherited in excess of 200 properties, mainly in the Moss Side area, from which rent was regularly collected. Since the death of their father, they had added to these assets, which was why we could afford to live the way we did.

In 1923 my father and uncle moved their offices to be closer to the centre of Manchester, setting up at 80 Mosley Street, near to the art gallery. Father's decision to sell the tennis court at the back of Church Bank enabled them to do this. A six-bedroom bungalow has since been built where the tennis court used to be.

My father would travel to work in Manchester each day and often call in to see his mother, who had remained at the family home on Demesne Road since the death of her husband. It must have been around this time my father and uncle had telephones installed both at their offices and in their homes, along with one at my grandmother's home in Whalley Range. My father had become increasingly concerned about his mother, as she was becoming rather frail. Although my aunt remained at the house to take care of her mother, Father had said it would put his mind at ease knowing she could get hold of him quickly if need be.

A few years later my uncle Robert, his wife and their three children moved into my great-aunt's house on Arnold Road, Whalley Range, in order to look after her in her old age. They would go on to have a fourth child at this house in 1929, and I think it was just after this that my uncle started to feel unwell. He and my father ended their business relationship at this time in order that my uncle could rest. My father then moved his offices one last time, into King Street.

As I became older, I enjoyed visiting my sister Kate after school. I was forced to lie to my mother about this as she would never have allowed these visits to take place, fearing Kate would be a bad influence on me. I'd tell her I was having tea at a friend's house and not to expect me home before 7 pm. I always made sure I was home at the time I'd said and was thankful Mother never questioned me. I hate to think what might have happened if she had found out where I really was.

During one visit, Kate had some news which she wanted to share with me. She was positive and excited about her news; I was less so. She and Frank were to move abroad. Frank had been offered a clerk's job in New Zealand, contracted to start later on in the year. They were to leave London by steamship on 5th February 1927 and spend a month or so in Australia before heading off to New Zealand. 'It will be a new start for us, Janet. Please say you're happy for us.'

'I am.' I squeaked, tears filling my eyes. 'But I shall miss you all terribly.'

'And we shall miss you, silly. But you can come and visit whenever you want.'

'If Mother will allow it,' I sobbed.

Kate pulled me to her and we embraced each other. Five-year-old Elaine pushed herself in between us, forcing us to part again. I ruffled her hair.

'Does Father know?' I asked Kate.

'Yes. I think he feels very much like you do, but he knows it's an opportunity that both Frank and I should not ignore.'

'Then I wish you all the best in your adventure,' I said, and we embraced again, this time with no interruptions.

The next few weeks were difficult as I tried to cram in as many visits to Kate as was possible. Father and I struggled to keep Kate's secret from my mother, as Kate had requested. The day before they left, Kate called round to the house with Frank to inform my mother. My mother reacted very little, seemingly unmoved by her eldest daughter's announcement that she would soon be departing this country.

'Maybe it's for the best, Kate,' was Mother's only comment.

Kate and Frank didn't stay long after that. There seemed little point. Mother would never approve of them, as Elaine had been born on 'the wrong side of the blanket': a phrase my mother had begun to use more frequently recently.

Father and I congratulated Frank, embraced Kate and wished them all a safe journey.

'Don't forget to write!' I screamed at Kate as she disappeared down the front driveway.

'As soon as I can,' she shouted back. Then she was gone.

She wrote separately to Father and then me, but both letters arrived on the same day. I was excited every time I received one of Kate's letters. Her first described the long journey on board the steam ship named *Oronsay* and how she had spent her twenty-seventh birthday suffering with sea sickness. Elaine had adjusted well during her time at sea and Frank too had been fortunate enough not to experience the motion sickness, but it sounded as though poor Kate had suffered for quite some days. In her letters she also included many facts about their visit to Australia.

Kate always seemed to have so much to tell me. I worried my letters would bore her, as nothing ever happened here, but within six months of Kate's departure much had happened and my letters to her finally held some content.

57

In September 1927 Rupert caught a steamship from London headed for Sydney, Australia. From there he was to travel across the Tasman Sea to visit Kate and her family in New Zealand. He was nineteen at the time and had pestered my father for the last two months about making the trip. He was desperate to get away from home. He had left school with few or no qualifications and done nothing with his life since. Father finally gave in, agreeing to pay for him to travel third-class only.

'When you return I expect you to know what it is you want to do with your life,' said my father. 'Speak to your sister. I'm sure Kate and Frank will be able to advise you.' Of course, he had already written to my sister, no doubt giving her instructions on how best to handle my brother and what to say to him.

Molly was next to leave the family home, in her late twenties. She had left school and trained to be a teacher, gaining herself her 'ticket'. Both my parents were proud of Molly's achievements but wondered if she would ever marry. She was working at a local primary school when she first started to walk out with Dennis Dickinson, a boy the family had known for some time. His family had lived on the corner of Heald Road and Stamford Road since before his birth in 1903 and Molly got on well with Dennis's sister, Kathleen. Our families had most probably initially met at St John's. I think Molly had been confirmed at St John's at the same time as Dennis.

Molly and Dennis had had a difficult relationship right from the start. There were always arguments which were quickly followed by making up. One time, Dennis had upset Molly when he'd been seen with another girl and for a while Molly had ended their friendship. They had started seeing each other again a few years later and seemed to get along much better.

Dennis visited Kenya in 1926, wishing to use his farming knowledge over there, returning full of enthusiasm for the country. Molly decided to accompany him on his return journey in late 1927.

On 4th February 1928 they were married in Mombasa. They decided to stay and make a new life for themselves in Kenya.

I was in my final year at Culcheth Hall School when my mother and father made the journey together by steamship to Mombasa, leaving me at home with Nora and Lucy. Their journey was arduous but they arrived just in time for Molly's wedding. Mother was terribly excited about the trip, having never travelled so far before, but she did not travel well and took to her cabin for almost the entire journey. Father, who I now know must have inherited his sea legs from his father, found the trip most enjoyable and made many new acquaintances. Their ship, the *Guildford Castle*, docked in Plymouth in April. Upon his arrival home my father said he couldn't wait to go back there. Mother was less enthusiastic.

After their trip away, Mother was called to her family home in Clarendon Road, as her father had been taken ill. He had lived alone for some time now and his health had recently deteriorated. Aunt Marion agreed to take on the care of my grandfather and when he died on 8th July 1928, she and my uncle Alan inherited over £1,000.

Mother and Father attended my grandfather's funeral. They were extremely solemn upon their return that afternoon. Mother disappeared to her bedroom and we did not see her until the following day, and my father made only one comment, saying my grandfather was a good man.

Later that year we received news that Molly was to have a child. Her first son was born on Christmas Day and they named him Gerald Noel. We were also informed that Kate now had a second daughter named Patricia, but Mother talked much less about that grandchild.

*

I finished school in the summer of 1928. After I left school my father wanted to know what I was going to do with myself. 'You must get yourself a ticket,' he said. I knew what he meant by 'ticket', of course, as I had heard him say the same thing to my sisters and brother on numerous occasions. The problem was I had no idea what it was I wanted to do with my life.

'I wouldn't think about it too deeply, my dear, as once you are married your husband will expect you to stay at home and look after your family,' my mother helpfully advised me. Mother could be so old-fashioned about things. She was living in a changing world and had no intention of trying to keep up.

My father was more practical. 'What do you enjoy doing, my dear?'

I thought about this briefly and replied, 'I like being here, at home. I enjoy the simple things in life, such as cookery and needlework.' Having very little experience of the larger world, this was all I really knew. Nora had experienced the same dilemma. Having left school with no particular qualifications, she had been unable or unwilling to further her prospects. Both Mother and Father had now given up trying to secure her a 'ticket'.

'I refuse to take the same course with you as we have with Nora. You will acquire a ticket. You are much more capable than your sister.' My father had enough determination for the two of us.

It was then Mother suggested I attend a domestic science college. 'I understand there is an excellent one in London,' she added.

Father's face was a picture. 'Hold your horses a moment, Ethel. How do you know about this college?' I could tell he was wondering how much it was going to cost him.

Mother evidently recognised that expression on his face as well. 'Do you want the child to secure herself a ticket or not?'

'Of course I do.'

'Then I think it is an excellent solution. She can learn about the things she enjoys doing around the house. It most likely will allow her to find some form of work afterwards, but it will certainly stand her in good stead for when she has her own family.'

So it was decided. I was sent to London. I stood little chance of changing their minds, so I decided not to even try.

The idea of visiting London for a year excited me. To get away from my parents for that amount of time thrilled me even more. I was ready for an adventure, yet I had no idea how hard I was expected to work.

I completed a one-year course which covered so much there was little time for exploration or fun. In needlework, I became competent in all areas of household sewing. I mastered the art of patching, darning and hemstitching, and my knitting skills improved significantly. I already knew how to sew and darn, as Mother had shown me, but I became quite accomplished at sewing pillow cases and towels. I could turn my hand to repairing just about any item of household linen, but, if I'm honest, I didn't enjoy sewing. Molly was far more interested in sewing than I was, and better at it.

Under the heading of home management I learnt about hygiene. We were taught how to wash dishes and saucepans, how to care for and clean metals and how to correctly lay a table. Personal hygiene was also taught and I learnt how to care properly for my hair, teeth and nails, but my favourite subject remained cookery. By the time I'd left the college, I was able to boil, steam, fry, bake, roast, sauté and stew just about anything.

I found a great deal of my time at domestic college a chore, but by the end of the course I had gained a qualification and had enjoyed time away from my parents to consider my options. Sadly, I was no closer to having made any definitive decision on my future and returned to Church Bank, to life with my parents.

While I had been away, it appeared a number of changes had taken place at home. My father had moved his office to King Street, reducing his rent substantially, and my mother's health seemed to have deteriorated. I had endured a couple of visits from my mother and father while in London, but it was not until I arrived home that I noticed the change in my mother. She had never been a slim woman, but in the last year she had gained some extra weight. I soon discovered she had also paid a visit to the doctor and was now taking tablets she called 'vitamins' each day. She told me they were for her heart. She had been experiencing a shortness of breath and some pain in her chest. The doctor had told her to lose weight, do less and get more rest. How he expected her to do all that, I'll never know. She struggled to lose weight, but I tried to do more for her. Having my recent training helped, especially as we only had one part-time domestic working for us at this time. My mother's health appeared to improve.

When Nora asked if she could go to Kenya to visit Molly, my father said he thought it a good opportunity for Mother to stop chasing after her all the time and to get some rest. Nora arrived in Mombasa in October 1929, eager to meet baby Gerald and see her sister again. She returned home in time for Christmas, full of stories about her trip, but had missed Lucy's wedding in the November. We spent the next few days swapping stories and catching up.

After her marriage to James Wiley at St John's church, Lucy went to live on Brooklands Road in Sale. James Wiley qualified as a doctor in 1920 and it was from their large home on Brooklands Road that he now conducted his private surgery. He was somewhat older than my sister, but Lucy seemed extremely happy with him and was soon expecting their first child.

One Sunday after church, when lunch was finished, I was relaxing with my parents in the front room of our home. Father was intent on catching up with his newspapers, which he liked to do every Sunday. Mother was flicking through the ones he had already read, and I had found myself a good book to read by Anthony Trollope.

Mother interrupted my concentration, asking my father, 'Have you seen this notice in the *Manchester Guardian*, Harry?' She handed him the paper. 'Did you know there are plans to pull down St John's in Manchester? Don't you have family buried in that graveyard?'

'Not in the graveyard, but I understand we have in the vault, under the church,' said Father. 'I did know about this. They want to get rid of the church and turn it into an open space for all to enjoy. The church is not needed any more.'

'What will they do with all the bodies that are buried there?' I asked.

'Too many to move,' replied Father, rather resigned to this fact.

When my father finished reading the announcement, I asked if I could take a look. In the article, Manchester Corporation stated they 'would leave the human remains interred in the vault and deposit in such vault any memorials not disposed of beforehand, filling in the vault with dry soil to ground level'.

'Filling in the vault seems terribly wrong and insensitive, Father. Don't you think?'

'They call it *progress*, darling.'

'It says here they are also going to lift and take away most of the gravestones and the ones that are left will be covered with soil to make flower beds or footpaths.'

'I think it disgraceful,' Mother commented.

I had to agree. All those poor people who must have been buried there, over the years, forgotten forever once the church and gravestones were removed.

'How many people do you think have been buried there, Father?'

'Thousands, I should expect.'

'That many?' asked my mother.

'It also says, "Any friends or relatives of any deceased persons of whom memorial tablets have been erected can arrange to have them removed at a reasonable expense." Do we need to do anything, Father?'

'I think we should leave well alone. That is their resting place and they will be none the wiser as to what is happening above ground.'

Those were my father's final words on the matter, but it made me realise, even when we are dead, it can be difficult to escape 'progress', as my father put it.

58

In 1930, when I was eighteen, I found myself repeatedly tied to my home when I had wanted to be out with my friends. It was a difficult period in my life. We never had prior warning of when Mother would take a turn for the worse. Some days she was fine; on others she was almost bedridden. My father was rarely at home and there was no one else to look after her, so this responsibility fell to me.

In the April, before my birthday, Mother's health improved slightly and my fifty-eight-year-old father made the decision to visit Kate in New Zealand. Rupert would also be there, as he had chosen to remain in the country after finding some farm work. My father travelled alone, as my mother had not wanted to accompany him, using her illness as an excuse.

Nora left the following month to visit Molly in Kenya. She too had more pressing things to do than stay at home in England. Molly was expecting another baby in the June and Nora had said she would be there to look after two-year-old Gerald. In truth, Nora was concerned for Molly, as Molly had confided in her during a previous visit, saying that since the birth of their first child, she and husband Dennis had been experiencing some marital problems.

In her excitement and apprehension to see her sister again, the last thing Nora expected to happen was that she should fall in love. She was on board the steamship *Madura* in the May of 1930, and also travelling second class was George Turner, one of many British Empire crown agents. Having worked with oversea governments for many years, George was used to travelling and took Nora under his wing. Apparently they hit it off immediately. As George shared his knowledge of Kenya and explained the many construction projects he was overseeing and what his role was there, Nora listened, captivated by this fascinating stranger. She explained she was visiting her sister in Kenya, so George asked if he could pay her some visits while she was there.

Molly's second child was another son, named Brian Darnley, this time given his grandmother's family name. My mother was very pleased to learn of this fact. George and Nora enjoyed taking the baby out for walks in his pram and the two became inseparable, according to Molly.

Soon after, my mother and father received a letter from Nora informing them of her marriage. Nora was not to return home. She had travelled with George out of Kenya, across the border and into Uganda. There they had settled in a place called Kampala. In her letter Nora described Kampala as having breathtaking scenery. She wrote, 'I have never seen so many miles of hills, valleys and open countryside, upon which there are scattered groups of corrugated iron shanties and sheds which the people there use for both shops and homes. Some of these areas were pretty poor and needed much building work to be completed.' George apparently was there to supervise some of this building work and oversee the completion of the railway line which was being built at Kampala.

While Nora was making a new life for herself out in Uganda, I was travelling with Mother between Church Bank and Brooklands Road, visiting Lucy, as her first child had been born in the August of 1930. Lucy now had a daughter, Anne. On the days Mother felt well, we would catch a train from Altrincham and Bowdon station to Brooklands station, and from there we would have a short walk to Lucy's house. At this time they had begun to test new electric trains on the line, but it wasn't until May the following year that the service became fully electric. Father, who returned from visiting Kate in the February of 1931, was rather impressed by these new trains. He said he could get to work a lot quicker now and wouldn't have to leave the house so early. The electric trains were faster and ran more frequently than the steam trains they replaced. Father said their only drawback was that they were busier now, as more people seemed to want to use them.

Father and I would often travel to visit Lucy at the weekend, if Mother wished to be by herself. These visits were always fun and I enjoyed playing with my little niece. Father got on well with Lucy's husband Jim. This may have been because he was older or perhaps because of his intellect and work as a doctor. I overheard Father asking Jim about my mother's affliction one day, but they stopped talking as soon as I entered the room.

Lucy and I were also getting on better than ever before. She had taken to motherhood very naturally and was very happy with her life. We became quite close during this time and she really appreciated my help with the baby. I loved pushing my niece's pram around the

261

local streets and along Baguley Brook on fine days. I smiled to myself as passers-by said hello, peering into the deep-bodied pram with little wheels, assuming the child inside was mine. I often went along with this fantasy, as it was far easier than having to explain.

In March 1931, my father received a sum of money after the death of his ninety-year-old spinster aunt. He was very private about things like this and would never have discussed the sum. She had for many years lived on Arnold Road in Whalley Range. She was my grandfather's sister, and my father told me that when he was a young child he could remember his aunt Ellen living with his family for a time. She had then moved to Arnold Road, where she had remained for more than forty years, during the last of which she had been cared for by my uncle Robert and aunt Evelyn. In return for her care, my great-aunt put her house into my uncle's name, so that it would pass to him when she died. My father visited his aunt most weeks, usually on the days he visited his mother. She had always been very fond of my father, which was why she had also arranged to leave a sum of money for him in her will.

*

When Rupert turned up at Church Bank completely out of the blue one day in the June of 1931, my mother was delighted to see him and eager to hear all about his time away. She had been feeling a little unwell that morning but appeared to suddenly improve upon Rupert's arrival. He had been gone for almost four years and had greatly changed. He felt almost a stranger to me. I could hardly think of the brother who had left all those years before as being the same person who stood before me that day. We had never been particularly close and he used to tease me as a child, but he could do no wrong in Mother's eyes. Father, on the other hand, had been a little less impressed by some of his antics over the years.

Rupert told us all about his visit to New Zealand to see Kate and how he had found himself a job working as a station hand on a large cattle farm. My father was little excited by his stories and asked, 'What are you going to do with yourself now that you have returned?'

'Let's not worry about that today, Harry,' interrupted my mother. 'Tell us what else you have been up to, darling.'

Over the next few months Rupert trained as a mechanic and found himself a job working in a local garage. He hadn't been there long when he started to get itchy feet and talked about another visit to Kate. On the 2nd January 1932 he left for New Zealand.

Kate was not very pleased about his swift return. I was furious. He left two weeks before my father's sixtieth birthday: a landmark occasion, we all thought, especially as my father had suggested he might soon retire from work. There was a small birthday celebration at the house, just for the immediate family, as Father didn't want anything too grand. I was cross with my brother for his obvious lack of compassion and found it hard to celebrate without thinking of Rupert and getting annoyed.

59

Soon after Rupert left, we received news from Nora. She and George now had a son. Once again a family name had been passed down to the next generation. My father was thrilled that it should be his this time. Robert Greaves had been born at the end of November and Nora promised in her letter that she would arrange a visit home with George and the baby before the year was out.

I was pleased to hear this news, as I had been feeling for some time that my mother's health was slowly deteriorating. I had expressed this much in recent letters to Kate, Molly and Nora. I didn't expect Kate to visit home. Mother would not have welcomed this, and Kate had said in her letter that it might even aggravate my mother's condition.

Molly had written back immediately enclosing news that her marriage was a sham. She knew her husband had been unfaithful, she suspected on more than one occasion. She explained how terribly unhappy she had been when she had been diagnosed with syphilis. She asked that I not mention any of this to our parents. Under the circumstances I felt she was probably right.

Molly arrived with her two young sons in mid-September of 1932. She had struggled to find the fare for the journey and felt unable to ask her husband for help as she was coming home to have treatment for her condition.

Mother and Father were delighted by her visit but were a little concerned that Dennis had not accompanied her and the boys. At first Molly explained her husband had work commitments. Later she confided in my mother about how miserable she was with Dennis but felt unable to reveal the full extent of what had been going on.

Molly took a great deal of convincing, but when she eventually left to return to Kenya, she told our parents she was willing to give Dennis another chance and they were hopeful she would be able to work things out.

December 1932 was a special time. Nora, George and one-year-old Robert arrived in England early in December, but firstly went to stay with George's family in Woking. They did not arrive at Church Bank until the Christmas week, after a four-hour journey by train. The whole house seemed to come alive upon their arrival and that Christmas remains very special in my memory.

Mother and Father were so excited to see Nora. They had never expected she would marry, let alone have any children. Nora, too, felt she had been blessed. I had never seen her looking so happy, and little Robert was a delight, such a happy boy. He was content to sit and watch the family, as though he could understand every word that was being said. Lucy, Jim and their two-year-old daughter also joined us for Christmas Day. Mother made a huge effort, ensuring everyone enjoyed themselves that Christmas. We were not to know it would be her last.

The house was adorned lavishly downstairs with holly, ivy and mistletoe and we had a huge, decorated Christmas tree with real candles that twinkled magically when lit. On Christmas Day we all went to church in the morning, then my sisters and I helped our mother to get the dinner ready. By early afternoon the dining table displayed a selection of foods fit for the King.

When King George delivered his Christmas speech over the wireless, it was as if Mother had been frozen in time. She had warned us beforehand that if anyone dared to even whisper during it, she would be most upset. We all sat as quiet as church mice throughout its duration. When the King had finished talking, Mother raised her glass to the wireless, saying, 'God bless the King and a happy Christmas to the royal family.' Finally we could all breathe and speak again.

I shall never forget that Christmas. We were all so happy and life was good.

*

The following year in April, Lucy had a second child, a son, named David. Once again Lucy embraced her role as mother and three-year-old Anne was thrilled to have a baby brother. Mother and I couldn't stay away, visiting Lucy almost daily. Lucy was pleased to have us there.

When the baby was a couple of weeks old, my mother, father and I spent the whole of one Saturday with Lucy. We all enjoyed a delightful day together, which included a spring walk amongst the blossom trees. Anne collected small posies of blossom and presented each of us with one. We laughed at her many entertaining mannerisms and were astounded by her abundance of confidence and wisdom.

'She knows far too much for a three-year-old,' my father commented, following this up good-humouredly with, 'She must get her intelligence from her grandfather.'

We all laughed and Anne asked what we were laughing at, becoming quite cross with her adult family members for being so silly. This of course increased our amusement and Lucy ended up having to pull her daughter to one side to calm the poor child down.

Upon our return to Church Bank later that afternoon, we were greeted on the doorstep by an unexpected visitor. Once again, out of the blue, Rupert had returned home. He had been away for almost eighteen months.

Rupert seemed a little subdued a day or two later, but I put that down to him not being able to walk back into his job at the garage. They had replaced him long ago and told him they had no other mechanic jobs available.

The next two weeks were difficult, to say the least. Father and Rupert did nothing but argue.

'When are you going to find yourself some work?' my father asked him almost every evening.

'I'm trying, Father. There doesn't seem to be much about at the moment. There is a recession on, you know.'

'I am fully aware of that, my boy, but it's hardly a skilled job you're looking for now, is it?'

'That's a little unfair, Harry. Rupert works very hard, I'm sure,' said my mother.

'Rupert doesn't work, *full stop*,' replied my father.

And so this continued for two weeks, until Rupert eventually found himself some short-term employment. That was the day before my twenty-first birthday.

On the Saturday morning of my birthday, my mother, father and I were having breakfast when Rupert decided to join us in the dining room. Our domestic had fetched in the post, along with the breakfast things, and Father was reading a letter from Kate. Its contents had clearly irritated him and his mood changed quickly from one of celebration for me to exasperation with Rupert.

'So this is why you've returned home with your tail between your legs,' announced my father, waving the letter high in the air for all to see. 'Your sister is well and truly fed up with your antics. No wonder she sent you home.'

'Do we have to do this now, dear? It is Janet's special day and it would be a shame to spoil it.' Mother spoke very quietly and slowly, and it wasn't until she spoke that it struck me she didn't look too well this morning. She had obviously been making an effort because it was my birthday.

At that very moment my father appeared to have the same

266

thought, for he backed off, saying, 'You're right, my dear. I'll discuss this with you later, Rupert. After breakfast, mind, so don't disappear.'

'Have you remembered it's your sister's birthday, darling?' Mother asked Rupert, ever hopeful.

'Of course,' lied Rupert, smiling sweetly at Mother. 'But she will have to wait until later for her gift. I have yet to pick it up.'

My father tutted.

I only caught snippets of my father and brother's heated conversation later, as I tried with difficulty to listen through the door. Piecing bits together, I realised Rupert had been up to no good with a number of women from a village close to Kate and Frank's home. I heard my father shout the word 'married!' a couple of times. It seemed Kate had become quite embarrassed about the whole thing and had sent Rupert packing.

When Rupert presented me with my gift that evening, it was a small heart-shaped gold locket on a gold chain. It was very pretty and I thanked him, suspecting he'd purchased it earlier in the day. Mother commented, 'How delicate it is,' and, 'Such a fitting gesture.' Father refused to acknowledge Rupert or his gift, choosing to hide behind his newspaper instead.

My mother and father had already given me their gift. Well, we had already discussed it, I should say. After much discussion and turning of pages in his atlas, Father and I had walked into Altrincham, where he had booked a fabulous cruise trip for later that year. To say I was excited could not even begin to describe how I felt. It was all I and my friends ever spoke about for the next few months.

60

By August my brother was showing a great deal of interest in my planned cruise trip and I got the distinct impression he too would like to travel again. He had moved out of Church Bank and was staying with a relation of Molly's husband on Willow Tree Road. He and my father had not been getting along. Rupert's job had come to an end and he had been unable to find another. He and Father argued all the time and my father, concerned for my mother's health, had asked Rupert to find somewhere else to live. This he had done with little resistance. I suspect he didn't want to be under the same roof as his parents any more, anyway.

Rupert would sometimes join us on a Sunday, for lunch. He would be on his best behaviour as my father had warned him any arguments may cause my mother's health to worsen.

After one lunch we were sat together in the sitting room. 'There's not long to wait now before your cruise, is there, Janet?' Rupert asked.

'I can't wait. I'm so excited.'

'I'm sure you are. I really enjoyed visiting Kate and experiencing what New Zealand has to offer. I miss it and the way of life over there. You mustn't say anything to Mother or Father, but I'm thinking of visiting Molly soon.'

'Are you?' I asked, not really surprised. 'When?'

'Hopefully later this month. I'm just finalising the details with Dennis.'

'Does Molly know you're going?'

'Of course. Dennis will have told her.'

I hope so, I thought.

Later that month, Rupert was furious when forced to change his plans, as my father asked him to temporarily move in with my grandmother. My grandmother had just undergone a small operation and, although my aunt Ellen could care for her, they needed someone who could lift and help to move her for a short time while she recuperated.

Father had no idea of Rupert's plans for travelling as he had not mentioned them to our parents. Rupert confided in me that he had already booked a place on a steamship leaving London on 25th August. He would now have to rebook this trip and possibly lose his money. I had little sympathy for him.

'It will only be for a few weeks. A month at the most,' my father told Rupert. 'It's not as though you have anything else to do now, is it? Janet has to look after your mother and has a cruise trip booked, so she cannot help. I have to go into work, but I will call in to see you as much as I can, and so will your uncle.'

Rupert reluctantly agreed. He'd always got along with Granny.

'I will just have to put my plans on hold for a month,' he told me quietly.

Rupert managed to rearrange his trip and, once Granny was better, he left London by ship on 22nd September, while I was away on my cruise.

I departed for my cruise on the SS *Voltaire* in the September and travelled to Madeira, Lisbon and Casablanca across the North Atlantic. It would have been too hot during the summer months. There I discovered that the island of Madeira is at the top of a massive shield volcano, so called because it resembles a warrior's shield lying on the ground. Because it is a volcanic island the soil is excellent for growing. The vegetation is a glorious emerald green. Exotic flowers of all colours line the roads and paths wherever you go.

After a seafood lunch on the island we were allowed to do some exploring. Many of the beaches there were black and rocky, scattered with boulders rather than shells, but we managed to enjoy a rest on one beach while admiring the spectacular scenery.

Next we travelled to Lisbon, admiring the coastline of Portugal as we approached. Lisbon was full of picturesque, narrow, cobbled lanes and back alleys, housing colourful old dwellings, and pretty beaches that sat below hilltop towns. Here we consumed more delicious fish and were able to visit a museum.

Casablanca also had great food, lovely restaurants and amazing architecture. We had enough time to look around a museum and art gallery.

I made many new acquaintances during my trip. One girl, named Muriel, would remain a firm friend of mine for many years to come.

*

After returning from my cruise, I noticed a further decline in my mother's health. Father suggested we all take a holiday to Wales and stay at our favourite bed-and-breakfast destination in Rhos-on-Sea. He booked this for the Christmas period. We had stayed with Miss Monroe for holidays for as long as I could remember. She and Father had always got along very well, and I wondered if at times my mother had been a little jealous of this fact. I had never warmed to the woman myself, but Father obviously liked her and what she had to offer.

'The sea air should do Mother some good,' I agreed.

'We can live in hope,' said Father.

'It's just what the doctor ordered,' my mother reassured us.

We left soon afterwards, packing extra layers for the winter months. At the station my father complained we were taking too much luggage as he struggled with the cases, but he was soon to realise our judgement had been accurate, as we enjoyed brisk, blustery walks along the sea front and promenade.

The week after we arrived in Wales, my mother's health quickly declined. Much to our horror, my father and I watched helplessly as my mother passed away on 18th December 1933. She had been in her mid-fifties; no age at all, really.

A few days after her death, we buried my mother in the cemetery of St Trillo, overlooking the sea. I had attended a number of services here with my mother in the past. She had commented one sunny morning, after the Sunday service, as we took a stroll across the graveyard, how this would be a pleasant spot to end up.

I don't wish to dwell on this time in my life, as it is too upsetting. Needless to say, everything changed that winter for me and my father. We had some adjusting to do.

I recall my father's impatience as we travelled home on the train, and the conversation he began about what he was going to do next and what I should do with my life. Father announced he was thinking about retiring from his job altogether. I wondered if this thought was a little premature. He had been into his office significantly less since my mother's health had deteriorated, and now he was saying he would like to spend more time travelling.

'We must find you something that will fill your time, my dear, take your mind off recent events.' At the time neither of us knew what this would be.

Then, a week or so after returning home to what was now a very different house, my father called me into the sitting room, wishing to share with me an advert for a college he'd come across in his paper. 'I think this will be just the *ticket*, my dear. You've always liked babies and children and it says here, "Suited for educated women who have a natural sympathy with young children." Do you remember how good you were with little Elaine? You adore Lucy's two. You'd move in with Lucy if she let you.'

I had to agree with my father. The advert he had come across excited me.

Over the next twelve months, my life was to change dramatically.

61

I began my training to become a nursery nurse at Withington's Princess Christian College in February 1934. The college had originally opened in 1901 in Kersal. By 1908 the college was firmly established and became a limited company, relocating to Wilmslow Road, and in 1919 it had moved premises again to 26 Wilbraham Road.

The college was residential, so I lived there for most of the time. Father suggested I stay with my sister Lucy on the occasions I came home, so it was her address I gave to the college. This enabled my father to travel, as and when he wished, without having to worry about me.

Father paid the college fees in two instalments, the first before the commencement of my training and the second within the first fifteen weeks. My training consisted of two terms of fifteen weeks each. Practical training was offered by the residence in the college of

271

several children under six years of age, as well as younger infants. The subjects taught included infant feeding, nursery management, domestic work, nursery laundry-work, nursery cooking, needlework, first aid, home nursing and general rules of health. Students had to be at least twenty years of age and unmarried. After obtaining my nurse's certificate, I would be required to find my own post and arrange my salary. At last, I had begun to feel excited about my prospects and my future.

My father took immediate advantage of my being away at college and booked a journey by ship to visit Kate, saying he would be back at the end of June to see how I was getting on. While he was away my grandmother, who had reached the grand old age of eighty-nine, took an unexpected turn for the worse after her operation and sadly died. Lucy and my aunts arranged my grandmother's funeral, which took place on 4th May at Southern Cemetery. It was decided not to send word to my father but to wait for him to return. My grandmother was laid to rest in the family grave, next to my grandfather. It was soon after this that my aunt Emily moved away to live in Colwyn Bay.

Upon my father's return, later in the year, Lucy was tasked with informing him of his mother's death. He was both shocked and devastated that he had not been with her when she had died.

During my break from college, Lucy was able to share some happier news. Two of our first cousins on our father's side, Marie Bradshaw and Frank Coates, had married in London. Marie was my uncle William's child and she had been born in Paraguay. Frank was son to my aunt Ellen. Lucy and I had no idea the pair had even met, but apparently they had at my uncle's funeral and instantly felt an attraction to one another.

'I think it's rather romantic, don't you, Lucy?' I asked at the dinner table, one lunchtime.

Lucy's husband replied instead. 'I happen to think it's rather unhealthy.'

When I asked Lucy later why her husband had said this, she

272

replied, 'He was being silly; just ignore him.' Nothing more was said about it.

When I discovered later that year the couple now had a son, I felt reluctant to discuss this with Lucy, as husband Jim was always around. I decided to write to my cousins instead, expressing my best wishes and congratulations, and enclosed a small gift for the child. I received a letter by return post, full of praise for my kind thoughts, and since that day I have remained in constant contact with my cousins.

While Father visited Kate in New Zealand, my brother Rupert was with Molly in Kenya. Rupert had been in Kenya since the end of September the previous year. It had been said, on more than one occasion, that he was making himself at home over there and enjoyed that way of life.

During this time the house at Church Bank stood empty. I hated to see it that way but since my mother had died, my father had wanted to spend less and less time there. I spent my summer break sneaking back to Church Bank from Lucy's home, the reason being that I had met a young man.

I had reluctantly agreed to go to a dance in Altrincham with some friends, which was where I met Gerald. Lucy had insisted I enjoy my break.

'You should get out of the house more and go and enjoy yourself. Why you should want to hang around here all the time with my two, I shall never know. It will be time to go back to college before you know it. Go and have some fun.'

I took her advice.

I talked and danced with Gerald for most of the evening, much to the amusement of all my friends. At the end of the evening, he asked if he could see me again and we arranged to meet. I saw Gerald almost every day during the four weeks I was away from college.

Gerald was four and a half years older than me. He had been born in 1907 in Stretford and shortly afterwards his family had moved to Vicarage Lane in Bowdon, where he'd grown up. His father was a pawnbroker's assistant and he had two sisters and one brother. He'd gone to Bowdon College, a boarding school which took day boys, on South Downs Road. He'd been brought up as a gentleman but had no trade. He had found it difficult to find work because of the depression. Now he worked for the *Altrincham and Bowdon Guardian*, at the Grafton Street depot, where he sold space in the paper for advertising.

Gerald had gone to school with a chap called Ted Ainsworth. They had remained good friends. Like Gerald, Ted had struggled to find work and now sold space for advertising. He had recently married a girl named Molly and the four of us went out a few times together during this period. Molly and I formed a firm friendship. She was so easy to get along with and we found we had a great deal in common.

My and Gerald's relationship moved quickly and before long we found ourselves in a situation there was no getting away from. Most afternoons we would make our way to Church Bank, chatting and enjoying one another's company. This particular afternoon, it was especially hot and we had taken some drinks out onto the lawn. Gerald kissed me, passionately. We had kissed before, but not like this. There was a hunger in his kiss that led us into the house, where we took our relationship a step further.

During our lovemaking, I could not have felt more at ease. I had never experienced such a rush of emotions, but afterwards I was taken over by a feeling of absolute panic.

As we lay in each other's arms, I wondered what my father would have to say if he knew. What would Lucy think of me? What if I was pregnant? A terrible feeling of shame and remorse came over me. I felt so guilty and Gerald could see I was unhappy.

'We should never have allowed that to happen,' I told him.

'There's not a lot we can do about that now, though, is there?'

'What if I'm pregnant?'

'You won't be. Stop worrying.'

'But what if I am? Have you done this before, Gerald?'

'What do you mean?'

'You know what I mean. Have you been with another girl in this way?'

'No. Of course not. You are my first.'

Although relieved by his admission, I still worried. 'What do we do now?'

'What do you mean, "what do we do now"?'

Was he trying to be stupid? 'What if I *am* pregnant?'

'If you're pregnant, then I'll marry you,' he said with some finality.

'You would do that?'

'Of course. In fact, why don't we just get married anyway? Ted and Molly seem happy enough. So why shouldn't we?'

This backhanded proposal caught me off guard. 'We can't!' I almost shouted.

'Why not?'

I thought about it. There was no reason why we couldn't. Who was going to stop us?

'Why don't we just get married?' he asked again.

So I agreed, but I insisted he tell no one.

On Friday 15th June we caught a train to Knutsford and were married at the registry office. It all happened very quickly and with little planning, as I was due to return to college on the Monday. I had never been one for a lot of fuss. We pulled two complete strangers off the street to witness the ceremony, then enjoyed our first stroll as man and wife around Tatton Park. Later, we had a meal at a local inn, where we spent our first night of marriage together. Gerald organised everything and made the day very special. He had purchased a gold wedding ring incorporating three diamonds, from his father's pawn shop, the day before, and I loved it.

I returned to Lucy's house the next day and she had no idea I had married. I had told her I'd been staying with a friend overnight and felt terribly guilty about lying to her. As soon as Father returned, I would tell him and Lucy my news, but for now I had to focus on returning to college and completing my second term. This would prove far more challenging than expected.

Gerald and I both knew it would be difficult to be apart from one another so soon after our wedding and to hide the fact that we were married, especially from the college. They would never have allowed me to continue with my training if we had told them, and my father would have been furious with me for wasting his money. We had no choice. I remained Miss Bradshaw, wearing my wedding ring upon a chain around my neck, hidden under my uniform. I could tell no one.

I did say I had plans to marry later that year, at least. I was pleased I had. It made my stay more bearable, as I was free to talk about Gerald.

However, the situation soon became much more complicated when I discovered I was pregnant.

62

As mentioned, my father was in New Zealand with Kate and Rupert was in Kenya staying with Molly. While he was away, my father received some devastating news. Molly sent a telegram addressed to Kate's home explaining my brother had been shot and killed. Kate later told me that Father had taken the news badly and for some time did not know what he should do.

I was sure the story surrounding my brother's death, as my father told it, was not the entire truth. He always maintained that my brother had tripped over his own gun, accidentally releasing the safety catch, while out hunting one day. Both Kate and Molly would later tell me it was suspected, although never proved, that Rupert's death had been due to an irate African farmhand, whose wife Rupert had been seen with on more than one occasion. Molly always maintained her husband Dennis had encouraged this behaviour in our brother. I then understood why my father had stuck to this story all his life. I felt terrible for my father, for first having missed the death of his mother while abroad and then having lost Rupert so suddenly and in suspicious circumstances.

*

I completed my training in the October of 1934. Miss Holloway, the principal, wrote a remark in my testimonial book upon completion of the course. It read, 'Miss Bradshaw has the makings of a good and efficient nurse but has rather lacked the incentive – due probably to excitement at the thought of her approaching marriage – and her work has sometimes suffered in consequence.'

I congratulated myself on keeping both my marriage and my pregnancy a secret while at college. I had discovered I was pregnant soon after my marriage, sharing this secret only with Gerald. Towards the end of my training, it had become more difficult to disguise my swelling belly. All I had to do now was inform my father.

Hearing the news that I had secretly married and was now with child at first shocked my father. He said very little. His silence frightened and concerned me. The poor man had endured a terrible year and I was afraid my news might push him over the edge. He was, after all, in his sixties now. I did not know it at the time, but he had also received some more distressing news from Molly.

After some minutes had passed, which in all honesty felt like hours, he asked, 'Can you give me some time to digest what you have told me?'

'Of course, Father. I am sorry if I have upset you.'

'I admit this was not what I had expected along with your homecoming, but you seem happy. Are you happy, Janet?'

'Very much so, Father. I would very much like you to meet Gerald.'

'I shall, my dear, all in good time. All in good time. I suspect you would much rather be with him than here right now. We can talk again tomorrow.'

My father accepted what I'd done and met Gerald two days later. It was during this meeting he told us he would be booking another trip to visit Molly in Kenya and, by his return, would have found somewhere else to live. I was shocked. My father also informed me he was to sign over the deeds of the house to me, if I wanted them. Gerald and I looked at each other in surprise.

'Where else are you going to live and bring up your family?' he asked.

Before his departure he'd signed the house over to me and secured himself rooms at a house in Hale. He appeared quite content with the decisions he'd made.

My father left for Kenya on 16th November 1934 on a ship named *Mantola*. He was away for a number of weeks. I assumed he had gone because of Rupert's death, but what I didn't know at that time was that Molly and Dennis had separated, shortly after Rupert had been killed. My father had gone to Kenya to support her and to make sure she was financially secure. Upon his return, my father reassured me that Molly was much happier now without Dennis, but said it was going to be difficult for Gerald and Brian to adjust without their father. He never disclosed to me the reason for my sister's separation, but I knew she held Dennis partly responsible for our brother's death.

My father brought home with him a photograph of Rupert's grave. A rather morbid thing to do, I thought, but it was something he obviously needed to have. He carried it around with him for some time afterwards and must have felt the loss of his only son far more than we all could have imagined.

While my father was away, Gerald and I spent Christmas with Lucy and her family. She had received news from Nora. Our sister now had a second son: 'a handsome little boy', according to his mother, whom they had named Edward. Nora had also mentioned the strong possibility of a visit to England the following year. I was excited by this prospect.

I passed on my sister's news to Father when he returned. I was also able to introduce him to another of his grandchildren, as I had given birth to a daughter at the end of February 1935, a matter of weeks before my father's return. Our daughter had been born at Church Bank, where Dr Craig and Nurse White were on hand to oversee events. We eventually settled on a name for her, but that was after much discussion. Gerald and I had no idea something as simple as a name would be so difficult to agree upon. I wanted to call my daughter Jane Claire: Jane after myself, using the English form of Janet, and Claire after Gerald's mother. Gerald was having none of it. We disagreed over the name for days after her birth.

'I know, let's call her Paddy,' Gerald said mockingly one evening. 'Paddy, the next best thing.'

'Stop it, Gerald. It's not funny any more.'

An American film named *Paddy the Next Best Thing* had been released in recent years and had proved very popular. It was a romantic comedy based on the novel written in 1912 by Gertrude Page, which as a child I had enjoyed immensely.

We eventually agreed on a name, but Gerald would insist on calling our daughter Paddy and the name soon stuck.

My father was thrilled with his latest grandchild. He couldn't wait to hold her. 'That makes nine grandchildren. Five grandsons and four granddaughters,' he announced with pride. 'Let me have a look at her, then. Pass her here.' He examined her close to. 'Doesn't she have dark hair and glorious brown eyes? She's a beauty.'

As I handed over my small daughter into the safety of my father's arms, I realised for the first time the importance of a family. I longed for my mother, wishing she too could have experienced this day with us. It was not until then that it suddenly struck me how much I missed her. Those strong feelings of euphoria and loss, combined, are not something you want to hang on to for long, so I brushed them aside, as I might the leaves on the path outside, and got on with the rest of my life.

A baptism was arranged for our daughter in April. Gerald insisted we hold it at St Vincent's church, where his family regularly attended. Among the guests were my father and his landlady; Gerald's parents and sister Kathleen, who was to be godmother; Gerald's work colleague, Frank Jordan, who was godfather; Lucy and her family, and, at Father's invitation, Miss Monroe. Among the many gifts our daughter received that day were a silver mug, a silver bowl and spoon and two serviette rings. My father had purchased a large pram for her.

Our friends Ted and Molly also had a daughter in the same year. She would be known as Jonquil. Molly had gone to her parents' home in Marple to have her daughter, so we did not see her for some time.

In the July of 1935, Gerald and I took our daughter on her first holiday to Rhos-on-Sea. We took her away for a holiday to the coast every year, during the summer months, for the next four years, until the war broke out. In the summer of 1939, we enjoyed two months in Rhos-on-Sea, before Gerald rushed to joined up for the war.

63

In 1935 my father was living at Thornville on Ashley Road, his landlady a widow woman named Mary Ayrton. Mary had three children: one older son, four years younger than me, then, following a gap of a decade, two other children under ten. Her husband, her senior by ten years, had died in hospital about three years before. According to Father, Mary gives a harrowing account of this time in her life. Her husband had been the manager of an estate office. He had been on his way to work when he had suffered a massive heart attack while sitting in his car, waiting at the level crossing in Hale. He had been rushed to the Greenwood Street hospital in Altrincham, but later died. Mary had then been forced to take in lodgers to make ends meet.

Father was instantly taken with this woman. They appeared to have very little in common but seemed to get along well.

Gerald and I were invited round to the house on a number of occasions. Although a great deal older, Mary's children were very taken with Paddy and she seemed to like them and the attention they gave her. I felt a little sorry for them, losing their father so suddenly and so young.

I learnt through discussion with Mary, for she was one to talk incessantly if allowed, that her childhood had been one of poverty. She had grown up in Timperley, her father a railway worker. I could see that she treasured her home and her belongings and having money was vital to her existence. She had done well to marry into wealth the first time round and, when her husband had died, he had left her comfortably well off, but I could tell she was concerned these funds would one day run out. I was sure she was now working on my father, considering him a potential husband, but she came across as pleasant enough and it was not my place to interfere.

Father had been back in the country for a matter of months when he announced he and Mary were to marry. To be honest, I was rather taken aback and unsure it was the right decision. I had never warmed to this woman and was concerned the only reason she wished to marry my father was because of his wealth. Of course, I was unable to share these feelings with my father. If I had, I would have run the risk of losing him, as he was completely under her spell by this time.

My sisters were informed and Nora and her family made the trip from Uganda to England in the August of 1935, to attend the wedding. As with their previous visit, they went directly to Woking, where they stayed with George's parents. In the September we all travelled to Colwyn Bay, where my father stayed with Mary and her children at Miss Monroe's and Nora and I found other accommodation, close to Aunt Emily's home. Nora was very taken with this area and I can remember her saying at the time that she could see herself living here.

My aunt Emily had moved to Colwyn Bay after the death of my grandmother and she was pleased to be able to join her brother on his wedding day. She invited us all back to her house after the ceremony for a cold buffet supper.

Father and Mary were married in Conway at the registry office. I felt animosity towards my father's choice of venue for this occasion, so close to where my mother had been buried. He might as well have stamped upon my mother's grave, for it appeared he had erased her from his memory. If I had been Mary, I would have insisted upon a different location for my wedding. The woman appeared to have no conscience and no one else seemed to be affected by this decision;

not even Nora seemed to understand my concerns. I found the whole experience quite upsetting and was pleased when Gerald and I were able to return to Church Bank.

I was soon to realise my father's marriage was not a particularly happy one. It appeared to be a marriage of convenience, both on my father's part and on Mary's. I couldn't understand why my father should want this type of relationship. He'd taken very few personal belongings with him when he'd left Church Bank and never once asked to move any of his furniture into Mary's house. Whether this was his choice or Mary didn't want it, I do not know. I had thought it strange at the time and a little sad.

The first obvious sign that all was not as it should be in my father's marriage came three months after his wedding. On 14th December 1935 my father boarded a ship named the *Madura* bound for Mombasa. He travelled alone to see Molly and Nora. He did not spend this first Christmas with his new wife. I am unsure as to whether Mary had refused to go with him or whether he preferred it this way. It may have been that this time of year held too many difficult memories for him, as it did for us all. He did not return until May 1936, so he was away for Paddy's first birthday. This turned out to be a good thing, as there was an epidemic of measles at this time and we were unable to have a celebration.

Upon his return, my father seemed determined to make his marriage work, remaining in this country for the next twenty-one months. He threw himself into his work and we soon discovered that was where he spent most of his days and some of his nights.

64

My uncle owned a large residence, situated on a tree-lined street called Dudley Road in Whalley Range. He and my aunt had moved there shortly after his aunt's death, when they had sold her house, enabling them to purchase this one. Their house had the name Summerlands.

Uncle Robert had been forced to give up working with my father some years earlier, when the doctor had told him, after a long illness, that he needed to rest more. I can never recall a time after this, when visiting my uncle, that he was not suffering from a dry cough or a cold of some description. On one occasion, we all became quite distressed, as he experienced a coughing fit and afterwards had difficulty catching his breath. It was after that particular attack that I was discouraged from visiting with Father any more. He preferred to call in alone on his brother after his day at work.

In July 1937, the month before his death, my uncle's health quickly deteriorated. He lost his appetite and, according to my father, lost a great deal of weight. He was having difficulty with his breathing, feeling lightheaded and coughing up mucus all the time. He had complained of chest pains to my father and the doctor, but all the doctor had told him to do was to get as much rest as possible and to drink plenty of water.

It was my aunt who informed my father of his brother's death. She told my father that his brother had taken to his bed feeling more unwell than usual. As she sat with him, he had experienced a terrible pain, held onto his chest and suddenly stopped breathing.

I was able to attend my uncle's funeral with my father, as I had recently enrolled Paddy at Highbury Preparatory School. Paddy had settled quickly there and I was relaxed about leaving her. Molly and Ted's little girl also attended this school and together they were always getting into mischief.

The recent years' events had taken their toll on Father, together with his difficult second marriage, and his health started to suffer. He was not his cheerful self for quite some time. Slowly his health improved, but it took him a long time to find the strength he needed to travel again.

By 1938 my father was spending less and less time at home with his wife. Father and Mary appeared to be living separate lives, although they still, on occasion, slept under the same roof. When my father travelled, he would always register his workplace in King Street as his permanent address, rather than Thornville. It had quickly become clear to him that this was Mary's home, and her address was recorded in local telephone directories as being the home of Mrs M Bradshaw: no mention of my father's name. I can only assume that at this time, less than three years into their marriage, it had already reached its conclusion. Little did I realise his marriage would not be the only one.

My father cannot have been happy that his marriage to Mary was not a success, but he shared few emotions on this subject. Instead he threw himself into spending all his free time with his daughters and grandchildren, roaming from one to the other, unable to find true contentment with any. The problem was that there was no one who would ever be able to replace my mother.

Father was desperate to leave this country again, but before he did, he was able to join us for a small party in celebration of Paddy's third birthday. Ted, Molly and Jonquil were also able to join us at Church Bank, along with Lucy and her two boys, David and John. Lucy's eight-year-old daughter felt she was too grown up and asked to stay at home with her father. Paddy enjoyed her special day, her grandfather spoiling her the most. She received many gifts: a doll's pram, doll's house, toy ironing board and toy ice cream cart, to name but a few.

My father's next trip took place at the end of February 1938. Now sixty-six years old, he caught a ship from Southampton to New Zealand to visit Kate. During his time away, Molly remarried in April. She had been through an unpleasant divorce from Dennis but thankfully found happiness with a gentleman named Charles Nicolson who was more than happy to take on her two boys and couldn't wait to add to the family. Together they purchased land, cleared it and created a large farm holding near Thompson Falls, employing many local families. Here Molly was mother, nurse and midwife to her many workers. Molly was excited, waiting for my father to fulfil his promise to visit Kenya later that year.

My father was away for a few months visiting Kate. Upon his return, he shared with me some unexpected news. After he had described in great detail his enjoyable trip home, his mood turned and he became rather serious.

'While I was staying with your sister, we made a discovery,' he admitted, then paused.

'Go on,' I urged him.

'I had been there a matter of weeks when it was Elaine's seventeenth birthday. Kate put on a great celebration and invited all Elaine's friends. We had a lovely day, sat outside in the sun. Kate had cooked up a delicious spread and, to round off the celebrations, had made a spectacular pink birthday cake, complete with seventeen candles. Elaine looked beautiful in her new dress and little Patricia, who is almost ten now, wouldn't leave my side. I think she felt a little left out, as I was the only one giving her any attention that day.'

I felt my father moving off track from what it was he was trying to tell me and I wanted him to get to the point. 'That all sounds perfect, Father, so what is the problem?'

'The day after the party, Elaine told her mother she thought she might be pregnant.'

I was shocked. 'And is she?'

'I'm afraid so. Kate took her to the local doctor and he confirmed it.'

Poor Kate, I thought. 'Is she going to allow Elaine to keep the child?'

'Kate and I had plenty of time to discuss this and, as you can imagine, it has stirred up many memories for her.'

'Of course.'

'Kate doesn't want Elaine to have to go through what she went through with your mother, so she has decided to support Elaine and keep the baby.'

'Is the father known?'

'On that front Elaine is keeping very quiet.'

'How is Elaine? What I mean is, is she healthy?'

'Extremely healthy. She's having regular check-ups now.'

'When is the baby due?'

'All these questions,' complained my father as he tried to remember. 'October, I think.'

'Not long, then.'

'No. Not long at all.'

It took a few days for this news to sink in before I found myself able to write to my sister. I had only admiration for her. How were all of them going to handle the shame? It is one thing, knowing you have done something wrong and feeling guilty for it. It is quite another once other people are aware of your secret. People were bound to make them feel ashamed and embarrassed, unless it was completely different over there, and I suspected it was not. I knew I wouldn't be able to deal with the humiliation. This surprised me, as I recalled what had happened with Kate and I realised I had changed. Now it appeared I agreed with my mother on this subject.

65

My father remained at home for less than a month before he was off travelling again in August 1938. He wanted to visit Kate, to be there to support her when Elaine's baby was born. While my father was travelling, Ted, Molly, Jonquil, Gerald, Paddy and I all enjoyed a short break in Prestatyn. The girls had hours of fun on the sandy beaches and splashing in the sea, while the men whiled away the hours in their deckchairs and in bars. Molly and I enjoyed the promenade entertainers and in the evenings there was time to catch up with each other's news.

In October, while Father was away, I had word from Kate. Elaine's baby was a boy and they had named him Alan. Kate wrote, 'There is still no father to mention, but mother and baby are healthy and that is all I can wish for. We are all taking one day at a time but Elaine seems to be coping well, under the circumstances. Father is well and will soon be on his way home to you.'

My father returned home mid-November. I was in the front room with Paddy when we heard a knock at the door. 'This might be Granddad,' I told her.

'Hellooo!' my father's voice shouted through the letter box.

Paddy's eyes suddenly lit up. 'Granddad!' she shouted, and she ran out into the hallway.

'I'm going to make you into pigeon pie!' boomed my father's playful voice through the letter box.

I opened the door.

'Don't be silly, Grandad. I'm not a pigeon.'

He scooped Paddy up and hugged her. 'How's my favourite girl?' he asked.

'I'm very well, thank you, Granddad.'

He kissed her on her cheek, then put her down, and she led him by the hand into the sitting room.

'I'm well also,' I muttered as I followed behind them. My father looked back and smiled at me.

I let my father sit down and chat with his granddaughter while I fetched something to drink.

'I've had some news from Molly today,' I announced, returning to the room and waving her letter in my hand. 'She's going to have another baby.'

'That's splendid. When?'

'Early January, she thinks.'

'I want to be there. First thing tomorrow I shall go and sort that out.'

'But you've only just got home. You'll make yourself ill with all this travelling.'

'Nonsense, my dear. On the contrary, it gives me great strength. It fulfils me to spend time with my daughters.'

I watched my father finish the drink I'd made him and as we talked some more, I couldn't help thinking how old he had started to look.

It seemed my father had been home only a matter of days before he was off again. He kept his promise and went to visit Molly and her new husband, Charles, in Mombasa during Christmas 1938. He was

287

there in early January for the birth of their first son, whom they named Charles Harry.

Upon his return my father was full of news about Molly, which he was bursting to share. He was very taken with her husband and couldn't stop talking about him.

'The man has the patience of a saint where those boys are concerned. They can be a bit of a handful, you know.'

'How was Molly?' I asked.

'She's fine. Very happy and content with Charles. He's a good man. It is obvious he cares for her considerably. They seem very much in love.'

'That's good.' I wished my father could feel the same satisfaction with his wife, but that was not to be. At least he looked well and rested, and had plenty of colour in his cheeks.

He went on to tell me Molly seemed like a new woman, that he had not seen her so content in a long while and his stay there had been extremely happy and restful. This was a good thing, as later this year everything would change when war was declared. Thankfully, my father had returned home safely before it all began.

Nora was travelling at this time also. She made the tiresome and treacherous journey by sea from Mombasa to England with her children in January 1939. She and George had decided it was best if she and the children move back to England, as there was serious talk of unrest and George might be sent anywhere at any time. They had agreed she should stay with George's parents in Woking. Nora was expecting a fourth child and George did not want to have to leave her alone in Uganda.

My father couldn't wait to meet his latest grandchild, Beryl Nora Marion, who was born late February in Woking, so in March a family holiday was arranged and we all went to Rhos-on-Sea.

Nora deserved a medal for taking care of her four. I took her two boys, Robert and Edward, off her hands as much as I could. I led them and Paddy on long, windswept walks along the beach for hours, to give her a bit of a break. Father would accompany us, if he felt like blowing the cobwebs away, or he would sometimes stay with Nora. She never had any time to herself; looking after two-year-old Stella and baby Beryl was a full-time job on its own.

66

With the onset of the Second World War, my father was soon prohibited from travelling abroad by sea because of aircraft strikes, submarines and torpedo attacks. Most passenger liners were being recruited for troop and hospital ships. They were quickly modified, installing bunk beds often stacked five deep, ripping out the luxury furnishings my father had become accustomed to.

Frustrated he was unable to travel, my father spent much of his time going back and forth between Lucy's house, Church Bank and Wales. Prevented from visiting his grandchildren abroad, he had to make do with the ones he had in England.

Lucy would have a fourth and final child during the war, giving my father five grandchildren locally, whom he could spoil, along with his grandchildren in Woking. Overseas he would eventually, by the end of the war, have another four whom he had never met, as Molly and Charles continued to build their family, regardless of the situation.

Many changes took place for the population during the war, and at Church Bank we were no exception. Gerald and two of his good friends, who had all attended Bowdon College together, joined the RAF. One of these friends was Ted.

Ted's wife Molly and I had become firm friends over the years. Both having daughters of the same age had cemented this friendship further. It seemed a sensible solution, therefore, that, while our husbands were away at war, we should live together at Church Bank, sharing the care of our daughters, the responsibility of finding paid work and the provision of food for the dinner table. As wives of servicemen, we actually had little choice. We just had to get on with it and make the best of things.

When Paddy and Jonquil had outgrown their preparatory school they had started at Culcheth Hall. Once the Second World War had started, both Molly and I moved our girls to Altrincham High School on Cavendish Road because it was a non-fee-paying school.

My role was to stay at home, to cook and look after the children: normally a role I would have relished and found simple, but with the war came rationing, and getting a decent meal on the table proved to be a challenge most nights. I also had a lunchtime job on the days the girls were at school, working at the Women's Voluntary Service British Restaurant in Bowdon Vale.

Molly had a job at Reyson's Milliners in Hale, Monday to Friday. Her wage helped us immensely throughout this time. In the evenings she swapped hats and worked as an ambulance driver around Manchester. She always had a story to tell about those evenings.

Molly and I worked as a team. The girls on the whole were well behaved, but on occasion, as they grew older, they could be rather challenging. It fell to me to keep them in check and to dish out all punishments, as it was I who was their main carer. To allow me some time off from the children, Molly would take them most Sundays to visit her mother, whom both girls referred to as 'Granny Sharp'. Molly and the girls would cycle to Crossfield Road in Hale, where they played in the garden and later had tea. Granny Sharp looked forward to their visits and, I have no doubt, spoilt them both sufficiently each time. Their time away gave me most of the afternoon to do as I wished, yet it more often than not involved catching up with the housework.

Before the war, Church Bank was already proving difficult to maintain. It was such a large house for just the three of us that most of the rooms were hardly used, and it was impossible to keep them all clean and in good repair. At the time I had been extremely grateful to my father for gifting the house to me, but as time went on it was becoming more of a headache and more of a burden.

I spoke to my father shortly after Gerald left for the war, asking him for some financial help with the general upkeep of the house. At first he refused, saying I needed to learn how to stand on my own two feet.

'Are you able to prove to me you need this extra money?' he demanded.

I wasn't surprised. Father never offered any financial assistance, even if he noticed I was struggling. If ever I needed anything, I would usually have to go on bended knee to him, prove that I really needed the help and be prepared to work for it. My father was harsh, but he was fair. 'You don't get anything for free in this life, Janet. The sooner you learn that, the better.' If I'd heard him say these words once, I'd heard them a million times over the years. I'd also heard him say them to my mother when she had been alive.

I explained my plight and asked if he might have any suggestions as to how I could make some extra money to pay the bills and look after the house.

Father eventually came up with a satisfactory solution and suggested I take in lodgers. He offered no financial assistance, but he did help me to refurbish part of the ground floor, fitting a new kitchen, and helped to find me some tenants, who quickly moved in. The Bagnall family were from the South. Mr Bagnall worked for the government and was married with two sons. They remained with us at Church Bank for the duration of the war.

I remember the Manchester Blitz in 1940. Air raids began in Manchester in August and September, when the Palace Theatre was bombed. The heaviest raids happened in December, just before Christmas, on consecutive nights, when 250 planes dropped their bombs, killing more than 650 people and leaving 6,000 homeless. Manchester Cathedral, the Royal Exchange and the Free Trade Hall were all terribly damaged in the raid. When Molly returned home after the blitz, she was exhausted and unusually quiet. She spoke little of what she had seen over those nights. Father was devastated about Manchester, yet relieved none of his properties had been damaged.

During this time the girls and I, and often our tenants, slept in the cellar of Church Bank. It was freezing cold but it felt a lot safer than being upstairs as the Luftwaffe flew over our heads, on occasion dropping their bombs on Altrincham on their way to and from Manchester.

As I was trying to keep my family safe from the threat of German invasion, Kate in New Zealand was experiencing a different kind of misfortune. By all accounts she had been very supportive of her eldest daughter when Elaine had given birth to an illegitimate child. Elaine had a son, but it was Kate who seemed to have taken on the role of mother to the child, with Elaine in the place of a sister. Kate saw to the boy's every need, while his mother appeared to continue with her own life, joining in with his care as and when she felt like it, usually avoiding the difficult moments and relishing the more congenial ones, according to Kate.

This situation would prove to be for the best, as when the child was only one year old, his mother was killed in a terrible accident. Elaine was on her way to meet friends when she was knocked over by a motorbike, later dying in hospital from her injuries. Kate was left devastated by the loss of her daughter, throwing herself passionately into bringing up her grandson as a way to get through her bereavement. This must have been a terrible time for Kate.

As Kate came to terms with the loss of her daughter, we came to terms with the prospect that the war could easily last a number of years more. Molly and I became extremely close during the war years, as we depended on each other for financial and emotional support. Our two daughters also grew close during this time. Attending school together and living together brought them as close as sisters. They did everything together, and that included getting into scrapes.

There was a siren situated on the police station roof, near to St Mary's church in Bowdon, to warn us of any raids by air. On one particular occasion, I was inside the house when I heard the siren going off and I quickly went to find the girls, to hurry them to safety in the cellar. I soon discovered they were outside in the garden and straining terribly over the top of our overgrown hedge to witness a dogfight which was taking place in the distant skies above. There was a dreadful amount of smoke in the sky and I remember grabbing both girls' arms and demanding to know what on earth it was they thought they were doing, while dragging them off to the cellar.

At Ringway Airport there was a parachute training school. Here the men of the RAF would train and then move on to Tatton Park, where they received the next stage of their parachute training. Men were lifted to 700 feet in barrage balloons, out of which they jumped, their parachutes gently bringing them to rest on the grass of Tatton Park. From the gardens of Church Bank, we could see these balloons floating majestically between the clouds. I would often notice the girls looking out across Langham Road towards Tatton Park, discussing these huge inflated whales.

Once the men had performed a couple of these jumps from a balloon they were ready to jump from a Dakota, and for many this was their dream job. A night drop was the final and most dangerous part of their training, before the men were able to collect their wings. Both Gerald and Ted had received similar training before becoming leading aircraftmen.

The war continued for five long years, yet I have some fond memories of this time, along with the more difficult ones. My father was constantly calling in and he was a godsend to have around, as our men were never there. Father was able to help with jobs around the house, the ones which needed doing urgently and couldn't wait until after the war. If he was unable to help for any reason, then he would make sure he found someone who could.

We had a leaking pipe in the kitchen one day. Father had gone to the kitchen to fetch something and shouted back to me in the front room, 'Should all this water be on the floor?' I rushed to the kitchen to find him standing in water almost coming over the top of his shoes. Mr Bagnall was out at work, so Father attempted to correct the problem, but just made things worse. I was left trying to mop up water which was leaking faster than I could mop. Eventually my father returned with a neighbour, who, armed with tools, repaired the leak, and order was restored to the house before the girls returned from school.

Molly and I saw our husbands only a handful of times during the war and, when we did, we rarely had any warning they were coming home. They would literally just turn up on the doorstep, although never at the same time. They'd be stationed at Wilmslow and on embarkation leave, which usually meant they would be at home for a number of days before being sent abroad again. Molly and I found these times both happy and challenging. With no warning our plans would suddenly have to change. The house would suddenly turn into a whirlwind of turmoil, as we all tried to readjust to their visit.

I think the children found it the most difficult. Their fathers were more or less strangers to them, as the girls had been only four years old when they had left for war. On one occasion, when Ted returned home on leave, there was some confusion as to whose father he was. I caught the girls arguing over him. It was a little embarrassing for Ted. Thankfully Molly and I found it funny. These forceful men, who craved attention, would turn up without warning and turn their children's young lives upside down. The girls were too young to understand about the war and the men were too preoccupied to care about their daughters.

During the war Ted was posted to Ireland. Gerald went to Palestine, where he claims to have met King Talal bin Abdullah of Jordan. He said the king asked if his son, Prince Hussein, the same age as our daughter, could climb into the armoured car Gerald was in. Gerald obliged, seating the child on his knee, demonstrating the controls and allowing the child to push and pull the levers and buttons. Gerald had many tales to tell during his visits home and it was often difficult to distinguish the facts from fiction. I understand he spent some time in Africa and Persia also.

Before this Gerald had been sent to Dunkirk in France, where he had been injured in the D-Day landings. Upon his return he explained how he and six others had clambered into a barge, with no engine, to try to escape from France. They had no food or water and remained in the barge for a number of days, floating around the coast of France, before ending up in the Bay of Biscay. Finally a plane flew over them and they were able to attract its attention. The problem was they had no idea whether the plane was friend or foe, and at that point Gerald said he was past caring. They were finally picked up and Gerald ended up in hospital in Eastleigh, Hampshire, for a few months. I knew nothing of this until his visit home.

In the summer of 1945 I received news from my cousins, Frank and Marie. Frank had joined the Royal Navy at the start of the war and Marie had moved herself and her two boys away from London and the bombs, to live in the country. Marie was writing to tell me she had now returned to live in the south-west of London and that she had just had a daughter. Frank was well, home on leave soon, and Marie was desperate for her husband's return as he had not met his youngest child as yet. Marie said she would be honoured if I might consider being godmother to her daughter and would let me know the date of the baptism in due course. This she soon did and I travelled by train to join my cousins on their special day. The child was a complete delight and the day most enjoyable. I returned home on the last train, on the Sunday afternoon, to find Molly and the girls waiting for me, bursting with questions about my day.

67

When the war ended, but before our men returned, I arranged a holiday for Molly, myself and the girls. I booked us into Mrs Reynolds' bed-and-breakfast accommodation near Helston in Cornwall. Molly and I were not stupid. We knew that once our menfolk arrived home everything would change, so we wanted to make the most of what time we had left together.

Two days before we were due to leave for Cornwall, the telephone rang and it was Gerald, announcing he would be home in a couple of days' time.

'We won't be here,' I declared.

'Why? Wherever will you be?' he demanded.

'I've booked for us to stay in Cornwall for a few nights.'

'All of you?'

'Yes.'

All went silent at the other end of the telephone, but I was not about to change our plans, as everyone had been especially looking forward to the trip.

'I'll give you the address and you can meet us there if you like,' I finally suggested. He reluctantly agreed and, so as not to disappoint anyone, I chose to keep this news to myself for the time being.

Before we left, the girls insisted on decorating an old sheet to read, 'Welcome home!' and hanging it up at the front of the house, just in case their fathers turned up at Church Bank while we were away.

When we arrived in Cornwall, I quietly warned Mrs Reynolds that Gerald might join us. Not having enough rooms to accommodate him, she kindly arranged for the farm down the road to rent us an extra room, should we need it. On the Saturday I received news that Gerald would be arriving by train on the Sunday, at which point I felt it only fair to warn my ten-year-old daughter.

The poor child was dragged around half of Cornwall on the Sunday morning in search of her father. I was, without doubt, not her favourite person that day, as we went looking for a man who was almost a complete stranger to her and whom she did not remember or recognise. We walked for miles in circles thinking we had missed his train, returning to our accommodation, hoping to find him there, only to turn back around and go straight out again. In my anxiety to find my husband, I quite forgot the trains only ran intermittently on Sundays.

Later that afternoon, Gerald finally stepped out into the street from the station and we saw each other for the first time in many months. We embraced and then he said hello to our daughter, who shied away from the stranger she saw before her. She was even less happy when I announced I was to leave her with Molly, while I went to spend the next two nights with her father at the farm down the road. It was rather a difficult and strained situation once Gerald had joined us: not the type of holiday I had envisaged.

Molly knew things would change quickly from this point and said to me, 'As soon as we get back to Church Bank, I will pack our bags and we will go and stay with my sister and her husband in Hale.'

'Thank you for being so understanding,' I told her, my eyes quickly filling with tears.

'We knew this day would come,' she said.

'Yes, but it would be nice to have had a little longer to adjust.'

'I'll only be down the road,' Molly assured me. 'I shan't abandon you totally.'

'Make sure you don't.' We embraced one another, but not for as long as we had wished, as Gerald entered the room. He would have thought we were being silly.

When Ted returned to Molly he went to work for Molly's brother, who, after the war, had opened a shirt factory. Ted was a salesman there. Gerald struggled to find work at first.

*

In late September 1946 Kate visited from New Zealand. She said she deserved a break and that caring for her grandchild was taking its toll on her. She had really missed our father's visits during the war and couldn't wait to see everyone in England. She travelled alone by ship, leaving husband Frank to his work and daughter Patricia to care for eight-year-old Alan.

It had been almost twenty years since I had seen my sister and for the first hour we kept hugging each other, unable to believe we were really in each other's company at last. Her visit was like a breath of fresh air, as two weeks before we had received some sad news. My father's very good friend and close associate for many years had died. John Gow had married my father's sister Mary before I had been born. Father and Uncle John had known one another for a great many years and always got along. My uncle's death had come as a terrible shock to both my father and my aunt.

My father confided to me, 'My sister might never get over her husband's death. They have always been so close. Aligned to one another's thoughts, words and deeds.' It seemed my aunt's heart had broken when my uncle had passed away.

Uncle John's body was taken to Salterhebble in Yorkshire to be buried, near to the home of his mother's family and to where he had lived as a boy. Father accompanied his sister to the funeral.

We told Kate about Uncle John's death and while she was staying with us, we all went to visit our widowed aunt in her great big house. My aunt was dressed head to toe in black and the house felt a very sombre place without my uncle.

When it was time for Kate to return home, none of us wanted to say goodbye. Father promised he would visit soon and Kate said she would look forward to it. There were many tears before she left. I hoped I would see her again and that I wouldn't have to wait another twenty years.

With the war over the Bagnall family moved out of Church Bank, returning to the South of England. Spare money was scarce for a time. Before he left, Mr Bagnall kindly found Gerald a job working at Salford Electrical Instruments at Peel Works, Silk Street, in Salford. As publicity manager, Gerald was involved with advertising for the company and travelled across the country quite a bit. His salary was helpful towards the upkeep of the house, but we still needed to rent out rooms to cover costs and money was often tight.

Paddy had not passed her eleven-plus exams and we had been forced to send her to Wellington Road School on Moss Lane in Timperley. She was unhappy with this arrangement as she was no longer with Jonquil, who had passed her exams. We also were unhappy and I began to save with enthusiasm in order to send her to another fee-paying school, somewhere I believed would be more appropriate for my daughter.

As Paddy was now older and much more independent, I decided I needed to find myself some part-time work in order to help me save more quickly. Using my Princess Christian training, in 1947 I managed to secure myself a job, three days a week, looking after two young girls whose mother wished for more time to herself. I was surprised by how much I enjoyed this work and stayed with this family for three years, until the children had outgrown me. Before ending my relationship with this family, I was engaged for two days a week to care for a one-year-old child who lived in Altrincham. This lasted for two months. The following year between January and May I cared for a two-and-a-half-year-old boy and his new baby sister in Hale. I was now able to put aside a tidy sum saved for Paddy.

The people of this country tried to adjust to life without war, a task you might expect to be easy. For me, having my husband back in my life was proving a challenge. Returning to normality was far more difficult than I had anticipated, as much had changed during the war years. Many did not want to return to the way things had been, and my daughter and husband were just two of the many.

It would be an understatement to say things at home were a strain. Gerald and Paddy clashed terribly, and by the time she was fourteen he had arranged for her to be sent away to boarding school. I did not like this idea, but Gerald convinced me it would be in everyone's best interest.

Even Father was a little shocked when I told him, and he asked if I was sure I was doing the right thing. 'It can be a difficult age,' he said. 'I'm not sure sending the child away to deal with it on her own is the best solution.'

Although I agreed with my father, I felt unable to go against Gerald's wishes as he was so adamant he'd made the right choice for our daughter. He was convinced that it was the best solution all round. So Paddy was sent to Tunstall Hall College for girls in Market Drayton.

I missed her terribly once she had left and tried to fill my time by taking up horse riding for a hobby. This worked, but only in the short term. We also took in more lodgers. Some alterations were made to the top floor of Church Bank and two young female teachers from Altrincham High School soon moved in. We also later managed to create a self-contained flat on the first-floor landing, complete with its own front door which led out onto the stairs. It was here the Smith family began to rent and would remain with us at Church Bank for many years.

68

When Paddy was fifteen, Gerald and I took her to Farnborough Air Show. Gerald was in charge of a stand at the show, selling electrical equipment for aircraft, and had taken this role every year since 1946. This was his fifth show since the end of the war and, to be honest, I was a little bored by the whole thing. It had been Gerald's idea for Paddy to experience the show during her summer break.

It cost Paddy and me three shillings each to enter, and there was plenty to see. The mighty Brabazon sat motionless upon the ground, but we were not allowed too close, restricted by a circle of ropes surrounding the aircraft. Others, such as cargo planes, we were allowed to climb into and take a look around. The Meteor NF.11 night fighter made its debut and de Havilland Mosquitoes with their Rolls-Royce engines flew overhead at speed. There were also planes flying in formation and the Venom left smoke trails behind it. There were other displays to watch, such as the men demonstrating their physical training. I was surprised that Paddy did not complain more during the day.

After the show, Gerald wanted something to eat and insisted we visit a local pub. I was unhappy about this. It was not a place an impressionable young lady such as my daughter should be introduced to. It was full of airmen, so Gerald felt quite at home. I, on the other hand, felt very uncomfortable throughout the inadequate meal which the establishment had provided. There was a table of airmen across from us and I was sure they were making eyes at my daughter. Thankfully Paddy seemed oblivious to this fact.

As we left through the main door of the scruffy, crowded public house, I said to Gerald, 'We're not going into that pub again.'

'Why ever not?' was his response.

'Those pilots were after our daughter.'

'Don't be so ridiculous, woman.' At which point he grabbed Paddy and give her a cuddle, saying, 'So what if they were interested? Paddy is a very attractive young lady.'

Paddy found her father's comments funny. I'm afraid I tutted at him and walked off in front of them. I hadn't realised until then that our daughter was indeed blossoming into a beauty and it had come as a bit of a shock, mainly because it made me realise how old I suddenly felt.

That day at Farnborough appeared to be the start of a much stronger relationship between father and daughter, and on occasion I did feel left out. After Paddy's first visit to a pub, Gerald encouraged it more and the two of them would often go to the pub together, returning home late for our Sunday lunch. This would infuriate me, although I tried my hardest not to let it.

I thought I had my daughter's life all mapped out for her. My plan for her, when her time at Tunstall Hall came to an end, was to send her to the Duchess of York hospital for sick babies on Burnage Lane in Levenshulme. They had an excellent reputation for women training as paediatric nurses and I believed the hospital could provide this ideal qualification for my daughter. Paddy, unfortunately, had other ideas. We had many disagreements on the subject and she flatly refused to do as I was asking. Night after night after night we argued, until in the end I was forced to concede.

Much to my distaste, Paddy went and found herself a job at Home Farm on the Dunham Massey Estate, where she began with the delightful job of potato picking. I don't mind telling you, I and her father were rather horrified that our daughter should want to do such a degrading job. But Paddy had decided she wanted to work on the land and there was no convincing her otherwise. She was very popular there by all accounts and made a great many friends. The young girls whom she brought back to the house and I got to meet were most definitely not of the same class, but what could I expect when she worked on a farm?

One year later I was still unhappy with the situation and wanted more for my daughter. I consulted my father for his opinion.

'If she is so determined to work on the land, then let her. She can gain a qualification by taking a course at Cheshire College of Agriculture in Reaseheath, near Nantwich.'

I had never heard of this college. With some persuasion, less than anticipated, we were able to convince Paddy. She enrolled in the September of 1952 but frustratingly was forced to give up in the February, returning home because she was suffering from appendicitis. Thankfully she made a full recovery, albeit a slow one, and agreed to return to the college the following September to resit the course.

By the end of 1954, now aged nineteen, Paddy found employment on a farm in Whitchurch, where she worked on the land and made cheese. Some months into this job she injured her finger on a thistle and was unable to continue with the cheesemaking. This process involved coming into contact with acid, which infected her wound, and she very nearly lost her finger.

I was at my wits' end with the girl, as it seemed she was unable to stick at anything for any length of time. 'Maybe you're just not cut out for farm work, dear,' I can remember saying to her, but my words fell on deaf ears.

Gerald and Paddy were more alike than I cared to admit, as Gerald was also finding things difficult at work. His company had taken on more staff and there was one particular co-worker with whom Gerald did not get along. 'I know he just wants to make his mark,' commented Gerald, one meal time. 'It's the way he's going about it that annoys me.' Gerald was becoming more and more irritated by this man every day.

Gerald's colleague had been allocated a role similar to his and in the same office. They were in effect sharing the workload. This man soon realised that it was Gerald who was getting the better deal and who was always the one to be given the jobs which took him travelling. Of course, when he confronted Gerald about this, he got nowhere.

After some months of unrest in the office, this other man took his concerns to his bosses. Soon, Gerald found it was he who was being left behind in the office while this other man claimed all the rewards. Gerald was the next to complain to his bosses, but it was no use. He was told, in no uncertain terms, that it was only fair. Gerald took it upon himself to walk out. I was furious with him when I discovered what he had done.

'There's nothing for it. You shall just have to eat humble pie and ask for your job back,' I said. But Gerald was having none of it and flatly refused to set foot on the premises ever again. He could be very stubborn when the mood took him.

Eventually he found himself a job, not unlike our daughter's, working on the land. It paid poorly, but he was too stubborn and proud, refusing to lower himself to working in a factory where the pay was better.

In 1955 Paddy started work on a pig farm in Northwich, but she found it rather dull and within a year had moved to live and work on a farm in Winsford. Here she was much happier, working as a land girl, with her many jobs including milking the cows, lambing, ploughing, gathering in the crops and managing poultry. I was of the same opinion as before, that my daughter could do better for herself than this, but it was difficult, especially as her father had now followed her into this profession. With Gerald also working on a farm, money was as scarce as ever.

When Gerald encouraged our daughter to purchase a motorbike, I thought it was the final straw. I turned to my father for support, only to be disappointed. He, like Gerald, thought it a great idea that Paddy should own such a machine and immediately insisted she allow him a turn. I had to go back inside the house; I couldn't watch as the three of them took it in turns to ride the contraption up and down Richmond Road.

Gerald seemed to keep doing things which irritated me. Without my prior knowledge he arranged to purchase a dog. He went into Manchester one morning, met a man at London Road station and returned with the hairy creature, whose name was Nicodemus.

'I'm going to call him Nico,' he announced proudly as the animal wriggled in his arms.

'And how much did he cost you?' I asked, dreading his answer, as I suspected this dog was a pedigree, with a name like Nicodemus.

'Not as much as he could have done,' was his answer as he lowered the dog to the floor.

'How much?' I demanded, but my words, once again, fell on deaf ears.

'He's a throwback. A blue merle collie throwback, not a proper pedigree,' he assured me. 'He came cheap at the price. He's too tall, has rough hair and eyes of two different colours, you see?'

'I see all right.'

'Isn't he a handsome chap?' Gerald smiled to himself as the dog rolled over submissively to allow him to rub its belly.

'And where is he to sleep? And what is he to eat?' I asked, stupidly hoping my husband had considered these things.

'I was just about to sort that,' he lied. Lifting the dog in his arms, Gerald scampered off with his tail between his legs in search of these answers.

Of course, Paddy was very taken with the newest member of the family when she first saw him. She disappeared for hours with her father some weekends, saying they were just going to walk the dog. I could always guarantee there would be a pub to quench their thirst at the end of their walk.

69

In April 1955 there was a knock at the door. Waiting on the doorstep was a handsome young man, grinning at me.

'Hello, Aunty,' he said. When I did not answer, he explained, 'It's Gerald, Molly's son.'

'Oh my word, I didn't recognise you. Come in, come in.' I had not seen him since he was about three years old.

'Did you not receive a letter from Mother telling you to expect me?'

'No, dear, I'm afraid I didn't. It must still be in the post. Oh, Lord, I have nowhere for you to stay. All my rooms are taken.'

'That's all right,' he said kindly. 'I'm not after a bed for the night. Mother has arranged for me to stay with Great-Aunt Mary. She hoped it might cheer the old lady up. I thought I might pay you a visit also, if that's all right?'

'Of course it is,' I said, relieved. 'And has your visit cheered up your great-aunt?'

'I hope so. I'm doing my best.'

'That's good to hear. How rude of me. I haven't offered you anything to drink.'

Gerald and I spent a good hour together discussing, amongst other things, his mother, his brothers and sisters and his work, that of engineer. I couldn't believe he would be turning twenty-seven this year. During his short time in England I was able to introduce him to many members of his family whom he had never met and spent time with Father, who was terribly excited to see his grandson.

The spring passed with few other incidents; the summer was another matter. In June my dear friend Molly died from cancer. It was a great shock to lose her so young and so suddenly. She must have been sick for some time, keeping it to herself, before going to see the doctor. When she had, there had been little he could do for her. It has taken me a great many years to get over her death. I often think about our times together and miss her terribly. We had become extremely close over the years, especially during the war, and I knew I would never have another friend like her.

Understandably, Jonquil and Ted were devastated. At this time they were living in Hale and Ted told me he was to dedicate the rest of his life to his daughter. But in less than two years he had remarried, and I don't think Jonquil has ever forgiven him for that.

Nora and her children moved from Woking to Wales once the war was over. George arrived in England some time in 1946 and they agreed to end their relationship. George returned to work in Nigeria while Nora rented rooms for herself and the children in The Towers on Abbey Road, Rhos-on-Sea. In 1949, George secured himself a job with Barclays Bank in Lagos, working as an accountant. Nora said they both had their separate lives now and she was happy with this situation.

By the early 1950s Nora was able to purchase a three-bed semi-detached property a little further along the coast, on a cul-de-sac named Rosemary Avenue in Colwyn Bay. Father, Gerald and I would visit as often as we could, my father more frequently than most. Once Paddy had her motorbike there was no stopping her. She would visit her aunt at the drop of a hat. She thought nothing of riding on that contraption for the seventy-mile journey, staying a few days, turning round and returning again to Winsford.

To have my sister Nora living in Wales proved to be a huge relief for me in 1957. After losing my best friend, Molly, I had turned to Nora, not just as a sister, but also for friendship. Towards the end of the spring, Paddy was due a brief weekend visit. Gerald and I had been drifting apart over the last couple of years and we seemed to do nothing but argue with one another. My father was abroad again and not due back until June, so I was looking forward to Paddy's visit, hoping she would be a breath of fresh air. However, things rarely go to plan.

When Paddy arrived at the house, I immediately knew something was wrong. You could call it a mother's instinct, but Paddy looked very pale. 'Are you all right, darling? Have you been working too hard?' I asked, concerned.

'I have to tell you something, Mother, and I suggest you sit down,' she said nervously.

She knew how I was going to react, possibly more so than I did. Her news shocked me terribly.

'I'm pregnant,' she announced. That was all she said. That was all she needed to say.

I actually thought I might die from the shame. She knew I considered this to be a sin. How could she do this to me? How could she bring such shame on the family? I was finding it hard to breathe when Gerald walked in.

For once, he seemed able to sense the atmosphere in the room. I don't think I had ever known him do that before. 'Everything all right?' he asked, hopefully.

'No, it most certainly is not!' I yelled. 'Tell him, then. Go on, tell your father what you've done!'

Gerald looked from me to his daughter. He had never seen me so angry and I suspect he knew what she had done before she told him.

'I'm pregnant.'

Gerald remained silent. Not a single word passed his lips.

How was I ever to forgive my daughter for putting me through this nightmare? I quickly made arrangements with Nora and Paddy was despatched to Wales before anyone could become aware of her condition. No one was ever to find out about her predicament. She had committed the most terrible sin.

At this time Nora was working at the Colwyn Bay Hotel on the promenade. She was the housekeeper there. The hotel had reopened its doors to customers in 1952 after being the Ministry of Food's national headquarters during the Second World War. Nora had arranged for Paddy to start working there as a chamber maid. Here she was kept extremely busy throughout her pregnancy, helping to keep clean the ninety-two bedrooms the hotel advertised.

Nora found Dr Owen, from Llandudno, to care for Paddy during her pregnancy, and he was responsible for finding a decent couple with whom to place the baby when it was born. This was all arranged and Paddy had little say in the matter. Once the child had been born, Paddy would be able to return home and no one would be the wiser. Nora said Paddy seemed to have accepted her fate and was happy to go ahead with the adoption.

All was going well, until one month before the child was due. The doctor paid Nora and Paddy a visit and informed them that the couple with whom he had planned the adoption had been offered another child, a baby boy, and they had accepted. At the present time, he had no one to take Paddy's baby, but he was certain there was enough time in which to find another suitable couple before the child was born.

Paddy stopped working at the hotel at the end of October 1957, and on 16th November I took the train to Colwyn Bay to visit her and my sister. Two days later, Paddy went into labour and the child was born.

I knew that it would be a strange day, one mixed with sadness and joy, but even I could not have predicted what would happen next.

After the child's birth, the doctor informed us that he had, as yet, been unable to find a couple to take the baby.

'That won't be a problem, doctor, because I'm keeping him, you see,' announced Paddy, with pure determination.

Nora and I looked at one another, unable to utter a single word.

'If you are sure that is what you want,' answered the doctor.

'Oh, yes. I'm quite sure,' said Paddy.

After the doctor had left, Paddy insisted, 'You'd better get used to the idea, Mother. I'm keeping him, no matter what you say.'

It was quickly clear I had little choice other than to accept the situation, but my mind was racing about how I was going to explain this baby to my friends and neighbours. I had thought I could get away with saying nothing and the problem would solve itself. It seemed this was not to be the case any more.

One month after returning home to Church Bank, Paddy was out for a walk with her son in his pram. I had been dealing with the grocer who, regular as clockwork, would turn up at the back door with the week's grocery order. I had just said thank you and goodbye to the man, and was watching him descend the back steps when Paddy appeared in the back yard with the pram. I watched as the grocer peered into the pram and said, 'What a bonny little chap. Is he yours or your mother's?'

Blushing, Paddy announced proudly, 'He's mine.'

That was it. We had managed to keep things quiet for one month, but now it would be all around the town within the hour. The shame of it.

There was nothing for it. I would just have to get used to it. It was what it was and we would all have to deal with it.

Gerald appeared to be dealing with the situation by staying away more and more. He was never at home to lend his support, so I just had to get on with it without him.

I very soon took on the role of my grandchild's main carer, as Paddy found work in Broadheath with a firm that made industrial detergents. She enjoyed it there and made some good friends. There were four other girls who worked in the office with her. They all got on well together and she told them all about her son. One evening, Paddy was invited out to a dance by one of the girls from her office. This friend had set her up on a blind date, and this was to turn out to be the evening she would meet her future husband.

Just as my daughter seemed to have found love, my marriage was reaching its conclusion.

70

In the late summer of 1958, Gerald left Church Bank and didn't return. I kept thinking he would return after a few days, but the days turned into weeks, then months, and then I started to believe I might never see him again. He had hurt me so much. Leaving like that without a word, without any explanation. Leaving me to pick up the pieces; how could he?

I had some support from my father, on the occasions he was home, but he had made a trip abroad almost every year now for over a decade, visiting his other daughters, and I wasn't a high priority. It was difficult for me to feel I could rely on any man for support. My father's final trip to see Kate brought him home in the June of 1959. He was, by this time, eighty-seven years old.

On 5th September 1959 Paddy was married at the local registry office. Nora and I arranged an informal reception for the happy couple afterwards, back at Church Bank. There were a number of Paddy's closest friends in attendance and, of course, relevant members of each family. My father did not attend. He had been feeling unwell and was at home with his wife. Mary had assured me he would be fit again in no time, and by October it seemed he was.

I don't mind admitting it was a relief to see Paddy married; nevertheless, I didn't for one minute think it would be easy for her.

In November my aunt Mary, a widow for some thirteen years, was taken ill. My father went immediately to be with his sister. I joined him there as often as I could. After a short illness, Mary Gow died at her home, South Downs, on the 19th November. My father and I were at her side.

'She's gone, my dear,' my father said. 'Her old heart has simply given up on her. She's at peace now.'

He was devastated at her loss. My aunt had made my father promise he would take her remains and have them buried in Yorkshire, not next to her husband's, but in the family plot at All Saints, South Kirkby.

Before he was able to fulfil her wishes, my father was also taken ill. He was rushed in terrible pain to hospital where, on the 23rd November, doctors operated on a stomach ulcer. I was sure the upset of my aunt's death had brought on this condition.

I was relieved when my father was finally discharged and appeared to be recuperating well at home with Mary.

Over the Christmas period my father began to deteriorate once again. At first he appeared melancholy and I put this down to him reminiscing about my mother over the Christmas period. Then, one day at Lucy's, just before the new year, we heard him vomiting in the bathroom after his lunch. Within the week he had been admitted into the Manchester Victoria Memorial Jewish hospital on Elizabeth Street.

Lucy and I visited our father on alternate days for the next two weeks. He was suffering from pneumonia and struggling to breathe easily. He was undernourished and looked very frail. It was heartbreaking to see such a strong, active man deteriorate so quickly.

Father passed away on 12th January 1960. Before doing so, he handed Lucy the responsibility of transporting my aunt's remains to

Yorkshire. By then we had been forced to have her cremated, which Jim had generously paid for. Lucy and Jim also arranged and paid for Father to be cremated in Altrincham and for our aunt's ashes to be laid to rest in Yorkshire.

I felt terrible that I was unable to help financially with these two funerals. Nora was in a similar predicament to me. At our father's funeral, we only managed to get through it because we had each other's support. Afterwards Nora said to me, 'When I die, will you see to it that my ashes go alongside Father's?'

'Of course,' I replied. 'And if I go first, I want to be placed next to Mother in Colwyn Bay.'

'That seems fair,' replied Nora.

We hardly saw my father's wife during his stay in hospital. She attended his cremation but made no attempt to speak to any of us. We assumed we would see very little of her after that, but we were wrong. Mary soon showed her true colours following my father's death. She contested his will. Father assumed he had been clever in already gifting large sums of money to his daughters abroad, many years earlier, while he was still alive. He had already given Church Bank to me and thought he could leave the rest of his fortune safely with his bank, to be divided amongst me, Nora and Lucy. This was his biggest mistake. Mary fought the courts and, although it took her months, she succeeded in securing my father's life savings all for herself, which amounted to more than £50,000.

A number of years after my father's death, I discovered something about him that I had never known. I had for many years believed that my father had been born in Manchester, but in a conversation with Kate she told me of his early childhood in Liverpool. She explained how our grandfather, a gruff man, according to Kate, whom she could scarcely recall, had been a seaman working from the port in Liverpool.

'Apparently it was common for seamen to drink as much as they could on the land, as it was frowned upon on the ship. A seaman caught drinking on board would undoubtedly lose his job.' Kate said Father had explained this to her once. He had disclosed to Kate that

311

when our grandfather arrived home on leave, he would drink heavily and could turn pretty nasty. 'Father said it was left to him to pick up the pieces. This is why we have never seen a drop of alcohol pass Father's lips.'

I have to admit, I was both surprised and upset by this revelation. I did not like to think of my father experiencing a difficult childhood. My father had always been so important in my life. It was difficult to imagine his childhood should not have been as happy as mine was.

'Did he say anything more about his father?' I asked Kate.

'He said that he used to enjoy trips to the local park with his parents to sail a small boat on the lake there. His father had brought it home after a trip abroad.'

'Couldn't have been all bad, then,' I replied.

'I think they got along better as he got older, but I get the impression no one dared to cross Grandfather Frank.'

The only photograph we have of my grandfather is from the early 1900s, the decade before I was born. He looks rather stern in the picture, yet also rather proud of his achievement: that of being able to afford one of the first cars ever driven around the streets of Manchester.

My mother and father are both in the picture, although I can hardly recognise them, as they are so young-looking. My father looks very handsome and I can see why my mother fell for him. Kate is also in the photograph but looks rather uncomfortable, having been placed between her grandparents in the front of the car. She said she could remember our grandfather shouting at everyone that day and this had quite upset her; it was the reason this memory had stayed with her.

Acknowledgements

Thanks to 'Paddy', without whom this book would never have been started or finished, for sharing her wealth of knowledge of the Bradshaw family, and to Christine Onions, whose family research set the foundations I was able to build upon.

Thank you to my ever-supportive husband, my mum for her helpful comments and corrections, my son and daughters for always 'finding something to do' in order that I could write, and my son's school for organising his residential trip, which allowed me to motor ahead to completion.

Thanks must again go to Miles and Rachel from the Choir Press and to Harriet for her insightful editorial suggestions.

Writing this novel has proved to be more challenging than anticipated. The endless research has increased my knowledge of the Manchester area and its rich history. I have made frequent visits to Manchester's Central Library, where archive staff were helpful and professional, remaining patient with my many requests, for which I would also like to thank them.

Finally, thanks should also go to Sale Library, Manchester's Gallery of Costume, Manchester Museum of Science and Industry, Beamish Museum and Quarry Bank Mill.

Every parent, if given the opportunity, would like to provide their child with a superior life to their own. We strive for our children to achieve the very best, often becoming blind to what it is our children really want. There is no malice in our attempt to provide our child with a 'better life', but we should remember they are distinct and unique and we should treat them so.

As humans the desire to prove and improve ourselves, to be happy and successful is forever strong, believing that it will be our generation which can achieve far greater things than the last.

With progress comes improvement, or so it is claimed. But with progress we can often lose the very foundations upon which we derive our good intentions.

www.ingramcontent.com/pod-product-compliance
Lightning Source LLC
Chambersburg PA
CBHW022220010726
47493CB00002B/531